DEADLINE

"And you're going to do what, exactly?" asked Becks.

She sounded sensibly wary. At least one of us was being sensible for a change.

"I'm going to earn my ratings," I said. Then the zombies were on top of me, and there was no more time for discussion. Quietly, I was glad.

There's an art to fighting the infected. It was almost a good thing that this mob had started off so large; we were cutting down the numbers rapidly, since we had the ability to think tactically, but the survivors were still behaving like members of a pack. They wanted to eat, not infect. "They wanted to kill me" may not sound like much of an advantage, but trust me on this one. A zombie that's out to infect will try to smear you with fluids. That gives it a lot more weapons, since they can bleed and spit—even puke, if they've eaten recently enough. A zombie that wants to eat you is just going to come at you with its mouth, and that means it has only one viable avenue of attack. That evens the odds, just a little.

Just a little can be more than enough.

By Mira Grant

Newsflesh Trilogy

Feed
Deadline
Blackout

Parasitology

Parasite
Symbiont

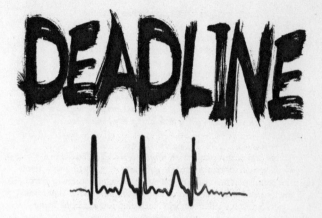

MIRA GRANT

www.orbitbooks.net

ORBIT

First published in Great Britain in 2011 by Orbit

7 9 10 8

A CIP catalogue record for this book
is available from the British Library.

ISBN 978-1-84149-899-7

Typeset in Garamond by M Rules
Printed and bound by CPI Group (UK) Ltd, Croydon, CR0 4YY

Papers used by Orbit are from well-managed forests
and other responsible sources.

MIX
Paper from
responsible sources
FSC® C104740

Orbit
An imprint of
Little, Brown Book Group
Carmelite House
50 Victoria Embankment
London EC4Y 0DZ

An Hachette UK Company
www.hachette.co.uk

www.orbitbooks.net

I am honored to dedicate this book to
Brooke Amber Lunderville
and
Rae Hanson.

The Rising would have been very different without them.

BOOK I

Point of Infection

Sometimes you need lies to stay alive.

—SHAUN MASON

The only thing we have in this world that is utterly and intrinsically ours is our integrity. If we give that away, we may as well stop fighting, because losing that battle is what loses the war. There's nothing worth that.

—GEORGIA MASON

I got another interview request yesterday from some brand-new baby blogger who's looking for a scoop and wants to know how I'm "coping." That's apparently the only thing anyone thinks I'm doing these days. I'm "coping." There are days when I feel like I'm never going to be allowed to do anything else. I'm going to walk through my life being Shaun Mason, the Dude Who Copes. Copes with a world filled with stupid people. Copes with a life that doesn't include the one person who ever really mattered. Copes with everyone asking him whether he's "coping," when the answer should be totally obvious to anyone with a brain.

How am I coping? I miss George, and the goddamn world is still full of zombies, that's how. Everything else . . .

Everything else is just details. And those don't really matter to me anymore.

—From *Adaptive Immunities*, the blog of Shaun Mason,
February 17, 2041

One

Our story opens where countless stories have ended in the last twenty-seven years: with an idiot—in this case, Rebecca Atherton, head of the After the End Times Irwins, winner of the Golden Steve-o Award for valor in the face of the undead—deciding it would be a good idea to go out and poke a zombie with a stick to see what happens. Because, hey, there's always the chance that this time, maybe things will go differently. I know I always thought it would be different for me, back when I was the one doing the poking. George always told me I was an idiot, but I had faith.

Too bad George was right.

At least Becks was being smart about her stupidity and was using a crowbar to poke the zombie, which greatly improved her chances of survival. She'd managed to sink the clawed end under the zombie's collarbone, which was really a pretty effective defensive measure. The zombie would eventually realize that it couldn't move forward. When that happened, it would pull away, either yanking the crowbar out of her hands or dislocating its own collarbone, and then it would try coming at her from another angle. Given the intelligence of your average zombie, I figured she had about an hour before she really needed to be concerned. Plenty of time. It was a thrilling scene.

Woman versus zombie, locked in a visceral conflict that's basically ground into our cultural DNA by this point. And I didn't give a damn.

The guy next to her looked a whole lot less sanguine about the situation, maybe because he'd never been that close to a zombie before. The latest literature says we're supposed to call them "post-Kellis-Amberlee amplification manifestation syndrome humans," but fuck that. If they really wanted some fancy new term for "zombie" to catch on, they should have made it easy to shout at the top of your lungs, or at least made sure it formed a catchy acronym. They're zombies. They're brainless meat puppets controlled by a virus and driven by the endless need to spread their infection. All the fancy names in the world won't change that.

Anyway, Alaric Kwong—the dude trying not to toss his cookies all over Becks's dead friend—had never been a field-situation kind of a guy. He was a natural Newsie, one of those people who are most comfortable when they're sitting somewhere far away from the action, talking about cause and motivation. Unfortunately for him, he'd finally decided that he wanted to go after some bigger stories, and that meant he needed to test for his Class A journalism license. To get your Class A, you have to prove you can handle life in the field. Becks had been trying to help him for almost a week, and I was rapidly coming to think that it was hopeless. He was destined for a life of sitting around the office compiling reports from people who had the balls to pass their exams.

You're being hard on him, Georgia chided.

"I'm being realistic," I muttered.

"Shaun?" Dave looked up from his screen, squinting as he turned in my direction. "Did you say something?"

"Not a thing." I shook my head, reaching for my half-empty Coke. "Five gets you ten he fails his practicals again."

"No bet," said Dave. "He's gonna pass this time."

I raised an eyebrow. "Why are you so sure?"

"Becks is out there with him. He wants to impress her."

"Does he now?" I returned my attention to the screen, more interested now. "Think she likes him back? It'd explain why she keeps wearing skirts to the office ..."

"Maybe," said Dave, judiciously.

On the screen, Becks was trying to get Alaric to take the crowbar and have his own shot at holding off the zombie. No big deal, especially for someone as seasoned as Becks. At least, it wouldn't have been a big deal if there hadn't been six more infected lurching into view on the left-hand monitor. I flipped a switch to turn on the sound. Not a thing. They weren't moaning.

"... the fuck?" I murmured. Flipping another switch to turn on the two-way intercom, I said, "Becks, check your perimeter."

"What are you talking about?" She turned to scan her surroundings, raising one hand to shield her eyes. "Our perimeter is—" Catching sight of the infected lurching closer by the second, she froze, eyes going wide. "Oh, *fuck* me."

"Maybe later," I said, standing. "Keep Alaric alive. I'm heading out to assist with evac."

"Empty promises," she muttered, barely audible. "Alaric! Behind me, *now*!"

I heard him swearing in surprise. The sharp report of Becks shooting their captive zombie followed immediately after. The more zombies you have in an area, the more intelligent they seem to get. If Becks and Alaric wanted to get out of there alive, they needed to reduce the number of infected as much as possible. I didn't see her make the shot; I was already heading for the door, grabbing my rifle from the rack as I passed it.

Dave half stood, asking, "Should I ... ?"

"Negative. Stay here, get the equipment secured, and get ready to drive like hell."

"Check," he said, scrambling from his seat toward the front of the van. I didn't really pay attention to that, either; I was busy kicking open the doors and stepping out into the blazing light of the afternoon.

When you're going to play with dead things, do it during the daylight. They don't see as well in bright light as humans do, and they don't hide as well when they don't have the shadows helping them. More important, the footage will be better. If you're gonna die, make sure you do it on camera.

The GPS tracker in my watch showed Becks and Alaric remaining in a stationary position roughly two miles away. Two miles is the federally mandated minimum distance between an intentional zombie encounter and a licensed traveling safe zone, such as our van. Not that the infected would avoid coming within two miles out of some sort of respect for the law; we just aren't allowed to lure them any closer than that. I did some quick mental math. If they'd already attracted a group of six, and the infected weren't moaning yet, that implied that we had enough zombies in the immediate vicinity to form a thinking mob. Not good.

"Right," I said, and swung myself into the driver's seat of Dave's Jeep. The keys were already in the ignition.

Unlike most field vehicles, Dave's Jeep has no armor to speak of, unless you count the run-flat tires and the titanium-reinforced frame. What it has is speed—and lots of it. The thing has been stripped down to the bare minimum, rebuilt, and stripped down again so many times that I don't think there's a single piece left that conforms to factory standards. It offers about as much protection during an attack of the infected as a wet paper bag. A very fast wet paper bag. It's evac only in hostile territory, and we haven't lost a man yet while we were using it.

I braced my rifle between the seats and hit the gas.

Large swaths of California were effectively abandoned after the

Rising, for one reason or another. "Difficult to secure" was one; "hostile terrain giving the advantage to the enemy" was another. My personal favorite applied to the small, unincorporated community of Birds Landing, in Solano County: "Nobody cared enough to bother." They had a population of less than two hundred pre-Rising, and there were no survivors. When the federal government needed to appoint funds for cleanup and security, there was nobody to argue in favor of cleaning the place out. They still get the standard patrols, just because letting the zombies mob is in nobody's best interests, but for the most part, Birds Landing has been left to the dead.

It should have been the perfect place to run Alaric's last field trial drill. Abandoned, isolated, close enough to Fairfield to allow for pretty easy evac if the need arose, but far enough away that we could still get some pretty decent footage. Not as dangerous as Santa Cruz, not as candy-ass as Bodega Bay. The ideal infected fishing hole. Only it looked like the zombies thought so, too.

The roads were crap. Swearing softly but steadily to myself, I pressed the gas farther down, getting the Jeep up to the highest speed I was confident I could handle. The frame was shaking and jerking like it might fly apart at any second, and, almost unwillingly, I started to grin. I pushed the speed up a little farther. The shaking increased, and my grin widened.

Careful, cautioned George. *I don't want to be an only child.*

My grin died. "I already am," I said, and floored it.

My dead sister that only I can hear—and yes, I know I'm nuts, thanks for pointing out the obvious—isn't the only one who's been worried about my displaying suicidal tendencies since she passed away. "Passed away" is a polite, bloodless way of saying "was murdered," but it's better than trying to explain the situation every time she comes up in conversation. Yeah, I had a sister, and yeah, she died. Also yeah, I talk to her all the damn time, because as long as I'm only that crazy, I'll stay sane enough to function.

I stopped talking to her for almost a week once, on the advice of a crappy psychologist who said he could "help." By the fifth day, I wanted to eat a bullet for breakfast. That's one experiment that won't be repeated.

I gave up the bulk of my active fieldwork when George died. I figured that might calm people down, but all it did was get them more worked up. I was Shaun Mason, Irwin to the president! I wasn't supposed to say "Fuck this noise" and take over my sister's desk job! Only that's exactly what I did. Something about shooting my own sister in the spine left me with a bad taste in my mouth when it comes to getting my hands dirty.

That didn't change the fact that I was licensed for support maneuvers. As long as I kept taking the yearly exams and passing my marksmanship tests, I could legally go out into the field any time I damn well wanted, and I didn't even need to worry about getting decent footage anymore. I was getting close enough to Becks and Alaric's position that I could hear gunshots up ahead, accompanied by the sound of the zombies finally beginning to moan. The Jeep was already rattling so hard that I probably shouldn't try to make it go any faster.

I slammed my foot down as hard as I could.

The Jeep went faster.

I came screeching around the final bend in the road to find Becks and Alaric standing on top of someone's old abandoned toolshed, the two of them back to back at the center of the roof like the little figures on top of a wedding cake. Only the figures on wedding cakes aren't usually armed, and even when they are—it's amazing what you can order from a specialty bakery these days—they don't actually shoot. They also aren't customarily surrounded by a sea of zombies. The six I'd seen on the monitors were quiet because they didn't need to call for reinforcements; the reinforcements were already there. A good thirty infected bodies stood between my people and the Jeep, and even more were shoving their way forward, into the fray.

Becks had a pistol in either hand, making her look like an illustration from some fucked-up pre-Rising horror/Western. *Showdown at the Decay Corral* or something. Her expression was one of intense and unflagging concentration, and every time she fired, a zombie went down. Automatically, I glanced at the dashboard, where the wireless tracker confirmed that all her cameras were still transmitting. Then I swore at myself, looking back toward the action.

George and I grew up with adoptive parents who wanted ratings more than they wanted children. We were a coping mechanism for them, a way of dealing with grief; their biological son died, and so they stopped giving a damn about people. Lose people, they're gone forever. Lose your slot on the top ten and you could win it back. Numbers were safer. We were a means to an end.

I was starting to understand why they had made that decision. Because I woke up every day in a world that didn't have George in it anymore, and I looked in my mirror expecting to see Mom's eyes looking back at me.

That won't happen, you idiot, because I won't let it, said George. *Now get them out of there.*

"On it," I muttered, and reached for the rifle.

Alaric was a lot less calm about his situation than Becks was. He had his rifle out and was taking shots at the teeming mass around them, but he wasn't having anything like her luck: He was firing three or four times just to take down a single zombie, and I saw a couple of his targets stagger back to their feet after he'd hit them. He wasn't taking the time to aim for the head, and I had no idea how much ammo he was carrying. Judging by the size of the mob around them, it was nowhere near enough.

Neither of them was wearing a face shield. That put grenades out until I could get them to move out of the blast radius, since aerosolized zombie will kill you just as sure as the clawing, biting kind. The Jeep wasn't equipped with any real defensive weapons of its own; they would have weighed it down. That left me with the rifle, George's favorite .40, and the latest useful addition to my zombie-hunting arsenal, the extendable shock baton. The virus that controls their bodies doesn't appreciate electrical shocks. It won't kill a zombie, but it'll disorient the shit out of it, and sometimes that's enough.

The mob still hadn't noticed my arrival, being somewhat distracted by the presence of already-targeted meat. Attempting to lure them off wouldn't have done any good. Zombies aren't like sharks; they won't follow in a group. Maybe a few would have followed me, but there was no way to guarantee I'd be able to handle them, and Becks and Alaric would still have been stranded. Recipe for disaster.

Not that what I was about to do was likely to be any better, in the long run. Moving to a position about ten feet behind the mob, I pulled George's gun from its holster and fired until the magazine was exhausted, barely pausing between shots. My aim might still be good enough for the exams, but it was getting rusty in field situations; seventeen bullets, and only twelve zombies went down. Becks and Alaric looked up at the sound of gunshots, Alaric's eyes widening before he started to do a fascinating variant on the victory shuffle.

Becks was more subdued in her delight over my brainless cavalry charge. She just looked relieved.

There was no time to pay attention to my team members. My shots had alerted the zombies to the presence of fresh, less-elevated meat. Several outlying members of the mob were turning in my direction, starting to lurch, shuffle, or run toward me, depending on how long they'd been in the grips of full infection. After snapping another magazine into George's pistol, I holstered it and raised the rifle, aiming for the point of greatest density.

Fact about zombies that everyone knows: You have to aim for the head, since the virus that drives their bodies can repair or route around almost every other form of damage. This is very true.

Fact about zombies that almost no one knows, because you'd have to be a damn fool to take advantage of it: an injured zombie *does* slow down, since you've just forced the relatively single-minded virus controlling the body to try its hand at double-tasking. What's more, the *right* kind of injury can make the difference between having time to reload and getting mowed down.

Bracing the rifle against my shoulder, I fired wildly into the throng. I was starting to get their attention; heads turned toward me, and the moaning changed timbre. I fired the last three shots in fast succession. Too fast to be productive, but fast enough to signal Becks. She hit the roof of the shed, dragging Alaric down with her. I dropped the rifle onto the seat and opened the glove compartment.

Using live grenades when you have people on the ground is antisocial at best and grounds for a murder charge at worst. Still, if you get the right kind—the ones that are calibrated to be explosive without being *too* explosive, since you want to minimize your aerosolized zombie bits—they can be damn handy. The wind still has to be with you, but as long as your people are more than eight feet up, you should be fine. I grabbed all four of the available grenades, pulling their pins one at a time as I sent them sailing into the thick of the zombie mob.

There were several loud, wet bangs as the projectiles found their targets, fragmented into multiple slammer pieces, and exploded. The zombies that caught shrapnel in the head or spinal column went down. Others fell as their legs were blown out from under them. Those last didn't stay down; they started dragging themselves forward, the entire mob now moaning in earnest.

Say something witty now, moron, prompted George.

I reddened. I never used to need coaching from my sister on what it took to do my job. I hit the general channel key on my watch, asking, "You guys mind if I join your party?"

Becks responded immediately, relief more evident in her voice than it had been in her face. Maybe she just wasn't as good at hiding it there. "What took you so long?"

"Oh, traffic. You know how it goes." The entire mob was moving toward me now, apparently deciding that meat on the hoof was more interesting than meat that wouldn't come out of its tree. I snapped the electric baton into its extended position, redrawing George's .40, and offered the oncoming infected a merry smile. "Hi. You want to party?"

Shaun . . . said George.

"Yeah, yeah, I know," I muttered, adding, louder, "You guys get down from there and try to circle to the Jeep. Hit the horn once you're in. There's more ammo under the passenger seat."

"And you're going to do what, exactly?" asked Becks. She sounded sensibly wary. At least one of us was being sensible for a change.

"I'm going to earn my ratings," I said. Then the zombies were on top of me, and there was no more time for discussion. Quietly, I was glad.

There's an art to fighting the infected. It was almost a good thing that this mob had started off so large; we were cutting down the numbers rapidly, since we had the ability to think tactically, but the survivors were still behaving like members of a pack. They wanted to eat, not infect. "They wanted to kill me" may not sound like much of an advantage, but trust me on this one. A zombie that's out to infect will try to smear you with fluids. That gives it a lot more weapons, since they can bleed and spit—even puke, if they've eaten recently enough. A zombie that wants to eat you is just going to come at you with its mouth, and that means it has only one viable avenue of attack. That evens the odds, just a little.

Just a little can be more than enough.

I used my baton to sweep a constant perimeter around myself, shocking any zombie that came into range and trusting the Kevlar in my jacket to keep my arm from getting tagged before I could pull it back. The electricity slowed them down enough for me to keep firing. More important, it kept them from getting positions established behind me. I could track Becks and Alaric by the sound of gunshots, which came almost as regularly as my own. I was taking out two zombies for every three shots. Not the best odds in the world. Not the worst odds, either.

The zombies pressed forward. I backed toward the Jeep, letting them think they were herding me while I kept thinning out their ranks. I realized I was grinning. I couldn't help it. Maybe facing possible death isn't supposed to make me happy, but years of training can't be shrugged off overnight, and I was an Irwin for a long time before I retired.

Aim, fire. Swing, zap. Aim, fire. It was almost like dancing, a series of soothing, predictable movements. When George's gun ran out of ammunition, I switched to my own backup pistol, the motion as smooth and easy as it could possibly have been. I couldn't hear gunshots anymore, so either Becks and Alaric had made the Jeep or my brain had started filtering out the sounds of their combat as inconsequential. I had my own zombies to play with. They could deal with theirs. Even George had fallen quiet, leaving me to move in a small bubble of almost perfect contentment. It didn't matter that my sister was dead, or that the assholes who'd ordered her killed were still out there somewhere, doing God knows what to God-knows-who. I had zombies. I had bullets. Everything else was just details, and like I keep saying, I don't care about the details.

"Shaun!"

The shout came from behind me, rather than over the intercom or from the inside of my head. I barely squashed the urge to turn toward it, a motion that could be fatal in the field. I put two bullets into the zombie that was lunging at me, and shouted back, "What?"

"We've made the Jeep! Can you retreat?"

Could I retreat? "Well, that's an interesting question, Becks!" I shouted. Aim, fire. Aim again. "Is there anything behind me? And what the fuck happened to honking?"

"Don't move!"

"I can do that!" I fired again. Another zombie went down. And hell opened up behind me. Not literally, but the sound of an assault rifle can be similar. Becks, it seemed, had found more than just ammo under the seat. Dave and I were going to have a long talk about making sure I knew what my assets were before we let me head into the field.

"Clear!"

"Great!" My throat was starting to ache from all the shouting. I surveyed the zombies remaining in front of me. None of them looked fresh enough to put up a real chase, and so I did exactly what you're not supposed to do in a field situation if you have any choice in the matter:

I took a chance.

I turned my back on the mob and ran for the Jeep, whacking anything that looked likely to move with my electric baton. Becks was in the back, covering the area, while Alaric sat in the passenger seat, looking shell-shocked.

Nothing grabbed me, and in just a few seconds, I was using the stripped-down frame to swing myself into the driver's seat. I didn't bother with the seat belt as I hit the gas, and we went roaring out of there, leaving the moaning remains of the Birds Landing zombie mob behind.

California is a fascinating place to live. Thanks to the weird geography and the microclimate zones, we have everything from mountain tundra to verdant forest, and that means we can be used as a case study for zombie preservation in almost any climate you can think of. We have some of the largest metro zones, and they're close to some of the first counties to be declared legally abandoned. It's like the whole state has multiple personality disorder.

Sometimes I think about moving someplace like New York or Washington, D.C., where the news is valued, but there aren't as many actual outbreaks to worry about. Only Shaun would be totally miserable if I did that, because he'd follow me. He'll always follow me, just like I'll always follow him. That's what being together means, right?

Neither of us ever has to be alone.

—From *Postcards from the Wall*, the unpublished files of Georgia Mason, originally posted January 9, 2041

———

So Becks and Alaric got themselves into a sticky spot today—for the moment-by-moment, uncensored report, check Alaric's status feed, but be prepared for lots of adult language. Did you know he knew some of those words? I did not know he knew some of those words! Our little boy is growing up.

But Becks and Alaric getting into trouble is practically old news around here, right? So what makes this such a big deal? Only the fact that our Lord and Master Shaun "The Boss" Mason made his triumphant return to the field to pull their asses out of the fire. And I have to say, seeing him out there . . .

It was good in a way I don't think I can put into words, and I do this for a living. Maybe we're going to recover from what happened last year after all. Maybe we can move on.

Maybe we're going to be okay.

—From The Antibody Electric, the blog of
Dave Novakowski, April 12, 2041

Two

I stopped the Jeep in front of the van before turning to really look at Becks and Alaric, scanning them for signs of visible injury or blood. Their clothing was filthy, but I didn't see any gore on either of them. "Either of you bit?"

"No," said Becks.

Alaric just shook his head. Poor guy still looked like he was going to puke.

"Scratched?" I hate this part. Before she died, George always took care of the post-field briefing and blood tests. I didn't want to deal with them, and she didn't make me. These days, I'm the boss, and that makes it my problem.

"Negative."

"No."

"Good." I leaned across Alaric to open the glove compartment, pulling out three blood tests. "You know what happens now."

"Oh, great," Alaric said, with a grimace. "Bloodshed. Because I haven't had nearly enough of that so far today."

"Stop your whining and poke your finger," I commanded, passing out the small plastic boxes.

Moaning and grumbling about needle pricks aside, I have to give the blood test units this: They're awesome pieces of technology, and they get better every year. The basic units I was handing out were ten times more sensitive than the units George and I were using in the field before we signed up to follow then-Senator Ryman's presidential campaign, where we'd had access to much better equipment. All we had to do was prick our fingers, and the sensors inside the disposable little boxes would go to work, filtering through our blood, looking for the active viral bodies that would signal an unstoppable cascade ending in amplification and zombification.

Blood tests are a part of daily life, especially if you're going out into the field. Most people don't consider them a big deal anymore, which is fascinating to me. This is a test where failure means death— no negotiation, no makeup exams. You'd expect there to be a lot more anxiety. I guess people just put the possible consequences out of their heads. Maybe it helps them sleep at night.

It sure as hell doesn't help me.

I popped the lid off my own test, saying, "One . . ."

Two, said George, half a second out of synch with Alaric.

I rammed my finger down on the test pad, closing my eyes.

"Three," said Becks.

I don't watch the lights on test units when I can help it. They flash between red and green while your blood is being examined to prove that either result is possible. It's partially a psychological device and partially to protect the makers of the test units from lawsuits. "I shot my wife, officer, but the green light on her unit didn't work." The man who could muster that defense would get a healthy settlement and possibly a movie deal. No one likes to get sued, and so any unit that finds a malfunction in either light will automatically reset itself, requiring you to try again. So the flashing makes sense, but I don't really give a shit. I've seen that light go red for real too many times. There are things that just hurt too much to be worth watching.

"Clean," said Alaric, relief naked in his voice.

"Me, too," said Becks.

"Good." I opened my eyes and looked at my own test. The light was shining green. No surprise there. Kellis-Amberlee won't ever kill me. That would be too merciful.

"Get back in the van before your new friends catch up with us," I said. "Dave's ready to get us the hell out of here. Aren't you, Dave?"

Dave had been eavesdropping, as I knew he would be. His response over the group channel was an immediate "Foot's on the gas, boss."

"You heard the man." I grabbed a reinforced plastic bag from the glove compartment, passing it around to collect the test units. "Becks, get these into the biohazard container. Both of you, start your footage cleanup while you're on the road, and we'll regroup at the office after cleanup and downtime."

"And what are you going to do?" asked Becks, somewhat warily.

"I'm getting the Jeep home. Now get out."

She looked like she wanted to argue with me. Luckily for my blood pressure, she didn't do it. "Come on, Alaric," she said, taking the shaken Newsie by the elbow and tugging him out of the Jeep as she climbed out of the backseat. "Let's get some walls between us and the idiots."

She didn't have to tell him twice. I'd never seen him move that fast. Becks and I exchanged a semi-surprised look as the van door slammed shut behind Alaric's retreat, and I actually laughed before waving her to follow him.

"Go on," I said. "I'll be fine."

"Sure thing, boss," she said, and turned to go.

I waited until she closed the door and I heard the van's engine turn over before starting the Jeep again. We were cutting it pretty close; I could hear the approaching moan of the hunting mob before the rumble from our vehicles drowned it out.

Good for ratings, George offered.

"Like that means anything?"

She didn't have an answer to that. Dave pulled the van back onto the road, such as it was, and I followed.

It was after midnight in London according to the clock on the dashboard. Bad, but not too bad, especially not when you're talking about professional blogging hours. "Time delay broadcast for editing," I said. My headpiece beeped to signal that my personal cameras were now being fed into a buffer, rather than recording live. Not as good for ratings as a live feed, but the only way to get even the pretense of privacy. I could delete anything I didn't want hitting the Internet. "Phone, dial Mahir."

"Local time in London is approximately twelve thirty-seven A.M.," said the automated operator, with mechanized politeness. "Ms. Gowda has requested that calls be held until eight A.M. local time."

"Ms. Gowda doesn't have the authority to block my calls, as I am, in fact, her husband's boss," I said amiably. "Please dial Mahir."

"Acknowledged," said the operator, and went quiet, replaced by the faint beeping of an international connection in process. I hummed under my breath, watching the abandoned California countryside rolling out on either side of me. It would have been pretty if not for, y'know, all the dead stuff.

"Shaun?" Mahir's normally smooth voice was blurry with exhaustion, making his British accent stand out more than usual.

"Mahir, my main man! You sound a little harried. Did I wake you?"

"No, but I really do wish you'd stop calling so late at night. You know Nandini gets upset when you do."

"There you go again, assuming that I'm not actually trying to piss off your wife. I'm really a much nicer person inside your head, aren't I? Do I give money to charity and help old-lady zombies across streets so that they can bite babies?"

Mahir sighed. "My, you *are* in a mood today, aren't you?"

"Been monitoring the boards?"

"You know that I have been. Or was, until I went to sleep." I also knew he'd called up the numbers the second I got him out of bed, because that was how Mahir's mind worked. Some men check their wallets; he checked our ratings.

"Then you know why I'm not in the mood for sunshine and puppies." I paused. "That expression makes no sense. Why the hell would I *ever* be in the mood for puppies?"

"Shaun—"

"I could go with sunshine, though. Sunshine is useful. It should really be 'sunshine and shotguns.' Something you'd actually be happy about."

"Shaun—"

"How'd the footage go over?"

There was a pause as Mahir adjusted to the fact that I'd suddenly decided to start making sense. Then, clearing his throat, he said, "We're getting some of our highest click-through rates and download shares in the last six months. There have been eleven outside interview requests, and I think you'll find as many, if not more, when you check your in-box. Six of the more junior Irwins have already been caught on the staff chats trying to figure out whether this means you'd be willing to do a joint excursion." A pause. "None were hired during your tenure as department head."

That meant they knew me, but had never worked with me in the field. I sighed. "Okay, so I won't shoot them. What's the worst headline?"

"Are you quite sure you want to do this while you're driving?"

"How did you—"

"You've gone to time delay, but there are still quite a few people watching you through the van's rearview window camera, hoping to see you get attacked again."

Of course there were. "There are days when I really think I should go be an accountant or something."

"You'd go mad."

"But no one would be staring at me. What's the worst headline, Mahir?"

He sighed, heavily. "You're sure?"

"I'm sure."

"All right, then. 'Shaun of the Dead, Part Two.'" He stopped. I said nothing. He must have taken that as a cue because he continued: "'Shaun Phillip Mason, the world's most well-known and well-regarded action blogger (known as an 'Irwin' to the informed, named in honor of a pre-Rising naturalist with a fondness for handling dangerous creatures), returned to the field today after almost a year of full-time desk duty. Does this mark the end of his much-debated 'retirement,' a career choice made during the emotionally charged weeks following the death of his adoptive sister, Georgia Mason, a factual news blogger? Or does it—'"

"That's enough, Mahir," I said quietly.

He stopped immediately. "I'm sorry."

"Don't be. I wouldn't have called if I hadn't expected them to be bad. At least this tells me what I'll be dealing with when I get back to the office." George was as pissed off by the world's refusal to leave me the fuck alone as I was, and she was swearing steadily in the back of my head. It was more reassuring than distracting. The things that get under my skin don't always get under hers, and I feel the closest to crazy when I'm disagreeing with the voice in my head.

"Are you all right?"

I paused before answering, trying to find the best words. If George had a best friend—a best friend who wasn't me, anyway—it was Mahir. He was her second-in-command before she died and gave him a promotion that he'd never wanted. Sometimes, I thought he was the only person who fully understood how close we'd been, or how much her death had broken me. He was the only one who never questioned the fact that she still talked to me.

Frankly, I think he was jealous that she never spoke to *him*.

"Ignoring the part where you know the answer to that is 'fuck, no,' I'm fine, Mahir. Tired. I shouldn't have gone out there."

"If you hadn't—"

"Becks had it under control. It's her department now. I shouldn't have interfered."

"You know that isn't true."

"Do I?"

Mahir paused before saying, "I was actually pleased to see you out there. If you don't mind my saying so, Shaun, you looked more like yourself than you have in quite some time. You might want to consider making this the beginning of a true . . . well, revival, if the word isn't in poor taste. You could do with something beyond spending all your time in an office."

"I'll take that under consideration."

No, you won't.

"No, you won't," said Mahir, in eerie imitation of George.

"Now you're ganging up on me," I muttered.

"What?"

Sometimes Mahir was a little too sharp for my own good. "Nothing," I said, more loudly. "I'm signing off now, Mahir. I need to concentrate on the drive."

"Shaun, I really think you should—"

"Tell the management I won't call back until it's a decent hour in your part of the world. Say, five minutes before the alarm clock?"

"Shaun, really—"

"Later." I hit the manual switch on the dashboard, cutting Mahir off midsentence. The silence that followed was almost reassuring enough to distract me from the fact that I was still apparently being filmed. I raised a hand and amiably flipped off the van.

Not nice, chided Georgia.

"George, please."

She fell sullenly quiet. For a change, I didn't mind. A sulking sister is better than a scolding sister, especially when I'm trying to wrap my head around the fact that the world wants me back in the field on a regular basis. One dead Mason just isn't enough for some people.

To distract myself, I hit the gas, sped up, and passed the van. It was a deviation from our standing driving formation, but not enough of one that it was likely to cause any real distress with the occupants of the van. With our viewing audience, maybe—especially the percentage that was hoping to see me fight off a horde of the infected through the rearview cam—but the staff would understand.

Hitting the gas harder, I sped off toward Alameda County, and home.

Prior to George's death, the two of us lived with our adoptive parents in the genteel Berkeley house where we were raised, a former faculty residence sold by the university after the Rising. I went back there initially, and quickly found that I couldn't take it. I could handle having George's ghost in my head, but I couldn't deal with the years of memory in those halls. More important, I couldn't handle watching the Masons hover around looking for ways to capitalize on the death of their adopted daughter. We always knew what they were to us and what we were to them, but it took George dying to really make me realize how unhealthy it was. I moved out as soon as I could manage it, renting a crappy little apartment in downtown El Cerrito. I moved again six months later, after the site really started pulling in the bucks. Oakland this time, and one of the four apartments in the same building that we'd rented under the name of After the End Times. One apartment for the office; one apartment shared by Alaric and Dave, who spent half their time as best buddies and half their time as mortal enemies; one apartment open for visiting staffers who needed a place to crash.

One apartment for me and George, who didn't take up any physical space but was so much a part of every room that sometimes I could fool myself into thinking she had just stepped out for some fresh air. That she'd be right back, if I were just willing to wait. If I were still seeing a psychiatrist, I'm sure I'd be getting lectured on how unhealthy my attitude is. Good thing I fired my shrink, huh?

Oakland's a pretty awesome place to hang your hat, whether or not you've got a dead sister to deal with. Twenty-five years ago—roughly, I'm not big on math—Oakland was an urban battlefield. They had a gang problem in the early nineteen-eighties, but that cleared up, and they were fighting a different war by the time the Rising rolled around. Oakland had become the site of an ongoing conflict between the natives who'd lived there for generations and the forces of gentrification that really wanted a Starbucks on every corner and an iPod in every pocket. Then the zombies showed up, and gentrification lost.

More things we learned from the Rising: It's hard to gentrify a city that's on fire.

The new folks turned tail and ran for the hills—the ones who lived long enough, anyway. But the people who'd grown up in Oakland knew the lay of the land, and they knew what it meant to fight for what's yours. Maybe they didn't have the advantages some of the richer cities started out with, but they had a lot of places they could hole up, and they had a lot of guns. Maybe most important of all, thanks to that gang violence I mentioned earlier, they had a lot of people who actually knew how to *use* the guns.

Oakland's inner city fared better than almost any other heavily populated spot on the West Coast. When the dust of the Rising settled, the city was battered, bruised, and still standing—no small accomplishment for a city that most of the emergency services had already written off as impossible to save. It's still a proud, heavily armed community today.

It's about fifty miles from Birds Landing to Oakland, and the safest route is even longer. Thankfully, having a journalist's license means never having to explain why you didn't want to take the safe way. I hit the first of the checkpoint entrances to I-80 after about twenty miles on the rocky, poorly maintained California back roads. According to pre-Rising records, the checkpoints used to be called toll booths, and they actually accepted currency, rather than automatically deducting usage fees from your bank account. Also, they didn't have armed guards or require a clean blood test for passage. Road trips must have been pretty boring before the zombies came.

Despite the ongoing decrease in personal travel—the number of miles logged by the average American goes down every year, with many people telecommuting and ordering their groceries delivered so that they'll never even need to leave their homes—we still need freeways for things like truckers and journalists. I-80 is actually fairly well-maintained, assuming you like your roads with concrete walls and fences all around them. Most accidents are fatal, not because of the other cars but because spinning out and hitting one of those walls doesn't leave much of a margin for recovery. It also doesn't leave much of a margin for reanimation. That's probably the point.

My GPS said that I was seventeen miles ahead of the van when I hit the freeway. I sped up, accelerating to the posted speed limit of eighty-five miles per hour. The van wouldn't be able to go that fast—not unless they wanted to risk flipping over. I could reach the apartment, get through decontamination, and hole up somewhere before they had a chance to grab me and ask me to do a post-run interview. The last thing I wanted to deal with was some idiot asking me how I was *feeling*, even if it was an idiot who worked for me.

Cameras mounted atop the I-80 gun turrets swiveled to follow me as I blazed down the road. Just one more government service, keeping the world safe from infection, the living dead, and the terrifying risk of privacy. For my generation, the concept of personal privacy was one more casualty of the Rising—and not one that many people take the time to mourn.

The Rising: casual parlance for the mass amplification and outbreak following the initial appearance of the mutated Kellis-Amberlee viral strain. It started three years before my sister and I were born, during the hot, brutal summer of 2014. More people died during that summer than have ever been properly accounted for, and they kept dying for five years.

Before the Rising, zombies were the stuff of fiction and crappy horror movies, not things that you could encounter on the street. The Rising changed that. It changed the world forever.

Oh, the world didn't change in the big, apocalyptic "tiny enclaves of people fighting to survive against a world gone mad" way most of the movies suggested it would, but it still changed. George used to say we'd embraced the culture of fear, willingly letting ourselves be duped into going scared from the cradle to the grave. George used to say a lot of things I didn't really understand. I understood this much, anyway: Most people are scared of more than just the zombies, and there are other people who like them that way.

I rode I-80 to another checkpoint and another blood test, even though it would almost take a miracle to amplify on a closed freeway system. Only almost: It's happened a few times. Spontaneous amplification is rare but possible, and that, combined with the culture of fear, keeps the checkpoints in operation. As I'd expected, my infection status hadn't changed during my solitary, zombie-free drive; also as I'd expected, the guards eyed my stripped-down Jeep like it was some sort of rolling death trap and waved me through just as fast as federal regulations would allow. I offered them a brilliant smile, making their nearly identical looks of discomfort deepen, and drove off the freeway to the surface streets.

My crew's apartment building is less than half a mile from the freeway, a quirk of location that makes it perfect for our needs and less desirable to the rest of the population, keeping the rent lower than it might otherwise be. We don't even have our own parking garage. Instead, we share a secure "community structure" with half the other buildings on our block. Every local resident and business pays into a neighborhood fund that goes to pay for security upgrades and salaries for the guards. It's definitely money well-spent. After the End Times regularly contributes extra cash, just to make sure things stay as close to top-of-the-line as possible.

I arrived to find James on duty at the guard station, his feet propped on the desk next to the monitor and the latest issue of *Playboy* open on his knees. He was studying the centerfold without shame, although he was paying enough attention to raise his head when I pulled up to the gate. Smiling, he hit the button for the intercom.

"Afternoon, Mr. Mason. Have a good day out there?"

"The best, Jimmy," I said, returning his smile. "You want to buzz me through?"

"Well, that depends, Mr. Mason. How do you feel about passing me your residency card and sticking your hand in my little box?"

"Pretty damn lousy, Jimmy," I said. Digging out my wallet, I produced my residency card and dropped it into the guard station's miniature air lock. It would be disinfected before James ever touched it, and he'd still wear Teflon-coated gloves when he picked it up to run it through his scanner. Protocol. Gotta love it, because anything else would lead to madness.

While James ran my card through his system and checked it for signs of tampering, I stuck my hand into the guard station's built-in blood test unit, gritting my teeth as the needles unerringly managed to hit right on top of my freshest puncture wounds. The worst thing about going into the field isn't the zombies or the driving. It's all the damn blood tests.

"Well, Mr. Mason, everything looks to be in order," James said, still cheerfully. He dropped my card back into the lockbox. "Welcome home."

"Thanks, Jimmy," I said, withdrawing my hand. His welcome was the only confirmation that I'd actually passed my blood test. Unlike the private units, which have to show you your results, business units often display only to the people who need to know—that is, the ones whose job it is to kill you if you fail.

Offering him a wave, which he amiably returned, I retrieved my card and drove on, leaving him to his comfortable Plexiglas box and his pornography.

Building underground in California isn't strictly safe, but neither is walking on the streets. That's the brilliant logic that led to the construction of underground tunnels connecting the community structures to their associated buildings. Our building's tunnel is about the length of a football field. As I walked along it, I amused myself by pondering just how many zombies would be able to pack themselves inside if there were ever a lapse in security. I had just reached the conclusion that the tunnel could hold somewhere around two hundred infected bodies, assuming they were all of average size, when I reached the door, swiped my residency card through the scanner, and was home.

The building consists of three floors and ten apartments: two on the first floor, four each on the second and third. My staff has three of the four third-floor apartments, and the fourth belongs to old Mrs. Hagar, who's so deaf that she probably wouldn't notice if we started holding weekly raves on the roof. Becks calls her "an old dear" and brings her cookies. In exchange, Mrs. Hagar no longer threatens to lob grenades at us every time we run into each other in the downstairs lobby. A few chocolate chips are a small price to pay to avoid getting vaporized while you're picking up the mail.

The manager has one of the first-floor apartments. He's almost

never there, and we're all pretty sure he has another residence somewhere outside of the city. Someplace safer. A lot of people think
they're safer in the country because there aren't as many bodies capable of amplification. Not as many bodies means not as many guns, as
George used to say. I'll take my chances with the cities.

The other first-floor apartment is mine. It's not much distance
from the staff apartments, but it's enough to let me feel like I have
a little privacy. A little privacy can make all the difference in the
world. I pressed my palm to the test pad for yet another blood test,
unlocked the front door, and stepped inside, alone at last.

Alone? asked George, sounding dryly amused.

"My apologies." Closing my eyes, I let my head tilt backward
until it hit the door. "Apartment, give me lights in the living room,
news scroll on mute on the main monitor, and prep the shower for
a decontamination."

"Acknowledged," said the polite voice of the apartment's computer system, following the word with a series of muted beeps as it
activated the various requested utilities. I stayed where I was for a few
more seconds, stretching out the moment. I could be anywhere in
that moment. I could be in my apartment. Or I could be back in my
bedroom in my parents' house, the room that was connected to
Georgia's room, waiting for my turn at the shower. I could be anywhere.

I opened my eyes.

My apartment is never going to win any beautiful-home compe-
titions. It consists of a living room full of boxes, computer
equipment, and racks of weaponry; a bedroom full of boxes, computer equipment, and racks of weaponry; an office full of boxes,
computer equipment, and racks of weaponry; and a bathroom where
the floor space is almost completely consumed by a top-of-the-line
shower and decontamination unit. No weaponry in there, at least—
just ammunition. Bullets are waterproof enough these days that I

could probably take them in the shower with me, if I were feeling particularly weird that day.

The air in the apartment always smells like stale pizza, gun oil, and bleach. Several people have said it doesn't feel like anybody lives there, and what they don't seem to understand is that I like it that way. As long as I'm not really living there, I never have to think about the fact that I'm living there alone.

It took me fifteen minutes to complete standard decontamination procedures and get myself into some clean clothes, leaving the old ones in a biohazard-secure bin for later sterilization. I checked the GPS readout on my watch. According to the van's tracking coordinates, the rest of the team was just now reaching the guard station and getting their chance to check out Jimmy's substandard taste in porn. Good. That meant I still had time to square myself away. Grabbing a clean jacket off a stack of survivalist magazines, I started for the door, swerving almost as an afterthought to pass through the kitchen and snag a Coke from the fridge.

Thanks, said George, as I stepped out into the hall.

"No problem," I murmured, cracking open her soda and taking a long drink before heading toward the door to the roof-access stairs. In most buildings, tromping around on the roof is likely to get you shot. Just another advantage of living where I do: Mrs. Hagar can't even hear us up there unless we're setting off land mines, and we've done that only once, for quality control purposes.

There used to be a padlock on the door leading to the roof-access stairs. As if the infected were going to be mounting a top-down attack? That stopped happening when the mass outbreaks stopped driving the wounded to the rooftops to wait for rescue that never came. The manager periodically realizes that the lock is missing and replaces it, and someone on my staff comes along and cuts it off the next day. That's the circle of life around here. Nothing stays locked away forever.

You're depressing today.

"It's a depressing sort of day," I said. George quieted, and I climbed the stairs in something that was chillingly close to solitude.

I don't deal well with being alone. Maybe that's why I decided to go crazy instead.

My crew's been working on converting the roof to suit our needs since we took over the third floor. It's one of those projects that's never going to be finished; there's something new every time I go up there. Dave has what he calls his "outdoor theater," a little grouping of folding chairs and a collapsible movie screen under a pavilion he bought at the Wal-Mart in Martinez. He brings out a projector on warm nights and shows pre-Rising horror movies. I think he's trying to lure Maggie out of her house and into the city by competing with her grindhouse parties, and if he keeps it up, he just may succeed.

Becks has a small firing range with targets designed for everything from basic handguns to her personal favorite weapon, the wrist-mounted crossbow. That girl reads too many comic books. Still, I have to say, the sight of a zombie's head catching fire after it gets hit with one of her trick arrows isn't something I'm going to forget anytime soon. Neither are our viewers.

And me? I have a corner of the roof where no one does anything else, where I can go and sit and drink a Coke and watch the clouds chase themselves across the sky, and where I don't have to be the boss for a little while. I can just be me. When I go up there, my staff'll move heaven and earth to keep anyone from following me, because they know I need the escape. They've mostly gotten over treating me like I'm made of eggshells, but there are exceptions.

A pigeon was sitting on the edge of the roof when I walked up, cooing contentedly to itself. It looked at me suspiciously, but waited to see what I would do before going to the trouble of flying away. When I just sat, it resumed its cocky back-and-forth strut without a second thought.

"Must be nice to be a pigeon," I said, taking another swig of Coke and making a face. "You sure I can't sell you on the idea of coffee? Nice, bitter, hot coffee that doesn't taste like going down on a hooker from Candyland?"

You never objected to me drinking Coke before, George replied.

"Yeah, George, but you didn't live inside my head before. You can use this stuff to clean car batteries. *Car batteries,* George. You think that's doing anything good to my internal organs? Because I'd bet good money that it's not."

Shaun, said George, in that all-too-familiar, all-too-exasperated tone, *I don't* live *anywhere. I'm not alive. Remember?*

"Yeah, George," I said, taking one last drink from the can of Coke before tossing it, still half full, off the edge of the roof. It sprayed soda in an impressively large arc as it fell. I leaned backward against the building's air-ventilation shaft and closed my eyes. "I remember."

As I've mentioned several times, I have a sister. An adopted sister, to be precise, fished out of the state system by Michael and Stacy Mason after the Rising left us both without our biological parents. That was George. She's the reason I got into blogging, and the reason we wound up running a site of our own. She was never meant to be one of nature's followers. And technically, I guess the tense is wrong there, because it ought to be "I *had* a sister." The death of Georgia Carolyn Mason was registered with the Centers for Disease Control on June 20, 2032. Her official cause of death is recorded as "complications from massive amplification of the Kellis-Amberlee virus," which means, in layman's terms, "she died because she turned into a zombie."

It would be a lot more accurate to say that she died because I shot her in the spine, spraying blood all over the interior of the van that we were locked in at the time. It might be even more accurate to say that she died because some bastard shot a needle full of the live

Kellis-Amberlee virus into her arm. But the CDC says she died of Kellis-Amberlee, and hey, we don't argue with the CDC, right?

If I ever find out who fired that needle, their official cause of death is going to be Shaun Mason. That's the thought that keeps me going. I sleepwalk through my job, I pretend I'm administrating our site while Mahir does all the work, I delete calls from my crazy parents, I hold conversations with my dead sister, and I look for the people who had her killed. I'll find them someday. All I have to do is wait.

See, when the zombies came, it was an accident. Researchers in two totally unconnected facilities were working on two totally unrelated projects that involved genetically engineering "helper viruses"—new diseases that were supposed to make life better for the whole damn world. One of them was based on a really fucking nasty hemorrhagic fever called Marburg, and was designed to cure cancer. The other was based on a strain of the common cold, and was supposed to get rid of colds forever. Enter Marburg Amberlee and the Kellis Flu, two beautiful pieces of viral engineering that did exactly what they were supposed to do. No more cancer, no more colds, just happy people all over the world celebrating the dawn of a new age. Only it turns out the viruses were just like the people who made them in at least one sense, because when they met, through the natural chain of transmission and infection, it was basically love at first sight. First comes love, then comes marriage, then comes the hybrid viral strain known as "Kellis-Amberlee." It swept the planet before anyone knew what was happening.

And then people started dying and getting back up to munch on their relatives, and we figured out what was happening damn fast. People fought back, because people always fight back, and we had one advantage the characters in zombie movies never seem to have: See, we'd *seen* all the zombie movies, and we knew what was likely to be a bad idea. George always said the first summer of the Rising was possibly the best example of human nobility that history had to offer, because for just a few months, before the accusations started flying and the fingers started pointing, we really were one people, united against one enemy. And we fought. We fought for the right to live, and in the end, we won.

Sort of, anyway. Look at the movies from before the Rising and you'll see a whole different world from the one that we live in; a world where people go outside just because they think that, hey, going outside might be fun. They don't file paperwork or put on body armor. They just *go*. A world where people travel on a whim, where they swim with dolphins and own dogs and do a hundred thousand things that are basically unthinkable today. It seems like paradise from where I'm sitting, a generation and a couple of decades away. If you ask me, that world was the single biggest casualty of the Rising.

The Rising didn't just showcase the nobler side of human nature; it was a war, and as long as there have been wars, there have been war profiteers. There's always somebody willing and waiting to make a buck off somebody else's pain. I'm not sure most of them meant to do what they did—I'm sure most of them really meant to do the right thing—but somehow, an entire world full of people who had managed to take arms against an enemy that was straight out of a Romero flick was convinced that what they really wanted was fear. They put down their guns, they locked their doors, they went inside, and they were grateful for all the things that they were scared of.

I used to think the Irwins were great warriors in the ongoing fight to live a normal life in our post-Rising world. Now I'm starting to suspect that we're just tools of some greater plan. After all, why leave your house when you can live vicariously through a dumb kid willing to risk his life for your amusement? Bread and circuses. That's all we are.

You're getting bitter, George observed.

"I got reason," I said.

Bread and circuses is what got George killed. We—her, me, and our friend Georgette "Buffy" Meissonier—were the original After the End Times news team, and we got hired by President Ryman to follow his campaign. He was Senator Ryman then, and I was a dumb, optimistic Irwin who believed ... well, a lot of things, but mostly, that I'd die before George did. I was never going to be the one who buried her, and I was sorry that she was going to bury me, but we'd both made our peace with that years before. We were chasing the news, and we were chasing the truth, and we were on the adventure of our lives. Literally, for George and Buffy, because neither one of them walked away from it. Turns out there were people who didn't want Ryman to make it to the White House. Oh, they were happy to have him elected. They just didn't want him to be president. They were backing their own candidate.

Governor David Tate. Or, as I prefer to think of him, "the fucking asshole pig that I shot in the head for being part of the conspiracy that killed my sister." He admitted it before he died. Well, before he injected himself with a huge quantity of live Kellis-Amberlee and forced me to shoot him. During the after-investigation, I got asked why I thought he'd decided to pull the classic super-villain rant before he killed himself. I got asked a lot of other questions, too, but that was the one I had an answer for.

"Easy," I said. "He was a smug fucker who wanted us to know how awesome the world would have been if we'd let him take it over, and he was stalling for time, because he knew that if he managed to inject himself, we'd never find out whom he was working with. He wanted us to think he was the mastermind. It was all him. But it wasn't. It never could have been."

They asked me why not.

"Because that asshole was never smart enough to kill my sister."

They didn't have any questions after that. What could they have asked? George was dead, Tate was dead, and I'd put the bullets in both of them. Before the Rising, a statement like that would have been an invitation to a murder charge. These days, I'm lucky no one tried to give me a medal. I think Rick probably convinced then-Senator Ryman that even the suggestion would result in me assaulting a federal official, and nobody wanted to deal with that. Although I might have welcomed the distraction.

Speaking of distractions, there was something poking me in the knee. I cracked one eye open and found the pigeon was now industriously pecking at my jeans. "Dude, I'm not a breadcrumb vending machine." It kept pecking. "Has Becks been putting steroids in your birdseed or something? Because don't think I don't know she's been feeding you. I found the receipt from the last time she hit the pet store."

"Since I haven't made any attempts to hide it from you, it would be a little bit upsetting if you didn't know," said Becks, from about three feet behind me. "As it is, you noticed the receipt and not the twenty-pound bags of birdseed in the office coat closet. That doesn't say much about your powers of observation."

"But it says a lot about my attention to detail." I twisted around to face her, sending the pigeon fluttering off to find a safer place to perch. "Is there a reason the sanctity of the roof has been violated?"

Becks crossed her arms across her chest in a gesture that was only semidefensive. I don't know why she looks at me that way. I've never hit her. Dave a few times, and I broke Alaric's nose once, but never her. "Dave says you've been up here for three hours."

I blinked. "I have?"

I thought you needed the sleep, George said.

"Gee, thanks," I muttered. You'd think having my dead sister living inside my head might have some helpful side effects, like, say, insomnia, but no such luck. I get all the negatives of being insane, with none of the bonuses.

"You have," said Becks, with a small nod. "We've been going over the footage. We got some great shots, especially from the sequence where Alaric was holding the crowbar. Before everything got bad, I mean."

"You checked your license allowances before you let him do that, right?" I asked, levering myself to my feet. My back was stiff enough to confirm that whole "three hours" thing; I'd been sitting in one position for way too long.

"Of course," she said, sounding affronted. "As long as I stayed within five feet and he was in no immediate nonconsensual danger, I was totally within my legal rights as a journalism teacher. What do you think I am, some sort of field newbie?" She sounded even more offended than the question would justify, because there was another question underneath it: *When did you stop being any fun?* Becks hired on as a Newsie under George and switched to my department almost before the ink on her contract was dry. She's one of nature's born Irwins, and she and I worked together really well. That's why I gave her my department when I stepped down. And that's probably also why she seems to really believe, deep down, that all she needs to do is find me a stick and a hole to poke it into and I'll be fine.

It's really a pity that I don't think it's ever going to work that way for me. Because damn, it would be nice.

"I don't think you're a field newbie, Becks, I just think there are some people who'd love to have an excuse to slap us with more violation charges. I mean, how much did we pay to get those 'standing too close to a goat' charges off Mahir's record? And he's in England. They still *like* goats over there."

"All right, fair enough," she admitted. "But still, Alaric did really well out there today. I think he's almost ready for his exams."

"Well, good."

"He just needs a senior Irwin to sign off on him."

"So sign."

"Shaun—"

"Was that the only reason you came up here to poke at me? Because it doesn't seem like enough."

You're trying to distract her.

I gritted my teeth and didn't answer. No one heard George but me; everyone heard me when I talked to her. Not exactly the fairest deal I've ever been a part of, but, hey, I'm the one who gets to keep breathing, so I probably shouldn't complain all that much. George wouldn't complain if our positions were reversed. She'd just glare at people, drink a lot of Coke, and write scathing articles about how our judgmental society called her crazy for choosing to maintain a healthy relationship with a dead person.

Becks gave me a sidelong look. "Are you all right?"

"I'm fine," I said, teeth still gritted as I willed George to shut up until I'd managed to get Becks to go away. "Just stiff. And that didn't answer my question. What else made you come up here?"

"Ah, that. You have company." Becks unfolded her arms, shoving her hands into the pockets of her jeans. She'd changed her clothes, which only made sense; the clothing she'd worn in the field needed to be thoroughly sterilized before it was safe to wear again. The logical need to change didn't explain why she'd put on new jeans and a flowery shirt that wouldn't offer any protection in an outbreak, but girls have never made much sense to me. I never needed them to. George was always there, ready and willing to play translator.

I raised an eyebrow. "Company? Define 'company.' Is this the kind of company that wants an interview? Or the kind of company I have a restraining order against?" Most people don't think I'm handling Georgia's death very well, what with the whole "hearing her inside my head even though she's not here anymore" aspect of things. Well, if I'm not handling it well, the Masons aren't handling it at all, since they've spent the last year alternately pleading with me to see reason and threatening to sue me for ownership of her intellectual property.

I always knew they were vultures, but it took someone actually dying for me to understand just how appropriate that comparison really was. They'd started hovering around before the man who paid her killer was even cold, looking for a way to make a profit off the situation.

I mean that literally. I checked the time stamps on the first e-mails they sent me. I don't think they even took the time to pretend to grieve before they started trying to make sure they'd get their piece of the action. So yeah, I took out a restraining order against them. They've taken it surprisingly well thus far. Maybe because it's done wonderful things for their ratings.

"Neither," said Becks. "She says she knows you from the CDC, and that she's been trying to get hold of you for weeks—something about needing to talk to you about a research program that Georgia was involved with back when you were—Shaun? Where are you going?"

I was halfway across the roof the moment the words "research program" left her lips, and by the time she asked where I was going, it was too late; I was already gone, hand on the doorknob, barreling back down the stairs toward the hallway.

My line of work, combined with George's virological martyrdom and my ongoing, if somewhat amateur, attempts to locate the people behind the conspiracy that killed her, has brought me into contact with a lot of people from the CDC. But there's only one "she" who has my contact information and would even dare to bring up George around me.

Dave was waiting outside the office apartment door, looking agitated. I stopped long enough to grab his shoulders, shake briskly, and demand, "*Why* haven't I been seeing her e-mail?"

"The new spam filters must have been stopping her," he said, looking a little green around the edges. It appeared that I was scaring him. I was having trouble getting worked up about that when

I was already so worked up about more important matters. "If she was using the wrong keywords—"

"Fix them!" I shoved him backward, hard enough that he smacked his shoulders against the wall. Turning, I opened the apartment door.

Alaric was in the process of handing my "company" a cup of coffee, making polite apologies about my absence. He stopped when I entered, turning to face me, and she half rose, a small, almost timid smile on her face.

"Hi, Shaun," said Kelly. "I hope this isn't a bad time."

There were many would-be saviors during the Rising, but some stand above the rest. One such is Dr. William Matras, a virologist working out of the Centers for Disease Control's Atlanta office. With a governmental decree forbidding any discussion of what they called "the Walking Plague," the CDC was unable to warn the populace of the coming crisis. Dr. Matras co-opted the one channel of communication he knew to be unmonitored: the blog of his daughter, Wendy. He posted everything he knew about the epidemiology of the Walking Plague, and he armed a world against the disease.

Dr. Matras was tried for treason, acquitted on all counts, and given a posthumous commendation for valorous service. His son, Ian Matras, is the current director of the WHO. His eldest daughter, Marianne Matras-Connolly, is an instructor at Georgetown University. Of his five grandchildren, three are in the family business, with the youngest, Kelly Connolly, currently studying under Dr. J. Wynne of the Memphis CDC.

We owe this family a great debt for everything that they have done. Without men like Dr. Matras, the future of the human race would be much bleaker.

—From *Epidemiology of the Wall*, authored by Mahir Gowda, January 11, 2041

Three

The last time I saw Kelly Connolly, she was delivering George's ashes for the funeral. The time before that, she was at the Memphis CDC installation where George, Rick, and I were taken into quarantine after an anonymous call claimed we'd gone into amplification. Not exactly the sort of encounters that lend themselves to easy companionship. I'm never really sure how to deal with people who aren't a part of my team and aren't trying to either kill or interview me. My usual tactics—gunshots and punches to the face—just don't seem to apply.

Kelly was looking at me expectantly, the cup of coffee she'd taken from Alaric still held in front of her. I almost wished she'd throw it at me, just so I'd have some idea of what I was supposed to *do*.

Say hello, George prompted.

"Why—" I began, and caught myself, snapping my jaws closed on my tongue so hard I tasted blood. Talking to George in front of my friends and coworkers was one thing: It weirded them out a little, but they were essentially used to it. Talking to her in front of someone who was still practically a stranger was something else entirely. I didn't have the time or the patience to deal with the questions it would inevitably raise.

Kelly was still looking at me with the same expectant air, now becoming slowly tinged with concern. I know that look. I get that look a lot. If I didn't say something soon, she was going to start asking whether I was all right, and then I was going to need to decide whether or not I was going to deck her.

Punching visitors from the CDC would be a new low for me. It wasn't one I was particularly eager to reach. I swallowed away the taste of blood and forced myself to smile as I stepped forward, offering my hand. "Dr. Connolly. It's nice to see you again."

Kelly took my hand, the edge of concern not leaving her face. Her handshake was surprisingly firm. I looked closer and realized that the concern was masking an even more pronounced expression of fear. Fear? She was with the CDC. Short of Kellis-Amberlee deciding to jump species and start infecting birds, what did she have to worry about?

"You don't need to be so formal, Shaun." Her smile tightened for a moment before she dropped it. She let go of my hand at the same time. I kept studying her face, taking note of the dark circles under her eyes. The good doctor hadn't been sleeping much recently . . . if she'd been sleeping at all. "I won't call you Mr. Mason if you won't call me Dr. Connolly."

"Deal." I stepped back, tucking my hands into my pockets. "Welcome to the madhouse, Doc. Have you had a chance to meet the rest of the team?"

"Well, I met Alaric here when he buzzed me into the building," she said, smiling brightly at him. He ducked his head, blushing and slanting a glance toward Becks at the same time, like he was checking her reaction. He shouldn't have bothered. Becks was staring straight ahead, giving Kelly her best "I am an ice-cold action bitch and you'd better not forget it" look.

Dave had managed to slink back into the room while I was gaping at Kelly. He hunched his shoulders as he sat down next to the bank of monitors, trying to make himself look small. If we hadn't had company, I would have rushed over to tell him I was sorry and promise—again—that this was the last time I'd ever lay a hand on him. I'd mean it, too, even if we'd both know I'd never be able to keep my word. Dave would say it was okay, that I hadn't actually hurt him, and we'd both feel better . . . at least until the next time I lost my temper.

That's how things worked around the office without George. We were used to it; comfortable, even. Having Kelly Connolly standing there, clearly waiting for an introduction to the rest of the team, was just screwing everything up.

"Uh," I said. "Well, that cool cat over on the news desk is one of our Irwins, Dave Novakowski." Dave raised a hand and waved. "Alaric here is Mahir's second-in-command. Mahir is . . . uh . . . Mahir Gowda runs the Newsie division remotely from London." I still couldn't bring myself to call him George's replacement. The word was just too bitter to say.

Kelly nodded, offering a quick smile in Dave's direction. Dave answered with a distracted nod, hands beginning to move rapidly across his keyboard. "Mr. Gowda interviewed me earlier this year," Kelly said, looking back to me. "He was a very nice gentleman."

"He did?" I asked blankly.

Alaric was staring. A note of excitement crept into his voice as he asked, "Wait—are you *the* Kelly Connolly?"

Becks and I exchanged a blank look, Becks mouthing "What the fuck?" I shrugged.

Kelly, meanwhile, was smiling half-smugly, with that look on her face that famous people always seem to get when they're pretending not to be pleased about being recognized. Mom used to walk around with that expression permanently locked in place. "I am."

"Oh, wow," said Alaric, eyes going even wider. "It's an honor to meet you, ma'am. I mean a real, genuine honor."

"Uh, excuse me for asking, but does someone want to explain to the nice Irwins," I caught the hopeful look in Becks's eyes, and hastened to clarify, "nice Irwins and *former* Irwins exactly what '*the* Kelly Connolly*' is supposed to mean? Because I have to say, I'm clueless."

"Truer words were never spoken," Becks muttered, almost under her breath.

"Dr. Matras was her grandfather," said Alaric, like that explained everything.

I paused, filtering through my recollections of college history seminars. Finally, I ventured, "You mean the CDC treason guy?"

They dropped the charges, George chided.

"Sorry," I said, automatically.

Kelly must have assumed the apology was directed at her, because she shook her head and said, "It's okay; that's how most people outside of epidemiological circles remember him. His trial was a pretty big deal. They made us watch the tapes when I was in medical school."

"Right," I said. I was starting to remember more, probably because George was practically yelling in my inner ear. "He's the guy who hijacked his kid's blog so he could get the word out." I could vaguely recall seeing Kelly in CDC press releases and interviews, always in the background, but pretty steadily there all the same. I always figured it was because she was photogenic. Turns out it was because she was an asset.

"His eleven-year-old kid's blog," said Becks, eyeing Kelly suspiciously. "You're at least twenty-one. How did you manage that?"

"My Aunt Wendy was the youngest of six," Kelly replied, with the ease of someone fielding an all-too-familiar question. "She was actually the flower girl at my mother's wedding. My mother is Deborah Connolly, born Deborah Matras, age twenty-five at the time of the Rising."

Becks nodded, her former Newsie's instincts mollified. "So what brings you to our neck of the woods?"

"Uh, guys?"

"Dave, I told you, we'll edit that report together in a minute," Becks said impatiently.

My phone beeped. Holding up a hand to excuse myself, I took a step backward and pulled the phone out of my pocket, clicking it open. "Shaun here."

"Why aren't you online?"

"Hello to you, too, Mahir. Why are you still awake? Shouldn't the Bride of Bollywood be threatening to withhold sex for a month if you don't put down your keyboard and crawl back to the nuptial bed?"

"She's asleep," he said, flatly. "No thanks to you. Why aren't you online?"

"There are a great many answers to that philosophical question, but for right now, I'm going to settle for 'because we have company, and my mama taught me it was rude to use your computer in front of company unless you've got enough for everybody.'"

"You're a bloody bad liar, Shaun Mason. Your mother didn't teach you anything of the sort."

"Maybe not, but she should have. Why do you need me online?"

"Guys?" Dave again, a little more insistent this time.

"Turn on the news and see for yourself. I'm blocking the live feeds out of the office and claiming site issues. You can thank me for it later."

Mahir hung up.

Mahir *never* hung up on me like that.

Frowning, I lowered the phone. "Dave? What are you trying to tell us?"

"I was looking for CDC-related reports from the last few days, to see if I could figure out why we have company, and there's a report from this morning of a break-in at the Memphis CDC."

"So?"

"So they're saying one of the doctors died."

I didn't need to ask which one. The answer was in Kelly's sudden pallor, and the way her eyes darted from side to side, like she was looking for an escape route from the apartment. There wasn't one. With the entire resident staff inside, the door had automatically sealed itself, and it wasn't going to open for anyone who didn't have a key.

Or couldn't pass a blood test.

I wasn't the only person who'd put two and two together. Alaric took two quick steps backward, nearly tripping over a beanbag chair someone had abandoned in the middle of the floor. Becks stayed where she was, tucking her hands behind herself. She always kept a firearm of some sort in a holster at the small of her back, where it wouldn't necessarily be spotted. I knew from field trials that she could have it out and aimed in under a second.

Take charge of this situation, or it's going to get messy. George sounded worried. That worried me, in a "less important than the possibly infected CDC doctor in our apartment" sort of a way. If my inner George was becoming more nuanced, did that mean I was getting more crazy? And if I was, did I mind?

"What do you want me to do here?" I asked, forgetting the whole "don't talk to George in front of strangers" rule in the face of a bigger problem.

You trained Becks and Dave. That means they'll shoot first and ask questions later. Alaric might have been helpful if this had happened yesterday, but he's too wound up from the field to think clearly right now. You need to settle them down.

Great. It wasn't enough that my sister was dead and living inside my head; now she was giving me orders. "It never stops," I muttered, and looked back toward Kelly. "If you died, want to tell us how it is you're standing here and not trying to eat us?" I paused, then added, "That wasn't actually a request."

"If you listen to the report, it doesn't say I died. It just says they found my body," she said, in a careful tone that I recognized from way too many press conferences. It was the voice people use when they aren't saying something.

The silence in the room for the next few seconds was almost palpable, as all four of us struggled with that statement. Dave spoke first, asking, "So you're listed as dead because you've started amplification?"

"No," Kelly said emphatically. "I'm not infected. I'm willing to submit to as many blood tests as you need in order to prove that."

She was technically lying: We're all infected. Anyone born after the Rising was infected in the womb, since Kellis-Amberlee is totally untroubled by the placental barrier. It's just that in most of us, the virus is sleeping peacefully, rather than taking over our bodies and turning us into something from a horror show. That's what the blood tests look for. Not infection; amplification. Which raised another question: amplification takes minutes, not hours. If Kelly was exposed to the live virus in Memphis, how could she possibly have traveled all the way to Oakland without fully amplifying?

"So why do they think you're dead?" Becks sounded pissed, like she was considering drawing on Kelly just to make the confusing situation stop. I shot her a warning look. She glared back.

George was right. I needed to take control of things before they got bad.

"Becks—" I said, cautioning.

"It's all right, Shaun. I knew I'd have to answer some questions." Kelly looked toward Becks, saying calmly, "They think I'm dead because the body they found was mine."

Pandemonium. I doubt there was anything else she could have said that would cause that much chaos, that quickly, amidst my staff. Even "Look, a zombie" would probably have inspired only general interest and a search for things to poke it with. It's only because we were viewing her as friend, not foe, that she didn't get a bullet in the forehead as soon as she finished speaking. As it was, the sentence was barely out of her mouth before Dave was on his feet, guns drawn and aimed in her direction. Becks provided a mirror image on the other side of the room. Meanwhile, Alaric was showing a rare degree of common sense for a Newsie and had resumed his retreat, taking cover behind the couch.

All three of them were shouting. Dave and Becks were coordinating their actions; Alaric was just yelling. And through it all, Kelly stood perfectly still, keeping her hands clearly in view. She was trembling, and the whites showed all the way around her eyes, but she didn't move. I had to admire that. It was the smartest thing she could possibly have done.

"Guys!" I clapped my hands. I didn't need to draw, since Dave and Becks were already holding guns on her. I could actually be the one playing Good Cop in the potentially life-threatening situation for a change. "She had to pass a blood test to get inside, remember? Chill the fuck out. I'm sure she has a good explanation." I glanced toward Kelly. "Just a friendly hint, Doc: This would be a really, really good time to say something that makes enough sense that it can keep my people from shooting you. Because around here, dead things are for target practice."

Kelly turned toward me, making the motion as economical as possible. Even so, Dave's hands twitched, putting the slightest degree of extra pressure on the triggers. Catching his eye, I shook my head. He eased off. Not enough. If Kelly didn't have a truly excellent explanation, we were going to need a new carpet.

"Cloning," she said.

That qualified as a truly excellent explanation.

"What?" I demanded, almost in unison with Becks's "You can't be serious!" and Dave's "No fucking way." Alaric stuck his head up from behind the couch, expression disbelieving.

"We've been using cloning technology in hospitals for fifteen years," said Kelly, a certain bitter amusement in her voice. "What makes you think this is so unreasonable?"

"Full-body cloning is illegal, immoral, and impossible," said Becks, slowly. "Try again, princess."

"If we can clone a kidney, why can't we clone a Kelly?" asked Kelly.

Becks didn't seem to have an answer for that.

"Actually . . . " Alaric stood up, eyes still fixed on Kelly. He wasn't coming back to the center of the room, but he was abandoning at least a small measure of cover. That was a good sign. "Full-body cloning isn't *impossible*. It's just illegal for anyone outside the three major medical research entities. They use clones to study the progression of Kellis-Amberlee. The World Health Organization, USAMRIID—"

"—and the CDC," I finished. Everyone turned to look at me, Dave and Alaric included. I shrugged. "I can count. So we can clone people?"

"Yes," said Alaric.

"And the CDC gets cloning privileges?"

"Yes," said Kelly.

"And they decided to clone you because . . . ?"

"I think at this point, it's going to be easier for me to explain if I can do it without people holding guns on me." Kelly glanced at Becks, licking her lips in agitation. "I'm not used to it."

"You're going to need to get used to it if you're planning to hang out around here." I crossed to the rack of medical supplies next to the weapons locker. Grabbing a high-end testing unit—not the best the market has to offer, but good enough that we could have faith in the results—I tossed it overhand at Kelly. She fumbled the catch, nearly dropping the unit before she got a good grip.

"Loss of manual dexterity is an early sign of amplification," said Becks.

"Loss of manual dexterity is also a sign of a lab rat surrounded by people who seem likely to shoot her in the face," I said. "You'd better go ahead and get some results for us, Doc, before one of my people decides they're done being civilized."

"You sure do know how to treat a guest," said Kelly. She popped the test open, shoving her hand inside.

"We try," I said.

Becks was right about the loss of manual dexterity: It's related to the virus basically hip-checking the brain out of the way and taking over. Once Kellis-Amberlee amplification begins, victims lose motor control at a fairly impressive pace. Viruses—even genetically engineered viruses designed to better the human condition—aren't all that smart, and they don't have to pass driver's ed before they get a shot at driving *us*. So zombies don't know how to use their fingers very well, and most of them are a little clumsy even when we're talking about things like "walking" and "not getting shot in the head."

About the only thing a zombie can do with any reliable accuracy is bite, spit, and scratch. The easiest routes to infection.

The lights on Kelly's test unit were just beginning to flash when my phone beeped again. I clicked it on, not bothering to check the caller ID. "Hey, Mahir."

"Is she still there?"

"Yeah, she's still here." I watched the lights flash between red and green, resisting the urge to look away.

"Is the situation contained?"

Red, green, pause. Red, green, pause. "I'm not sure. Dave and Becks have guns trained on her head right now."

"What, only the pair?"

"Alaric's busy hiding behind the couch—"

"Hey!"

"—and I figured I'd try being the reasonable one for a change."

"Really? How's that going, then?"

Not well, muttered George.

"Not bad," I said, wishing I had a way to glare at the inside of my own head. The lights were slowing down, lingering on green for longer and longer periods of time. "We're just about done with the blood tests over here. Do you want to video conference in or something? Because it's time to play twenty questions with Doc, and you might have some good ones."

"I can't." There was genuine regret in his tone. This was news, happening right in our company headquarters, and as the head of the Newsies, Mahir had a serious jones for information. That was part of what made him so good at his job. "This is a secure connection, but if I go for a video link, it'll attract attention, and I'll have to answer questions."

"I take it from your tone that this would be a bad idea right about now?"

The lights on Kelly's unit settled on a firm, unblinking green. She held it up, smiling a little, like she'd known the answer all along. Dave lowered his guns, sliding them back into their holsters. Becks lowered one of hers, hesitated, and lowered the other. I gave her an approving nod. The Masons may not have taught me much about how to treat a guest, but they taught me not to shoot at them unless it was absolutely necessary.

Mahir sighed. "Yes. A very bad idea."

"I told you not to marry her, Mahir."

"I'm not having this conversation again."

"Just saying, you didn't have to worry about this shit when you lived the happy bachelor life. Look, I need to go—the Doc's just checked out clean, so it's probably time to find out what she's doing here."

"Call me when you know what's going on."

"Got it," I said, and clicked off.

Kelly lowered her test unit, apparently satisfied that everyone had seen it, and said, "I'm clean. Do you have a biohazard receptacle I can dispose of this in?"

"It's next to the medical supplies." I walked toward the kitchen. "I need a Coke. Anybody else need anything before story time commences?"

No one did.

The kitchen gave me just enough privacy to feel comfortable saying quietly, "Can we try to keep the interjections down for a little bit? I don't want Kelly thinking I'm crazy." I paused. "Not yet, anyway."

You have a plan? asked George.

"More making it up as I go along," I replied, and grabbed my soda before turning to walk back into the living room.

When I got there, Kelly was on the couch, Alaric was sitting on the beanbag he'd tripped over before, and Dave was back at his terminal, watching the scrolling data feed with one eye while remaining half-turned toward the room. Only Becks was still standing, eyeing Kelly like she expected the other woman to spontaneously amplify at any second.

"Aren't we a cheery bunch?" I grabbed a folding chair from against the wall and set it up in front of the entrance hall. Nobody was getting in or out without going through me, and that wasn't exactly an easy proposition. Potentially entertaining; not easy.

"I'm cheerier when there isn't a corpse sitting on the couch," said Becks, before moving to her computer chair and slowly sitting down.

"Most people are." I turned to Kelly. "That brings us back to story time. Well, Doc? What's going on?"

Kelly sighed. It was a soft, exhausted sound, conveying a vast amount of information in a very small amount of time. This was a woman who'd been run to the limits of her endurance before being forced to find reserves she didn't think she had. Now even those reserves looked about to run out. Maybe the word "corpse" was more accurate than it sounded. I tensed, waiting for the other shoe to drop.

"Dr. Wynne sends his regards."

There it was: the other shoe.

Dr. Joseph Wynne was Kelly's supervisor at the Memphis CDC. He was also the man who answered when George called the CDC for help on the night Buffy died. We knew we'd been set up—it was hard to miss that part, what with people shooting at our tires and everything—but we didn't realize how thoroughly screwed we were until we talked to the CDC. Somebody else called them before George did. That first caller reported that we'd all gone into amplification, not just Buffy. Since we were outside in a confirmed outbreak by that point, Dr. Wynne would have been legally justified in ordering our immediate executions. He didn't do it. That meant, in a strange sort of sidelong way, that I owed him.

"Does he?" I asked, as neutrally as I could.

"He sent a data card for you to review." She picked up her brief-case from the floor next to the couch and popped it open, rummaging for a second before producing a plain white plastic rectangle. I raised an eyebrow. A smile ghosted across Kelly's face as she offered the card to me. "What, did you think I managed to grow a full-body clone and stage my own death without *help*?"

"Guess not," I said. "Alaric, run the card." He jumped to his feet, snatching the card from her hand and running for his terminal so fast that I almost expected him to leave skid marks on the floor. I snorted with amusement before turning back to Kelly. "Now it's *really* story time, Doc."

"Yes, it is," she agreed. She took a stack of manila envelopes from the briefcase and stood, walking a loose circuit around the room. Each of us got an envelope before she returned to the couch and sat, looking almost serene. I know that look. That's the look I get from people who've done their civic duty by reporting the zombie outbreak to the local news media and are now planning to sit down and let it be our problem instead of theirs. It's the expression of someone who knows, deep down inside, that the buck is about to be passed.

Buck-passing rarely comes with handouts. I peered into the envelope, natural paranoia demanding that I confirm it wasn't filled with mousetraps or funny white powder before I removed the contents. Paper. Some paperclipped reports, a few loose memos, and a few sheets of statistical data. I didn't understand most of what I saw, which really wasn't surprising. I never was much of one for the numbers.

I looked up. Kelly was watching me intently. Everyone else was flipping through the contents of their respective envelopes. It looked like it was up to me to keep her talking. I waved a sheet of statistics and asked, "What's all this?"

"It's the story." She sagged back in the couch, closing her eyes. The "passing the buck" expression faded, replaced by one of deep and abiding weariness. She kept her eyes closed as she began to talk. It may have been because she was concentrating on getting her facts straight, but I don't think so.

I think she just didn't want to risk seeing the look on my face.

"The first cases of confirmed Kellis-Amberlee occurred in 2014. That's when the viruses were introduced to the biosphere, met, and managed to successfully combine. The viral substrains are either descendants of different initial cases of Marburg Amberlee or the result of very minor natural mutation, occurring within isolated geographic areas. Everywhere in the world, Kellis flu met Marburg Amberlee, and Kellis-Amberlee was the result. It's not natural virus behavior. Neither of the pathogens involved was a natural virus. Kellis-Amberlee has been stable, and effectively identical, since it was 'born.'"

Becks looked perplexed. "Did we sign up for a seminar or something?" I held up a hand for quiet. She snorted, and subsided.

Kelly continued: "The first cases of confirmed Kellis-Amberlee infection going 'live' in isolated parts of the body—the reservoir conditions—were identified in 2018. They may have been cropping up before then, but we didn't have the capacity to track them. The infrastructure was still too broken down for that to be an option."

"Makes sense," I agreed. The Rising left the medical community in tatters. Frontline doctors and nurses were among the first to be infected, leaving the hospitals of the world severely understaffed even after the initial battles of the Rising had been fought and technically won. I say "technically" because it's hard to call a conflict with that kind of casualty rate a victory. There are still hospitals and people who can use them, so I guess we'll have to count that as a win, for now.

A smile tugged at the edges of Kelly's lips. "I could start listing the index cases for the known reservoir conditions, but I doubt you really care, and they aren't that applicable in this situation. They showed up one by one, they didn't follow any perceptible pattern, and they were as incurable as the parent virus. That's what matters to the story: Once you have a reservoir condition, you have it for the rest of your life."

She's got that right, said George bitterly. She developed retinal Kellis-Amberlee while we were little, and she had it until the day she died. Kids in our high school used to tease her about it and threaten to steal her sunglasses. They never did, though. There was always too much of a chance that her "cooties" might be contagious.

That's bullshit, by the way. You can't catch the live form of Kellis-Amberlee unless you come into contact with it, and George didn't sweat the live virus. It just lived inside her eyes, all the time. Waiting for the day when it would get loose to play with the rest of her body.

Which it eventually did.

I had to force myself to start talking again, before I could really start dwelling on what had happened to George. This wasn't the time. "So what's the moral of our story?" I asked, relieved when my voice sounded halfway natural. "Reservoir conditions suck?"

"Reservoir conditions represent a viral behavior with no known purpose or explanation," contributed Dave. Everyone but Kelly turned to look at him. He shrugged. "I took a couple of virology courses before I went to Alaska. It seemed like it might help with that whole 'not dying' thing."

"Ah." Dave was in Alaska last year when half the staff died. He was probably safer on the frozen, zombie-infested tundra than we were in Sacramento. There was something ironic about that. I paused. "Wait, are you saying no one knows what the reservoir conditions *do*?"

"There are theories." Kelly sounded suddenly evasive. I eyed her. Her expression was practically a mask; with her eyes closed, she could have been thinking anything at all.

She should get some sunglasses if she wants to pull that trick, said George.

I didn't say anything. I just waited.

Kelly gave a small shake of her head and continued: "I've spent the last year studying reservoir conditions. The CDC tracks anyone with a KA-related medical condition, but nothing's ever really been done with the data. So I thought I'd start."

"Hey, that's not true," I protested. "George was in all kinds of studies. There was always some new specialist asshole wanting to poke her in the eyes and see what happened."

"There have been studies of the individual *kinds* of reservoir conditions, but nobody's really looked into the syndrome as a whole." Kelly sank, if anything, farther back into the couch. "Why does it happen? Why does it happen in specific parts of the body? How is it that the virus is contained? Everything we know says that anyone with a reservoir condition should amplify immediately, but they don't. They just keep going until they die. It doesn't make sense."

"And that's what you were studying?"

A marginal nod. "Uh-huh. That's when I found it."

"Found what?" asked Alaric.

"Look at the statistics." Kelly sighed, tilting her face up toward the ceiling. "The first column is population. The second column is percent of population with a known reservoir condition—type is irrelevant in this instance."

I squinted at the numbers. I'd seen the number on the third column somewhere before. I hazarded a guess: "Column three is KA-related deaths in the last year?"

"Yeah."

"So what's the fourth column?"

Becks spoke, voice heavy with dawning horror. She'd managed to figure things out just a little faster than the rest of us, and she didn't sound happy about her epiphany. "Oh, my God. It's—that's the number of people with reservoir conditions who died, isn't it?"

Kelly nodded.

I squinted at the numbers. They didn't seem to mean anything. I was about to open my mouth when George said, very quietly, *Look at column two again, Shaun.*

I looked. And I understood.

"This can't be right," I said, suddenly cold. Reservoir conditions don't increase the odds of viral amplification; they actually tend to reduce them, since most people who suffer from a latent form of KA wind up even more paranoid about infection than the rest of the population. People like George, who went out into the field, or Emily Ryman, who kept raising horses even after she developed retinal KA, were the exception rather than the rule.

Kelly sighed, opening her eyes for the first time since her lecture had begun. "That's what I thought," she said, looking right at me. "I ran the numbers over and over. I had an intern pull the census data six times. It's all accurate."

"But—"

"Less than eleven percent of the population suffers from reservoir conditions. Last year, they accounted for thirty-eight percent of the KA-related deaths." Kelly's tone was grim. Suddenly, her exhaustion was starting to make a lot of sense. "Statistically speaking, this can't be happening."

"Maybe it was a glitch," suggested Dave. "Statistical anomalies happen, right?"

Becks snorted. "Yeah, and respected CDC doctors totally help their employees fake death by clone over statistical anomalies. It happens all the time."

"The data goes back ten years, and it's consistent all the way through. Every year, more people with reservoir conditions die than can be supported by reasonable projections—not from spontaneous amplification, not because they were stupid, not for any reason that I can find. And no one's ever said, 'Hey, maybe something's wrong here.'" She paused, shaking her head a little. "That's not right. There have been project proposals that would have addressed these numbers, and somehow they always get shut down. There's always something more important, more pressing, more impressive. Politics get involved, and the reservoir conditions get pushed to the back burner. Again, and again, and again."

"So what, you think it's intentional suppression?" asked Alaric.

"Last year, there was a six-billion-dollar study on a new strain of MRSA that's cropped up in two hospitals in North Carolina. We could have done it on a third of the budget and half the manpower. It was busywork. There's so damn much busywork." She rubbed her temple with the heel of one hand, frustration evident. "The CDC is supported by the government. We're supposed to be an independent organization, but that isn't how the funding works out."

"Was Tate involved?"

The question was soft, reasonable; it took me a moment to realize that I'd asked it.

"Not with that study," said Kelly. Hope flared and died immediately as she continued: "He was one of the supporters of continuing cancer research. You know, since cancer will become a threat again once Kellis-Amberlee has been cured. So more and more of our budget goes to things like that, and reservoir conditions just get ignored."

"How big a chunk of the CDC budget are we talking about?" asked Alaric.

"Eleven billion dollars."

Dave whistled, long and low. "That's not chump change."

"No, it's not. I'd say maybe twenty percent of our research budget is actually being spent on research into Kellis-Amberlee-related conditions. The rest of it keeps getting siphoned off into studies that look good, but don't *do* anything." Her frustration was evident. "It's like we're being stopped from finding out what this virus really does."

Probably because you are, said George.

"I didn't know that was possible," I said. "You're the CDC."

"And somebody has to pay the bills."

"Right." I stood abruptly, stalking back into the kitchen with my mostly full Coke in one hand and the stack of papers in the other. Behind me, Kelly started to ask where I was going, and was quickly hushed by Becks. Becks understood. Becks always understands.

The kitchen was cool and dark and, most important, empty. I put my things down on the counter, turned to face the wall, and began, methodically, punching it as hard as I could. The sound echoed through the room, gunshot-loud and soothing. My knuckles split on the fourth blow. I started feeling a lot better after that. I generally do. Pain clears the fog in my head, enough that I can *think* again. Besides, as long as I'm punching walls, I'm not punching people.

Someone was using the CDC's budget to control their research.

Someone was funneling research *away* from Kellis-Amberlee, into diseases that weren't an issue anymore and problems that shouldn't even have been on the CDC's radar. And Governor Tate had been involved. The man who killed my sister. The man who changed everything. If Tate had his bloody little fingers in the pie . . .

If Tate was involved, so was whoever he worked for, said George, as calmly as I couldn't. *We have to help her. We have to find out what's going on. This could be our chance, Shaun. This could lead us straight to the ring-leaders.*

"Yeah." I stopped punching the wall, taking a shaky breath as I studied the new dent I'd created next to the half a dozen that were already there. We lost our security deposit a long time ago. "I know."

Good.

If we helped Kelly, we could find out who was manipulating the CDC. We could find the people who ordered Tate to kill George. After that . . .

Maybe after that we'd both be able to rest.

I rinsed my hand in the sink, applying gauze and antibiotic cream before returning to the living room. There was no point in freaking Kelly out any more than the pounding noises doubtless already had. "Sorry about that," I said. "I just needed to work through a few things."

"It's okay, boss," said Dave. Alaric and Becks nodded their agreement.

Kelly bit her lip. "Is . . . is everything okay?"

"Not really, but we can pretend." I walked back to my seat, belatedly realizing that my things were still in the kitchen. Oh, well. "So no one ever tried to figure out why so many people with reservoir conditions were dying?"

"Um." Kelly blinked, apparently thrown by my return to the earlier topic. Then she nodded. "We got a new crop of interns recently. Very enthusiastic, very eager to prove themselves. One of them noticed the statistical anomaly while he was doing some filing, and he brought it to Dr. Wynne. What he said just didn't sound right. I asked if I could look into it. Dr. Wynne was as surprised as I was, and he agreed."

"That's how you got started on this?" asked Alaric.

"I thought it was bad data. I thought I was chasing down a reporting error. Instead . . . this was huge. I put together a team of people I trusted once I realized what I was really looking at. Someone's killing people with reservoir conditions in truly terrifying numbers." She took a shaky breath. "And when my team started digging, they started killing us, too."

"What?" Becks demanded.

Oh, shit, said George. I privately echoed the sentiment.

"There were eight people on my team when I started this study. Now I'm the only one left." Kelly sniffled. I realized without any real surprise that she was on the verge of tears. "I need help. I didn't know where else to go."

Becks and I exchanged a look. Dave and Alaric did the same. Then everyone turned toward me, like they expected me to make the call. Oh, wait. With George gone, they did.

Crap.

It seems like everyone I work with has some great story about how their family shows support of their career in the news. Alaric's father paid for his college education, no strings attached—scholarship by Daddy. Dave comes from this huge Russian family, and they're all so proud of him they could explode. Maggie's parents buy her everything her little Fictional heart desires, and Mahir's parents are so happy with what he does that they send care packages to the office. Care packages from *England*, sent to an office where he doesn't even work. That's how cool with things they are.

Shaun may hate the Masons, but at least they supported what he chose to do with his life. No cotillions, no coming-out parties, no "Oh, honey, this is just a phase" or "Please, darling, it's just one night." Just one night, just one dance, just one silk dress, and the next thing I knew, I'd be just one more product of the Westchester Trophy Wife Factory, proudly producing quality goods since the days of the Mayflower. I am a card-carrying Daughter of the American Revolution. I can foxtrot, quickstep, waltz, and tango. I know how to plan a cocktail party, make small talk, and overlook a man's personality, manners, and hygiene in favor of what matters: his bloodline and his bank account.

These are the things my parents taught me. They raised me to be just like my sisters—sweet, pliant, pretty, and available to the highest bidder. It's too bad I had other ideas. I am the shame of my family, the bad seed whose name will be quietly erased from the family tree the day after my picture gets posted on the Wall. I am the one who couldn't be content playing nicely with the other children, and who had to go out and get her hands all dirty.

It's days like this when I miss Georgia most of all. I may have abandoned the Newsies to go Irwin the second the opportunity presented itself, but she understood what I meant when I talked about my family, about not being sorry that I let them down. The things that made her a pretty lousy friend made her an excellent boss, and I think this would all be a hell of a lot easier if she were here.

Mom, Dad? The next horrible thing I do in public is for you. I hope you choke on it.

—From *Charming Not Sincere*, the blog of Rebecca Atherton,
March 8, 2041

Hello, darlings! I hope you're ready for some sizzling romance, swashbuckling adventure, tragic love, and mysterious happenings, because all those and more are on the schedule for this week. I'll be on the live chat every night from seven to ten Pacific time, and I'm always happy to talk about anything your little hearts desire. I'm your private Scheherazade, and I'm here to tell you stories all night long. Welcome to Maggie's House of Horrors—I hope you're planning to stay for a while.

After all, you know I always miss you when you're gone.

—From *Dandelion Mine*, the blog of Magdalene Grace Garcia,
April 11, 2041

Four

What are we going to do?"

Becks asked the question, but all three of my staffers were looking at me with near-identical expressions of impatient expectation on
their faces. It was all I could do to not turn and flee the room. They
were expecting me to give them a direction; they were expecting me
to make the call; they were expecting me to be George.

"What are we going to do?" I echoed, hoping they'd take the
question as rhetorical.

The person it was aimed at didn't. There are small mercies. *We're
going to find out what's going on, and we're going to scream it from the moun-
taintops,* said George. I repeated each word a half-beat behind her,
creating a weird delay that no one outside my head could hear. *We're
going to do our jobs. We're going to go out there, and we're going to get the
news.*

All four of the people in the room were staring at me by the time
I—we—finished our little speech. Alaric was the first to look away,
ducking his head slightly as he turned back to his computer screen.
Dude always wanted me to be my sister when it came time to make
a decision, but he was never okay with it when I actually did.

"That's great and everything, but there are a few things to work out," said Dave. He held up a finger. "What do we do with Doc here?" A second finger. "If we don't know whether it's safe to talk to the CDC, where the hell are we supposed to start?" A third finger. "What are we going to say to the rest of the site? This isn't you and a little team and a van anymore. This is a business. We can't go chasing a story we can't talk about, maybe even disappear on everybody, and expect them to be cool with it."

"Call Rick, see what he says," said Becks.

"I'm pretty sure we can't call the vice president of the United States with 'Hey, we have a dead CDC researcher who says somebody's trying to suppress her research,'" I replied. "We're going to call Rick, but we need more than we have before we do it."

Becks looked mollified. Rick Cousins used to be one of our staff Newsies. Now he's helping run the country. That gave us a certain degree of access to the president, but if we were going to announce that the sky was falling, we needed to have some proof.

"And the rest?" asked Dave.

"Starting with your third question, we're going to tell Mahir, because he already knows, and we're going to tell Maggie," I said. "We can figure out the rest as we go."

Dave frowned. "Why are we getting Maggie involved?"

"Because she's in charge of the Fictionals. If there's any chance this is going to end up getting big enough that we have to bring the whole site in on it, I want her to have had time to figure out how she's planning to tell her people," I said.

Plus, it's the right thing to do, added George.

"Well, yeah," I muttered. "I knew that."

My team had learned not to comment on my conversations with George. Kelly hadn't. Frowning, she asked, "Are you wearing an earpiece?"

"What?" Shit. "Uh . . . no, not exactly."

"Then who are you talking to?"

There was no way out but straight ahead. Shrugging, I said, "Georgia."

Kelly hesitated, emotions chasing themselves across her face like a gang of zombies chasing a government hunting party. Finally, she settled for the easiest possible answer: "I see."

The urge to get up in her face and try to start something was almost too strong to suppress. That's how I usually dealt with people who gave me the look that she was wearing now, that horrible mix of surprise and shock and pity. Six months ago, I probably wouldn't have been able to stop myself. Six months ago, I was thinking a lot less clearly. Maybe I'm crazy. But I'm going to be the kind of crazy that's careful until it blows everything in its path to kingdom come.

"We all cope in our own ways," I said briskly. "Dave, is Maggie online? We can conference her in right now."

"Negative," he said, without a moment's hesitation. I gave him a curious look. He shrugged. "She had a movie party last night. She won't be up for another few hours."

"Is she actually nocturnal or just trying to train herself to act that way?" asked Becks. Glancing to me, she added, "I'm not sure I'm comfortable with this."

"What, with telling Maggie?"

"With not telling everyone else."

"How many people work for this site?"

Becks paused. "Uh . . . I'm not sure."

"That's why we have to do things this way, because right off the top of my head, *neither am I*." I gestured at the server bank. "Like Dave says, this isn't just me and a team that fits in a van anymore; this is a *business*. You know why corporate espionage keeps happening, no matter how bad they make the penalties for getting caught?"

"Greed?" ventured Alaric.

"Poor judgment brought on by possession of insufficient data?" said Kelly.

"People stop caring," said Dave.

I pointed at him. "Give that man a prize. People stop caring. Once you reach the point where you're working with more people than can comfortably go for drinks together, folks stop giving as much of a shit. Politics creep in. Do I trust everyone who works for us with the day-to-day? Yeah. I'd trust every Irwin we have at my back in a firefight, and every Newsie we've got to tell the truth according to their registered biases. But we go dangling a giant cherry of a story like 'The CDC has illegal clones, and their dead researcher isn't really dead, oh, and maybe there's a conspiracy blocking certain research paths,' somebody's going to leak it. They'll do it for profit, they'll do it because it gives them the leverage to get a better job with another site, or they'll do it because it's just too damn good not to share. Every person we bring in on this is another chance that this gets out before we're ready, and we're all fucked."

"Some of us more than others," muttered Kelly, sotto voce.

"You trusted us with Tate," said Becks.

"We didn't have a choice with Tate, and we didn't understand the stakes the way we do now," I said. "We tell Mahir, we tell Maggie, and we stop there until we know what's going on. Anyone really feel like arguing?"

No one did.

"Good," I said, after taking another look around the room. "Doc? From what you're saying, the CDC's out of the picture. I'm assuming that means WHO is also compromised."

She nodded marginally. "WHO and USAMRIID. There's no way we can go to them without the CDC finding out what we're doing. But . . . " She hesitated.

"But what?" asked Becks. "I'm sorry, Doc, you can't just show up here with your corpses and your conspiracy and your craziness and not give us at least a place to *start*."

Kelly wiped her eyes, managing to do it without smearing her mascara, and said, "I mentioned that the funding wasn't really there for researching the reservoir conditions. My team had the director's blessing, and we were still working on a shoestring budget. Our interns kept getting reassigned, our lab spaces ... anyway. That doesn't matter. What matters is that almost all the specialists have gone into the private sector to pursue their own research. I have a list."

"Thank you, God," said Dave, rolling his eyes theatrically toward the ceiling.

"Dave, cut it out." I focused on Kelly. She was holding it together better than I would have expected. Pure researchers don't usually do well when suddenly hurled out of their labs and into the real world. "Is that everything, Doc?"

Kelly took a deep breath, and said, "No one outside the CDC knew what my team was researching."

Dead silence engulfed the room as Dave and Alaric stopped typing and Becks and I just stared. There was a moment where I wasn't sure I'd be able to control my temper—a moment where her statement was one thing too many in the "Why didn't you say that first?" column. Was it her fault? No. But it was suddenly our problem.

Calm down, cautioned George. *We need to keep her talking.*

"Says you," I snapped. Kelly blinked, looking to Becks, who shook her head. My team's had time to learn the difference between me talking to them and me talking to George. Thankfully.

It's not her fault.

"I know." I whirled around and punched the wall. Kelly jumped, making a small squeaking noise. That was satisfying, even as it made me feel worse about the whole situation. Like she wasn't scared enough already? "Sorry, Doc. I'm just ... I'm sorry. I was a little surprised, is all."

"It's okay," she said. It wasn't—not according to the look in her eyes—but it was going to have to do.

I shook my hand to ease the ache as I counted to ten, considering the implications of Kelly's words. We'd always known somebody inside the CDC was involved with Governor Tate's doomed attempt to claim the presidency through the use of weaponized Kellis-Amberlee; Kelly's information just confirmed it. What we'd never had was the proof necessary to make a concerted inquiry into one of the most powerful organizations in the world. "Get me facts and I'll convince the president," that's what Rick had said. But the facts had been awfully slow in coming.

As for me . . . I'd been ready to take the CDC on single-handedly, if that was what it took. Mahir and Alaric talked some sense into me. Getting myself killed wouldn't bring George back. If we wanted the people responsible for her death punished, we needed to be slow, we needed to be careful, and we needed to nail them to the wall. Kelly's information didn't change any of that, and at the same time, it changed everything, because it meant the conspiracy was still alive and well. If someone inside the CDC decided that the study needed to stop, then someone inside the CDC was involved in whatever was raising the death rates among individuals with reservoir conditions.

Somebody *knew*. Somebody knew George was in danger—before the campaign, her condition pre-existed the campaign by years—and they didn't do a thing. Somebody *knew*—

Shaun!

Her tone was sharper this time, cutting cleanly through my anger. I took another deep breath, counting to ten before I straightened, tucking my bruised hand behind my back. "Doc, give Dave the list." I paused. "Please."

"Sure." Kelly produced a flash drive from her briefcase and leaned over the back of the couch to pass it to Dave. He took it without a murmur of thanks, slamming it straight into a USB port and beginning to type.

"Thanks. Now take off all your clothes."

"*What?*" demanded Kelly, eyes going wide. "Shaun, are you feeling all right?"

"I'm fine. I just need you to strip."

"I'm not going to take off my clothes!"

"Actually, princess, you are," said Becks, standing and moving to stand beside me. "We need to check you for bugs. Don't worry. You don't have anything we haven't seen before."

Being asked by another woman seemed to do the trick, even if it was overly generous to call what Becks was doing "asking." Kelly sighed deeply and began removing her clothing, holding each piece up to show us before dropping it to the floor. Finally, when she was standing stark naked in the middle of the living room, she spread her arms and asked, "Happy?"

"Ecstatic." I glanced to Becks. "Take her clothes with you." Becks nodded, and grabbed a laundry bag before beginning to gather Kelly's things.

"Wait, what?" Kelly dropped her arms. "Where is she taking my clothes?"

"Don't worry, you're going with them. Becks, get the counter-surveillance kit from the closet and take her to the bedroom. I want everything she has swept for trackers, bugs, anything that might transmit. Don't bring her back until you're sure she's clean." I gave Kelly a reassuring look. "It's not personal, Doc. We just need to know."

Kelly surprised me: She didn't argue. She just sighed, looking resigned, and said, "I understand decontamination procedures," before picking up her briefcase and turning to Becks. "Where do we go?"

"This way." Becks slung the laundry sack over her shoulder and led Kelly from the room. The door closed behind them with a snap as Becks engaged the interior locks. They'd be a while.

Alaric and Dave were watching me warily when I turned to face them. I smiled faintly. "It's a fun day, isn't it? Alaric, turn on the wireless speaker. I want the two of you to hear this."

"Hear what?" he asked, beginning to type again.

"I'm going to play the concerned citizen and call the Memphis CDC. I want to extend my heartfelt condolences to my good friend Joseph Wynne," I said blandly, pulling out my phone. "Dave, start the server recording."

"It's on," he said.

"Good." With all the necessary steps taken, I flipped my phone open. Most guys my age have girlfriends and drinking buddies on their speed dial. Me, I have the Memphis CDC. Sometimes I really think I never had a chance in hell of having a normal life.

"Dr. Joseph Wynne's office, how may I direct your call?" The receptionist's voice was bright, perky, and generic. I might have spoken to him before; I might not have. Office staff at the CDC seemed trained to behave as interchangeably as possible.

"Is Dr. Wynne available?"

"Dr. Wynne has asked not to be disturbed today."

"And why is that?"

"There has been a recent personnel change, and he is attempting to redistribute tasks in his department," said the receptionist pertly.

That was the coldest way I'd ever heard to describe somebody's death. Rolling my eyes, I said, "Tell him it's Shaun Mason calling with condolences for his recent loss."

"One moment please." There was a click and the speaker was suddenly playing the elevator music version of some bloodless pre-Rising pop hit. Removing the lyrics and most of the subliminal bass actually improved the song.

Dave and Alaric got up and came to stand beside me, as much for the psychological benefit as to hear what was going on; the speaker was broadcasting every tortured, tuneless note to the entire room, and it kept broadcasting as the music clicked off, replaced by the tired, Southern-accented voice of Dr. Joseph Wynne: "Shaun. I wondered when you'd be calling."

"I just finished processing the news, sir. How are you holding up?"

"Oh, as well as can be expected, I suppose," he said. Someone who thought Kelly was dead might have taken the strain in his voice for grief. Since Kelly was in the next apartment showing Becks parts of her anatomy that only her gynecologist would normally see, I recognized his hesitance for what it was: fear.

I was talking to a man who was scared out of his mind.

"What happened?" I asked.

"We don't rightly know yet, although I wish we did. There's a group of folks here from the Atlanta office going over our security tapes and checking all the facilities. There's no way anyone should have been able to get this far into the building, but they managed it somehow."

"I'm so sorry, sir," I said, exchanging a nod with Dave. It was good tactical thinking. Set up a convoluted enough break-in and distract the security teams with picking it apart, rather than looking too closely at "Kelly" while she was still in the morgue. The body would be cremated almost immediately—hell, it might have been cremated already, depending on her family's wishes—and any chance of them identifying it as a clone would be lost. Sure, Dr. Wynne would be fucked beyond belief if the break-in was revealed as a fake, but Kelly would be in the clear.

"I'm still a bit in shock," he said. "I'm sorry to say it, Shaun, because I know the wounds are still raw for you, but it's like Georgia all over again."

Shit, hissed George.

"George?" I said, automatically.

Luckily for me, Dr. Wynne was one of the few people I knew who hadn't received the "Shaun has lost his marbles" memo. Him and my parents. "The way we lost her was just so damn sudden," he said, continuing our conversation without missing a beat.

He's saying it was an emergency evacuation, you idiot, said George. *She may not know it, but he got her out to save her life. God, I wish there was a way you could ask if he was sure she wasn't bugged.*

"Uh, yeah," I said. "It really was. Was there any way anyone could have predicted this was coming?"

"I don't think so," said Dr. Wynne, quickly. Not quickly enough. I could hear the hesitation in his voice, that split second of uncertainty that told me everything I'd been hoping I didn't really need to know. Did he think he'd managed to get Kelly out clean? Yeah, because if he didn't, he wouldn't have risked sending her to us. But was he absolutely one hundred percent sure that he'd succeeded?

No, he wasn't.

"Let us know if there's anything we can do over here, but you may have to wait a little while for a response," I said. "The team and I are going on location for a little while. I'm not sure when we'll be back."

"Really?" There was deep reluctance in his voice as he asked the natural next question: "Where are y'all heading?"

The reluctance was the last piece of evidence I needed to support the idea that Kelly might not have gotten out as cleanly as she thought she had. Dr. Wynne didn't want to ask in case I was serious about the trip; he didn't want me to tell him the truth about where we were going. "Santa Cruz," I lied. "Alaric's testing for his field license soon, and we want to get some footage of him on his provisional to build into a supporting report. We're trying to up his merchandise sales among the female demographic, and our focus groups agree that the best way to do that involves getting him shirtless in a pastoral setting. Danger is just a bonus." Alaric shot me a confused look. I waved him down.

"You kids," said Dr. Wynne, with a forced chuckle. "Y'all be careful out there, all right?"

"As careful as you can be when you're looking for the living dead," I said. "Take care of yourself, Dr. Wynne."

"You, too, Shaun," he said, and disconnected the call.

I took a second to just stand there with my phone in my hand, closing my eyes and listening to George swearing in the back of my head. "Here we go again," I said, voice barely above a whisper.

"What?" asked Dave.

"Nothing." I opened my eyes, slamming the phone into my pocket before stalking back into the kitchen for a fresh Coke. I popped the tab and downed half the can in one large, carbonated gulp. The frozen sweetness made my molars ache and snapped the world back into a semblance of focus. "I need you to tear down your workstations, and then get started on everybody else's," I said, returning to the living room. "Dave, where are you with that list?"

"It's encoded. I need—"

"Forget what you need. Upload it to the main server and the mirrors; pack the physical drive."

"Boss?" asked Alaric, uncertainly.

"Gear up like you're never going to see this place again. Alaric, as soon as Becks confirms that there's nothing standard on the Doc, I need you to take over. Do a second scan of everything she brought with her. You find anything that looks like it might be related to something that might be a bug, kill it." I raised a hand before he could protest. "Don't study it, don't dissect it, don't try to subvert it, *kill* it. We don't have time to risk the sort of heat that might be coming after her."

"But—"

I turned away from him to open the closet door. The shelf on the right was crammed with ammo boxes. I started grabbing them three at a time. "He said it was like George, Alaric. Not like Buffy, who was actually unexpected; not like Rebecca Ryman, or any of the other people he and I wound up having in common."

"So what?"

Go easy on him, said George. *He wasn't there. He doesn't really under-stand.*

"I know," I muttered darkly. More loudly, I said, "So there were people at the CDC who were involved with what happened to her, and we never caught them. George had a reservoir condition. I thought you were the Newsie here. Do I have to draw you a picture?"

My favorite hunting rifle was leaning against the closet wall. I grabbed it, relaxing slightly as its satisfying weight fell into my hand. Letting it rest against my shoulder, I went back to grabbing ammo.

"Fuck," muttered Dave.

"My thoughts exactly," I said. "Go tell Becks she needs to hurry it up; we're getting out of here. Any bugs she can't find without a subdermal sweeper, she's not going to find with an extra ten minutes."

"On it," said Dave, and trotted out of the room.

We got to work, Alaric dismantling the equipment that wasn't needed for final uploads, while I emptied and packed down the contents of the closet. Dave came back and started helping Alaric break things down. I was filling a backpack with protein bars and spare laptop batteries when the bedroom door opened and Becks emerged, followed by a rumpled-looking Kelly.

"She's clean," Becks announced, tossing Kelly's briefcase to Alaric. He caught it and turned back to what remained of his workstation, reaching for a scanner.

"Good. We roll in twenty. Grab whatever you think you're going to need, and pack like we're not coming back."

"Where are we going?" asked Becks.

"Maggie's," I replied. She nodded, looking relieved. Even Dave and Alaric relaxed a little. If we were heading for Maggie's, they knew that we were at least going to wind up someplace safe.

Maggie lives in the middle of nowhere and has the best security money can buy. Literally. Some of the systems on her house are military grade or better, and her parents make sure she gets the latest upgrades. Hell, sometimes I think the latest upgrades are designed specifically for her and then just shared with everybody else. She started out as one of Buffy's friends—and Buffy had interesting friends.

The apartment buzzed with renewed activity as Dave and Alaric redoubled their work. Becks started picking up stray ammo boxes. Only Kelly stayed where she was, looking utterly confused. "I don't understand," she said.

"We're leaving," I informed her. "Which sort of brings up the next question on the table: Do you have a cover story that lets us take you with us, or are we going to be smuggling you out and then shipping you off to one of the Amish compounds to live a camera-free existence?"

"They always need trained medical personnel who don't have a major addiction to electricity and running water," said Becks sunnily. Kelly shot her an alarmed look before turning to me. She seemed to view me as the stable one in the room. I might have found that comic under better circumstances.

"I have a cover story," she said. "A whole ID, even. Dr. Wynne paid to have it built for me. The files are on that card I gave you."

"Who did he pay?" asked Dave, sounding suddenly wary. Alaric didn't say anything; he just stiffened as both of them turned toward Kelly. They looked like they were waiting for something to explode.

Their reaction wasn't surprising or as over the top as it might look. Dave and Alaric wound up taking over the bulk of the computer maintenance after Buffy died, at least until we could hire some permanent IT staff. They never approached Buffy's level of competence—she was some kind of crazy computer virtuoso, and those don't come around very often—but they'd learned a lot, and they hadn't exactly started out as idiots. If anyone knew how easy it was to crack a cheap cover story, it was them.

"I don't know who did the programming," said Kelly, with increasing annoyance. "Dr. Wynne mentioned 'the Brainpan' once, but that was all. Everything was done through electronic transfer and encrypted messages. I never saw a face."

Dave and Alaric exchanged glances, saying, almost in unison, "The Monkey."

"It's creepy when you two do that, so stop." I raised a hand. "Somebody want to share the reason this makes us not panic?"

"The Monkey is possibly the single best identity counterfeiter in the country." Dave shook his head. "If you want an ID that can stand up to anything, you find a guy who knows a guy who might be able to put you in touch with one of the Monkey's girlfriends, provided you're willing to pay a deposit on faith."

"How much 'anything' are we talking here?" I asked.

"Scuttlebutt says one of the news anchors at NBC has three felony convictions and an ID by the Monkey," said Alaric.

"First, never say 'scuttlebutt' again," I said. "Second, good to know. All right, Kelly, you've got an ID. So who, exactly, are you supposed to be?"

"Mary Preston," she promptly replied. "Dr. Wynne's niece."

"Right. Alaric, can you—"

"Already on it," said Alaric, turning to one of the computer terminals that had yet to be torn down.

"Good. So 'Mary,' does this mean you have a paper trail?" I turned back to Kelly, who was starting to nod. "How much of a paper trail?"

"Mary's a real person, and she's really Dr. Wynne's niece," said Kelly. "Born in Oregon, joined Greenpeace straight out of high school, and got her conservationist's pass to move across the Canadian border five years ago. Last Dr. Wynne heard, she was working on one of the dog preservation farms and had no intention of ever coming back to the States."

"So she's disreputable enough to get along with journalists, and unlikely to come demanding her identity back when you're still using it." I looked over at Alaric. "Well?"

"Damn. I mean, just . . . damn." He was staring at his screen in open admiration. The rest of us took that as an invitation and put down whatever we were holding as we clustered around to peer over his shoulders, leaving Kelly by herself. Alaric shook his head. "I've never had a confirmed piece of the Monkey's work to look at. This is . . . it's not just amazing; it's *elegant*."

I frowned. "What are we looking at?"

The entire screen was filled with pictures of Kelly. Kelly in elementary school. Kelly at what looked like her senior prom. Kelly holding up one end of a banner that read STOP SHARK FISHING in big yellow hand-painted letters. Pretty standard snapshots, the kind you'd find on anybody's personal site or bias page.

Look again, prompted George, sounding exasperated.

I looked again, and actually saw what I was looking at. "Holy . . . are all those pictures fakes?"

"Yes and no," Alaric said, pulling up another set of pictures, including what looked like a still frame from an ATM's security camera and a shot where she was clearly drunk and flipping off the camera. "They're not really pictures of the Doc," he nodded toward Kelly, "but they're real pictures. The Monkey must've taken every picture of Mary on the entire Internet and somehow forced Kelly's physical isometrics over them. Seamless transition. Add the paperwork I'm finding, and—"

"No one ever knows the difference," Becks finished. "Slick."

"I'm glad you all understand what the fuck that means, because I don't," I said sharply.

"Magic computer pictures make old Mary go bye-bye, put pretty new Mary instead. Now pretty new Mary not get shot by CDC for failure to be her own dead clone," said Dave, in the lilting voice of a children's teaching-blog host.

"Great. So you've got an ID that's unbreakable as long as some chick in Canada doesn't get homesick, a bunch of numbers I don't understand, and a bunch of dead researchers. Oh, and folks like George are dying way too fast for anything short of a massive conspiracy. Okay, people, can anyone come up with a way to make this day any worse?"

That's when everything started to happen at once.

The building's siren began blaring almost at the instant that my phone started screaming with Mahir's emergency ringtone. I smacked it without taking it out of my pocket, triggering my headset to pick it up. "We're having a situation here, Mahir," I snapped. I could see Dave and Alaric out of the corner of my eye, rushing through the effort of tearing down our gear. "Sirens just started going off. We don't know why yet."

"Yes, well, I bloody well do!" he shouted. "Your building's surrounded, you've got no evac routes, and the civic authorities are declaring a state of general emergency through the surrounding cities! I don't know how you're supposed to do it, but you need to get the hell out of there, and you need to do it *now*!"

"Wait—Mahir, what the fuck are you talking about?" Becks started to say something. I held up a hand for quiet. It was already hard enough to hear Mahir over the siren.

"Good God, man, you mean you didn't know?" Mahir managed to sound horrified and unsurprised at the same time. It was a nifty trick, but I didn't have long to appreciate it; his next words took all the appreciation out of the world:

"There's an outbreak in Oakland, Shaun. And you're right in the fucking middle of it."

The formation of the modern health-care system was an organic process, guided almost entirely by the stresses imposed by the Rising and by the panic of the general populace. Given the death rates at hospitals during the worst of the outbreak, it wasn't a surprise that people would be afraid of them. Given the risk of amplification, it wasn't a surprise that people would need medical attention more than ever. The answer was complex, involving the restoration of house calls and private care, increased access to home medical technology ... and the sudden semi-autonomy of the CDC and the World Health Organization. If they couldn't do what needed to be done, when it was needed, there was the risk that none of us would live long enough to make a better choice about how things should be handled.

The CDC enjoys relative freedom from all ethical medical laws and local restrictions. The WHO enjoys absolute freedom in almost every nation in the world. Maybe it's time we stopped and thought about that a little more.

—From *The Kwong Way of Things*, the blog of Alaric Kwong,
April 15, 2041

Five

I dropped my phone and lunged for the window, swearing. The sirens were making it difficult to focus on anything but the noise. Outbreak alarms are supposed to get your attention and make you focus on the problem at hand. They work well for the first, and not so much for the second. Behind me, Alaric and Becks were shouting at Dave to shut the damn thing off already, while he shouted at them to be quiet, he was trying, and they were making it harder for him to concentrate.

Only Kelly seemed to realize that my reaction meant something was seriously wrong. She clenched her hands together, stress-whitened knuckles resting against the underside of her jaw, and watched me with eyes that seemed suddenly too large for the rest of her face.

I jerked the window as far open as it would go before leaning out over the fire escape and looking down at the street. The siren in the apartment stopped shrieking as Dave finally managed to crack the case and yank out the wires, but with the window open, the neighborhood sirens were right there to take its place—and so was the screaming.

At least the sirens took the edge off the screams. At least the sound of gunfire meant that someone was still standing.

At least.

Oh, fuck me, said George.

"My thoughts exactly," I muttered. "Guys?"

"What?" asked Alaric.

"I think it's time for an evacuation. Nice, easy, and oh, say, yesterday." I pushed away from the window. "I hate to say it, but this is not a drill."

There was a moment of relative silence as everyone stared at me, trying to rationalize what I'd just said. Then they exploded into motion, Becks and Alaric lunging for the weapons cache in the closet, Dave lunging for his keyboard. Only Kelly stayed where she was, hands still clenched beneath her chin.

Shaun—

"I'm on it," I said, and started for the server rack.

It had been almost fifteen years since the last major outbreak in Oakland. You want the recipe for a relatively zombie-free existence? It's easy. Take an armed population, give them an ingrained bunker mentality, and tell them they can't depend on anyone outside the community. They'll police their borders so well that you'll probably never need to worry about them again. Trouble is, that sort of border patrol can wind up hurting as much as it helps. Sure, Oakland had all the security features you'd expect to find in a major urban center, but most people didn't know exactly how they worked or how to take full advantage of them. They could handle their home defense systems. The public defenses were a little more difficult.

At least half the storefronts I'd seen during my brief survey of the street had been standing open, with their emergency gates fully retracted. Some of the blast shutters had managed to descend, but not nearly enough of them to make a difference, especially when the doors weren't locked. Sealed blast shutters on a building whose doors were standing open wouldn't save anyone. They'd just make sure no one could get out once the infected got in.

About half the unsealed windows had been broken—shatterproof glass is a much more academic concept when the infected are involved. They don't have any functioning pain receptors to slow them down, and they'll keep beating themselves against the glass until something gives way. When you're talking about civic-use storefronts in a relatively low-income neighborhood, it's going to be the glass that gives. There had been blood splashed all around the sidewalk, and there wasn't much screaming coming from our immediate vicinity. For most of the locals, it was long past too late.

I stepped up to the server rack and started to disconnect drives and flip the switches to transfer as much of our data as possible to secured off-site backups. There are some files we try never to keep live on an out-facing network, including most of the research we've done into the conspiracy that killed my sister. Even that data gets backed up daily, both to the drives I was shoving into my pockets and to other, off-site drives, stored in safety deposit boxes, hidden caches, and stranger places all over the Bay Area. I feel I've earned my paranoia.

I could hear the reassuring sound of Becks loading her rifle behind me, underscored by the equally reassuring sound of Alaric emptying the contents of the primary weapons locker onto the apartment floor. He might not be a field man, but he's one of the most well-informed weapons geeks I've ever met. That's not a contradiction in terms. Being comfortable on the firing range doesn't mean you'll have a damn clue what to do when a zombie comes at you. The belief that the two skill sets translate directly gets a lot of people killed.

You're getting distracted, chided George. She sounded anxious. I couldn't blame her. *Focus, asshole. This would be a stupid way to die.*

"I know, I know." I shoved the last of the drives into my pocket. Time to start moving.

The sound of my voice snapped Kelly out of her fugue. "What do we do?" she asked, in a low, tightly controlled voice. Her gaze darted around the apartment like she expected zombies to come bursting through the walls. She'd probably never been in an actual outbreak before. Talk about your trial by fire: from illegal cloning and faking your own death to trying to survive your personal slice of the zombie apocalypse in just one afternoon.

I'm man enough to admit that under most circumstances, I might have enjoyed watching the biological error messages flash across Kelly's face. Maybe it's cruel, but I don't care. There's nothing funnier than seeing somebody who thinks of the infected as somebody else's problem realize that they, too, could join the mindless zombie hordes. Most medical personnel fall into that category; by the time they have hard proof that they're not somehow above all harm, they're usually either dead or infected. Either way, they're not exactly making reports after that.

There's a time and a place for laughing at the suffering of others. This wasn't either. "We get the hell out of here," I said, striding toward Dave. "What's the situation at the parking garage? Do we have vehicle access, or are we just fucked?"

"They managed to take out the human security, but the autolockdown kept them from getting inside," Dave reported, his eyes never leaving the screen. His fingers flew across his keyboard and the ones to either side of it like a concert pianist in the middle of a symphony, never missing a beat. The screens connected to the secondary keyboards flickered windows and blocks of code so fast that they were almost strobing. None of it seemed to bother Dave. This was his element, and he was damn well in control of it. "The tunnel's clear—for the moment. The building's automated defense systems include bleach and acid sprayers. I've managed to suppress the acid. I can't stop the bleach."

"That's what gas masks and goggles are for. You sure there's nothing in the parking garage?"

"It should be clear all the way to the van." His hands didn't slow down once. "Outer perimeter hasn't been breached yet. I give it fifteen minutes if they keep slamming on the doors the way they are. Ten minutes if anybody gets bitten, panics, and drives their car into one of the fuse boxes on the street."

"How likely is that?"

"Move fast."

"Got it." I turned. "Alaric, Becks, status?"

"Almost ready." Becks tossed me a grenade. I clipped it to my belt. "We could blast our way out of anything, but . . . "

"But we need to assume the entire population of Oakland now wants to eat us. I know the drill. Alaric, how are we for gas masks?"

"Good." He looked up, face flushed. "Kelly, what's your weapons rating?"

She blanched. "I—it wasn't a priority for lab work, and so I didn't—"

All activity stopped as people turned to stare at her. Even Dave's fingers ceased their tapping. The screams and sirens from outside seemed louder without our preparations to blur them.

"Please tell me you didn't let it expire," I said, quietly.

"It wasn't necessary for lab work," she said, her voice practically a whisper.

I didn't need to swear. George was doing it for me, loudly and with great enthusiasm. The fact that no one else in the room could hear her was purely academic; it was making *me* feel better, and at the moment, that was all I gave a shit about. "That changes things," I said. "Alaric, you're on Kelly. Where she goes, you go, at all times. And Kelly, before you make the privacy protest, there are no potty breaks during a zombie outbreak."

Becks raised her eyebrows, looking at me.

"You've got another job to take care of." Dave's typing resumed as I spoke. The sound took the edge off the screaming from outside. Gesturing toward the pile of weaponry, I said, "Suit up, take what you need, and hit the garage. I want that tunnel absolutely secured, and I want a thorough sweep of the vehicles before we get out of here. You're going to be taking the van."

Her eyes widened as she realized what I wasn't saying. "Oh, no."

"Oh, yes."

"Shaun, you're not driving a motorcycle out through an active outbreak. That's not just stupid; that's suicidal."

"You've all been saying I was suicidal for months now, so I guess it's time I proved you right." I shook my head. "This isn't open for negotiation. Get ready, and get moving. Alaric, after you're done dealing with the ammo, go up and check the roof, see if any of our neighbors are up there, and check for helicopter evacuations on the nearby buildings. Once you've got an idea of the situation, regroup downstairs next to the door to the parking garage."

"Got it," he said, nodding once. He didn't argue with my orders or try to negotiate for leaving Kelly behind; he just stood and headed for the door. George trained her people well, and Alaric started out as one of hers.

Kelly hesitated on the cusp of following him into the hall, clutching the police baton Becks had shoved into her hands against her chest like a child would clutch a teddy bear. "Where are you going?"

"My apartment." I grabbed the rifle I'd taken from the closet, resting it against my shoulder. "I need to get something."

Dave glanced away from his keyboard. "Shaun—"

"Don't. Stay here, keep the network traffic moving, keep shifting the files we're going to need later, and just don't." Kelly stepped out into the hall, following Alaric. I looked from Dave to Becks, shaking my head. "I'll be right back."

I don't believe you just said that.

"I've been saying it all my life," I muttered, and left the apartment.

The emergency lights were on all the way along the hall, bathing it in bloody red light that was supposed to "convey a feeling of urgency" while "reducing the mental trauma of possible biological contamination." Government doublespeak for "red freaks people out so they move faster" and "it's harder to see what you're stepping in that way." To make matters worse, the emergency shutters on our building had activated, at least in the public areas where we hadn't bothered to install any overrides. The shutters blocked out the screaming. They also blocked out the daylight.

Leave it, Shaun. It's not that important.

"Pretty sure me being the one with the body means I get to decide what's important." The stairs were clear. I took them two at a time, ready to start shooting if anything moved in a way I didn't like. Nothing did.

Shaun—

"Shut up, George," I said, and opened my apartment door.

Every blogger keeps a black box in case something goes wrong. No, that's not right. Every *good* blogger keeps a black box in case something goes wrong. Every *sane* blogger keeps a black box in case something goes wrong. Every blogger you should be willing to work with keeps a black box, because every blogger you should be willing to work with understands that "things going wrong" isn't an *if*. It's a *when*.

Black boxes take a lot of forms. They're named after the boxes the FAA puts on airplanes to record information in the event of a crash. The idea behind a blogger's black box is basically the same: That's where we record the information that we need to survive when nothing else does. George's black box was built to withstand every known decontamination protocol, and a few that were still just theoretical. It was the first thing I got back from our van after she died. Becks and the others might think it wasn't worth going out into the open for, but they'd be wrong. It was the only thing worth going out into the open for.

George and I basically grew up online. What with the Masons

cheerfully exploiting our childhoods for ratings and our own eventual entry into the world of journalism, we never had many secrets. Everything we ever did wound up in somebody's in-box. Almost everything, anyway. There were always the things we didn't want to share, or didn't know how to. That's why we kept paper journals. It was the only way to steal ourselves a little privacy. That "we" is intentional, by the way; George was always the thinker, while I was always the doer, but we kept one diary between us for almost twenty years. We still do. I write my pages, and then I close my eyes and let her take care of hers.

I don't read them anymore. It's better if I just imagine that they're real.

The black box contained our paper journals. Her medical records, her extra sunglasses, her first handheld MP3 recorder, and data files from the start of the campaign up until the point where she stopped recording. Her bottles of expired pain medication. All together, it was the most physical part of my sister that I had left, and there was no way I was going to run off and leave it behind.

Getting my shit together took less than five minutes. I crammed the black box into a duffel bag, along with all the weapons I could grab, and crammed extra ammo into the space remaining. There was a picture of us on my bedside table. I grabbed it and slipped it into the pocket of my jacket. Whenever you have to evacuate, there's always the chance that you won't be able to come back. Take whatever you're not willing to live without.

I paused at the door, glancing back at the boxes and the barren walls. Everything I cared about could fit in one bag, the pockets of my coat, and my head. There was something tragic about that. Or there would be, if I let myself think about it.

Don't, whispered George in the back of my head, almost too softly for me to hear.

It's scary when she fades out like that. It reminds me that, technically, her presence makes me crazy, and sometimes, crazy people get sane again. "I won't," I said brusquely, and pulled the door shut as I hurried toward the stairs.

My headset connector started beeping angrily when I was only halfway there. I unsnapped it from my collar and jammed it into my ear, demanding, "What?"

"We've got a problem." Dave sounded so calm that he might as well have been telling me to update the shopping list. "Alaric just got back from the roof."

"That was fast." I kept walking, stretching my legs until I was taking the stairs three at a time. It still didn't feel fast enough. It was the best I could do.

"Well, it turns out that he's had enough field training to know that when you open the roof door on a mass of the infected, you should stop and turn around."

My toe caught on the lip of the stair I was stepping over, sending me tumbling forward. I grabbed the railing, banging my elbow in the process. "*What?!*" I barked, in almost perfect unison with George.

"There's a mob up there. Kelly says twenty, Alaric says eleven, I'd say the real number is somewhere in the middle." Dave paused. "He got a positive ID on Mrs. Hagar before he slammed and barred the door. The rest didn't come from this building."

"Meaning what?" I asked, picking myself up and resuming the trek toward the third floor.

Meaning this "outbreak" is somebody's idea of cleaning house.

"Somebody had to put them there," said Dave, unknowingly supporting George's statement. "There's no way our building is generating spontaneous zombies."

Swearing steadily now, I took the last of the steps in four long strides, kicking open the door to the apartment. Kelly jumped, staggering back against Alaric. She was as white as a sheet. Alaric's complexion was too dark to let him pull the same trick; he was settling for turning a jaundiced yellow-tan. Dave didn't even turn around. He just kept typing, hands moving across his conjoined keyboards like he was conducting the world's biggest orchestra.

"Prep for evac," I snapped. "We're out of here as soon as Becks gets back."

"Why don't we go meet her?" demanded Kelly, a thin edge of hysteria slicing through her voice. "Why do we have to wait up here? There's a *live outbreak* on the roof! Those people, they're *infected*!" The hysterical undertones were getting louder, like she wasn't sure we understood that this was supposed to be a big deal.

Deep breaths, counseled George. *Count to ten if you have to.*

I actually had to count to thirteen before I felt calm enough to speak without shouting. "We're aware of outbreak protocol, Dr. Connolly," I said. My tone was cold enough to make Dave glance away from his screen and shake his head before going back to work. "Rebecca is currently confirming whether it's safe for us to proceed, or whether we need to find an alternate route. The rooftop door is locked, and the front of the building is sealed. We're safer sitting here than we would be rushing blindly toward what we think might be an exit."

"The building design makes that tunnel a perfect kill-chute," added Dave. "If there's anything down there, Becks is probably clearing it out before she reports back. If not, she's confirming that we can get out of the garage without dying."

"Actually, she's right behind you."

We all turned toward the sound of Becks's voice. She was standing in the doorway, smelling of gunpowder, with a grim set to her expression. I raised my eyebrows in silent question. Becks held up a bagged blood testing kit, lights flashing green, and tossed it to the floor next to the biohazard bin. That was an answer in and of itself: She wouldn't have ignored proper biological waste disposal protocols if she thought there was any chance we'd be staying.

"Three guards and two civilians who had no good reason to be there, all infected. None of them made it within ten feet of me. The rest of the garage is clear, and our transport's prepped and ready."

"Excellent." I glanced around the apartment one last time, looking for things we might have missed. Our outbreak kits have always been well-maintained and ready for something to go wrong. That doesn't stop the feeling that something major has been forgotten. "Everyone, grab your masks and goggles. We're out of here."

Suiting up for a run through a tunnel that might or might not fill with bleach while we were inside it took only a few minutes—God bless panic, the best motivator mankind has ever discovered. Kelly looked oddly calmer once she had her goggles on and a gas mask bumping against her collarbone, waiting to be secured over her nose and mouth. Maybe it reminded her of being back at the CDC, where all the "outbreaks" were carefully staged and even more carefully controlled. She'd need to get over that eventually. Now wasn't the time. If pretending this was all a drill would keep her calm, I was all for it.

We left the apartment in a tight diamond formation. I was on point and Becks was at the rear, with Dave and Alaric flanking Kelly in the center. If there were any other people in the building, they didn't show themselves as we descended. That's the right thing to do when you're caught in an outbreak and don't have an evacuation route: stay put, stay quiet, and wait for the nice men with guns to come and save you. Sometimes they'll even show up in time.

We were halfway down the last flight of stairs when the sirens changed, going from a continuous shriek to a rising series of piercing air-horn blasts, like a car alarm with rabies. Alaric stumbled, knocking Kelly into Becks and nearly sending all three of them sprawling. I took two more steps down to get out of the way, and then turned, looking back toward the others.

That's not a good sound.

"I know," I muttered, before saying, more loudly, "Dave? What's going on?"

Dave might as well have been a statue. He was standing frozen, eyes gone wide in a suddenly pale face. My question startled him back into the moment. He blinked at me twice, shook his head, and whipped his PDA out of his pocket, fingers shaking as he tapped the screen.

"We should be moving," said Becks.

"We should be waiting," I replied.

"We should be praying," said Dave, glancing up. "This block has been declared a loss."

Alaric closed his eyes. Becks started swearing steadily in a mixture of English, French, and what sounded like German. Even George got into the action, uttering some choice oaths at the back of my head. Only Kelly didn't seem to share the group's sudden distress. Sweet ignorance.

"Meaning what?" she asked. "Why are we stopping?"

"Meaning they salt the ashes," said Becks, before starting to swear again.

Dave swallowed, squaring his shoulders as he looked at me. "Boss . . ."

"No."

"Yes."

"There's got to be another option."

There isn't, said George, quietly. *You know that. You have to let him.*

"I can delay the lockdown. Not forever, but long enough."

I shook my head. "No. There's got to be—"

"There's not," said Alaric. I turned toward him, not quite fast enough to miss the mixture of terror and relief washing over Dave's face. Alaric had pulled off his goggles, presumably so we could see his eyes. He was looking at me with something close to pity in his expression. "The computers in the apartment are wired into the building's security systems. They can't be controlled remotely, but they work just fine if you're tapped directly into the cable. He can do it. But only if he does it from up there."

"Do you know what you're asking me to do?" I demanded. "You're asking me to let him kill himself."

"I'm asking you to let me do my job." Dave's voice was quiet, almost serene. "I didn't become an Irwin because I wanted to live a long and happy life, boss. I sure as shit didn't stay with this site because I thought it was going to be a cushy job. The math's pretty simple. It's me or it's everybody. Pick one."

"Can't someone else—"

"Unless you're planning to bring Buffy back from the dead, no."

My hand clenched into a fist. I forced myself to lower it, gritting my teeth all the way. "You're trying to piss me off," I accused.

"Yeah, I am," Dave agreed. The air-horn blasts were getting louder and closer together, breaking up our conversation like gunshots. "Keep fighting me, and we all die here." And then, the killing blow: "You'll never find out who killed your sister."

I stiffened. There was a moment where it could have gone either way; a moment where I could have grabbed him and dragged him along with us, where we would have been caught in the government lockdown when it hit our building.

Please, George whispered.

The moment passed.

"Who has the ID Dr. Wynne made for Kelly?" I demanded. Kelly blinked as she produced the card from her pocket. I snatched it from her hand and passed it to Dave. She started to protest. I cut her off, saying, "You're not carrying any trackers, and your equipment checks clean. This is the *only* thing with circuitry we can't decode, and somebody traced you here. Understand?"

Mutely, she nodded, face gone white with increasing terror. I'm not sure she'd realized before that moment that she could still be followed.

Dave shot me a pained look, saying, "Shaun—"

"Just don't. You fucker, you better make this count." I turned my back on him and continued down the stairs, snapping, "Move out!" to the others. I heard steps going up as he started back toward the apartment. Then the others were moving with me, Alaric and Becks hustling Kelly along.

We were halfway down the tunnel when the bleach jets came on, but that was all; no acid, no nerve toxins designed to target the infected and the healthy alike. We just got decontaminated, and then we were out, moving through the empty garage to our vehicles. Becks got Alaric and Kelly into the van while I donned my helmet and straddled George's bike, shoving the key into the ignition.

Cameras ringed the parking garage; cameras with feeds that plugged into the building's security system. I turned to the nearest of them, blinking back the tears that were suddenly threatening to blur my vision, and saluted.

"Move it or lose it, boss," said Dave, voice cracked and distorted by the speakers in my helmet. "You've got ten minutes at most before the fire rains down."

"Don't you dare move into my head after you die, you fucker," I said. "It's crowded enough in here."

"Boss?"

I closed my eyes. "Open the doors."

Whatever whack-ass computer voodoo he'd worked on the security system was good; the doors slid open as soon as I gave the command. Only a few of the infected were visible on the street outside, but they'd start to mob soon enough. I gunned my engine, waving for Becks to follow, and roared out into the light. She followed about fifteen yards behind, both of us cutting a path toward the closest major street—Martin Luther King Boulevard—and our hopeful survival.

Dave was wrong about one thing. We didn't have ten minutes. The building went up in a pillar of flame six minutes later, along with every other structure in its immediate vicinity. Slag and ash rained down on the entire neighborhood. Collateral damage for a major urban outbreak; the only way to be sure the infection wouldn't spread.

We were outside the quarantine by that point, outside the kill zone, but the light from the explosion was still enough to hurt my eyes. I pulled off to the side of the road and kept watching it all the same. When the glare got to be too much, I put on the extra pair of sunglasses George always kept in a case clipped to her handlebars, and I kept watching.

I kept watching while Oakland burned, and a good man burned with it. A lot of good men, I'm sure, but only one who'd answered to me. The first man lost on my watch, instead of on my sister's.

"All right, George," I said. "Now what?"

For once, she didn't have an answer.

BOOK II

Vectors and Victims

Life's more fun when you take the chance that it might end. I have no regrets.

—DAVE NOVAKOWSKI

A martyr's just a casualty with really good PR. I'd rather be a living coward any day.

—GEORGIA MASON

—transmitting? You fucking useless piece of crap, don't you cut out on me n—

—fixed it. I hope that means I fixed it. If this is getting out, this is Dave Novakowski reporting live from the headquarters of the After the End Times. Well. This *was* Dave Novakowski reporting live. By the time this report finishes bouncing to our servers, and Mahir sees it and clears it by the boss, I'm going to be long d—

—shit, the sirens just stopped. That means they're not letting evacuees out anymore. Too late, ha-ha, joke's on me, couldn't get out if I wanted to. I take my hands off the controls, the building goes into lockdown. I stay here, I can let people out—or I could, if there were any people left—but I can't escape. Irony in action, ladies an—

—dalene? Even if this entry stays in-house, I know you'll see it, somehow. God, Maggie, I'm sorry we screwed around so much. We should've just gone for it. That's what people ought to do. They should just go for it. I loved you a lot. I loved my job a lot. I guess that makes me one of the lucky ones. I guess—

—can hear the bombs now; I can hear them coming, I can he—

—From *The Antibody Electric*, the blog of Dave Novakowski,
April 12, 2041. Unpublished.

Six

Maggie's place is located six miles outside a town called, I swear to God, Weed. Weed, California, one of the smallest urban areas intentionally reclaimed after the Rising. What made them so special? Choice of location: Weed offers convenient access to three of California's major rivers, and with red meat permanently off the menu, the fishing industry is one of the hottest things going. If you want river-fished trout to be one of your menu options, you need to reclaim your fishing towns. Weed was rescued from the oblivion that claimed most of the towns and cities built too close to the wild, and it was rescued *because* it was so close to the wild. Sometimes, logic just doesn't work.

Driving from Oakland to Weed takes about four and a half hours if there aren't any quarantine barriers on I-5. According to the GPS, we were looking at clear sailing the whole way. I signaled for Becks to follow and pulled back onto the road, turning north. It was time for us to get the hell out of Dodge.

Shaun?

"I'm not in the mood right now, George." The roar of the wind ripped my words away as soon as they were spoken, but that really didn't matter; she'd hear me. She always heard me, even when I didn't say a word.

I lost him, too.

"He died on my watch, George. *My* watch. That's not supposed to happen."

Bitter amusement tinged her tone as she replied, *So, what, they're only supposed to die on mine?*

I didn't have an answer for that, and so I didn't answer her at all. She took the hint, falling silent as the bike chewed away at the miles between us and our eventual destination. The van stayed visible in my mirrors, following at a close but careful distance. There were no other cars to be seen anywhere along the highway in either direction. A reflective yellow sign caught the light and threw it back at me as we went roaring past: CAUTION—DEER HABITAT.

Deer can grow to more than forty pounds and meet the standards necessary for Kellis-Amberlee amplification. We can't wipe them out wholesale—ecological concerns aside, they're herbivores, which means their food supply hasn't been compromised, and they breed like the world's biggest rabbits. Periodically, somebody introduces legislation to firebomb the forests and take care of the deer problem once and for all, and promptly gets shouted down by everyone from the naturalists to the lumber industry. I don't have an opinion one way or the other. I just find it interesting that kids apparently used to cry when Bambi's mother died. George and I both held our breaths, and then cheered when she didn't reanimate and try to eat her son.

A small orange light started blinking at the top right-hand corner of my visor, signaling that the van was trying to open a connection. Did I want to talk to any of the people who were in the van? No. No, I did not. Did that mean I could get away with ignoring the call?

Unfortunately, no, it didn't. Smothering the urge to hit the gas and drive away from the trappings of responsibility as fast as I could, I said, "Answer call."

Becks spoke in my ear a moment later, voice rendered irregular and crackly by the sound of the wind whipping by outside my helmet. "Shaun, you there?"

"No, it's the Easter Bunny," I said. "Who do you expect is going to be answering my intercom? What do you want, Becks? We're a long way from Maggie's."

"That's actually what I wanted. We didn't have time to prep the vehicles for another road trip before we left the—" She stopped, choking off the sentence with a small hiccup. Her voice was softer when she spoke again, making it even harder to hear above the roaring of the wind. "I mean, we're not all that good for gas over here. I don't know what your status is, but we've got about another fifty miles, tops, before we're going to have an emergency."

Fuck. "What does the GPS say?"

"There's a truck stop about twenty miles up the road that takes journalist credentials and has a good safety rating. Clean, reliable blood tests, no outbreaks in the past nine years."

With our luck, we'll fix that for them.

"Probably," I said, my shoulders sagging with relief. George had been quiet since I told her I wasn't in the mood, and I'd been irrationally afraid that somehow, the trauma of losing someone else who mattered to me had combined with my anger and managed to repair my brain, making me fit the normal standards for "sane." Screw sane. I don't want anything that makes her stop talking to me. That would drive me crazy for real.

"Shaun? What was that?"

"Nothing, Becks. The truck stop sounds fine. Why don't you call ahead and let them know we're coming?" If the truck stop was ready for our arrival, they'd have someone waiting at the gate to run the blood tests and let us inside. Much faster and more convenient than calling from the driveway and chilling our heels while some underpaid attendant tried to pull himself away from his coffee.

I was about to hang up when a thought struck me, making my stomach drop all the way to my toes. "Fuck—what about the Doc? She's legally dead, and her only clean ID just went up with Oakland."

She's died twice in under a week, commented George. *Even I never managed that.*

"Hush," I muttered.

Becks ignored my interjection as she replied, "We're way ahead of you. Alaric dug out one of Buffy's old clubbing IDs for her. It won't hold up to major scrutiny, but it'll do until we get to Maggie's and he can find something more stable."

"Awesome. Get a hat or something on her—we don't want anybody getting a good look at her face. And she stays in the van; somebody else can buy her drinks."

"Got it," said Becks. "Terminate call." There was a click, and I was alone with the sound of the wind once more.

The wind and the voice that lurked inside my head. "George?"

Yeah?

"Is it always like this? Losing somebody that counted on you?"

You say that like it happened all the time.

"You did it first."

Yeah. A long pause, and the faintest sensation of a sigh at the back of my mind. *But what else is new?*

George always did everything first. She talked before I did, read before I did . . . about the only thing I ever did first was figure out the game the Masons were playing with us, and that was as much luck as anything else. She was the one who decided to become a professional journalist, hauling me along in her excitement. I went along with it in the beginning to make her happy, and later because it turned out I was actually pretty good at poking things with sticks for the amusement of others. It was the first thing I'd ever found that I was really good at, that I really enjoyed doing, and I never would have found it if it weren't for her. She was the one who suggested we follow Senator Ryman's presidential campaign. She was the first one to recognize what it had the potential to do for our careers.

She was the first one to die.

I drove quietly, giving her time to collect herself. Finally, slowly, she said, *It's different every time. Losing Buffy was . . . It was basically the end of the world, but I held it together. I had to hold it together.*

"Why?"

Because, she said, like it was the most obvious thing in the world, *you needed me to.*

There was nothing I could say to that. I put my head down, gunned the throttle, and drove straight down the highway until the neon sign of a truck stop beckoned, promising food, fuel, and lots of burly rednecks with guns who were just aching for the chance to put down an outbreak. Everyone's got the places where they feel safe. My top three would probably be the middle of an Irwin meet-up, inside a CDC lockdown facility, and any truck stop in North America. You want to talk scary survivalist mentality, go find yourself a trucker, and then get back to me.

Three guards in oil-stained denim met us at the gates with hand-held blood testing units. One guard for me, two guards for the van. My attendant was an unsmiling, pimple-faced teenager whose nametag identified him, probably inaccurately, as "Matt." I didn't bother trying to engage him in conversation. I just pulled off my glove and held out my hand to let him do his job. He grunted appreciatively at the professionalism, jamming the test unit over my hand without pausing to make sure my fingers were straightened properly. It wouldn't change the test results; all one of those boxes cares about is blood. I winced as he bent my pinkie, but didn't say a word. Better to let him take care of things before I made him think of me as a person.

The lights on the top of the unit cycled from red to green,

stabilizing. A grin split his cratered face, transforming it into something that was almost endearing. "Looks like you're clean and clear, Mr. Mason," he said, further confirming that Becks had radioed ahead with our credentials. "Love your site. Those reports you sent out of Sacramento last year? They were amazing." He paused before adding shyly, "I was really sorry to hear about your sister."

I plastered my best "Gosh, no, it doesn't hurt at all when you bring up George randomly in conversation. Thanks so much for checking with me first" smile across my face, glad that the helmet's visor mostly obscured my eyes, and said, "Thanks. It's been an interesting time."

"Well, welcome to Rudy's. I hope we've got everything you need."

"Thanks," I repeated, and tugged my glove back on before starting the bike and rolling past the gates, into the truck stop proper. The other two guards were still busy testing the occupants of the van; maybe even double-checking Kelly's credentials. I felt better knowing that she was using something Buffy built. The Monkey might be the best in the business, but Buffy was the one whose work I knew and trusted.

I set my bike to auto-fuel while I ducked into the truck stop's generously designed convenience store, wandering past racks of real artificial cheese nachos and withered all-soy hot dogs to find the sodas. I paused in the act of opening the Coke cooler, looking longingly at the pot of coffee simmering next to the hot dogs. That stuff was probably ancient, tarlike, created through the slow compression of the bones of prehistoric creatures until their fossilized blood was pumped up from the very center of the planet to fortify long-distance truckers.

Go ahead.

"Huh?" I stopped where I was, blinking like an idiot. Not exactly a safe thing to do, since disorientation and jerkiness are early signs of Kellis-Amberlee amplification. My team may be used to my conversations with my dead sister, but the rest of the world isn't quite so understanding.

You want coffee. Get some coffee.

"But—"

I already made you drink a hooker from Candyland once today. I can show a little mercy. There was amusement tinged with sadness in her tone. It took me a while to learn to read how she was feeling—I wasn't used to watching for cues in a disembodied voice—but now that I knew, I couldn't un-know. *Besides, you've earned it.*

"Blow up one employee for one cup of coffee, huh?" I murmured, stepping away from the coolers and heading for the steaming pre-historic coffee. George always hated the taste of the stuff. I just don't understand why anyone would want to get their caffeine in a less-efficient form.

Alaric must have lost the "who has to leave the car" coin toss; he was coming into the convenience store as I was coming out, the biggest cup of coffee they were willing to sell me clenched firmly in my hands. Alaric glanced at the steaming cup and blinked, raising his eyebrows. The question was clear in his expression. Lucky for me, I've had a lot of time to practice being the oblivious one.

"I'm going to go double-check the bike and make sure all the windows on the van are clean while you take care of things in here." I sipped my coffee, reveling in the feeling of it searing its way down my throat. It was as thick and bitter as I'd hoped. "Make sure you remember to get something for Becks and the Doc to snack on. It's a long way to Weed, and Maggie may not have dinner on the table when we get there."

Alaric frowned. "Boss—"

"Go ahead and use the company card. When I get the bill, I'll tell me that I authorized it, and I'm sure I'll be willing to let the charge stand." I offered him a bright, disingenuous smile and brushed quickly past as I left the convenience store, heading for the fueling stations.

The sun was dipping lower in the sky; we'd be making most of the drive to Weed in full darkness. Even in today's safety-oriented society, there aren't lights on most of I-5; just around the exits to inhabited areas. Those are also the places where the guard stations are actually staffed, and where nice men with guns will be happy to "help" if you go and get yourself infected. Good Samaritans, every single one of them. Thanks to the laws regarding infection, they don't even have to be certain before they shoot; anything that can stand up as reasonable doubt in a court of law is enough to excuse them putting a bullet through your skull. The farther into the wild you go, the less reasonable that doubt has to be.

"Night-riding," I said, sipping my coffee again. "Gosh. That's just what I was hoping I'd be doing tonight. Driving down a deserted highway in the dark is always superfun."

I'd do it for you if I could.

"I know," I said. Alaric was coming out of the convenience store, practically staggering under his load of junk food and bottled sodas. I tossed my half-full coffee cup into the nearest trash can and pulled my helmet over my head, offering him a quick salute as I kicked one leg over my bike. The faster I made for the gate, the less time we'd have to talk about what happened. There'd be time for talking when we got to Maggie's place. We wouldn't be able to help it. For now, all I wanted to do was drive, and I didn't even particularly feel like doing that.

I had my bike pulled out from the pump and idling by the time Alaric reached the van. He dumped the supplies into the passenger seat and waved to me, a questioning expression on his face. I've learned to recognize the "Do you want to talk about it?" look—God knows I got it enough after George died. I shook my head, jerking a thumb toward the gate.

My team knows my signals as well as I know theirs. Alaric nodded, getting into the van. A moment later, Becks flashed me the thumbs-up signal out the driver's-side window and started the engine. The van pulled away from the pump and stopped behind me, waiting for my sign.

"Amateurs," I muttered, and gunned the engine.

The rest of the drive to Weed was the sort of uneventful trip that leaves every nerve on full alert, ready to freak out at the slightest provocation. Pre-Rising horror movies used to build suspense before a big scare by making the audience wait. They'd do something horrible, maybe kill off a few protagonists, and then make people sit around waiting for the next terrible thing to come along. They called it "setting up a jump scare." Well, the drive to Weed felt exactly like that. We blasted down the abandoned length of I-5, and with every mile that passed without something going wrong, the paranoia grew.

It was almost eleven when we pulled off the freeway and onto the surface streets of Maggie's hometown. Floodlights lit a billboard located near the city center, large block letters proclaiming CON-GRATULATIONS JAMES! WEED'S CITIZEN OF THE MONTH!

There's something in the mentality of small towns that I'll never understand. Shaking my head, I signaled for the others to follow as I turned onto the frontage road leading to Maggie's.

Houses took on a distinctly utilitarian feel after the Rising, as people suddenly figured out that maybe being able to withstand the zombie apocalypse was more important than having a showy picture window. I've always had a soft spot for pre-Rising buildings. Sure, they're basically death traps and most of them should be torn down before something goes horribly wrong, but they're death traps with *style*. Pre-Rising houses are the Irwins of the architectural world. Maggie's place, well ... it could easily win a Golden Steve-o just for existing.

We turned off the lackadaisically maintained frontage road and onto the smooth pavement of Maggie's two-mile driveway, which wound like a ribbon through the trees to make an almost perfect circle around the house. Less impractical than you might think: Every segment of the driveway was surrounded by automatic sensors and motion trackers, right up until you hit the wall, which looked like stone but was actually specially treated polymer over a steel core. The gates were set to slam shut in less than half a second, and they were guaranteed to shear straight through anything short of a tank. The twisting driveway sliced the surrounding woods into sectors, and each sector contained a series of trip wires and cameras that would make sure nothing ever snuck up on Maggie or her guests.

I stopped the bike just shy of the first gate, shifting to neutral and activating my helmet's intercom. "Uh, Becks? Did anybody call Maggie to tell her we were coming?"

A long pause greeted my question before Becks said, "No. I thought you did."

"Slipped my mind." I sighed, starting forward. "Let's see if her security system kills us, shall we?"

The first two gates were set to open for anyone with After the End Times credentials. The third required a blood test—you could get into the kill chute after you were infected, but you'd be stopping there in a hurry. The fourth performed a mandatory ocular scan. George never had the occasion to visit, which was a pity. It would have been fun to watch the hard-coded security system try to deal with her retinal KA. Maggie might have needed to actually call some of the live guards out of the woods where they usually lurked unseen.

We could see the house after we passed the third curve in the drive. Every window was lit, and the yard was illuminated by floodlights concealed in the carefully manicured garden. It was practically bright enough to be daylight. The light led us the rest of the way up the hill. I started to relax after we'd passed the fourth gate without anything coming out of the trees to kill us all. The fifth gate—the final gate—was standing open. I drove through to the yard, parking to the side in order to leave the van with plenty of space to pull in past the gate.

The front door opened while I was taking off my helmet and Becks was parking the van. A small flood of furry bodies poured out into the yard, Maggie walking at the center of the rollicking, barking pack. I had to smile. I couldn't help it.

The barrier weight for Kellis-Amberlee amplification—that is, how heavy something has to be before it won't just die, but will also come back from the dead and have a go at eating Grandma—is forty pounds. That seems to be a reasonably hard cut-off point; some things may not reanimate under fifty pounds, but nothing reanimates under forty. Logically, you'd think this would mean the dog fanciers of the world would go, "Gosh, aren't teacup poodles nice?" Logic has never been the human race's strong suit. Breeding programs sprang up the minute the risk of apocalypse was past, with people all over the world trying to miniaturize their favorite canine companions.

George used to say it was disgusting, and that people should get over themselves. Me, I've always found Maggie's miniature bulldogs endearing, in a fucked-up, epileptic sort of a way. The miniature bulldog's tendency to develop epilepsy is actually the reason rescues like Maggie's exist, since a surprising number of families wanted a dog "just like Grandpa's," but didn't read the new breed specs.

"Hey, Maggie," I said, shifting my attention from the sea of bulldogs to their owner. "Are we too late for dinner?"

"Not if you like emu meatloaf," she said, with a forced attempt at a smile. Her eyes were red and slightly swollen, like they'd been wiped too many times in the past few hours. "I assume you guys are planning to stay for a while?"

"If that's all right with you." She looked miserable, standing there in the midst of her little swarm of rescue dogs and trying to seem like nothing was wrong. I wanted to comfort her. Only I didn't have any idea how.

I was better with that sort of shit when George was alive, because I had something to protect. She didn't like touching people, so I touched them for her. She didn't like emotional displays, so I took up the slack. Only without her around to give me an excuse, it was like I didn't even know where I was supposed to start.

We always figured she was the one whose emotional growth got stunted by the way we were raised. It was sort of weird to realize that the damage extended to cover both of us.

Alaric saved me from needing to figure out what I was supposed to do. He was out of the van almost before Becks had the engine off, running toward Maggie with total disregard for the dogs surrounding her. Luckily, miniature bulldogs are smart enough to get out of the way when they're about to be stepped on, and he made it to her without incident. Putting his arms around her shoulders, he pressed his face into her shoulder. She did the same to him, and they simply held each other. That was all. That seemed to be enough.

Breathe, George said.

"I'm trying," I murmured. Watching Maggie and Alaric embrace felt weirdly like spying. I turned away.

"Hey," said Becks, stepping up beside me. Kelly was close behind her, clutching one of the spare blankets we kept in the back of the van around herself for warmth. They both looked exhausted, but of the pair, it was Becks who looked like she was going to be okay. The circles under Kelly's eyes were deep enough to be alarming, and her face was pale.

"Hey," I replied. Nodding toward Kelly, I asked, "Doc get through the drive okay?"

"I slept some," said Kelly, in a distant tone.

"No," said Becks, half a second later.

"Didn't think so." I glanced over to where Alaric and Magdalene were still clinging to each other, and said, "Maggie made emu meat-loaf. It's inside. Maybe we should join it."

"That sounds like an excellent idea to me," Becks said. "I'll get my bag."

Now Kelly began to look alarmed. "Wait—this is where we're *staying*? Here?"

"Yup," I answered, turning to unhook the bike's saddlebags and sling them over my shoulder. "Welcome to Maggie's Home for Wayward Reporters and Legally Dead CDC Employees."

"But this isn't—it's not—" She waved her hands, encompassing the wide green lawn, the patches of tangled, seemingly untended greenery, and the trees outside the wall. "This isn't safe!"

Becks and I exchanged a look. Then, almost in unison, we started to laugh. It had the ragged, almost hysterical edge that always seems to come with laughter that's halfway born from exhaustion, but still, it felt damn good to laugh about *something*. Just about anything would have been okay by that point.

Kelly looked between us, eyes widening with alarm that turned quickly into irritation. "What?" she demanded. "What are you laughing at?" That made us laugh harder, until I was bent almost double, and Becks was covering her face with her hands. Even George was laughing, an eerie, asynchronous echo inside my head. Alaric and Magdalene ignored us, lost in the private world of their grief.

Becks was the first to get control of herself. Wiping her eyes, she said, "Oh, Shaun, I don't think anybody ever bothered to tell the Doc here exactly where it was that we were going."

"Apparently not," I said, rolling my shoulders back and forcing my expression to sober as I turned to Kelly and said, "Doc, we are fortunate enough to enjoy the hospitality of Miss Magdalene Grace Garcia."

"Please don't steal the silver," added Becks.

Kelly's mouth dropped open.

If Kelly's family was responsible for many of the medical advance-
ments of the past twenty-five years, it was Maggie's family who made
sure they had the equipment they needed to keep moving forward.
Her parents were heavily into software before the Rising; their company had already made millions when the dead began to walk. They
were savvy people, and they saw the writing on the wall: Either
everybody was about to die, in which case money had just become an
outdated concept, or we were going to beat back the infected, and
folks were going to get real concerned about their health. They managed to shift most of their financial capital into medical technology
before the markets froze. They didn't make millions. They made *bil-
lions*, and that was after taxes.

They weren't only heavily into software: They were also heavily
into philanthropy, and their contributions were a large part of what
made saving Weed possible. Of course, that left them owning a controlling share in two of the town's four major fisheries, as well as most
of the hospital. We're talking about the kind of people for whom a
thousand dollars is a perfectly reasonable price for a bottle of wine.
When Maggie turned twenty-one, they asked her what she wanted,
said that the sky was the limit, nothing was too good for their precious little girl.

She asked for the farmhouse that belonged to her grandparents, a
military-grade security system, a private T1 line, and permanent
access to the interest generated by her trust fund. Nothing else. And
her folks, being the sort of people who try to keep their word, agreed.
We might have been safer in an underground CDC bunker. Maybe.
If it was protected by ninjas or something.

"But . . . " Kelly said finally. "Shouldn't she be doing something,
I don't know, important with herself?"

"She is," I said, and smiled. "She hosts grindhouse film festivals
and writes for me. Come on. Last one to the table has to do the
dishes." I started for the door, skirting a wide circle around Alaric and

Maggie. Kelly followed me, still looking confused, and Becks came after her. She left the front door standing open. The privileges of security are many, and not always visible.

None of the other Fictionals were evident in the large, bookshelf-lined living room, which was cluttered with boxes of dusty papers, dog beds, and comfortable-looking couches. That was unusual; Maggie was almost never home alone, having opened her house on a semipermanent basis to all the Fictionals working for the site, as well as a few of the Irwins and Newsies. She liked company, Maggie did. She grew up in a level of society where it was still possible to be a party girl, and even though she walked away from her roots in a lot of ways, she couldn't walk away from everything she'd learned. Normal people like being alone. Being alone means being safe. Maggie got lonely.

Kelly stuck close behind me, drinking in her surroundings with a coolly assessing expression that I recognized from watching Irwins sizing up hazard zones. Most homes are decorated for utility these days, resulting in a lot of sleek lines, brightly lit corners, and modernistic furniture that looks like it came from a pre-Rising horror movie, all of it designed to be easy to disinfect. Maggie decorated in antiques and homemade furniture, with clutter covering every surface, and dust covering all the clutter.

I've always assumed that Maggie lives the way she does partially out of sheer contrariness. If everyone expects her to run around partying with the kids she grew up with, moving in a virtual bubble of overpaid security guards and the sort of safety that only money can buy, fine; she'll live in the middle of nowhere with a pack of epileptic dogs instead of a purse poodle and a posse. If people expect her to have three brain cells to knock together, she'll become a professional author and manage a crew of twenty more. The list goes on. She's a fun girl, our Maggie, even if the way she lives implies that her sanity is somewhat dubious.

The thought barely had time to form before George interrupted it, saying, *You're one to talk.*

I didn't mind. At least she was talking to me. And she sounded amused, which is always nice. It's good to know that I can still make my sister smile. "Hush, you," I said.

Kelly gave me a startled look. "I didn't say anything," she protested.

"It was George," I said, with a quick shake of my head.

"You know," said Kelly carefully, "if it's anxiety that leads you to continue conversing with her, there are medications that will—"

"New topic time," I said pleasantly. "Continuing this topic is going to lead to somebody getting punched in the face. It could be you."

"Shaun has no compunctions about hitting girls," said Becks.

"You try growing up with George, see how many compunctions about hitting girls you come out with." I led our motley little parade into Maggie's kitchen. It was decorated like the rest of the house, in middle-class pre-Rising shabby. Maggie hadn't been kidding about the meatloaf. It was sitting on the kitchen table, alongside a platter of sliced vegetables, a big bowl of mashed potatoes, and half a sponge cake.

"I'll get the plates," said Becks.

When Maggie and Alaric finally came in fifteen minutes later, they found the three of us seated around the kitchen table, stuffing our faces. Becks and I were stuffing our faces, anyway. Kelly was watching us with a sort of horrified bemusement, like she couldn't believe her life had gone so terribly wrong in just one day. She'd catch on. If she lived long enough.

Maggie and Alaric had clearly both been crying, although it showed more on her than it did on him; her eyes were puffy and her cheeks were even redder, whereas Alaric looked about as normal as he ever did. He tried to explain his consistently camera-ready appearance to me once, but I didn't listen. Largely because I didn't care.

"Alaric tells me you're the dead girl from the CDC," said Maggie, arrowing in on Kelly with the laser-point accuracy that has made her editing skills feared throughout the Fictional world. "Nice trick. Explain it."

"Hello to you, too, Maggie," I said brightly, reaching for the mashed potatoes. "Do you need an introduction to our guest, or do you prefer the tornado approach? Just so it's said, she's had a pretty shitty week, and I wouldn't blame her if she freaked out on you. I mean, it's been a shitty day for all of us, so I'd really appreciate it if you could take it easy on the Doc."

Maggie stiffened. I looked at her calmly, waiting to see which way the dam was going to break: raging flood or anguished trickle.

Finally, her shoulders dropped, and she said, "Mahir kept Dave's last post from going live, but he sent me a copy and said he thought you might be coming here. That's why I sent everybody home."

"That was a good idea," I said, neutrally.

"I didn't get to say good-bye, Shaun." Maggie shook her head. "I should've been able to say good-bye. I should've been able to tell him . . . I should've been there."

That was the sort of grief I can handle. Sadly enough, it's the kind I've been on the inside of, because even saying good-bye isn't enough. There's always one more thing you should have had the time to say, or do, or ask. There's always going to be that one missing piece.

I put my fork down and stood, shifting dogs out of the way with the side of my foot as I walked over to Maggie. She looked at me. I nodded, once, and put my arms around her, feeling the tension in her shoulders. "I won't tell you it's going to be all right, because it's not going to be all right," I said. "I won't tell you I understand what you're going through, because nobody who isn't inside your head can understand, and I won't say that we're here to help. We're not. We're here to save our asses, and we're here to find out what the fuck is going on. But I'll say this: Dave made his decision, and they're going to put him up on the Wall with all the other heroes. He's going to be there forever because of what he decided was the right thing to do. I guess I can't be too angry at him for that. George wouldn't have hired him if she didn't think he knew how to make the hard calls, and I wouldn't have kept him if she wasn't right."

"I think I loved him," said Maggie, her voice soft and almost muffled by her face pushing up against the side of my shirt.

I sighed deeply, looking over her head toward the others. Becks and Alaric had barely had time to get over being the walking wounded after losing Buffy and George. I'd barely had time to learn how to look like I was coping. And now it was all starting up again. The conspiracy theories, the confusing evidence, the deaths, the whole fucking mess.

The worst part was that deep down in my heart, in the part of me that no one got to see but George, I was glad. Because if all the old shit was starting up again, that meant that we were moving again. Moving toward an answer to the question that kept me from sleeping at night, and probably kept me from killing myself:

Who really killed my sister?

Kelly met my eyes and looked away, expression guilt-stricken. I'd have to talk to her about that. This wasn't her fault, any more than it was mine, or Alaric's, or Maggie's. She was a victim, just like the rest of us. None of us did anything wrong. But that could be dealt with tomorrow, when we'd had time to sleep, reassure Mahir that we were still alive, and really look at Kelly's data.

"I think we all loved him at least a little," I said, with complete honesty, and I stood in that homey-smelling kitchen surrounded by the remains of my team, and I held her while she cried.

Screw you, David Novakowski. Screw you for being noble and good and earnest and staying in that damn building, and screw you for that last transmission, and screw you twice for taking so fucking long to say anything. You idiot. You stupid, stupid idiot.

I loved you, too, you idiot.

I can't post this. I want to post this. I can't post this. But writing it down helps, a little, because writing it down is what we *do*. They're on their way here—they have to be, because if they're not ... I won't think about it. The house feels so empty. God.

—From *Dandelion Mine*, the blog of Magdalene Grace Garcia, April 12, 2041. Unpublished.

———

I'm sorry, my darlings, but I won't be able to make tonight's chat. I know, I promised, and I'm sorry, but Auntie Maggie has a headache right now and needs to have a nap. Normal transmissions will resume tomorrow. Be good. Be kind to each other. And if there's somebody you love, tell them. The world always needs more love.

—From *Dandelion Mine*, the blog of Magdalene Grace Garcia, April 12, 2041

Seven

"Shaun?"

I raised a hand to rub my temple as I raised my head, trying to ward off the headache I could feel brewing there. I'd turned off most of the lights when the rest of the house went to bed, but I hadn't stopped reading. Maybe that wasn't such a good idea. "In here, Maggie." I was sitting on the living room floor, back against the couch. I'd been sitting long enough that I wasn't sure I could still stand.

Maggie made her way down the darkened hall to the doorway without tripping over anything. I had to admire how well she knew where everything was. I couldn't have navigated that hall without causing my shins some serious damage. "How's Mahir?"

"Relieved that we're not dead. Broadcasting some old camping footage George and I took the last time we went to Santa Cruz. As long as he strips the dates, he should be able to make it look like we were all off having a grand time with the infected when they fire-bombed our building."

Maggie swallowed. "And Dave?"

"Stayed behind to take care of the servers. We figure the cleanup on Oakland should be done by morning. They'll contact his family, and we'll announce it after they contact us." It was heartless. It was unforgivable. It was the only choice we had. "I figure we can fake being out in the field for three or four days before we need to find somewhere else to be."

"Don't be an idiot." The edge on her voice was surprising. I blinked. Drawing her tattered terrycloth bathrobe around her shoulders like it was a form of armor, Maggie scowled at me. "You'll stay right here. My security systems can bounce your signal anywhere we want it to be."

"Maggie—"

"Don't you dare tell me it isn't safe, Shaun Mason. Don't you *dare*." She stalked to the nearest overstuffed armchair and sat, curling her legs under herself and eyeing me like an aggravated cat. "I've never been safe in my life. I'm not planning to start now."

"You can't tell me that," I protested. "I've seen your security system."

Maggie's laugh was rich, bright, and surprising. "I'm going to inherit enough money to buy a small country someday. My parents don't have anyone else to leave it to. There's a reason I live in the middle of nowhere and surround myself with reporters. Do you have any idea how good the security on this place *really* is? If I scream, someone comes. They can't fake an outbreak on us here that won't be immediately obvious as a setup. So unless the dead decide to rise en masse again—"

"Which is thankfully not very likely."

"Exactly. You won't be safe when you leave here."

I looked at her measuringly. "Nice cage you've got here."

"Thanks." She smiled thinly. "The food's pretty good, but, man, does the company suck."

"We do our best." I sighed. "I'm really sorry about all this."

"Don't be. Just get some sleep." Maggie pulled her almost waist-length braid over one shoulder, picking aimlessly at the trailing end. "You've had a long day."

"Yeah, well. Objects in the rearview mirror don't get smaller just because they're getting farther away." I held up one of the folders from Kelly's briefcase. "I'm trying to make sense out of all this crap while nothing's catching on fire. I figure that won't last for long."

"It never does," Maggie agreed. "How bad is it?"

"On a scale of one to oh fuck, we're all gonna die?" I flipped the folder open and read, "'Considering the risk of mutation, the concept of the reservoir conditions as the next stage in Kellis-Amberlee's evolution cannot be ignored. We would be severely remiss to ignore the opportunities, and dangers, that such an evolution may present.'" I closed the folder, but didn't look up. "What the fuck does it even mean? Somebody's killing the folks with reservoir conditions. The numbers aren't lying, even if everybody else is. But what does it *mean*?"

"It means we have a job to do, I guess."

"Yes." I glanced toward the hall. "Everybody else asleep?"

"Yes, they are. I think a few of them may have helped themselves get that way with chemical aid, but whatever works."

"Good."

Maggie had prepared the guest rooms while we were still on the road, swallowing her grief long enough to break out fresh bedding and clean towels. I'm pretty sure the process was a sort of good luck charm for her; if she got the rooms ready, we'd show up alive. As it was, when bedtime came, she apologized for having only three guest rooms, since the other two spare rooms had been converted, respectively, into a home theater and a study. Like there's anything "only" about a house with six bedrooms. George and I grew up in a house with three, and ours were connected enough to practically count as a single room. Three guest rooms meant one each for Alaric, Becks, and the Doc. I've slept on couches before. It doesn't bother me.

Besides, I wanted to stare at those numbers until they started making sense. After almost two hours, I wasn't getting any closer. I sighed. "I'm missing something. I know I'm missing something."

Don't be so hard on yourself, said George. *You're tired.*

"That's easy for you to say," I snapped, before I could stop myself. Then I froze, casting a careful glance toward Maggie. I was expecting . . . I don't know what I was expecting. I get a lot of reactions to the fact that I still talk to my sister. Most of them aren't good ones.

Maggie's fell somewhere in the middle of the spectrum. She was looking at me thoughtfully, head tilted slightly to one side. "She really talks to you, doesn't she?" she asked. "It's not just you talking to her. She talks *back*."

"Hell, half the time she starts it," I said, half-defensively. "I know it's weird."

"Well, yes, it's weird. Technically, I think it's insane. But who am I to judge?" Maggie shrugged. "I live in a house most people view as the setting of a horror movie waiting to happen, with an army of security ninjas and a couple dozen epileptic dogs for company. I don't think I'm qualified to pass judgment on 'weird.'"

That's a new one, said George, bemused.

"Tell me about it," I muttered, adding, louder, "That's, uh, different."

"At least you know that you're crazy. That means you have the potential to recover."

I hesitated. There are a lot of people who'd say that my steadfast refusal to give up on George means I'll never get over my grief. I sort of hope they're right. I don't want to get over it. "Well, um, thanks," I said. The words sounded even lamer outside my head than they did inside.

Maggie didn't seem to notice. She was gazing off into one of the darkened corners of the room, expression gone even more wistful. "I knew Dave loved me, you know," she said, with a studied casualness to her tone. Whatever she was going to say, she was going to say it whether she got the right conversational prompts from me or not. I was an audience, not a participant. "But I was still getting over losing Buffy, and Dave and I, we were doing this . . . this weird circling thing, like we needed to figure out every single line of the script before we could even start the movie. I knew, and he knew, and we didn't do a damn thing about it." She sniffled. A very small sound that seemed loud in the sudden silence of the room. "It's like we thought everything had to be perfect, or it wouldn't work. Like it was a story."

I wanted to say something, but there was nothing to say. I sat frozen, my fingers twitching slightly on the folder I still held. I wanted to reach for her. I wanted to take her hand. Only I knew it wasn't her hand I wanted—the hand I wanted had been reduced to ash and chips of bone before being scattered down the length of California Highway 1—and so I didn't move.

"Have you ever been in love?" Maggie looked back toward me, the faint light glittering off the tears running down her cheeks.

There's never been a good answer to that question. I didn't even try. I just shrugged.

"Love sucks," said Maggie, and stood. "Everyone I fall in love with dies. Try to get some sleep tonight, okay, Shaun? And . . . thanks for listening. I can't post that." She chuckled, the sound barely managing to escape turning into a sob. "You know, it seems like every time I wind up with a real tragic love story to tell, I can't post it. It wouldn't have been fair to Buffy, and now it wouldn't be fair to Dave. It's . . . there's so little that's personal anymore."

"Yeah," I said, swallowing past the dryness in my throat. "I'm pretty sure he knew you loved him, too. He had this theater thing set up on the roof—"

"I know." Her smile was brief, but it was real. "Get some sleep. Tomorrow's not going to be any better."

Can't be any worse, muttered George.

I swallowed the urge to answer George, and said, instead, "I'll try."

"Good enough for me," said Maggie, and turned to go, leaving me alone with my pile of folders, my tiny pool of light, and the voice of my sister echoing inside my head.

You used to make me sleep, said George.

"Yeah, well, you had a body then." I looked at the folder in my hands, willing it to open of its own accord. That way I wouldn't actually have to decide whether or not I was going to stop. Once it was open, I could just read.

Shaun—

"Leave it."

She sighed. I knew that sigh. I knew all her sighs. This was the "Shaun, stop being stupid" sigh, usually reserved for when I needed to be pushed into doing something she considered sensible. *I won't let you dream.*

I froze.

George didn't say anything after that. I could feel her waiting at the edges of my mind, eternally patient, at least where my well-being was concerned. I swallowed again before I leaned back in the chair, closing my eyes. "You can still surprise me," I said.

Good. Now get up, and get on the couch.

"Yes, ma'am."

Maggie's couch proved to be surprisingly comfortable once I'd cleared everything off it and piled it all on the floor. I turned off the light before taking off my shirt and shoes, leaving my jeans on, just in case we needed to make an early-morning getaway. I was asleep almost before my head hit the pillow.

George was true to her word. If I dreamed that night, I don't remember it.

I woke to the sound of voices in the next room, pitched at that harsh semi-stage-whisper level that everyone seems to think is unobtrusive, despite being impossible to ignore. Something about the sound of people whispering touches off a primordial red alert in the back of the brain. I probably wouldn't have noticed if they'd just spoken quietly in normal voices. At least no one was screaming; that meant we'd all probably managed to live through the night. Survival is always a nice thing to wake up to.

Sitting up was hard. My back was stiff from spending several hours on the bike, followed by several more hours sitting on the floor and trying to study. I may not spend as much time in the field as I used to, but that hasn't made me a bookworm or anything. Who knew being a geek would *hurt*? Groaning, I braced my elbows on my knees and dropped my head into my hands. The voices from the kitchen stopped. Zombies don't groan, they moan, but the two can sound almost identical to the untrained ear. Of the four people in the house with me, only Becks had the field experience necessary to know that whatever had made that sound was alive. Just cranky.

Becks and Alaric both had enough general experience working with me to know better than to come poking before I was at least standing under my own power. The voices from the kitchen resumed, a little louder now that they knew they didn't have to worry about waking me anymore. Leaving my head cradled in my hands, I considered my options. Going back to sleep was at the top of the list and had the extra added bonus of not requiring me to think about anything. Unfortunately, whoever was killing the people with reservoir conditions wasn't going to wait around for me to get my shit together, and if anyone realized Kelly was still alive, we probably didn't have all that much time.

There was always the possibility that time had already run out. If Kelly's original fake ID was compromised, they might have tracked her across the country with it. That didn't explain why they waited for her to reach us before going on the offensive, but maybe she just hadn't held still long enough before that. They wouldn't be tracking her that way again. Her fake ID was so much slag in the remains of Oakland, and nobody outside the team knew she was alive.

Now we just had to keep it that way.

The outbreak could have been triggered in response to my call to Dr. Wynne, but that didn't seem likely. The timelines didn't synch. That level of outbreak would take time to set up. Even if it had started the second my call was connected to the CDC, there wasn't time for all those people to amplify and get into position. Whoever targeted us—assuming it was a "who," which had to be my operating assumption, at least until something came along to make a strong case for coincidence—had more time than my phone call gave them.

I lifted my head, groaning again, and stood. One of the bulldogs had turned my discarded shirt into a makeshift doggy bed, probably as revenge for my taking up the entire couch. It opened one eye to watch me as I approached, and made a small "*buff*" noise that might have been intimidating, if it hadn't been roughly the size of an overweight housecat. "Whatever, dude," I said, putting up my hands. "I wasn't that cold anyway."

Alaric, Becks, and Kelly were gathered around the kitchen table when I came shuffling in, making a half-hearted attempt to push my spiked-up hair back into a semblance of order. All three looked over at my entrance. Becks raised her eyebrows.

"You're looking bright and shirtless this morning," she said, dryly. "Did you decide that clothes were for sissies?"

"Dog took my shirt," I replied. "Where's Maggie? Is there coffee? If Maggie's hiding because she drank all the coffee, it's not going to be pretty."

"Ms. Garcia is, um, out back, in the garden," said Kelly. She gestured toward the back door as she spoke, looking distinctly uncomfortable. Understandable. She'd probably never been in a private residence open to the scary, scary outside world before.

Sometimes I think George was right when she said that people want to be afraid.

"Coffee's on the stove," said Alaric, before adding quickly, "Do we have a plan, or are we just going to sit around here drinking coffee and waiting to see what happens next?"

"That depends on the Doc." I walked over to the stove. A half-full pot of coffee was on the central heating plate. "We know what happened yesterday wasn't just bad timing. So I guess the question is, Doc, were they after us, or were they after you?"

Silence fell behind me. I took a mug from the rack and poured myself a cup of coffee, taking a slow, patient sip as I waited for someone to say something. The liquid was almost hot enough to be scalding, and it tasted like it had been brewed just this side of Heaven. I'll drink Coke for George all day if I have to, but there's nothing like that first cup of coffee to get the morning started.

Finally, in a small voice, Kelly said, "Dr. Wynne thought we were managing to get me out before our plan could be compromised. With most of my team dead, it's not like there were that many people who knew about the clone, or what we were going to do with it. It should have been a clean escape. He did say . . . When I left, he said you were probably in danger anyway, because of . . . "

She stopped. A lot of people have trouble talking about what happened to George when I'm in the room. I can't decide whether it's because they don't want to remind me that I was the one to pull the trigger, or if it's because they can't deal with the fact that she's still with me. Maybe they just don't feel like getting punched in the face.

The *why* doesn't matter much to me. The end result is the same: George stays dead, and no one talks about it.

"You knew we were in danger before you reached us?" I recognized the warning in the tone Becks was using. She started as a Newsie, and she processes facts a little faster than most Irwins. That gives her the ability to sound very reasonable, and the more reasonable she sounds, the more danger you're in. "And you didn't say anything?"

"There will be no killing the Doc," I said, walking over to the settle at the table. "She's just as screwed as we are, so play nicely, okay? This isn't her fault."

Kelly nodded firmly, looking more frustrated than anything else. "I *tried* to say something. I was e-mailing you for three weeks before we hit the point where I couldn't hang around in Memphis anymore."

The spam filters, said George quietly.

I winced.

"A secure phone line would have been noticed in a facility as locked down as the CDC," Kelly continued. "When Dr. Wynne evacuated me, I wound up drugged and stuffed into the back of a truck that was hauling dry goods to California. I barely had a pulse for a few thousand miles. I definitely wasn't in any condition to make phone calls."

"You could still have opened the conversation with the fact that we might want to evacuate," said Becks.

"Would you have listened?" asked Kelly.

Becks looked away.

Kelly sighed. "I thought not. Look: I had no way of knowing things would get that bad, that fast. The world doesn't work like that in the lab. Things go slower there." She took a shaky breath, calming herself. "Our research team was down to three when we realized none of us were safe. We had to get someone out alive if we wanted to preserve our results. Dr. O'Shea wasn't willing to take the risk, and Dr. Li had a family. It had to be me. So I went to Dr. Wynne."

"And he had you cloned," I deadpanned. "Naturally. Why didn't I think of that?"

"I had to seem to die—it was the only way that I'd have a chance at getting away with our results. Dr. O'Shea was working on a nerve study that required full-body subjects. She set up the clone. It was supposed to be her DNA."

"Swap-off happened at the techie level?" asked Alaric, suddenly paying attention. He always paid attention when something started smelling like a story.

"Yes," said Kelly. "One intern handed the sample to another intern, who handed it to a lab tech when Dr. Wynne asked him to run an errand instead, and by that point, it was easy enough to get the sample from the incubator and swap in one of my own samples instead."

Ask her why the source DNA matters, prompted George.

"Right," I muttered, before saying, in a more conversational tone, "Why does the source DNA matter? I thought the CDC was exempt from the prohibition against cloning."

"Clones are illegal for moral reasons. The CDC's dispensation allows researchers to do full-body cloning for research purposes, and the moral questions are skirted by permitting only self-cloning," said Kelly. "That way the question of the clone having a soul can be politely ignored, and the religious community doesn't feel the need to shut us down."

"Because presumably there's just one soul per genetic pattern, and the original donor holds the copyright?" I asked. Kelly nodded. I snorted. "That's a fun piece of bureaucratic jump rope if I've ever seen one. So fine, they think they cloned this other lady, and they actually cloned you. What's going to keep somebody from doing the math when they crack the factory seal on her and there's nothing there?"

"Dr. O'Shea died two weeks ago. There was an error in her car's electrical system and she lost control on the freeway." Kelly looked at me, lips drawing back in a smile that looked more like a rictus. "It was very sad. Our superiors were quick to offer their regrets and let us know that if we wanted to shut down the program, they'd support our moving on to other research projects. An immediate destruction notice was issued on her clone, since the original was deceased. It was officially destroyed four days before my 'death.'" She hesitated before adding, much more softly, "Dr. Li was killed in a lab accident the day after that."

"How come no one noticed they were short a clone?" asked Becks.

Kelly shrugged, shaking off her brief malaise. "Clones are considered lab waste. Anyone can dispose of them."

"So you disposed of the clone that didn't exist."

"Exactly."

"What did I miss?" asked Maggie, coming in with a basket full of tomatoes over one arm. "Hey, Shaun, you're up. Can I get you anything? Toast? Omelet?"

"An omelet would be great, and you got here just in time to hear the Doc explain how they broke her clone out of storage and slaughtered it like a chicken so she'd be free to come and make herself our problem." I took another drink of coffee and stopped, grimacing. "Also, you got any Coke?"

Alaric and Becks exchanged a look. Maggie simply nodded, saying, "I'll get you one in a minute," as she continued across the kitchen to begin fussing with her harvest. "Keep talking, everybody. I'm sure I'll catch right up."

"Great." I looked back to Kelly. "Carry on, Doc. We're burning daylight here, and you've just made that a rare commodity around these parts."

"My clone wasn't slaughtered like a chicken," she protested. "Dr. Wynne knows some people. Professional people. He hired them to break in and shoot the clone after we'd decanted it. They guaranteed a kill on the first shot. It didn't have time to suffer."

"And then you ran for us."

"And then I ran for you." Kelly glanced away. Her gaze fell on the open door and she grimaced, looking down at her lap instead. "Your . . . There were a lot of records detailing the progression of

Georgia Mason's retinal Kellis-Amberlee. The particular nature of your mutual upbringing provided an invaluable source of data."

"Meaning what, exactly?" asked Maggie, putting a skillet on the stove.

"She means there were cameras on us all the time when we were kids, and we got a lot of med tests so we could follow the 'rents into proscribed areas." I watched Kelly. Kelly kept watching her lap. "It made George a great case study, without any of those pesky release forms getting in the way."

"Mm-hmm," said Kelly, looking up. "That also makes you a great case study."

"Me?"

You, confirmed George, quietly. *Prolonged exposure to someone with a reservoir condition is odd enough, but for you to be my—*

"—makes your immunological reactions uniquely fascinating," said Kelly, her words overlaying Georgia's until she drowned out the voice in my head. I managed not to jump. My hand still shook hard enough to slosh the remainder of my coffee dangerously close to the edge. I put the cup down on the table. Kelly didn't seem to notice. "We would have been asking you to come in for some tests later this year if our study had been allowed to develop normally. Just to see if there were any deep abnormalities that might explain why she developed retinal Kellis-Amberlee and you didn't. Of course, with Georgia dead, there's always the possibility whoever's killing the people with reservoir conditions could come after you, instead. We don't know what the motive is there."

"So combine Shaun's possibly fucked-up immune system with all the footage we've got, and our known connections to the research team, and we're a target, is that it?" asked Becks. "Note for the future? This is the sort of shit you should maybe lead off with. 'Hi, nice to see you, just faked my own death, and PS, the people who want me dead are probably after you, too.'"

"Yes," said Maggie pleasantly, as she started cracking eggs into the pan. "It might've saved Dave's life."

"That's not fair," interjected Kelly.

Maggie ignored her. "Two eggs or three, Shaun?"

"Three, please. I doubt we're going to be stopping for a big lunch."

"Good. Will you need to bury her body in the forest behind my house tonight, or will you be keeping her around a little longer for informational purposes?" This question was asked just as pleasantly as the last. Maggie's tone didn't hold anything to indicate that killing Kelly was of any more or less importance than my omelet.

Maggie can be like that sometimes. She's grown beyond her upbringing, for the most part, but sometimes she's still a spoiled little rich girl whose response to things she doesn't like begins and ends with getting rid of them.

It's better not to argue with her when she gets that way. "Informational purposes, but I promise to let you know when that changes," I said. Kelly paled. I decided that the polite thing would be to ignore it. "Any news out of Oakland?"

"The announcement of Dave's death went up about an hour ago," said Alaric, quietly.

"Okay." I looked at my coffee, and sighed. "What do our site stats look like?"

"Up five percent globally, Dave's reports are up thirty-five percent, and we have three syndication requests for his Alaska material from last year." Alaric sounded a lot more confident in this answer. That wasn't surprising. Next to Mahir, there's nobody who tracks our standings as carefully as Alaric does.

"Did Maggie fill you in on the cover story?" Everyone nodded. "Good. Has anyone posted?" Everyone shook their heads. "Not so good. I need you all online. We were camping in Santa Cruz, our apartment got blown up, we're shaken, we're going to stay in the field for a few days while we recover. Maggie, I want you to make it clear that you're here alone. Tack on a poem I don't understand, with lots of creepy-ass death imagery—the usual—and then if you can double security, that would probably be a bonus. Nobody say anything about the Doc. She's not here."

"I'll get right on that," Maggie said, walking over and slapping a can of Coke into my hand before putting the plate with my omelet next to my discarded coffee cup.

"Good. Becks—"

"Come up with some believable outdoor footage." She stood, picking up her plate. "I'll set up out in the van."

"Good. Alaric—"

"Ground-level analysis of the Oakland tragedy, short memorial piece on Dave." He rose as he spoke, expression already far away. "I should be able to cobble something together fast enough to let me hit the forums and do some damage control after."

"That's excellent. Now what are we going to do about the Doc?"

"I thought you'd ask that," said Alaric, looking briefly smug. He likes being efficient. "I checked Buffy's stock of precoded IDs. Kelly looks enough like Buffy did that she can use most of them."

"Any of them come with medical credentials?"

"No strict medical, but three scientific. I have an ichthyologist—a fish scientist," Alaric added, seeing my look of blank incomprehension. "Also a theoretical physicist and a psychologist."

"I minored in psychology," said Kelly, sounding relieved to have something to contribute to the discussion. "I've never practiced, but I can fake it if I have to."

"Great. Alaric, get the ID up and running, make sure it passes any surface checks people are likely to run, and go from there. You're still a doc, Doc. We're going to hire you to replace Dave as soon as we come back to civilization." Kelly looked faintly alarmed. I grinned. "Don't worry. Mahir will ghostwrite your articles, and we'll just publish them under—what byline are we publishing these under, Alaric?"

"Barbara Tinney."

"Great. We'll publish them under the Barbara Tinney byline. It reinforces the impression that you're legit—and we can just call you 'Doc' in public."

"You're crazy," pronounced Becks.

"And you're carrying eight guns," I replied. "Now that we've covered what everybody knows, can we move on? When I post, I'll say a few words about Dave and how honored we all are to have worked with him, bullshit, bullshit, blah, blah, blah." I waved my free hand vaguely before cracking open the Coke and taking a deep drink. The acidic sweetness hit the back of my throat like a slap. I choked a little, getting my breath back, and finished: "I'll hit the staff boards. Give everybody the edited version of the situation. Be done with your reports and ready to roll by ten."

"Where are we going?" asked Kelly, looking like she couldn't tell whether she should be relieved to be getting away from Maggie or worried about what was coming next.

"And why are we going *now*?" asked Alaric.

I couldn't blame him for the question. He wasn't there when we lost Buffy, or when we lost George. I took a deep breath, held it long enough to be sure I'd stay calm while I answered him, and said, "If we sit here until we feel ready to move, we're never going to move again. We're going to get comfortable, and we're going to stay here until we die. We don't want to run off half-cocked, either, but there's a line between the two, and if we don't find it, we're fucked. As for where we're going . . . " I turned a predatory smile on Kelly. "That's what the Doc here is going to tell me."

"Me?" she asked, sounding surprised.

"You. Come on. We're using the living room terminal, and you're going to explain what I'm not getting out of all those lovely notes you brought for us." Picking up my omelet, I added, "You have your assignments, everybody. Two hours. Be ready."

Kelly followed me to the living room and sat next to me at the desk. "Perk up. It's not like you went out of the frying pan and into the fire. It's more like out of the frying pan and into the industrial-strength toaster."

"I don't understand." She shook her head, looking perplexed. "This is our chance to go to ground. Why aren't we doing it?"

"And where would we go? Canada? We're not going to get any answers there. I trust Maggie's system to keep us off the grid, and whoever arranged to have Oakland deleted is going to have trouble sweeping it under the rug if they pull it a second time. I know my job, okay?" I tapped the side of my head, smile fading. "I've got a few brain cells still working up here."

"I didn't mean—"

"Don't start. My mood stays better if you don't start." I turned to the keyboard. The terminal turned itself on as soon as its sensors "saw" me looking at it, and I typed my password to unlock the home network.

"Noted," she said. She didn't sound like she approved, but at the moment, that was at the bottom of my priority list.

"Good." All Maggie's computer equipment was top of the line. Having parents with money and Buffy Meissonier as your original technical consultant will do that. "I spent a few hours after the rest of you went to bed going through those files you brought us last night. Didn't understand half of what I was reading, but George managed to explain some of it for me."

Kelly's expression went very still, like she was fighting an inner battle to keep herself from pointing out that George couldn't explain anything, because, guess what, George was dead. I've seen that look a lot since the funeral. As long as she could keep herself from saying anything, I could keep myself from getting angry that she'd want to.

"Really," she said finally, in a neutral tone that could have meant just about anything.

Good enough for me. "Really," I confirmed. "What I'm curious about is the list of labs. How many of those are going to be safe for us to visit? Where can we go to get the fieldwork side of the equation?" Kelly's files gave us numbers, but they didn't give us the rest of the picture. If we were going to understand, we needed to talk to someone who could confirm or contest the data—and if the CDC had been steered away from researching the reservoir conditions for as long as Kelly said, the labs on our list might have pieces of the puzzle we didn't even know existed yet.

"All the labs on list A are ones with head researchers a member of the team worked with directly at some point, either before or after they went into the private sector," she said, sounding much more relaxed now that she was dealing with verified facts instead of crazy reporters. "List B contains the labs where someone had personal experience with the supporting researchers, but not the head of the lab, and list C is made up of the labs where we had only secondhand information on the people working there. Reputations, credentials, whether or not they bothered to check their sources . . . "

"What about list D?" My hands were moving as we spoke, spewing out line after line of borderline coherent claptrap. It was the day after a death. We'd be expected to update—nothing was going to get us out of that, not even actually dying; George's blog may have changed names when she died, but her backlog of files meant she missed less than a week. That didn't mean we were expected to be profound.

"Ah." Kelly's tone was disapproving enough that I actually glanced toward her. Her lips were pursed into a tight moue of distaste. "That would be the labs where the researchers have been confirmed as following less than ethical paths in their research."

"What, vivisection? Human test subjects?" I pressed Post on my first entry of the day, switched from my own feed to the administrative, and started typing again as I asked, "Full-body cloning?"

"It's different when the CDC does it," she said sharply. "We have a dispensation."

"So?" I shrugged, continuing to type. "That doesn't make it right. How many of the labs on list D would have been on list A if you weren't being judgmental?"

Kelly sighed. "Two, at most."

"Okay. Either of them anywhere near here?"

There was a horrified pause as she realized what I was asking. "Shaun, you don't understand! These people were blacklisted from reputable scientific circles for a lot of reasons, and not all of them were as petty as you seem to think! These are not the secret heroes of some underground resistance against the evil CDC—they're bioterrorists and crazy people, and they're *dangerous*. We could get seriously hurt if we go to them. We could get *killed*."

"And we could get killed if we stay here. I'm not seeing a difference in results." I picked up George's Coke and took another swig. "Your objections are noted. Can any of these people be trusted? At all? Or do I just pick one at random and hope they aren't on the Frankenstein end of the 'mad doctor' scale?"

Kelly swallowed, throat working as she struggled against some clear inner impulse not to answer. Finally she said, "Dr. Abbey. I read some of the work she did on reservoir conditions before she went off the grid. I think she'd be able to help us."

"Fine. Where is she?"

She sighed. "Portland, Oregon."

"That's a five- or six-hour drive if we take the direct route," I said, sipping again from the can. "Annoying, but manageable. What was the big crime that got them blacklisted?"

"Unethical experiments involving the manipulation of the viral structure of Kellis-Amberlee. None involving human subjects, thank

God, or she and her staff would be in federal prison for the rest of their lives."

"I'm surprised they aren't in federal prison anyway. How much blackmail material did she have?"

"Enough." Kelly shook her head. "I don't know much—it was all before my time—but she worked for Health Canada. Joint research team, theirs and ours. Some bad things happened, and she quit. Ever since then, she's been pretty careful about who she lets get anywhere near her or her research."

"Better watch out, Doc. That sounded almost like respect."

"I like people who are serious about their work." She shrugged. "Dr. Abbey was devoted to figuring out Kellis-Amberlee."

"Somebody has to be." I swung back around to the keyboard. "Better go see if Maggie's got something you can wear, Doc. We're going on another road trip."

We made it out of Oakland alive. I'm still not sure how we did it, except that my team is made up of some of the best people I've ever known, and I don't deserve them. I keep making it out of places alive. I think the universe is fucking with me.

I did something during the evacuation that you shouldn't ever do. I went back for George's black box. I'd do it again, too. Because there's already not enough of her left in this world, and I'm running out of things to hold onto.

Fuck, I miss her.

—From *Adaptive Immunities*, the blog of Shaun Mason,
April 12, 2041. Unpublished.

———

Santa Cruz is gorgeous this time of year. I realize it's a zombie-infested wasteland, but hell, at least the rents are good, right? Besides, there's a reason this used to be one of the state's most popular vacation destinations, and I doubt it had very much to do with their boardwalk, no matter what the old tourism brochures try to tell you.

We're still working on getting Alaric ready for his field trials. Next up, Becks is going to take him down to the beach and see if they can find a zombie seal to poke at. Never a dull moment around here. Oh, well. It's better than a desk job.

—From *Adaptive Immunities*, the blog of Shaun Mason,
April 12, 2041

Eight

Maggie didn't look *happy* about being sent off to outfit the Doc, but she did it; that was really all I could ask of her. I stayed in the living room, getting a few posts up on the site and making it clear that we'd been nowhere near Oakland when the bombs came down. While I was at it, I surfed over to the medical blogs to see what they had to say about the "death" of Dr. Kelly Connolly. With the way they were going on about her—lost scion of one of the CDC's proudest heritage families, rising young star of the virology world—you'd think she'd been on the verge of curing Kellis-Amberlee, not just slaving in the CDC salt mines with the rest of the peons.

That's the power of good press, said George dryly.

I chuckled, and got back to work.

Alaric came into the room with a half-eaten piece of toast in one hand as I was firing off an e-mail to authorize the continuing sale of Dave's merchandise line. "Did you see the crime scene photos on the gossip sites?" he asked. I nodded. He continued: "This is, like, *Invasion of the Body Snatchers* levels of scary. I always knew cloning technology was better than we saw here on the fringes, but the CDC employs the best doctors in the world, and even they couldn't tell it was a clone."

"Could be worse."

"How?"

"I have no idea. But it can always be worse." I glanced toward the kitchen door. "Where's Becks?"

"She's helping Maggie with Dr. Connolly." He took a bite of toast, sitting down at the monitor next to mine. "I don't think she wanted to leave them alone together."

"I always knew she was smart."

Alaric grunted as he logged on and started working the message boards. I leaned over to "supervise," which really meant "look over his shoulder, drinking a Coke and pretending to pay attention." He ignored me. I took his tendency to shut me out while he worked personally at first, until George assured me that he'd always done the same thing to her. He was just one of those people who really liked to focus on his work.

I love how you ignore the inherent impossibility of me telling you something you didn't already know, George said.

"Don't start with me," I said, and took another drink of Coke. That's normally enough to shut her up for a little while. When that doesn't work, I zone out in front of the news feeds. Comforting for her, educational for me. Everybody wins.

It's true.

"It's a shitty thing to say and you know it."

Alaric ignored my conversation with the air. He learned the hard way that sometimes it was best to turn a blind eye. During our first few months in the office, he asked who I was talking to every time I forgot and answered George aloud, and he pointed out that she was dead more than once. He stopped after I finally lost my temper and introduced my fist to his face, resulting in skinned knuckles on my part and a broken nose on his. He still flinches if I move too fast. Guess I can't blame him. If my boss were a potentially crazy man with a mean right hook, I'd probably be a little jumpy, too.

The title of one of the threads caught my eye. I leaned forward, tapping Alaric's screen. "There. Can you expand that thread?"

"Sure." He clicked the header line: *CDC Safety Precautions Insufficient?* "I don't see what it has to do with——"

"Just scroll."

"Right," he said, and started scrolling.

The thread started as a discussion of the break-in at the Memphis CDC and devolved into a discussion of CDC security precautions over the course of half a dozen posts. As I'd hoped, the posters quickly started naming names, citing every CDC doctor, intern, affiliate, and publicity person to have died during the last eighteen months. "Alaric, can you grab the names of the deceased and start calling up obituaries and circumstance-of-death reports? If anyone looks at you funny, you can say you're basing a report off this thread."

"Sure," he said, warming to the idea as he saw where I was going with it. "I can do you one better. I still have a few of Buffy's old worms live and functional. I'll set one of them digging for connections between the deceased employees, Kelly Connolly, Joseph Wynne, and any other unusual or unexplained deaths in their circle of friends."

"Just don't get caught or traced and you can do whatever you want."

"Awesome." Alaric bent forward, starting to type. He had the same focus I've seen from George, Rick, and every other Newsie I've ever met. I could probably have danced naked on his desk without getting him to do more than grunt and shove me out of the way of his screen. Content that I'd done something useful, I got up and walked to the kitchen. A fresh Coke would keep me from thinking too hard about the tools he was using to do the job.

There are people who say that Kellis-Amberlee and its undead side effects are going to bring about the end of the human race. I tend to disagree with this perspective. I'm pretty sure that if the zombies were going to destroy humanity, they would've done it back in 2014, when they first showed up. I think that if anything destroys the human race at this point, it's going to be the human race itself.

With my posts done, Alaric working, and Becks and Maggie sequestered with Kelly, I didn't know what to do with myself. I settled for sitting at the kitchen table with my fresh can of Coke, waiting for something to happen. My patience was rewarded about fifteen minutes later, when something happened.

Footsteps descended the stairs and Becks appeared in the kitchen doorway, hands raised in a warding gesture. Not the best sign. "Okay, Shaun, before you freak out, this was the best way to do it."

I raised an eyebrow. "That's a really shitty elevator pitch, and I would never buy your project based on that. Just so you know."

"I'm just saying, don't freak out." She finished stepping into the kitchen, looking back over her shoulder. "Come on, Kelly."

"I feel like an idiot," said Kelly. She moved into view, Maggie half a step behind her.

I stared.

Buffy left a lot of her shit to me and George when she died. Her parents gave us even more. We were her best friends, and they couldn't think of anything else to do with her collection of gaudy jewelry and hippie skirts. The fact that I'm not a cross-dresser and George wouldn't have been caught dead in that sort of thing didn't matter: They were grieving parents, we were Buffy's friends, and we got it all. Only we didn't have much room in the apartment, and the idea of getting rid of her things left me feeling sick. So we stored them at Maggie's.

Becks was looking at me with rare anxiety, clearly waiting for me to say something. I swallowed the lump that was blocking my throat and said the first thing that came to mind:

"Wow. That's ... different."

Kelly was wearing a multicolored broomstick skirt, a white

peasant blouse, and a patchwork vest with little mirrors sewn all over it. They twinkled when she moved, not quite as gaudily as the dozen or so bangle bracelets crusted with LED "jewels." There were matching "jewels" on the straps of her sandals, which looked entirely impractical. I knew better. Buffy was an idealist and sort of an idiot, but she knew the importance of being prepared, and she didn't own a single pair of shoes she couldn't run in.

God, I miss her, said George, almost too quietly for me to hear.

"Me too," I murmured, just as softly.

Georgette "Buffy" Meissonier was the original head of the Fictional News Division. She designed almost all of the After the End Times network and computer systems. She was one of the only people I ever met who could make George smile on a reliable basis. She was sweet, and she was funny, and she was smart as hell, and she was an enormous geek, and every time her name comes up, I have to remind myself that she didn't do any of the things she did on purpose. Sure, she let Tate's men into our system, and sure, a lot of people got killed because of that, but she had the best intentions.

Buffy died because of what she did. On the days when I'm really getting my crazy on, that seems like sufficient payment. Of course, those are the days when I can convince myself that George isn't dead, just, I don't know, mysteriously intangible and pissed off about it. Most of the time, well . . .

I'm just a little bit bitter.

Either Maggie or Becks—I was betting on Maggie—had hacked off most of Kelly's hair, leaving her with a spiky mess that stuck up in all directions. I'd never been so glad a woman was blonde in my life, because that was exactly the way George always wore her hair— too short for the zombies to grab, long enough to be controllable with a minimum of effort—and if Kelly had been a brunette, I think I would have screamed.

"Well?" asked Maggie.

"Right." I swallowed several more possible responses, starting with "dead friend's clothes, dead sister's haircut, good job" and going downhill from there. "She definitely looks, uh, really different." That seemed insufficient, so I added, "Good job."

Becks grinned, looking unaccountably pleased.

Kelly, meanwhile, reached up to touch her hair with one hand, saying, "I haven't kept my hair this short since I was a little kid. I don't even know what to do with it."

"Better cropped than arrested for hoaxing the CDC, Doc," I said.

Kelly sighed. "I wish I could argue with that."

"I wish a lot of things," I said, and stood. "Come on, gang. Let's get moving."

Herding everyone out of the house was more difficult than it should have been, since Kelly was exhausted and wanted to stay behind, leading to loud protests on Maggie's part. She said she didn't trust people alone with her dogs. What Kelly was supposed to do to a pack of epileptic bulldogs wasn't entirely clear to me, but Maggie was firm: No one was staying home unsupervised—and, apparently, the enormous army of security ninjas lurking in the bushes didn't count as supervision. To complicate matters further, Maggie refused to stay behind.

"I just lost Dave," she said. "I'm not letting you drive off and leave me here. If I'm going to lose everyone, I'm going to go with you."

I couldn't really bring myself to argue with that.

After a lot of shouting, some plea bargaining, and an outright threat to leave Alaric sitting by the side of the road, we wound up with Becks driving the van, Alaric manning the forums from the passenger seat, and Kelly riding in the back. I drove the bike, Maggie riding pillion. She insisted, probably because she didn't trust herself in an enclosed space with Kelly. Dave's death wasn't the Doc's fault. Maggie would realize that eventually. I hoped.

I'd never driven any real distance with a passenger—not unless you counted George, who didn't actually change the way the bike was balanced, or make it necessary for me to compensate for additional weight. Oh, I'd *been* a passenger on the bike often enough, back when George was doing the driving, but it wasn't the same thing by a long shot. It didn't help that Maggie wasn't used to riding a motorcycle and didn't know to shift her weight to help me keep us balanced. If we'd encountered any real problems, we would have been screwed.

There aren't many real problems along I-5. The combination of tight security, large stretches with little to no human habitation, and most motorists being unwilling to drive more than a few miles has done a lot to make distance travel safer for those of us crazy enough to attempt it.

Buffy died during a long-distance road trip, when a sniper shot out the wheels of the truck she was riding in. But beyond little things like that, it's perfectly safe.

Safe. Now there's a laugh.

Nearly six hours and fifteen security checkpoints later, we were approaching Eugene. I-5 is the fastest route to damn near any major city on the West Coast, but it has its downsides, like the constant barricades. We had to stop every time we drove into or out of a city, or even too close to one, by whatever the local definition of "too close" happened to be. It was always the same song and dance: Where are you going? Why? Can we see your licenses? Can we see your credentials? Would you like to submit to a retinal scan? Do you really think you have a choice?

The CDC had no reason to be tracking our movement—not yet, anyway. Our papers were in order, and every checkpoint wound up waving us through, but the stops still made me nervous. I was being paranoid. After the past twenty-four hours, I figured it was justified.

The orange light in the corner of my visor started blinking, signaling an incoming call. "Answer," I said.

"Hey, boss." There was a note of tension under-scoring Alaric's
normally laid-back tone. "We're an hour and a half out of Portland,
according to the GPS. You going to give us the actual address soon,
or are we going to play guessing games with the surface streets?"

"We're not going to Portland," I said. Becks started swearing in
the background. I almost laughed. "Tell Becks to keep her panties on.
We're going to a town *near* Portland. It's called Forest Grove. We're
heading for an old business park that got shut down during the
Rising and never officially reopened. The address is in the GPS. I
uploaded it under the header 'Shaun's secret porn store.'"

Charming, commented George.

"Ew," said Alaric. "Okay, accessing coordinates now. Is there anything else we need to know?"

"You know what I do, and you can pump the Doc for information
if you need to." I swerved to avoid a pothole, feeling Maggie's arms
tighten around my waist. She was staying amazingly calm for a
woman who almost never left her house. I was starting to wonder
exactly what was in that "herbal tea" she drank right before we left.
"We're heading for an illegal biotech lab to talk to somebody the
CDC is too afraid of to fuck with. What could possibly go wrong?"

There was a long silence before Alaric said, "I'm hanging up on
you now."

"That's probably for the best."

"You're fucked in the head."

"That's probably true. See you in Forest Grove." The amber light
flicked off. I allowed myself a grim chuckle and hit the gas. Our little
road trip of the damned was well under way.

Do you have a plan? asked George.

"You know better," I replied. I wasn't worried about Maggie hearing me talk to myself; the roar of the wind would keep my voice from

reaching her. Weird as it might seem, George and I actually had a measure of privacy, despite having another human being with her arms wrapped around my waist. If Maggie had been driving, I might have actually been able to fool myself into thinking everything was the way it was supposed to be, even if the illusion would only last until the bike stopped.

George laughed. I smiled, relaxing, and kept on driving. Next stop: Forest Grove.

The Caspell Business Park was located at the edge of town, in what was probably considered an area ripe for expansion before the dead decided to get up and walk around. It was built on a model popular before the Rising, all open spaces and broad pathways between the buildings. I'd be willing to bet that more than half those buildings had automatic doors at one point, totally unsecured against the shambling infected. It was no wonder the local authorities hadn't bothered trying to reclaim the place; if there was anything remarkable about it, it was that it hadn't been burned to the ground.

According to the Doc's instructions, the place we were looking for was in the old IT complex, where the buildings had been constructed according to much more sensible schematics: airtight, watertight, no windows, no real danger of contamination if you remembered to lock the damn doors. Georgia and I went to preschool in a pre-Rising IT complex, and we were just as secure as we could possibly be. Locating the lab in that sort of structure made a lot of sense, especially with the rest of the business park providing excellent, if hazardous, cover. Not even the bravest Irwin was going to stumble on the place by mistake, and the ones who were dumb enough to think it was a good idea would all be eaten before they arrived.

The parking garage had developed a worrying leftward tilt. I eyed it, shook my head, and kept driving. The last thing we needed was to get a parking garage dropped on our heads, or worse, dropped on our vehicles while we were inside the building. On the other hand, we'd be dead if the garage fell on us, and we wouldn't have to worry about this shit anymore.

You're in a fabulous state of mind today, said George.

"Enjoy it while it lasts," I said, and continued to blaze a trail through the deserted business park. Maggie clung a little tighter every time we hit a bump, but she didn't jerk around enough to make me lose my balance. That was a good thing. The broken pavement was littered with rusted metal, broken glass, and other debris; if we went sprawling, we'd be lucky to get away with just a tetanus shot.

The loading dock behind the IT complex was clear and showed signs of semi-recent upkeep. That was promising. I pulled up and killed the engine, waiting for Maggie to dismount before deploying the kickstand and sliding to the relatively unbroken pavement. My thighs ached from too many hours on the road, but my head was clearer than it had been in weeks. Knowing that I'm actually *doing* something has that effect on me.

The van pulled up a few yards away. The side door was open before the wheels had fully stopped turning, and Alaric jumped down, fumbling his field pack on as he trotted toward us. I pulled off my helmet and smirked at him. "Did you have a nice drive?"

"I hate you," he said flatly.

"That's nice," said Maggie. Alaric shot her a look, and she smiled, removing her helmet. Her pupils were slightly enlarged—not in the exaggerated manner that would indicate a live infection, but in a softer, more relaxed manner that I recognized from dealing with high-strung reporters at press conferences. Her herbal tea definitely contained a few extra ingredients.

I considered pulling her aside for a talk about taking psychoactive substances before going into the field and decided to let it pass. It wasn't like she was a combatant. She and Kelly were so much dead weight if we got attacked. She might as well be pre-anesthetized dead weight, in case things went poorly. As it was, she was only legal to be with us because the town zoning regulations made this place technically safe. Very technically.

Becks was the next out of the van, her own field pack already in place. Her scowl looked like it had been permanently affixed to her face. "You owe me," she said, coming to a stop next to Alaric.

"Me or Maggie?"

"*Yes*. No. I don't know. The only way to keep her quiet was to keep the radio turned to the medical news channel. If I'd been forced to spend another minute listening to the exciting new developments in the world of pharmaceuticals, I would have taken her head and—"

Kelly's hesitant emergence saved us from the details of what Becks would have done to her. She gave the parking lot a horrified look before hurrying toward us, demanding, "What are we doing *here?*"

"This is the address your file said we should be at, Doc."

"There must be some mistake."

"Nope. Underground lab, underground facilities." I tucked my helmet under my arm, looking at the low-slung buildings spread out around us. "Can anybody see the numbers on these things? We're looking for eleven."

"You can't mean we're actually going to go *inside*," said Kelly.

"No, Doc, we just drove a couple hundred miles to pose on the sidewalk." Becks shook her head before turning to stalk off toward the buildings, scanning for more signs of habitation.

Kelly sighed. "This day just gets better and better."

"Don't worry. I'm sure that soon, we'll be looking back on this moment as one of the good times." I followed Maggie, Alaric close behind me. Kelly stayed where she was for a few moments, staring after us. I could see her out of the corner of my eye. It was all I could do to not start laughing—which would have been entirely inappropriate, true, but it would have felt so damn good.

Be careful, George cautioned. *Push her too far and she'll freak out. We need her to stay calm, stay cooperative, and keep talking.*

"I thought she'd already told us everything," I muttered, as Kelly started running to catch up. Alaric cast a glance in my direction, but didn't say anything.

You're not that dumb.

There was nothing I could say to that. I kept walking, assessing the buildings surrounding us as I moved. I wasn't exactly expecting a big sign that said ILLEGAL VIROLOGY LAB HERE, but it would have been nice. The buildings in the IT complex seemed to be essentially identical, all square, boxy, and in reasonably good repair, as long as you weren't judging by the paint jobs. The building closest to us even had its original set of cell tower repeaters bolted to the roof, their narrow antennae making a familiar lightning-jag outline against the afternoon sky.

I stopped in my tracks. Looking bemused, Alaric did the same. "What year did we go to block-by-block private cell towers? Anybody know?"

"Uh . . . two thousand twenty," said Alaric, after a long pause to do the math inside his head. "I remember when they put ours in."

"Uh-huh. This is a pre-Rising complex. So who installed that?" I jerked a thumb toward the antennae.

Alaric's eyes went wide. "Oh."

"Yeah, oh. Over here, guys." I waved for the others to join us and started up the cracked pathway leading to the building door. Locked. No real surprise, that; if I were running an illegal biotech lab, I wouldn't exactly want scavengers or thrill-seekers dropping in on me unannounced. I rapped my knuckles against the metal of the door itself, hearing the echoes they sent ringing dully into the space beyond.

No one answered. That really wasn't a surprise, either. "Maybe we should shoot the lock out," suggested Becks.

I gave her a dubious look. "Did you just suggest discharging a firearm into a door that may be attached to a lab? Like, 'explosive chemicals and weird machinery and God knows what else' lab?"

Becks shrugged. "At least we'd be doing something."

"We *are* doing something. We're getting inside." I knocked again. After a several-second pause, I cleared my throat, and shouted, "This is Shaun Mason, from After the End Times. We're here to speak to Dr. Abbey. Is she available? It's about the reservoir conditions."

The echoes of my knock were still ringing when the door swung open, revealing a short, cheerfully curvy woman with spiky brown hair streaked with bleach-white lines that looked more accidental than anything else. She was wearing an electric orange T-shirt that read DO NOT TAUNT THE OCTOPUS, jeans, and a lab coat, and was pointing a hunting rifle at the middle of my chest.

"Got any ID?" she asked. Her voice was light, even charming, with an accent I couldn't quite identify. She followed the question with a pleasant smile that didn't warm her eyes. This was a woman who wouldn't hesitate to pull the trigger if she thought we were giving her reason.

Not the friendliest greeting ever, and yet, not the least friendly, either, said George. Kelly gasped, either in shock or indignation. I wasn't sure which, and I really didn't care; it gave me something to respond to that wouldn't convince the woman with the large gun that I was insane right off the bat. That could come later, when she no longer had a weapon aimed at us.

"Hush," I said, making sure to slant my eyes toward Kelly, to at least give the impression that I was talking to her. Looking back to the woman in the doorway, I asked, "May I reach into my jacket for my press pass? I promise to do it slowly."

"Fine by me," she said, still smiling. "Joe! Come over here, boy." The largest dog I'd ever seen came ambling up behind her, its flapping jowls oozing strings of gooey white saliva. Its head looked like it was bigger than my chest. That may have been shock speaking, but there was no way I was going to volunteer to do the measurements. It didn't help that the damn thing was solid charcoal black, making it look unnervingly like the classic hellhound.

Kelly drew her breath in again. This time, I didn't blame her. Even Becks gasped, and I heard Maggie mutter something that sounded suspiciously like "Holy shit."

"Joe, guard," said the woman with the rifle. The massive canine obediently padded out onto the walkway, standing between her and the rest of us. It wasn't growling, glaring, or doing anything else actively hostile; it was simply standing there, being enormous. That was more than enough.

Reaching slowly into my jacket, I asked the most sensible question I could come up with under the circumstances: "Lady, what the *fuck* is that?"

That's right. Antagonize the woman who accessorizes with Cujo. I was tired of being the only dead one in this relationship.

I ignored her, choosing instead to focus on the woman who had the capacity to kill me. Call me single-minded. I tend to pay more attention to the immediate threats to life and limb, and leave the sarcastic dead people for later.

"That's Joe," said the woman, keeping the rifle aimed solidly at my chest. "He's shown me his ID. He's in no danger of getting himself shot."

"He's an English Mastiff," breathed Maggie, almost reverently. She started to step forward, one hand outstretched in a gesture I'd seen her use on her video blog whenever she was adding a new rescue to her miniature pack. She froze midgesture, eyes darting toward the woman with the rifle. "Is he friendly?"

"He will be, once I've seen your ID." Still, shotgun lady's smile took on a slightly more honest edge. "Joe's a good boy. He only eats the people I tell him to eat."

"How encouraging," I muttered, and held out my journalist's license. "Here. All my credentials are on file. Just run the code."

"And your people?" She jerked her chin toward the others, not bothering to take the license from my hand.

"Rebecca Atherton, head of the Irwins. Magdalene Garcia, head of the Fictionals. Alaric Kwong, he's with the Newsie division; the actual division head lives in London and isn't with us today. And this is—" For a sickening moment, I couldn't remember Kelly's alias.

Barbara Tinney, prompted Georgia.

"—Barbara Tinney," I echoed. "She's a social scientist on loan to the site for a few months. Getting some field experience."

From the look on the woman's face, she wasn't buying it. "Uh-huh. What are you folks doing here? Take a wrong turn on the way to a real story?"

I had two choices. I could try to come up with a plausible lie or I could tell her the truth. Once, I would have gone straight for the lie, the more interesting the better. I'm not really comfortable with that sort of thing anymore. "We came to see Dr. Abbey," I said, still holding out my license. "I have some files from the CDC that I need to have explained to me, and I thought she might be the person who could do it." Her brows lifted slightly; she was interested. I decided to press my luck. "I don't know if you follow the news, but my sister, Georgia Mason—"

"Retinal Kellis-Amberlee, wasn't it? I remember her. That was a real tragedy. I was very sorry to hear about it." The rifle wavered slightly. "I need a better reason for you to be here, and not at a 'real lab' somewhere."

Tell her. George's mental voice held a venom I rarely heard from her, even when she was alive. Then again, I couldn't blame her. The CDC's secret keeping might be the reason she was just a voice in my head.

In for a penny, in for a pound. "Barbara Tinney is a cover ID for

Dr. Kelly Connolly of the CDC. The researcher who was killed in a break-in recently—that was a full-body clone. The real Dr. Connolly wasn't killed, and this is her." This time, Kelly's horrified expression was more than a bit betrayed. I did my best to ignore it. "She's how we got the files, and those same files identified this lab as being disreputable enough that no one would suspect we'd go to you, while still having staff who know how to find their asses with both hands. It didn't mention the giant dog, or we might have gone somewhere else. Now, are you Dr. Abbey, or can you tell us where to find her? I'm getting a little uncomfortable standing out here in the middle of nowhere."

"Well, why didn't you just say so?" The spiky-haired woman lowered her gun, suddenly smiling with genuine sincerity. "I'm Dr. Abbey—you can call me Shannon—and it's a pleasure to have guests. Especially guests with such interesting connections." Her smile dimmed as her gaze fell on Kelly, who was too busy staring at me to notice. "How about you all come inside, and we'll sort this out."

Alaric managed to find his voice, swallowing hard before he asked, "Will—will the dog be coming?"

"Of course he will. Joe's my lab manager, aren't you, Joe?" The enormous canine responded with a bark loud enough to make my ears hurt, tail beating against the ground. Maggie looked like she was physically restraining herself from running over and throwing her arms around his neck. Catching the look, Dr. Abbey laughed. "He doesn't bite. Joe, guest passes for all these folks. Got it?" The dog stood, tail still wagging.

"Does that mean I can pet him?" asked Maggie eagerly.

"Can you pet the moving legal violation after we get inside?" I asked.

"Come on." Dr. Abbey stepped aside, waving a hand at the open door. "Ladies first."

"That means us, princess." Becks looped her arm through Kelly's, tugging the reluctant doctor along with her as she went striding through the door to the lab. Maggie followed, still casting longing looks at the dog. Alaric gave me an uneasy glance and went after her, presumably unwilling to leave her alone in the company of a bona-fide mad scientist.

Dr. Abbey crooked an eyebrow, studying me. "Will you be joining us?"

"Yeah. Thanks." I did my best to swagger as I walked toward the door, even going so far as to give her enormous pet a pat on the head as I passed him. "Good doggie."

Joe made a deep buffing sound in the back of his throat. I hoped that meant he was happy, rather than planning to bite my hand off at the shoulder. The law forbidding urban ownership of any domestic animal large enough to undergo Kellis-Amberlee amplification was named after my family. That means I never got much experience with dogs beyond Maggie's epileptic teacup bulldogs.

Dr. Abbey snorted with amusement and followed me inside. Joe padded after her, killing any lingering hope that I might have had about the big dog staying outside to, I don't know, guard the sidewalk or something.

I was so busy watching what the dog did that I walked right into Becks, bumping her forward a half step. "Hey, watch it," I began.

Shaun, hissed Georgia. *Look.*

I looked. And promptly understood why the rest of the team was standing frozen in their tracks at the end of the short entrance hall, staring into the gutted warehouselike depths of the former IT building. I'd been expecting a dingy little basement operation, something barely more technically advanced than a bunch of kids running their own pirate news site out of their parents' house. This was a functional lab, operating totally outside all sane safety precautions, but still equipped way beyond anything I might have anticipated.

All the interior walls not essential for structural support had been knocked out at some point, replaced with a maze of cubicles, portable isolation tents, and live animal cages. Racked computer servers stood side-by-side with rabbit hutches. Hydroponic beds studded the floor, growing healthy-looking crops of things I vaguely recognized from Maggie's garden. The light was an even, brilliant white, and about half the people I could see moving around the computers were wearing either sunglasses or the clear plastic bands hospitals sometimes used to protect the eyes of individuals with reservoir conditions.

Kelly was staring at the scene with her lip curled upward, looking utterly disgusted. "This is ... horrific," she breathed, turning toward me. "We have to get out of here. This is an abomination. It's a violation of so many medical and ethical regulations that I can't even start to count them, and—"

"And it's not under CDC control, which means it's not okay to break the rules, is that it?" asked Maggie. Her tone was icy.

Kelly stopped midtirade, taking a shaky breath. "You don't understand," she said, slowly. "This is ... the things they could do here, with this sort of equipment, are practically unthinkable. That's a genetic sequencer." She indicated a machine I didn't recognize. "They could build a whole new version of the virus, if they wanted to."

"Let's not antagonize the nice people, okay?" I asked. "You can be offended by their ethics later. When we aren't outnumbered." A lab this size would make body disposal distressingly easy. The last thing I wanted to do was give Dr. Abbey a reason.

The massive dog—Joe—ambled up and stopped beside me, panting amiably. Maggie promptly knelt down and offered her hand, knuckles first, like she was trying to attract the attention of one of her own, much less scary-looking, canines. Joe deigned to sniff it. A moment later, he was slobbering all over her palm, tail wagging with delight as she used her other hand to start scratching behind his ears.

"Most people are a lot less relaxed about Joe," said Dr. Abbey, rejoining the rest of us. She'd shed her rifle somewhere between the door and the lab floor, but she was still wearing the lab coat. At least some of the overhead lights must have been using George's beloved blacklight frequencies, because the fabric fluoresced slightly in the glare.

"Most people don't like risking infection when they don't have to," said Kelly.

"Well, those people have sticks shoved half a mile up their asses," said Dr. Abbey. "Besides, Joe's no threat. He's immune, aren't you, sweetheart?" The mastiff looked around at the sound of his name, tail still wagging frantically back and forth.

The rest of us, with the exception of Maggie—who was still deeply involved in her dog-worshipping duties—turned to stare at her. Surprisingly, it was Alaric who found his voice first, asking, "Are you serious? Immune? But he's got to weigh more than sixty pounds. How can he possibly be immune?"

Dr. Abbey shrugged. "He's got the canine forms of five reservoir conditions, and the initial signs of developing a sixth. He's never going to be a daddy, since the fourth one he developed was testicular Kellis-Amberlee—I had to have him neutered after that, poor guy—but he's never going to amplify fully, either. He's immune."

My thoughts raced as I tried to absorb her words. It didn't help that George was shouting in my head, demanding answers and denying the possible truth of Dr. Abbey's claims at the same time. Kelly turned to look at Dr. Abbey, her mouth moving silently as she tried to form a protest that wasn't willing to come out. Even Becks was just staring, looking as surprised as I'd ever seen her. That was saying something, because Becks doesn't *do* surprised. No one who's done field time as both a Newsie and an Irwin goes around being easy to knock off balance.

Maggie looked up from her enthusiastic worship of Joe, a narrow line forming between her eyebrows as she considered Dr. Abbey. "Five reservoir conditions in one dog?" Dr. Abbey nodded. "But how? I've never heard of anything, canine or human, developing more than one."

"Oh, that part was simple," said Dr. Abbey, and beamed. This smile was pure professional pride. "I induced them."

All of us fell silent at that, even George. Maggie's hands stilled, dropping away from the dog. The distant beeping of the computers, the occasional squeal or bark from a lab animal, and the footsteps of the other technicians provided a strange sort of background music. Joe looked between the humans and let out a resonant, echoing bark.

Dr. Abbey reached down to pat him on the head. "Well, since we've obviously got a lot to talk about, why don't you come to my office? There's cookies and tea, and I can tell you all about how I've managed to pervert the laws of nature. Come on, Joe." Waving for the rest of us to follow, she walked forward, into the bustling lab.

"Are we going with her?" asked Alaric.

"Got a better idea?"

"Nope," he said, glumly.

"All right, then. Following the crazy lady to our deaths it is." I shrugged and walked after her, trying to look nonchalant. The day was getting more interesting by the minute. I just had to hope it was the sort of interesting we'd live to talk about later.

The nature of the so-called reservoir conditions has never been fully explained, although a great many theories have been proposed, some reasonable, some not. Why does the KA virus manifest its live state in certain parts of the body? Why does that live virus then fail to spread the infection according to the laws that govern all of its other manifestations? Why is retinal KA most common in females, while cerebro-spinal is most common in males? Nobody really seems to have a clue.

We do know that reservoir conditions are becoming more common, with reported cases of retinal, cerebro-spinal, ovarian, testicular, and pituitary KA in both human and animal hosts up by more than eighteen percent over the last eleven years. There are rumors of new reservoir conditions manifesting themselves, conditions with scary names like "cardiac" and "pulmonary." Yet still, no one knows why.

Taken all together, it's enough to make one question whether we truly dodged the end of the human race . . . or merely delayed it by a decade or two.

—From *Epidemiology of the Wall*, authored by Mahir Gowda, January 11, 2041

Nine

Dr. Abbey's "office" was a euphemistically named cubicle only slightly larger than the ones around it. It didn't help that it was jammed with file boxes, outmoded computer equipment, and—best of all—clear plastic tanks full of assorted insects and arachnids. I don't have a problem with spiders. Spiders can't carry Kellis-Amberlee. Ditto giant hissing cockroaches and squiggly things with way too many legs. Becks didn't share my disregard. Every time the squiggly things moved, she sank farther back into her chair.

It's called a millipede, said George.

"It's called comedy," I muttered, and turned my attention back to Dr. Abbey.

She had shrugged out of her lab coat before pulling a bag of Oreos out of a filing cabinet and dumping them onto a paper plate. Now she was rummaging through the minifridge shoved under her desk, crouching in a way that I recognized as designed to put a minimum of stress on her knees. Joe the Mastiff was stretched out between her and us, enormous head resting between his forelegs. His pose was relaxed, but his eyes were alert, focusing on whoever had moved most recently. That meant his focus was mostly on Becks, who couldn't stop flinching.

"So there's apple juice, water, beer, and something unlabeled that's either a protein shake or algae." Dr. Abbey looked up. "Who wants what?"

"I want to know how you managed to induce a reservoir condition," volunteered Kelly, the need for knowledge apparently overwhelming her reluctance to work with unsanctioned researchers.

Dr. Abbey fixed her with a flat stare. "That's not a beverage. *I* want to know how you managed to justify violating a couple dozen international laws when you used a clone for personal benefit. Don't they train you out of that at the CDC? I thought that was their job. That, and restricting research to party-line channels while people were dying."

"I'll take an apple juice," I said.

"Nothing for me, thanks," said Alaric. He was looking at Dr. Abbey with the same sort of intent focus that Joe was turning on the rest of us, eyes slightly narrowed.

"Uh, water," said Maggie.

Becks said nothing. She was too busy watching the millipede.

"Got it." Dr. Abbey straightened, passing a bottle of water to Maggie and a bottle of apple juice to me before sitting in the chair next to her dog. "So you're finally here about the reservoir conditions. Damn. I've had a bet going with Dr. Shoji in Oahu for years now. He's been swearing you'd come someday. I thought you'd just keep treading water until we were all completely fucked."

"Shoji?" asked Alaric, eyes narrowing further. "Would that refer to Joseph Shoji, the director of the Kauai Institute of Virology?"

"Why are you asking me questions you know the answers to already? Nobody here needs the exposition." Dr. Abbey picked up her own drink, sipping calmly before she said, "If you think you can sell me to your government, think again. They already know who I'm in contact with, how often, how we communicate, basically everything but how often I change my underwear. If they wanted to take me, they'd take me. They just don't want to risk it."

"Actually, I sort of need the exposition, since I have no clue what you people are talking about," I said. "Why doesn't the government want to risk it? I mean, no offense, but it's not like you're sitting on a nuke here or anything."

"Oh, but I am." Dr. Abbey's gaze went to Kelly, and stayed there, guileless and steady as she continued: "See, the CDC knows damn well and good that something's wrong. I don't know how many of the people working there know what it *is*, but you can't have half a brain, work in the medical field, and not realize that something's not right."

"That's not fair," protested Kelly. "The research—"

Dr. Abbey cut her off: "That's an excuse."

"You're talking about the reservoir conditions," said Becks. It was a relief to have her join the conversation. Her training was a lot more analytical than mine. I didn't know what questions to ask. She and Alaric did, and that could save our asses.

"Exactly." Dr. Abbey kept looking at Kelly. "What do you know?"

"I don't know who Dr. Shoji is," I volunteered. "But I know that people with reservoir conditions are dying faster than they should be, and I know that my sister was one of those statistics, so we're here because we need you to tell us what the CDC doesn't want to say."

Kelly shot me a look. "Control of sensitive information is a key duty of all government organizations," she said. "Given your own need for information security, I would have thought—"

"Drop the party line, Doc," I said pleasantly. "I still don't have a problem with hitting girls."

Her mouth snapped shut with an audible click.

Dr. Abbey studied me for a moment before looking toward Alaric, nodding in my direction, and asking, "Is he for real?"

"He's for real," said Alaric. "Infuriating, impossible, and probably insane, but for real."

"Huh." Dr. Abbey took another sip of her drink. "Joe has five fully developed reservoir conditions. Retinal, cerebro-spinal, cardiac, testicular, and my personal favorite, thyroid. He's the first documented case of a canine thyroid reservoir condition, aren't you, Joe?" Joe turned his massive head toward her, tongue lolling as he drooled agreement with her words.

"You said you induced them?" said Becks.

"That's impossible," said Kelly. "The virus doesn't behave that way."

"It's not impossible. It's just hard," said Dr. Abbey. "I started injecting him with the live-state virus when he was six weeks old. That gave his body time to learn to deal with it before he got big enough to amplify. The first two conditions developed on their own, as a consequence of the inoculations. The others took more doing, since they had to be induced after adulthood."

"I just don't understand," said Kelly. "I mean, the risk of amplification alone—"

"Who says he didn't amplify?"

We all turned toward Maggie—I'd almost forgotten she was there, I was so busy trying to understand what the hell was going on—who was looking at Dr. Abbey with wide, solemn eyes.

"What?" asked Kelly.

"Who says he didn't amplify?" repeated Maggie. She picked up her water, took a thoughtful drink, and continued: "I mean, if you can induce reservoir conditions . . . You said he'd never amplify *fully*. It seems like there's only one way you could know, and that's by testing it. I'm not sure how you'd do it; it's not like I'm a doctor, but it seems . . . possible."

"Doesn't it?" asked Dr. Abbey. "Gold star for you."

A slow, horrifying picture was beginning to come together in my head, a picture that I didn't want to see. George was silent, making it even harder to ignore the conclusions my mind was drawing. Whatever those conclusions were, she was drawing them, too, and she didn't like them any more than I did. My mouth was suddenly desert-dry, as parched as the ground outside of Memphis, where snipers opened fire on our convoy, where Buffy died . . . where the CDC took us in for the very first time.

"Dr. Abbey?" I asked. She looked toward me, expression that of a teacher who wanted to encourage a favorite student to come up with the right answer before the final bell. "What do the reservoir conditions really do? Do you know?"

"Of course I do." She smiled, setting her drink aside as she stood. "Come on. I think it's time I took you for a tour of the lab. You need to understand what we're doing here."

"I've always liked a good perversion of science," said Becks. At least one of us was remembering to keep things light. "Let's take the tour."

Yes, said George, sounding oddly subdued. *Let's.*

Kelly didn't say anything. Maybe that was for the best.

We left our drinks behind and followed Dr. Abbey from her cramped cubicle to the main floor of the lab. Joe padded along at the rear of the group, claws making an unnerving clacking sound against the bare linoleum. It was impossible to forget that he was there, or that he was—all protests aside—more than large enough to undergo full amplification. He could kill us all before anyone had a chance to reach for a weapon.

But he won't, said George, picking up on the thought. *I don't think Dr. Abbey's quite that crazy.*

"Says the one with the least to lose," I muttered.

Dr. Abbey looked back at me, brows raised. "What was that?"

I offered her a sunny smile. "Just talking to my dead sister. She lives inside my head now. She says you're not crazy enough to let your dog go zombie and eat us all."

"She's right," Dr. Abbey agreed, seemingly unperturbed by the fact that I was talking about carrying on conversations with a dead person. It was weirdly jarring. "Even if Joe *could* amplify—which he can't, after all the work we've done—I wouldn't let him do it outside a sealed room. There's too much here that he could damage."

"Like these?" Alaric stopped, frowning at a tank that contained about a dozen things that looked like guinea pigs with too many legs. Becks followed his gaze and let out a shriek, jumping backward.

"Goliath tarantulas," said Dr. Abbey. "Average weight of the specimens in that tank is between four and six ounces. It's taken generations to breed them up that large."

"Why would you *want* to?" demanded Becks. "They're horrible."

"They're infected," said Dr. Abbey. We all turned to stare at her. She continued blithely, "The biggest female has amplified twice so far. Once she got sick enough that she started displaying stalking behavior and infected three other spiders before she could be contained. One of them didn't recover. A pity. He was from a very encouraging line. Come on, there's a lot to see." She resumed walking, obviously trusting us to follow her.

"Spiders can't amplify," said Kelly, sounding uncertain.

"Keep telling yourself that," said Dr. Abbey, and kept walking.

The rest of us hurried to catch up, with Joe once again lingering long enough to bring up the rear. I found myself wondering what would happen if one of us tried to split the party, the way they always seemed to do in the horror movies Maggie and Dave liked so much. Given the size of Joe's head, and the number of teeth it contained, I wasn't in any real hurry to find out. Let Becks take the suicidal risks. She was the group's remaining Irwin, after all.

Dr. Abbey waited for us at the head of a narrow alley that smelled of salt water and damp. "I was starting to think I needed to send search parties," she said, and ducked between the racked-up tanks, starting into the darkness.

"I don't like this," said Alaric.

"Too late now," I replied, and followed her.

The source of the smell quickly became apparent: The tanks making up the sides of the alley were filled with salt water and contained a variety of brightly colored corals and plastic structures. I paused to peer closer and recoiled as a thick, fleshy tentacle slapped the glass from the inside. Dr. Abbey snickered.

"Careful," she said. "They get bored sometimes. They like to mess around with people's heads when they're bored."

"They who?" I asked, pressing a hand against my chest as I waited for my heart to stop thudding quite so hard against my ribs. There was a distinct heaviness in my bladder, telling me that I needed to find a bathroom before I lined myself up for too many more exciting surprises. "What the fuck is that thing?"

"Pacific octopus." Dr. Abbey tapped the offending tank. The tentacle responded by slapping the glass again, before it was joined by two more near-identical appendages, and a large octopus slithered out from a crack between two pieces of coral. "We do a lot of work with cephalopods. They're good subjects, as long as you can keep them from getting bored enough to slither out of their tanks and go around wreaking havoc."

I glanced to Becks. "Isn't this the part where you should run screaming?"

"Nah," she said. "I've got no problem with octopuses. It's bugs and spiders that I don't like. Octopuses are cute, in their own 'nature did a lot of drugs' sort of way."

"Girls are fucking weird," I said.

You should know, George replied.

I smirked and leaned in for a closer look at the octopus. It settled against the glass, watching us with its round, alien eyes. "That is a freaky-looking thing," I said. "What's it for?"

"Barney here is for testing some of the new KA strains we've been developing," said Dr. Abbey, removing the cover from the tank. The octopus promptly switched its focus to the surface of the water. She stuck in a hand, and it reached up with two tentacles, twining them firmly around her wrist. "We haven't been able to infect him yet, although he's shown some fascinating antibody responses. If we can just figure out what's blocking infection in the cephalopod family, we'll be able to learn a lot more about the structure of the virus."

"Wait, you mean you're actually *trying* to develop new strains of the virus?" Kelly looked at her with wide, baffled eyes, like this was the last thing she could imagine anyone wanting to do.

Dr. Abbey took her attention away from the octopus—which was now trying to pull her arm all the way into the tank—as she frowned at Kelly. "What did you think we were doing here? Growing hydroponic tomatoes and talking about how nice it'll be when the CDC finally decides to get around to saving us all?" She began untangling her hand from the octopus's grasp, not appearing to take her attention off Kelly. "Please. Are you really going to stand there questioning my medical ethics while you tell me you people haven't been working with the structure of the virus at all?"

Kelly bit her lip and looked away.

"Thought not." Dr. Abbey pulled her hand out of the tank and replaced the lid. The octopus settled back at the bottom in a swirl of overlapping arms, appearing to sulk. "If you'll all walk this way, I think we're about ready to conclude our little tour. You should have all the information you need by this point." She turned and strode down the alley, shoulders stiff.

"Think we should follow?" asked Alaric, sotto voce.

"I'm not sure Joe here is going to give us a choice." I glanced at the mastiff. He was sitting calmly behind our little group, blocking the only other exit from the narrow row between the tunnels. "Besides, we've come this far. Don't you want to find out what the big secret the Wizard has to share with us is?"

"Maybe she's planning to give you a brain," deadpanned Becks.

"If she does, I hope that means you're getting a heart," I replied, and started walking.

Behind me, Alaric said, almost mournfully, "I just want to go home."

Kelly and Maggie didn't say anything at all. But they followed, and that was more than I had any right to ask of them.

Dr. Abbey was waiting on the other side of the alley, in front of a wide safety-glass window that looked in on what was obviously a Level 4 clean room. The people inside were wearing hazmat suits, connected to the walls by thick oxygen tubes, and their faces were obscured by the heavy space-helmet-style headgear that's been the standard in all high-security virological facilities since long before the Rising. Dr. Abbey was looking through the glass, hands tucked into the pockets of her lab coat. She didn't turn as we approached. Joe trotted up, and she pulled one hand free, placing it atop his head.

"I started this lab six and a half years ago," she said. "I've been waiting for you—or someone like you—ever since. What took you so long? Why didn't you show up years ago?"

"I didn't even know you were here," I said. "I still don't really understand."

Yes, you do, said George. Her voice was small, subdued, and almost frightened.

"George?" I asked. My own voice sounded almost exactly like hers had.

"We should go," said Kelly, sounding suddenly alarmed. She took my elbow. I looked down at her hands, but she didn't let go. "Or we should ask her about the research. You know, what we came to ask about."

"Dr. Abbey?" asked Alaric. "What's going on? What are you doing here? Why did you give your dog reservoir conditions, and what do you mean when you say he can't amplify? And what does it have to do with the deaths of the people with the natural reservoir conditions?"

"The Kellis-Amberlee virus was an accident," said Dr. Abbey, still looking at the pane of safety glass. Her hand moved slowly over her dog's head, stroking his ears. "It was never supposed to happen. The Kellis flu and Marburg Amberlee were both good ideas. They just didn't get the laboratory testing they needed. If there'd been more time to understand them before they got out, before they combined the way that they did . . . but there wasn't time, and the genie got out of the bottle before most people even realized the bottle was there. It could have been worse. That's what nobody wants to admit. So the dead get up and walk around—so what? We don't get sick like our ancestors did. We don't die of cancer, even though we keep pumping pollutants into the atmosphere as fast as we can come up with them. We live charmed lives, except for the damn zombies, and even those don't have to be the kind of problem that we make them out to be. They could just be an inconvenience. Instead, we let them define everything."

"They're zombies," said Becks. "It's sort of hard to ignore them."

"Is it really?" Dr. Abbey's hand continued caressing Joe's ears. "There's always been something nasty waiting around the corner to kill us, but it wasn't until the Rising that we let ourselves start living in this constant state of fear. This constant 'stay inside and let yourself be protected' mentality has gotten more people killed than all the accidental exposures in the world. It's like we're all addicted to being afraid."

Ask her about the reservoir conditions, prompted George.

"George—I mean, *I* want to know, what do the reservoir conditions have to do with any of this?" My voice sounded unfamiliar to my own ears, like someone else was asking the question.

"The immune system can learn to deal with almost anything, given sufficient time and exposure. How else could we have stayed alive for this long?" Dr. Abbey turned to look at me, eyes dark and very tired beneath the erratically bleached fringe of her hair. "The reservoir conditions are our bodies figuring out how to process the virus. How to work around it. They're our immune responses writ large and inconvenient, like the autoimmune diseases people used to suffer from before the Rising."

Just about everyone with an autoimmune syndrome either died during the Rising or found their suffering greatly alleviated as the body's immune responses got something much better to waste their time on than attacking their own cells: the sudden burgeoning Kellis-Amberlee infection doing its best to wipe out everything in its path. Autoimmune disorders still crop up, but they're nothing compared to their numbers before the Rising turned the medical world on its ear.

The facts flashed across my mind like puzzle pieces falling inexorably into place, each of them notching smoothly into place with the ones around it. The things Kelly was surprised by. The illegally massive dog with the induced reservoir conditions, and the casual way Dr. Abbey said he wouldn't amplify, like she knew, absolutely, what she was talking about. The spiders, the bugs, and the octopuses with their grasping limbs and their staring, alien eyes. All of it made sense, if I just stopped trying to force it.

I turned toward Kelly before I realized that I was intending to move. Her eyes widened, and she took a step back, almost pressing herself against Maggie. Maggie gave her a puzzled look as she stepped out of the way.

"I don't know what he's so pissed about, but I'm not going to get in his way," she said, in a tone that bordered on the sympathetic. "Better you than me."

Alaric and Becks were watching me with confusion. Dr. Abbey turned to watch me advancing on Kelly, and there was no confusion in her expression, just calm satisfaction, the teacher's face once more watching her student finally understand the lesson.

"The reservoir conditions are an immune response," I said. It wasn't a question; it didn't need to be. I could see the confirmation in Kelly's widening eyes. "They're the way the body copes with the Kellis-Amberlee infection, aren't they?" She didn't answer me. "*Aren't they?!*" I shouted, and slammed my hand into the safety glass.

Maggie and Alaric jumped. Becks stepped up beside me. And Kelly flinched.

"Yes," she said. "They are. They just ... they just happen. We think it has something to do with exposure in infancy, but the research has never been ... it's never ... "

All my sympathy for her was gone, like it had never existed at all. I wasn't seeing a person anymore. I was seeing the CDC, and the virus that took George away. "I'm going to ask you one question, Doc, and I want you to think really hard about your answer, because you're legally dead, and if we want to hand you to this nice lady," I gestured toward Dr. Abbey, "for her experiments, well, there's really not much you can do about it. Don't lie to me. Understand?"

Kelly nodded mutely.

"Good. I'm glad to see that we have an agreement. Now, tell me: The reservoir conditions. What do they do? What do they *really* do?"

"They teach the immune system how to handle an ongoing live Kellis-Amberlee infection," said Kelly, meeting my eyes at last. She sounded oddly relieved, like she'd known we were going to wind up here and just hadn't known how to force the issue on her own. "They teach the body what to do about it."

"Meaning what?"

Alaric spoke abruptly, his own voice glacially cold: "That's the wrong question, Shaun."

"All right, you're the Newsie. What's the right question? What should I be asking her?"

"Ask her what would have happened if you hadn't pulled the trigger." Alaric looked at Kelly for a long moment, and then looked away, like he couldn't bear the sight of her. "Ask her what would have happened to Georgia if you'd just left her alone in the van and hadn't pulled the trigger."

Kelly's answer was a hushed whisper, so soft that, for a moment, I couldn't believe what I was hearing. The words seemed to get louder and louder as they echoed inside my head, repeating over and over again until I couldn't bear the sound of them. I slammed my fist into the safety glass as hard as I could, so hard I could feel my knuckles threaten to give way. Then I turned on my heel and stalked away, back down the dank-smelling alley where the octopuses watched with their alien eyes, back past the tanks of massive spiders, past the working lab technicians, who barely even looked up as I passed them. I was running by that point, running as I tried to outpace the words still echoing in my ears—those horrible, condemning, world-destroying words. It didn't do any good. No matter how fast I ran, no matter how hard I hit the world, nothing could take those words back again.

Those five small, simple words that changed everything:

"She would have gotten better."

Shaun and I had one of those awkward talks today—the ones that hurt the most because they're the ones you don't want to have, ever, but *have* to have eventually. This one was about our birth parents. Who they were, why they gave us up, whether they survived the Rising, all those things they say adopted kids are supposed to ask. Whether they wanted us. That's a big one for Shaun. He's always been more forgiving of the Masons than I am, but for some reason, it's really important to him that we were wanted before we wound up here.

I know what triggered it. I got the same e-mail he did, from a service promising to "reunite the orphans of the Rising with their families." According to the e-mail, these people would—for a modest fee, of course—run blood and tissue samples through every public and military database in the country, looking for a genetic match. Satisfaction guaranteed; they were clear on that point. We Find Your Family, Or Your Money Back.

That sort of scam fascinates me, but I don't want the answers that they're offering. I've had my genes tested for every nasty recessive and surprise health hazard we can test for, and that's most of them—anything they don't have a chromosome type for is so damn rare that at least it would be interesting to write about as it killed me. I have no pressing need to find the family that created me. The one thing I have in this world, the one thing I'm not willing to risk losing, is Shaun. And if I went out and found another family, I'd run the risk of losing him.

Whether the Masons rescued us from certain death—like the press releases say—or stole us, or hell, bought us on the black market, I don't *care*. The girl I would've been if I'd grown up with a mother with my nose and a father with my funny-looking toes never got the opportunity to exist. *I* did. *I* was the one who got to grow up, and I grew up with Shaun, and that's all I give a damn about. We got lucky. If he doesn't see it, well ... I guess there's no way to make him.

But I still know.

—From *Postcards from the Wall*, the unpublished files of Georgia Mason, originally posted May 13, 2034

———

The good thing about Kellis-Amberlee, as a virus, is that it only goes after mammals. I mean, think about it. Can you imagine an infected giant squid? It would be like the Sea World Incident of 2015 all over again, only this time with bonus tentacles. Not my idea of a good scene. If that doesn't disturb you, consider this: The average crocodile is well over the amplification threshold.

Yeah. That was my thought, too.

The bad thing about Kellis-Amberlee, as a virus, is that it goes after *all* mammals. From the smallest field mouse to the largest blue whale (assuming there are any blue whales left down there), if it's a mammal, it's a carrier. That means that any cure we devise will also have to work for all mammals, because otherwise there's always the chance that Kellis-Amberlee can mutate and come back for another try. Viruses are tricky that way. At least we're used to dealing with this form of the disease. I'm not sure how quickly we'd adjust if it somehow changed the rules.

—From *The Kwong Way of Things*, the blog of Alaric Kwong, April 12, 2041

Ten

The outside air slapped me hard across the face as the door to Dr. Abbey's lab clanged shut behind me. I stumbled to a stop, realizing two things at the same time—first, that I was alone in the middle of a mostly abandoned industrial park, and second, that while I had my standard field arms, I wasn't wearing any armor beyond my basic motorcycle gear. It was like a recipe for suicide, and while it might have been acceptable when I was too out of it to realize what I was doing, that moment had passed. I let my gaze flick wildly around my surroundings, looking for signs of movement. I didn't find any. What I did find was the van, sitting like an island of serenity among the ruins.

I took another step forward, barely aware that I was going to do it until it was already done. The van. That's where I was going when I ran away. To the van, where George and I saved each other's lives a thousand times . . . where I pulled the trigger and killed the woman who was my sister, my best friend, and my only real family, all with a single bullet.

She would have gotten better, whispered Kelly's voice, in the black space behind my eyes where only George was supposed to speak. The world blanked out again.

The sound of the van door slamming forced me back into my surroundings for the second time. My index finger was slightly numb, with the deep, subcutaneous ache that meant I'd taken—and passed—a blood test to open the doors. No amplification for me. Not yet, anyway. I looked dully around the van's interior, eyes flicking toward the ceiling in an automatic check for the Rorschach test that was formed by George's blood immediately after I pulled the trigger. For a moment, I could see it, streaks of red trending into a dozen shades of brown as it dried. Then I blinked, and the blood was gone, replaced by pristine white paneling.

"Breathe, Shaun," said George. Her voice came from behind me, rather than from inside my head. It was calm, soothing, even slightly amused; she was just talking me down from a panic attack. Nothing important, all part of a day's work. I've never been terribly prone to that kind of episode, but when you spend your days playing with dead things, one or two flip-outs are bound to come with the territory. "You're going to give yourself an aneurysm."

"Didn't you hear her?" I demanded, clenching my hands into fists. The urge to look toward the sound of her voice was nigh irresistible. I kept looking at the ceiling instead, waiting for the blood to repeat its flickering appearance. "You would have gotten better."

"Says her," George said. The amusement vanished, replaced by the barely chained irritation that was practically her trademark. "The test results were locked in—the CDC knew I was dead. If you'd walked away, something would have happened, and you know it. Worst-case scenario, you would have been treated to the delightful sight of men in hazmat suits dragging me into the open while I screamed for them to take another test. My last post might not have gone out. The *truth* might not have gone out." She paused before delivering what I was sure was meant to be the killing blow: "Tate might have walked away clean."

"You don't know," I said. "We could have claimed there was something wrong with the test. It's happened before."

"How often?"

I didn't answer her.

George sighed. "Three times, Shaun. With a top-of-the-line test, three times. In all three cases, there was proof of mechanical failure—and in two of the cases, the people were killed anyway. Their families won their suits on the basis of secondary testing units. We both know what a secondary test would have shown in my case. There's no point in pretending that we don't."

That was too much. The blood flickered back into visibility a second before I spun around, feeling my fingernails cutting into my palms as I shouted, "For fuck's sake, Georgia, there was a *chance*!" The empty chair would fix it. I'd see the empty chair, and she'd go back to being a voice in my head, just a voice in my head, because she was dead, I killed her. I just had to see the empty chair.

Instead, I saw George.

She was sitting in her customary place at the counter, her chair turned to face me. The computer monitor behind her framed her head like a technological halo, and the position, the lighting, all of it was so familiar that I didn't know whether I wanted to laugh, scream, or thank God that I'd finally gone all the way insane. She was wearing her usual fashion-impaired ensemble: black jacket, white dress shirt, black slacks. Only her face was wrong—no, not even her entire face; just her eyes. Her sunglasses were missing, and her eyes were the clear, undistorted coppery-brown that I remembered from the years before the progression of her retinal Kellis-Amberlee turned her irises into outlines.

I stared at her. She ignored it, the way she always did when she wasn't willing to wait for me to catch up. "Was," George agreed. "Not *is*. There *was* a chance. But we're past that now, aren't we? We're way, way past that."

My mouth went dry, and the room, already unsteady, started to spin. "George . . . ?"

"Glad to see you haven't suffered any major head injuries lately," she said, wistfully, and smiled.

I kept staring until she sighed and said, "It's not like we have all day, you know. They're going to come looking for you sooner or later—probably sooner—and you really don't want them to find you like this."

"They're used to me talking to myself," I said quietly.

"To yourself, yes; to me, no." George shook her head. "Don't get me wrong, we both know that I'm not really here. There's no such thing as ghosts. But if you're actually *looking* at me, they're going to have a harder time taking you seriously, and you have a lot of work to do. *We* have a lot of work to do."

I decided against asking how "we" could do anything, if we both knew that she wasn't really here. If I did that, she might decide to stop talking to me altogether, and then I really would go crazy. The kind of crazy that puts you in a rubber room, rather than chasing conspiracies and running a news site. I forced a smile of my own, wondering how believable it would be, and said, "It's good to see you."

"I'd say it's good to be seen, but it's not," said George, looking at me steadily. "Just how crazy are you?"

"On a scale of one to ten?" I bit back a laugh. "Crazy enough that we're having this conversation. How's that for a starter?"

"Can you function?" She leaned forward, bracing her elbows against her knees. It was such a familiar gesture that my chest tightened, making it hard to breathe. "The way I see it, this is either where you man up and stop letting yourself freak out, or where you admit that you're too cracked to do the job and hand things over to somebody else. It's your call. You're the one who isn't actually dead."

I winced a little at the word "dead." "Can you not—?"

"Can I not what? Call myself dead? It's true, you dumb-ass. You're talking to me because I represent the part of you that still has a fucking clue how bad things are going to get. You've been fucking around since Tate decided to play martyr, and I'm tired of it. The team needs you. *I* need you. You can either step up, or you can step down, but you can't keep treading water like this."

She would have gotten better, whispered Kelly.

"Be quiet," I muttered.

"You're only saying that because you know I'm right," said George implacably. Apparently, the voices in my head couldn't hear each other. That was just another slice of crazy pie. "God, you never could take an honest critique. You would never have made it as a Newsie."

"Then it's a good thing I never tried to." My knees were shaking. I sagged back against the counter on my side of the van, resting my weight on my hands. It was as much to keep myself from trying to grab hold of my hallucination as it was to keep from falling over. "How do you expect me to step up for something like this? This wasn't the plan."

"No, the plan was to make me do it." She looked at me solemnly, alien eyes wide and grave in that familiar face. "We always knew one of us was going to be finishing things alone. Maybe we didn't know why, exactly, but we always knew this would happen somehow." Her solemnity broke, replaced by the half smile that meant she didn't want to be as amused as she was. "I have to admit, even when I was being self-important, I never thought they'd put 'assassinated to conceal a massive political conspiracy' on my Wall entry. I always figured it'd be something less . . . I don't know. Something less your department."

"Yeah, well." It was hard to swallow past the lump in my throat. It was the damn smile that did it. I knew she was a hallucination. I just didn't *care*. "You zigged when you should've zagged."

"What's done is done. So are you up for this?"

I didn't say anything.

More sharply: "Shaun? Are you even listening to me?"

"I miss you so much." I looked down at my feet. I couldn't keep looking at her, not if I wanted to hold on to what little was left of my sanity. "I mean, you know that, and I know I've been talking to you this whole time, but I also know it's because I'm really not all here without you, so I'm talking to myself in order to pretend I can ever be all the way here again, and this isn't even really a sentence any-more, so I'm going to stop now, but God, George, I miss you so much." I stopped, and hesitated before adding, very softly, "I don't think I know how to do this without you."

"You have to." I heard her stand, heard her footsteps as she crossed the van to stop in front of me. Her knees were on a level with my field of vision. If there's a rating system for quality of hallucination, I can say I was definitely scoring pretty high; I could see the wrinkles in her slacks where they fell over her knees, and a bit of carpet lint sticking to the sole of one sensible shoe. "Shaun, look at me."

I raised my head. This close, her eyes were even more alien . . . but they were still her eyes. It was still her behind them.

"Step up or step down," she said, very quietly. "Those are the choices."

I swallowed. "Do I get anything more than that? Step up or step down?"

"This isn't a news story, Shaun. The only reward you get for making it to the end is making it to the end—you get to know the truth, and that's it. I don't come back. The last year doesn't unhap-pen. Life doesn't go back to the way that it was; life never goes back to the way it was, no matter how hard we try to make it. But you'll know. You'll have the truth. You'll have the pieces that we're still missing." She smiled again, despite the tears welling up in her eyes. I'd never seen her cry, even when we were kids. The retinal KA atrophied her tear ducts years before her eyes actually changed in a visible way. But she was crying now. "The only happy ending we can have is the ending where you take the bastards down and make them pay for what they did to us. Can you do it? Because if you can't, I need you to call Mahir and tell him that he's in charge now. Someone has to find the truth. *Please*."

"I can do it," I said. My voice was unsteady, but it was there, and that was really all that I could ask. "For you, I can do it."

"Thank you." She leaned forward. My breath caught as she pressed a kiss against my forehead and stepped away again, leaving me with a clear path to the exit. "I miss you, too."

I stood, glancing up as I did. The blood on the ceiling was gone. When I looked down again, so was George. I wiped my cheeks with the palm of my hand until it came away dry, still looking at the spot where George had been. She didn't reappear. That was probably a good sign. "Love you, George," I whispered.

She would have gotten better, hissed Kelly's voice, but its power was gone. Oh, I was still going to have to deal with the reality of it, but I'm good at dealing with stupid shit. If the CDC wanted to play hardball, we'd play hardball. And we'd win.

I was unsurprised to find Becks standing outside the van with her pistol resting against her knee, lazily sipping from a bottle of water. She straightened when I stepped out onto the blacktop, asking. "Everything okay?"

"I think I just had a minor psychotic episode or maybe a breakdown or something, but it's cool; I'm feeling basically okay now," I replied, closing the van doors. "You?"

Becks blinked at me, momentarily thrown by the flippancy of my reply. Even after working with me for as long as she has, she hasn't learned to take statements like "minor psychotic episode" in stride. I'll give her this: She recovered fast, saying, "Well, I just watched my boss have a minor psychotic episode, and I thought I'd come out and make sure he didn't get his damn fool ass eaten by a zombie before he settled down." She hesitated, then added, "I didn't shoot her. After you ran out of the room? I didn't shoot her."

I wasn't sure whether she was looking for praise or expecting me to condemn her for showing mercy. I elected for the praise. "Good call," I said, nodding. "We're going to need that pretty little head of hers intact if we're going to crack it open, pry out all its secrets, and use them to bring down the CDC."

"Right," said Becks, slowly. "Were you on the line to Mahir just now? Because I thought I heard voices in there."

"Psychotic break, remember?" I shrugged. "Look, Becks— Rebecca—you know what you're getting out of this team. We're damaged goods, some more than others. I'm so damaged I'm practically remaindered. If you can cope with that, I can promise you the ride of your life. If you can't, I have the feeling that when we go back in there," I hooked a finger toward the door to Dr. Abbey's lab, "you lose the last chance to cash in your ticket on the crazy train."

"I like trains," said Becks. Her expression sobered before she added, "And I loved your sister. She was the first person who gave me a chance to prove myself in the field. She was a damn good reporter. So if you're a little nuts, so what? I think it's pretty obvious that we're all mad here."

"Great," I said. We were the only things that moved as we walked toward the door. "She didn't want to let you go. I had to haggle like a bastard to get you away from the Newsies."

"She recognized talent when she saw it," said Becks, with a small smile.

"Yes, she did," I replied, with utter seriousness. Becks blinked, smile fading as she saw the look on my face. "So did I. I'm about to ask all of you to go all-in—put up or shut up, because we're done treading water." I was echoing some of what George had said to me, but that was okay. She was a figment of my insanity, and she probably wouldn't sue me for plagiarism. "Not all of us are going to walk away from this one alive."

"You're kidding, right?" Becks actually laughed out loud, the sound echoing through the empty structures around us. "If there's one thing I've learned since I started working with you people, it's that no one gets out alive." She leaned over, kissing me lightly on the cheek and then speed-walking the rest of the way to the door. "No one," she repeated, and was gone.

I stopped, touching my cheek and staring after her in bewilderment. "What the fuck was that?"

A complication, said George. She sounded amused. *Also, a girl thing.*

"Right." I dropped my hand. "Glad to see you're back where you belong."

I'm right here. Until the end.

"Great." I started forward again. "Come on, George. Check this out."

BOOK III

The Mourning Edition

Here's how it used to work: George told you the unvarnished facts, no matter how nasty they were or how lousy they made you feel, and then I came in to dance like a monkey and make you feel better about this shitty world we're living in. I was the carrot, and she was the stick. Well, guess what, folks? The stick got broken, and that's not how things are going to work anymore. Those days are behind us.

This is the new deal: I'm going to tell you the unvarnished facts, no matter how nasty they are or how lousy they make you feel . . . and that's it. If you want news that makes you feel good, go somewhere else. If you want wacky adventures, laughter, and an escape from your miserable life, go somewhere else.

If you want the truth, stay here. Because from here on out, that's all I'm going to give you. No more carrot-and-stick. No more dancing monkeys. Just the truth. And if it kills us, well, at least this way we died for something. It's better than the alternatives.

—**From *Adaptive Immunities*, the blog of Shaun Mason,**
April 15, 2041

Eleven

Becks was half a step behind me as I stopped at the end of Octopus Alley to take in the scene. Kelly was sitting in a folding chair with her hands clasped white-knuckle tight and resting on her knees. Alaric sat across from her, watching her like he thought she'd start making sense to him if he waited long enough. Best of luck with that, buddy. Maggie and Dr. Abbey leaned against the safety-glass window, watching this little tableau. Only Joe didn't seem to be disturbed by the current mood in the room. He was sprawled at Dr. Abbey's feet, gnawing on a massive length of animal bone.

Dr. Abbey offered me a nod. "Welcome back. Feeling better?"

"No, but I think I'll live. That's more than some people can say." Kelly shot me a look. I ignored her. "Dr. Abbey, how secure is your network? If we made a call, could it be traced?"

"A call to, say, the CDC?" She straightened. "I have a few burn phones I've been saving for just such an occasion. Wait here." Dr. Abbey made a complicated gesture toward Joe, who was in the process of standing, presumably so he could follow her. The dog subsided, staying where he was as she turned and strode out of the room.

Kelly looked at me with open alarm. "Shaun? What are you going to do?"

"Break your fucking jaw if you don't shut up, right now," I said, pleasantly enough. "I'm not ready for you to talk to me yet."

"That means it's time for you to be quiet," said Maggie.

There was a time when I would have told her not to taunt the Doc. That time was over and done with. "Becks, why don't you make sure the Doc stays quiet while I take care of things. I wouldn't want her to get any funny ideas about saying hi."

"My pleasure." Becks drew her pistol and moved to stand behind Kelly, adopting an easy, comfortable-looking stance. She could stand that way all day if she needed to. I'd seen her do it in field recordings.

Kelly stared straight ahead, unflinching. If I hadn't been so mad at her, I might have been impressed. As it was, I couldn't really look at her without wanting to punch her face in.

Dr. Abbey walked briskly back down the hall and slapped a phone into my hand. "This is voice activated and will stay untraceable for about five minutes. Give it the number you want and tell it to dial. You might also tell it to set itself to speaker, since I'd like to know what my resources are being used to do."

"Happily," I said. I pulled my normal phone from my pocket and brought up Dr. Wynne in my address book, reading off the numbers in a slow, clear voice before saying, "Dial and set to speaker."

The phone beeped. Three rings later, a CDC receptionist came on the line, perky as always as he said, "Dr. Joseph Wynne's office, how may I direct your call?"

"This is Shaun Mason. Please connect me to Dr. Wynne."

"May I ask the nature of your call?"

"No, you may not. Now connect me to Dr. Wynne."

"Sir, I'm afraid I—"

"*Now!*"

Something in my tone must have made it clear that I wasn't fucking around. The receptionist stammered an apology before the line gave a click, replacing his carefully cultivated blandness with the hum of hold music. That lasted only a few seconds. There was another click, and Dr. Wynne said, "Shaun, thank God. Now what the blazes is going on? You nearly gave poor Kevin an attack."

"I'll be sure to send a nice card and some flowers." The acid in my voice surprised even me. I thought I was better trained than that. "I left several people in Oakland before the outbreak, so you'll forgive me if I'm not on my best behavior."

There was a pause as Dr. Wynne took in what I was saying: that Dave hadn't been the only casualty of Oakland. It was a lie, sure, but it was one he had no reason not to believe. "Oh," he said finally, voice gone soft. "I see. I'm so sorry to hear that."

"It is what it is. Look, I've been doing some research, Dr. Wynne, and I wanted to confirm the results I'm getting. Got a second to answer a few questions for me?"

"I'm always happy to answer questions for you."

"Maybe not this time." I glared at Kelly as I spoke. Tears were starting to roll down her cheeks as she stared at the wall, expression otherwise remaining impassive. I didn't care. Bitch deserved to cry. "Dr. Wynne, are reservoir conditions an immune response?"

He hesitated. When he spoke again, his tone was slower, more careful, and more heavily accented. "Well, I suppose it depends on who you ask. Some people think they might be."

"What do *you* think?"

"I'm not sure that's relevant."

"I think it is. So what do you think? Are reservoir conditions an immune response or not?"

"Shaun . . . " He sighed heavily. "Yes. I think they are."

"So if Dave had managed to scan and e-mail me some documents before Oakland went kerplooey, and if the people I'd gone to with them said that George would have recovered if I hadn't decided to go ahead and shoot her, would they be fucking with me? Or was that little slice of good news somehow omitted from my handbook?"

He was silent.

"Fine. Whatever." Making my voice light was almost impossible, but I did it. Somehow. "I guess I'll just publish everything I've got here, let people with a more scientific background than mine sort it out. Right?"

"Shaun . . ." He sighed again. "Yes. Yes, she might have recovered. *Might*. The tests we ran on her blood were inconclusive."

My vision flashed red. The CDC had George's blood for weeks after her death. Logically, I knew they'd been using that time for tests, as well as decontamination, but I'd never really allowed myself to think about it. The idea of them doing God knows what to her had never been a pleasant one, and the more I knew, the less pleasant it became. "You're an asshole," I said, conversationally. "We trusted you."

"Shaun—"

"Fuck off." I hung up and tossed the burn phone back to Dr. Abbey. "Thanks."

"You're welcome." She tucked the phone into the pocket of her lab coat. "Satisfied now?"

"No. But it's a start." I turned to Kelly. "It's your turn to talk, Doc. Make it count."

"I . . ."

I glared at her. "*Talk.*"

She talked.

She kept her eyes on the floor the whole time, her voice tight and bordering on monotone. It was like she was trying to convince herself that she was giving a lecture, rather than being interrogated at gunpoint. The few times she did glance up, her eyes were filled with guilt, darting between us almost too rapidly to be followed. Then she'd look down again, her monotonous monologue never stopping. The expression on Dr. Abbey's face—calculating and predatory—probably didn't help. Then again, the fact that Becks was holding a gun pointed at the Doc's head probably helped even less.

"The first reservoir conditions were identified in 2018. Four years isn't long in human terms, but it's centuries in virus generations. The Kellis-Amberlee virus had been replicating the whole time. Spreading. Changing. I mean, the first infected didn't demonstrate mob behavior, but they started by the early twenties. That wasn't an adaptation on the part of the infected. It was an adaptation in the behavior of the viral substrains driving them. Six of the fifteen strains we had identified by that point would cause the pack behavior. Nine wouldn't. Ten years later, we could find only two strains that didn't come with that instinct to infect before eating. Outside the ones we had stored in our freezers, that is." She hesitated, shoulders tightening for an instant. Then, like some impossibly difficult decision had been made, she continued: "We tried cross-infection. Well. When I say 'we,' I mean scientists working at the CDC and USAMRIID. I wasn't working with . . . I wasn't a part of that project." Kelly glanced up again, eyes searching desperately for a sympathetic face. "I wasn't involved."

"That's when Dr. Shoji went off the reservation—he stuck it out as long as he could, but those cross-infection tests were the last straw," said Dr. Abbey, in a casual, matter-of-fact tone. "You want to talk about the cross-infection tests? What those entailed, precisely? I'm sure these nice people would really love the gory details."

Kelly took a deep breath as she looked back down. "They took . . . volunteers . . . "

"Prisoners," said Dr. Abbey.

"They volunteered," said Kelly, a stubborn note in her voice. "Yes, they were prisoners. They had no chance of parole, no chance of ever being released back into the public, and use of human test subjects has a . . . it has a long and time-honored place in medical science. Sometimes it's the only thing you *can* do. That's how they discovered that yellow fever was spread by mosquitoes, you know. How . . . how they proved that smallpox inoculation worked. A lot of people's lives were saved by human testing. When there wasn't any other choice. When there wasn't any other way."

"How many lives did this save?" asked Dr. Abbey.

"What did you *do*?" asked Alaric.

His was the question Kelly chose to answer. Darting a glance toward him, she said, "The choice was offered to certain inmates whose viral profile matched the criteria. Let us inject them with a potential vaccine and, if they recovered, we'd enter them in the witness-protection program. Whole new identities. Whole new lives. They could start over."

"If they lived," said Alaric, softly.

Kelly winced.

"Come on, princess," said Becks. "Story hour isn't over yet. I want to know what happens next."

"The volunteers were injected with a serum containing deactivated viral particles from the opposing strain. The theory was that maybe one strain would destroy the other. Best-case scenario, they'd *both* destroy the other, and we'd finally have a treatment. Worst-case scenario . . . " Her voice tapered off.

Dr. Abbey took up the thread when it became clear that Kelly wasn't going to, saying, "Worst-case scenario is what they got. Not only did every single one of their 'volunteers' go into spontaneous amplification when the two strains met, but they bred a new strain—one that increased mob behavior in exposed infected. They fucked up gloriously. And then they swept it all under the rug, with the rest of their failures."

"What did you want us to do?" Kelly's head snapped up, eyes narrowing as she glared at Dr. Abbey. "Did you want us to just sit back and watch the virus do its thing, not even *try* to find the answer? Yes, people died. Yes, mistakes were made, and mistakes will *be* made, and someday, maybe, because of those mistakes, we'll have a cure. Wouldn't you like that? A cure? An end to all the fear? Because that seems like a really good thing to me, and if I have to work with the CDC to make it happen, that's what I'm going to do."

"I'd love that idea, if I thought it was anything but a pipe dream." We all turned toward Maggie. She'd moved to sit on the floor next to Joe, one arm slung lazily across the dog's back. She looked completely at peace, despite the fact that she was leaning against an animal that could take off her face with a single bite. "People laugh at me because I watch a lot of horror movies, but horror movies are educational, if you know how to pay attention to them. They tell you about societal trends—about the things that people are afraid of. In the ones before the Rising, they were afraid of actual *things*. The new ones . . . they're just afraid of not being afraid."

Kelly snorted. "No one makes horror movies anymore."

"Yes, they do," said Maggie. "These days, everything's a horror movie."

"To get back to the original point, before we went on this fascinating and informative tangent, you said the virus was adapting," said Alaric. He leaned forward, eyes fixed on Kelly. The Newsie in him sensed blood in the water. I could see it in his face. "No mob behavior, then, mob behavior. What are the reservoir conditions supposed to *do*?"

"No one really knows." Kelly stole a glance in my direction, testing my reaction, before focusing on Alaric. She sounded less like she was lecturing and more like she was trying to make herself understood, like it suddenly *mattered* that we understand. "We think they stem from exposure to the live virus that somehow fails to cause full amplification. You see it mostly in people who risked exposure when they were under the threshold weight, although there have been exceptions. We're still trying to figure out what causes the exceptions. Why it happens in some adults, and not in others. We don't really know yet, and it's not the sort of thing you can easily test."

"So wait," said Becks. "Are you saying that people who got exposed when they were really little, they get reservoir conditions instead of getting the whole zombie combo pack?"

Kelly nodded. "Exactly."

My eyes were normal until I was almost at the amplification threshold, said George thoughtfully. *The retinal distortion didn't kick in until then.*

"I know," I mumbled, keeping my voice low, so as to hopefully avoid reminding my team that I was crazy. Louder, I asked, "What does that mean, exactly?"

"It means their bodies were exposed to live Kellis-Amberlee when they were still incapable of suffering the full effects of the virus," said Dr. Abbey. There was a lunatic good cheer in her voice, like being allowed to make that statement was a great and glorious gift. "Ever hear of chickenpox?"

"Well, yeah," said Becks. "It's part of the standard set of field vaccines."

"For a long time, they didn't have a vaccine for chickenpox—it was a childhood disease, and almost everybody caught it. Only that was a good thing back then, because most kids get over the chickenpox pretty easy. They itch for a week and then they're fine. Better than fine. Having the virus once makes them resistant to catching it again, and for adults, chickenpox is no laughing matter. It can cause permanent nerve damage, severe scarring, all sorts of nasty side effects." Dr. Abbey looked placidly at Kelly. "People used to have chickenpox parties, where they'd deliberately expose their young children to somebody who was already sick."

"That's disgusting," said Becks.

"Now that we have a vaccine, sure. Back then, it was a way to save your children from suffering a lot more. It wasn't safe—kids died of chickenpox—but it was a damn sight better than the alternative."

"I don't understand," I said.

I do, said George, very quietly.

"I do," echoed Alaric. I turned to look at him, and he said, "When infants are exposed to live Kellis-Amberlee, they can't amplify, but they still get sick. Only they can get better, can't they? They can actually recover from the virus."

"Bingo." Dr. Abbey, touching her nose with her left index finger while she pointed at Alaric with her right. "Princess CDC, tell the nice man what he's won!"

Kelly was silent.

I swallowed away the dryness in my throat, and said, quietly, "Please."

My voice seemed very loud in the enclosed space of the lab. Kelly turned to face me and said, "Yes, sometimes early exposure can lead to individuals successfully fighting off a live Kellis-Amberlee infection. It's impossible to run a standard blood test on an infant, because they can't amplify, so we can't find the usual amplification markers. But they'll get sick. It's been seen. And then, after a little while, they aren't sick anymore." Kelly stopped, choosing her next words with care: "Most of the individuals who undergo a potential infectious episode as infants develop one of the reservoir conditions when they get older, because their immune systems are preconditioned to respond."

"Their bodies remember that the virus is bad, and they set up their own little kennels, filled with their own little packs of domesticated viral bodies," clarified Dr. Abbey, leaning down to thump Joe on the side. He looked up at her adoringly, tongue lolling. "That's what humanity does when faced with wolves. We take them in, tame them, and teach them how to keep us safe."

"Yes," agreed Kelly. "The reservoir conditions are a marker that the immune system has learned it needs to fight back when Kellis-Amberlee starts taking over."

"That's why you said she would've gotten better, isn't it?" Kelly didn't answer. I slammed my fist into the safety-glass window, hard enough to make everyone jump—everyone but Dr. Abbey, who looked like she'd plugged herself into some inner reservoir of contentment. "Answer the damn question, Doc."

"Yes." Kelly looked up at me, expression drawn. "Dr. Wynne and I reviewed her test results. Her immune system was already starting to respond to the new infection when the test was taken. The chances that she would have been able to fight off the infection were very good. Better than eighty percent."

"Spontaneous remission," said Alaric, sounding awed.

I didn't take my eyes off Kelly as I said, "Explain."

"It's supposed to be an urban legend. Supposedly, there are people who've been infected—like, full-on ready-to-eat-the-neighbors infected—but they miraculously recovered before they could be put down. Nobody ever seems to know anyone who's had a spontaneous remission. It's always a guy who knows a guy who used to know a guy. But the stories keep cropping up, and then the CDC reminds everyone that there's no cure and they get written off again."

"Guess it's not that much of a legend, huh, Doc?" I glanced toward Dr. Abbey. "Is that what we're talking about here? This remission thing?"

"The CDC is telling the truth about one thing: There's no cure for Kellis-Amberlee, and if someone offered me one, I wouldn't take it, for a lot of reasons. They're also lying, because if you can live with the virus from the time you're born, why the hell should it be able to wake up but not able to go back to sleep?" Dr. Abbey smiled encouragingly. "Isn't story hour fun?"

"Like a heart attack," I said.

"Two in ten thousand," said Kelly sharply.

"What?" I asked.

"Two in ten thousand." She stood, ignoring the gun Becks had trained on her. "That's how many people *with* existing reservoir conditions are likely to recover from a live infection. Two in ten thousand. No one who didn't have a reservoir condition has ever recovered. The rate of recovery seems to be tied to the density of the viral particles in the individual reservoir, but we don't have any hard-and-fast proof of that. It's not like we've had much opportunity for study, since you can't exactly get volunteers for that sort of thing."

"Not even from the prison system," deadpanned Maggie.

Kelly winced again. I didn't really give a fuck. If she wanted to feel guilty, she'd damn well earned her guilt. "It's not like that," she said.

"Bullshit," said Dr. Abbey. "There are plenty of ways to test that sort of thing. Take Joe. I exposed him as a puppy: He got sick, he got better, he developed his first reservoir condition. I exposed him again when he hit amplification weight: He got sick, he got better, he developed his second reservoir condition. At this point, I could bathe him in the damn virus and he wouldn't amplify. He might get a little dehydrated and have some chest pains, but they'd pass quickly. Test passed."

"How many puppies did you start with?" countered Kelly.

Dr. Abbey looked uncomfortable for the first time. "Joe wasn't the first subject, true. But he's been the most successful."

"So wait a second," said Becks. "Are you people saying what I think you're saying?"

"That depends. Rebecca, do you think they're saying that a person with a pronounced enough reservoir condition can come back from zombie-dom, and that we could intentionally give babies reservoir conditions by exposing them before they're big enough to go zombie? Because that's what *I* think they're saying. But I'm the big, dumb Irwin, remember?" I punched the window again. "George was the smart one. Too bad she's the one who died."

"Two in ten thousand," repeated Kelly, like it was some sort of magic charm. "Could you have pulled the trigger if you had that figure? Could you have put the gun to her head and let her go to keep anybody else from getting hurt if you knew there was a chance—even a tiny, tiny little chance—that she'd get better?"

No, said George.

"Yes," I said, but there was no strength behind the word. I think everyone knew that I was lying. I don't think any of them had the right to blame me.

Kelly shook her head. "Society would collapse. Everyone would start to think *they* were special, *they* would be the ones whose mothers or fathers or children would get better. They'd start hesitating before they fired."

"Shoot first, ask questions later," said Becks, very quietly. "I hate to say this, Shaun, but she's right. If people stopped shooting, it'd be a bloodbath. Nobody would be willing to risk killing somebody who might recover."

"And while they're sick, they're really sick. The virus isn't any kinder to their bodies than it would be to yours, or to mine," said Kelly. "They can hurt people, and they can infect people, before their fevers start to go down. Can you imagine? Getting bit, and then coming out of it and learning that you'd killed and eaten your entire family? And what happens if your family isn't actually dead, just sick? As soon as you stop registering as part of the mob, they'll rip you apart. We won during the Rising because we learned that once someone gets bitten, you shoot. Take that away, and we're all going to die."

"Nice speech, but there's something you forgot, Doc," I said, as mildly as I could.

"What's that?"

"She," I hooked a thumb toward Dr. Abbey, "managed to give a dog a reservoir condition. So why the fuck aren't we starting a program to do that for people? Why are we just sitting back and . . . and not trying to change things?"

"Ask her how many of the puppies didn't have to get bitten before they amplified," Kelly countered.

"Aw, hell," said Alaric. "Rick's kid."

"What?" asked Becks.

"He had a son. He also had a wife with ovarian KA. He did a piece for the site about it, before he went off to become vice president. Their son amplified as soon as he hit the threshold weight. He was born with the live virus in his blood, and he never managed to fight it off." Alaric looked to Kelly. "That's what you're talking about, right?"

"It is." She lifted her chin a little, trying to look confident. She was only succeeding in looking scared. "We can't start a vaccination program unless you want to start turning every baby into a little time bomb. Maybe they'll fight it off and just have messed-up eyesight or weird headaches. Or maybe they'll stay sick, and then one day, they'll turn around and try to rip your throat out. We don't have enough control over the virus to do it. And we can't tell people because it changes things too much." She shot a pleading look in my direction. "Your sister was passionate about the truth, Shaun, but there are truths the world isn't ready to hear. There are truths that are just too big."

"Who made you the judge of that?" I asked quietly.

"Nobody." She shook her head. "There was nobody we could ask."

"Boo-hoo," said Dr. Abbey. "Let me know when you people want to grow a pair and join the scientific community. We're looking for answers. We'd love access to your lab equipment."

"You mean join the mad scientists," spat Kelly, guilt turning into anger in an instant.

"You say potato, I say pass the jumper cables," said Dr. Abbey.

Alaric looked at her thoughtfully. "You said Dr. Shoji left the mainstream medical community after the cross-infection trials. What made you do it? Why aren't you working with the CDC, trying to take them over from the inside out?"

"Simon Fraser University," said Dr. Abbey.

Kelly stiffened before sinking back into her seat and covering her face with her hands. Alaric's reaction was nowhere near as dramatic. His eyes widened slightly, and then he nodded, sympathetic comprehension filling his expression. "Who did you lose?"

Dr. Abbey looked down at Joe the mastiff. Maggie was stroking his ears, and he looked utterly blissful. "My husband," she said calmly. "Joseph Abbey. He was a software engineer. I was still working for the provincial CDC back then, looking for solutions through 'safe' channels. I followed protocol, I maintained my lab at their professional standards, and I was stupid enough to think that meant something."

The name of the school was familiar, but it wasn't connecting to anything, and for once, George wasn't helping. "Somebody fill me in," I said.

"Joe used to give lectures to software engineering classes. They said it was good for the students to deal with someone who had 'real-world experience.' I always thought it was partially to remind them that there was a world off campus." Dr. Abbey glanced my way. "Simon Fraser was a closed school. No student or faculty in and out during the semester. You came in clean, you stayed clean, you left clean. Pretty much the only risk of infection came from the outside speakers and the maintenance staff, and they were tested in every way possible. Joe used to say he couldn't sit down for a week after he did one of his lectures." She fell abruptly silent.

"There was an outbreak," said Alaric, taking up the thread where Dr. Abbey left off. "The security footage was mostly destroyed, but what we have indicates that it must have started in the gym. Maybe someone pushed themselves a little bit too far and had a coronary. We'll never know."

"Oh, fuck," I said.

"My thoughts exactly," said Dr. Abbey.

An outbreak is never good, but an outbreak on a sealed campus is close to a worst-case scenario. The healthy would be locked in with the infected until someone could come and let them out, and the mop-up would probably take weeks, if not months, after which the school would almost certainly be decommissioned for several years while they waited for the hazard level to go down again. "What was the student body size?"

"About eleven thousand," said Dr. Abbey. "It was a larger school before they closed it to nonresident students. Add another three hundred or so for the faculty and staff."

"How many got out?" asked Maggie.

"None," whispered Kelly.

"None," echoed Dr. Abbey. "See, the outbreak started near the school walls, and they were located on a hill that made it difficult to get to the campus any way but via the main road. Whoever was in charge that day—whatever genius was at the switch—decided that it was too dangerous to try for an evacuation. That the infection was already too close to breaking out. So they called down the wrath of fucking God on that little school."

"I remember that," said Becks, sounding faintly awed. "We studied it when I was in training. Almost all the security footage went missing, even the stuff that should have been beamed straight into the Health Canada and CDC databases. It was just gone."

"Except for the pieces that somehow ended up on private servers," said Alaric. "I've seen some of the footage. It's clearly an outbreak, but it doesn't look . . ."

"It doesn't look that bad," said Dr. Abbey. She seemed to have regained a bit of her composure. She looked challengingly around at our little group before she continued: "It looks like the sort of thing you handle with an insertion team and a general quarantine. Not by

ordering a firebombing on Canadian soil. My *husband* was in that
school. He called me fifteen minutes before they hit the news, and he
was *laughing*. He said there was 'a little ruckus' near the track, and
that he'd be home in time for dinner. Told me to get an ice pack
ready for the bruises left by all those blood tests they insisted on running. Everything was fine, and that was *after* the outbreak started.
But they treated it like the end of the goddamn world."

"So you went rogue?" I asked.

"Is that what they're calling it these days?" Dr. Abbey shook her
head. "I tendered my resignation immediately. They refused it. Three
times. Said that I was a 'valuable researcher,' and that they'd be happy
to give me the time I needed to get my affairs in order before I
returned to work. So I got my affairs in order. I packed my things,
I emptied out my lab, and I left while they were still congratulating
themselves on being so understanding in my time of need."

"You quit," said Kelly.

"You never started," countered Dr. Abbey. "Don't you look at me
like that, you little Barbie girl with your big moral ideals that go out
the window as soon as you think you know best. My husband died
because a bomb was cheaper than a cleanup squad. That's the simple
truth of things. Joe died because somebody didn't want to pay the
bill. His sister," she jabbed her finger at me, "died because you people
won't do the research into the reservoir conditions that needs to
happen if we're going to survive this damn virus. As a species, and
as a society. You may think you're doing the right thing, and hell,
you may even be right, but when you don't let anyone watch over
your shoulder, how the fuck are the rest of us supposed to know?"

Kelly took a slow breath, visibly calming herself before she said,
"I wouldn't be here if I was still willing to play by their rules."

"And again bullshit." Dr. Abbey slid off the desk, taking a quick
step forward. "You don't make them, but you're sure as shit defend-
ing them, and it's time to stop. Because if you're far enough off the

reservation to be sitting here, they're not going to let you come back. It's cheaper to drop the bomb than it is to offer medical assistance, remember?" She leaned in until her face was almost up against Kelly's, and said, voice suddenly soft, "I was you, once upon a time. Remember that. I was *you*, and the organization you still believe in made me who I am now. They'll do the same to you, if you don't get smart in a hurry."

Kelly gaped at her. Before any of us could formulate a response, Dr. Abbey was turning and striding off down the hall. Joe lumbered to his feet and went trotting after her, nearly knocking Maggie over in the process. The rest of us joined Kelly in gaping.

We were still staring when she shouted back, not turning, "I want you people out of my lab in ten minutes!" Then she was gone.

I glanced at Alaric. "I think I like her."

I think I do, too, said George.

Becks eyed the rest of us with poorly restrained impatience. "Well?" she asked. "Now what the fuck are we supposed to do?"

"That part's easy." I smiled, slowly. "We have a conspiracy. Let's go bust this fucker open and see what comes tumbling out."

But when the springtime turns to dust
(A thousand shades of blood and rust)
And everything is ash and stone
(Contagion writ in blood and bone)
Then what exists to have or hold?
(What story, then, has not been told?)
Let this be my sacred vow
(Oh Mother Mary, hear me now):
I will not fail, I will not fall
(Though Heaven, Hell, and Chaos call).
We are the children of the Risen.
This world our home, this prayer our prison.

**—From *Dandelion Mine*, the blog of Magdalene Grace Garcia,
April 16, 2041**

————

I am officially tired of camping. I am tired of eating fish. I am tired of watching the boys wander around scratching themselves and pretending that we're "roughing it" while living out of a van that's better appointed than many mobile homes. I am tired of shooting zombie deer that wander past our safety zone. Well, okay. I'm not really tired of that part. That part is pretty cool. Suck it, Bambi.

So I'm going to do something else today. No, I'm not going to tell you what; you're going to have to tune in and find out for yourself. But I promise you, you're going to have a *blast*.

**—From *Charming Not Sincere*, the blog of Rebecca Atherton,
April 16, 2041**

Twelve

Most major cities have their own CDC offices, although three out of four are just satellites, built mostly to keep people calm. The big offices are rarer, and they're the ones with the real resources—they're the ones where things get *done*. The nearest big office was smack in the middle of Portland, which conveniently put it less than an hour's drive from Dr. Abbey's lab.

Less conveniently, we couldn't exactly pull up stakes and go running straight to the CDC to start shaking them down for answers. "They're a government agency," said Becks. "It's their *job* to make things confusing."

"Besides, if we just go charging in there, we're all going to die," added Alaric.

"I hate trying to argue with you when you use logic on me," I said. The sun had dipped substantially lower in the sky while we were getting our Virology 101 from Dr. Abbey, and the shadows were long enough to have become menacing. Sunsets were considered beautiful before the Rising. Now they just mean night is coming, and staying out after dark is a good way to get yourself killed. "We need to get in there. We need to plant some bugs and see if we can knock the CDC off balance enough to tell us anything."

"This isn't a good idea," said Kelly. There was no room for disagreement in her tone. "The CDC has the right to shoot first and ask questions later. All they need to do is formulate a reasonable case for you having been a threat."

"Then I guess we'd better not be threats, huh?" I looked at her and shook my head. "We're going in there, Doc. We need to."

Seeing that Kelly still wasn't following me, Alaric said, "It's like putting together an academic defense. Sometimes you need to look for negative results, as well as positive ones. If we don't learn anything from the CDC, we get footage of them outright denying what everybody will eventually know is true. If we do learn something, we've made progress."

"And I need to know how much of the CDC is involved."

Kelly looked between us, frowning slightly. "You're all insane," she said.

"Yeah." I unlocked the van doors. "But look at it this way: At least you don't have to come."

Kelly snorted and got in.

Sadly, I meant what I said. No matter how pissed I was at Kelly, she was the one who spoke their language, and having her with us would have made things infinitely easier. But with Dr. Wynne assuming she'd died in Oakland, and everyone else believing she'd died in Memphis, we couldn't exactly march her into the office and expect to get actual answers. Shot at, yes, but answers, no.

Alaric was the one to come up with the obvious solution: "It's too late for us to do anything serious tonight. Why don't we get a couple of hotel rooms, and then you can leave me and Maggie to babysit Dr. Connolly while you and Becks go off to wreak havoc."

"I'm not normally in favor of splitting the party, but I have to say that Alaric's plan is a good one. It also keeps those of us—namely, me—who don't have much field experience from standing in the line of fire," added Maggie. "I'd rather not have the CDC call my parents to report that I've come storming their castle."

I nodded. "All right. Let's get out of here. Of course, if there's anyone who'd like to skip their all-expenses-paid ticket on the crazy train, you're welcome to stay here. At that point, your options are going back to the lab and trusting Dr. Abbey not to turn you into her private Frankenstein, or staying out here and praying that whatever comes to find you is in a killing mood, rather than an infecting one."

"Actually, Frankenstein was the doctor, not the monster," said Maggie. "Common misconception."

"Way to ruin the moment, Maggie." I walked over to the bike, picking up my helmet. "Everyone cool?"

"I still say this is a very poorly conceived idea," said Kelly. "I mean, maybe you'll get lucky. Maybe the CDC will let you walk out alive. But I wouldn't place bets on it."

"Maybe *you'll* get lucky and they'll let us leave," I corrected, gently. "Becks here may be the one voted most likely to point a gun at somebody's head just for kicks, but Maggie . . ."

"They'll never find the body," said Maggie. Her tone was blithely chipper, like she was talking about the latest fund-raiser for the Bulldog Rescue Association. That made it worse. "Not that anyone's going to be looking, since you're legally dead, but even if they looked for you, they'd never come close. All I'd need to do is call my father and tell him I finally had a problem he could fix. You could be the best Father's Day present I've ever given him. He's *so* hard to shop for."

Kelly's eyes widened, fear flickering in their depths. "Is she serious?"

"Almost certainly, but I wouldn't worry about it just yet," I said. "Come on, crew. Let's find us a hotel."

In the end, we wound up checking into the first hotel we found in downtown Portland, a nondescript little Holiday Inn whose front door boasted about their recent security upgrades. I was barely picking up any wireless frequencies, which meant "recent" was probably more like ten years ago, but that didn't matter. Their clearances were up-to-date, and the local review sites said that the rooms were generally clean. We didn't need five-star accommodations. We just needed a place to stash our semi-hostage and regroup without being attacked by zombies.

We got two rooms, one for the boys, one for the girls. If Alaric was uncomfortable about rooming with me—and hence with George— he didn't say anything about it. He just started hooking up his equipment and plugging things in to recharge, while Becks marched Maggie and Kelly into the room across the hall with all the tenderness of a drill sergeant. Maggie took the barked orders gracefully, while Kelly just looked unsettled. I found myself feeling sorry for her, even after everything. After all, I liked her before she told me what the reservoir conditions really meant. It wasn't like she designed the disease.

She's out of her element, said George.

"We all are," I muttered. Alaric glanced my way but didn't say anything. He just kept connecting cables, getting the mobile office of After the End Times up and online.

The message boards had been busy while we were off gallivanting around the Pacific Northwest, harassing mad scientists, and uncovering corruption in the CDC. I skimmed the comment feeds as I waited for my mail to finish downloading. The usual cadre of trolls, assholes, and conspiracy nuts were out in force, almost drowning out the more reserved forum participants. Mahir and the rest of the Newsies had them essentially under control. Technically I'm in charge of the site, but it can be easy to lose track of how big we really are these days. It used to be me, George, and Buffy. Now it's dozens of people, half of whom I've never met and probably never will.

Thank God for Mahir. Without him, we'd fall apart, becoming another fringe site clinging to the edges of extinction. He manages the marketing and merchandising that George used to handle, and somehow all the bills get paid. Even the ones relating to ammo supplies for the Irwins, which I know from experience can get pretty damn expensive.

"Anything on fire?" asked Alaric.

"Not as such, but that's okay. I'm sure tomorrow's field trip will supply us with plenty of matches." I put my laptop on the bedside table, stretching until I felt my shoulders pop. "For right now, I'm going to see about catching a little sleep before I go back to professionally risking my life. You have things under control on your end?"

"Yeah. I'm going to write up a few articles on medical ethics and the lack of high-level oversight; I figure Mahir should be up by the time I finish, and I want to check in with him before I crash." As the head of the Newsie division, Mahir was Alaric's direct superior and the one who actually approved his articles. They worked together well, which was a relief. I don't know how I would have dealt if they'd hated each other. Probably by punching the walls until the two of them settled down and said they'd play nicely.

You never did have any people skills, said George, tone managing to be dry and fond at the same time.

"You're one to talk," I mumbled, and closed my eyes, sinking into the too-soft hotel mattress. The sound of Alaric typing away was soothing, helping me relax even further. George and I shared a lot of rooms exactly like this one, one of us dozing while the other kept working, the staccato click of keys providing the white noise that meant it was safe to sleep.

Hush, chided George. *You need to get some rest. You're running yourself too hard.*

"I learned from the best." I sighed, letting out my breath in a deep, slow exhalation. Somewhere in the middle of breathing out, the world slipped away, and I slipped into sleep.

In my dreams that night, George had coppery eyes that she didn't need to hide behind her sunglasses, and we walked in the sunlight, and we didn't have to be afraid. Everything was perfect. Those are the worst dreams of all, because in the end, I can't stay asleep forever.

I woke to the sharp, sweetly metallic tang of gun oil. It had managed to perfume the entire room, overwhelming the less-intrusive smells of toast and greasy hotel turkey bacon. I scrubbed my eyes with the back of a hand, clearing the gunk away before sitting up and squinting at the figure perching on the end of the bed.

"I was starting to think you'd sleep until we got attacked again," commented a female voice. For a single, heart-stopping moment, it sounded like George—but the moment passed. Becks raised her eyebrows at my expression, asking, "You see something green, Mason? Or are you just pissed that I messed up your beauty sleep?"

"Some of us don't *need* beauty sleep, Atherton," I shot back, pushing myself into a sitting position and reaching for the room-service tray someone had kindly placed on the bedside table next to my laptop. "What's the status?"

"Alaric's in the other room keeping an eye on the princess while Maggie makes a grocery run and checks in with the staff at her house. She's worried they'll forget to feed the dogs if she doesn't remind them." Becks continued wiping a silicon cloth along her gunstock, removing the marks her fingers left behind. Her entire kit was open in front of her, explaining the scent of gun oil in the air.

"And the princess herself?" I started making a sandwich from fake bacon and dry toast. It didn't look all that appetizing, but I was hungry enough not to give a damn.

"Awake, anxious, the usual." Becks started packing up her kit. "She's a good kid, but she's also a liability. We should find a safe house and turn her into someone else's problem."

"She's a useful liability—and what do you mean 'kid'? She's the same age you are. We need her, at least for now."

"I wish I were as sure about that as you are."

"I thought you were the one who started out as a Newsie." I took a bite of my sandwich, swallowing before saying, "She knows things we don't know—and if worst comes to absolute worst, I bet she knows the layout of the Memphis CDC pretty darn well. Whoever tracked her to Oakland may not have thought to rekey the biometric sensors to take her retinal scans and fingerprints off the security locks yet. Everyone thinks she's dead, right? So why waste the money to do a rekey when they don't have to?"

Becks blinked before admitting, "I hadn't thought of that one."

"That's why I'm in charge." A drop of hot grease hit me below the collarbone. I hissed and wiped it away, realizing as I did that I'd managed to remove my shirt sometime during the night. This led to the unpleasant but suddenly important question of whether or not I was wearing pants. "Kelly has more to tell us, and she's *going* to tell us. We just have to give her time to realize that she doesn't have a choice."

"I don't like it."

"Never asked you to. Look, I'm pretty sure I don't trust Dr. Wynne, but I still have to admit that he's a damn good doctor, and she worked with him. Maybe she's not the most efficient data-delivery mechanism ever. She still risked a lot to come here and help us out. She's a dead woman walking. She's got nothing left to lose. That makes her a damn good ally."

"It also makes her a damn big suicide risk." Becks stood, taking her gun kit with her. "How long before you're ready to roll?"

"Give me twenty minutes to shower and clean up. We want the CDC to let us in, don't we?" I gave her my best camera-ready smile. Becks rolled her eyes, looking unimpressed, and stomped out of the room.

The door slammed behind her. I yanked the sheets off, relieved to see that I'd managed to keep my jeans on through the night. Accidentally flashing my female colleagues has never been one of my secret aspirations.

The hotel might be shabby, but it was good enough to have a full decontamination shower, with an attached clothing sterilization unit for people who didn't have sufficient gear for fieldwork. It was a nice touch that probably didn't get used too often. I stripped down and shoved my clothes into the sterilizer, hopping into the shower and triggering the bleach nozzle. The water came on at the same time, spraying me down with a heated combination of sterilizing chemicals, bleach-based antiseptics, and something that smelled like cheap lemon disinfectant. I squeezed my eyes tightly shut and started scrubbing.

The amount of bleach in the average shower is why blonde highlights have become so common. They're almost a badge of safety for some people—"See, I've been decontaminated so many times that my hair has lost all natural color." George always hated that. She re-dyed her hair at least twice a month, keeping it dark brown and snarling at anyone who said she was being girly. I always liked the way her hair dye smelled, caustic and sweet at the same time. A lot like George.

The shower finished running the decontamination cycle a few seconds after the clothing sterilizer beeped to signal that my clothes were once more safe to wear around other humans. I dried off, dressed, and stepped back out into the main room to find Alaric waiting for me in an eerie, unintentional imitation of Becks.

"Ready to go?" he asked.

"Ready to stay?" I countered.

To my surprise, he shook his head, and said, "No. Maggie and I were talking, and we want to take the van—and the Doc—back to the house while you're at the CDC."

"Why?" I asked, as I moved to shut down my laptop and start packing it to go.

"Maggie's starting to get twitchy about being away from home this long, and I'd rather not be in the city when you make your trip." Alaric shrugged. "Maybe I'm being paranoid, but if things go wrong, I don't want Dr. Connolly this close to a CDC installation."

"Afraid she'll run for cover? Pretty sure that ship has sailed."

"Afraid they'll come and take her away from us."

I froze in the act of zipping my laptop case. "Fuck. I didn't even think of that. You really think it's a risk, even after we torched her first ID?"

"It depends on whether she's here to play decoy and herd us into danger, or whether she really was sent because they're afraid someone's killing CDC researchers." Alaric shrugged. "Any institution large enough to have different departments is going to have infighting. I don't think she's here to stab us in the back, and that means she's in danger as long as she's in Portland—and we're in danger as long as we're here with her."

"Damn." I chuckled, shaking my head as I shoved the laptop case into my bag. "I bow before your logic. Yeah, take Maggie and the Doc and head for Maggie's place. Becks and I will meet you there after we finish up at the CDC, assuming they don't shoot us on sight. If we haven't checked in by five o'clock this afternoon . . . " I paused before finishing. "Run. Got it?"

"Got it." Alaric stood, picking up his own laptop as he did. "Kinda like old times, huh, boss?"

"What, walking into certain danger with eyes open, one hand on the recorder, and one hand on the gun?" I flashed him a quick smile. "Exactly like old times."

"I wish—" He faltered before finishing lamely, "Anyway, you and Becks be careful out there today, okay?"

I nodded. "Do my best. Drive safe."

"Will do."

Maggie, Becks, and Kelly were waiting in the hall. Becks cast a thin smile my way. "So you're good with the plan?"

"You guys don't have to conspire against me, you know," I said, shaking my head. "It's a good plan; I am good with the good plan. Maggie, I want you messaging Mahir every twenty miles until you get home, you hear me?"

"No problem," she said. Taking Kelly by the elbow, she said, "Come on. Let's get out of here before somebody gets hurt."

"Where's the fun in that?" asked Becks, and turned to lead the way down the hall and out of the hotel.

Watching the van drive off with Alaric at the wheel left me strangely numb, like somehow their departure meant I would never see them again, like this was some sort of an ending, rather than another step along the road to learning why George really died. I stood frozen in the parking lot, staring after them, a hard lump blocking my throat when I tried to swallow.

"Hey." Becks touched my elbow. I turned to face her. She raised her eyebrows. "Are you okay?"

I managed a small smile. "I'm always okay. You ready to go and piss off the CDC?"

"Why, Shaun," she said, flirting her eyelashes coquettishly, "I thought you'd never ask." She turned to head for the bike. After a moment's pause, I followed her.

The Portland CDC was located in its own facility, a large, meticulously clean collection of low, white-painted buildings that could easily have been repurposed as a hospital or maybe a medical college. From a distance, it looked friendly and inviting, the sort of place that would make a routine checkup almost enjoyable. That first impression didn't survive getting close enough to see barbed wire topping the fence that circled the entire installation, or the small yellow-and-black signs indicating that the fence itself was electrified. Pre-Rising, they would have used a low wattage and backed it up with guard dogs.

Post-Rising, well, let's just say they probably cranked things up to lethal levels at the slightest excuse.

Becks kept her arms looped around my waist as I pulled the bike up to the guard station. It was a small, featureless gunmetal booth that gave no indication whether it was occupied or automated. I held up our IDs, careful to keep both of my hands visible, and said, "Shaun Mason, After the End Times, and Rebecca Atherton, same."

"Please place your identification in the slot," said a mechanized voice. A slot hissed open in the side of the guard station, right next to the speaker. I dropped our ID cards into the slot, which hissed shut. "Please wait."

"Because I was totally planning to zoom off and leave you with our IDs," I muttered.

Shaun, said George warningly. Becks pinched me on the back of the neck.

"Your identification has been confirmed," announced the guard station. The slot opened again, allowing me to reclaim our cards as the first gate began sliding open. "Please proceed onward for blood testing and examination."

"How I love the CDC," I said, passing Becks her ID card and hitting the gas.

The procedure from there was exactly as the guard station threatened—sorry, "indicated." We reached a second gate about ten yards onto the campus, this one accompanied by men wearing Kevlar vests and clutching assault rifles. There were also blood testing units waiting there, one for each of us. We both passed our blood tests, robbing the sentries of the chance to use the weapons they clutched so carefully, and drove on to the third station, where the retinal scanners were waiting.

"I'd think this was excessive if I hadn't just been to Maggie's place," I muttered to Becks, who snorted with quiet laughter. I wasn't kidding, either; I wouldn't be surprised to learn that Maggie and the CDC get their security designs through the same firm. God knows her family has the money, and they've never been shy about spending a few extra bucks for the sake of a little bit more safety.

Finally, after running the security gamut, we were allowed to enter the CDC parking lot, where I parked in a space marked VISITOR in large yellow letters. Becks slid off, removing her helmet and producing a hairbrush from her pack while I was still getting the kickstand positioned. She began briskly brushing out her hair, making adjustments in accordance with some secret set of female rules that even George had never been willing to share with me.

"You look fine, especially for this sort of visit," I said, securing my own helmet to the handlebars. "Nobody's going to be looking at your hair."

Becks gave me a frosty look. "So says you," she said stiffly. "I've found that good hair can open many doors for the female investigative reporter. It certainly doesn't hurt my ratings when I take steps to avoid looking like I just rolled out of bed."

I had to admit she had a point: Becks paid more attention to her appearance than any other Irwin I knew, male or female, and her merchandise sales were even higher than mine. She wore her hair longer than was strictly safe for fieldwork, with blonde highlights and dark brown lowlights that made her otherwise medium-brown hair seem somehow exotic, especially in the sort of light conditions she was usually filming under. Combined with naturally green eyes and a fondness for wearing tight white tank tops, well, it wasn't a mystery why eighty percent of her viewers were male. It was more of a mystery that she seemed to want me to approve of it. I was never going to get that one.

Let her brush her hair so we can get moving, said George.

"Fine," I said, digging my equipment out of the bike's saddlebag more briskly than was strictly necessary.

"What?" asked Becks.

"Nothing."

"Right." She shoved the brush back into her bag. "There, all done."

"Really?" I lifted my eyebrows, giving her an appraising look. "You sure you don't need to touch up your makeup or something before we can go in?"

Becks flashed me a sunny smile that didn't come close to masking the sarcastic lilt in her voice as she said, "Nope. My mascara's designed to stay on for twenty-four hours in a heavy rainstorm under combat conditions. My eye shadow practically has to be removed with an acid wash, and this lipstick is so long-lasting that I haven't seen the natural color of my lips since I was fifteen. I'm totally ready."

"I'm sure the CDC will be thrilled to know that you made such an effort on its behalf," I said, and started down the path that was labeled ENTRANCE in more large yellow letters. At least these ones were on a sign, not painted onto the pavement. Becks made an entirely unladylike snorting noise, and followed me.

After all the security checks required to get to the parking lot, walking up to the front doors of the Portland CDC was almost anti-climactic. They were clear glass, making a point with their total lack of reinforcement—this was the CDC. If the infected made it this far in, the city was already lost, so why bother wasting money that could be put to better use elsewhere? These were *scientists*. They didn't feel the need to squander public funds on fripperies.

Those fripperies included furniture for their front lobby. A wave of comfortably chilly climate-controlled air hit us as we walked into the building, so devoid of character that it might as well have been an unused movie set. The floor was black marble, and the walls were white, except for the large steel sign proclaiming this to be the

Portland office of the Centers for Disease Control. "Got that part, thanks," I muttered, arrowing toward the one piece of furniture in the room: the sleekly futuristic reception desk.

The receptionist herself was also sleekly futuristic, possibly because she felt the need to live up to her workstation. Her hair was pulled into a bun so severe it looked almost molded, her jacket was impeccably cut, and the eyes behind her black-framed glasses were cold. "Names and business?" she asked as we approached. Her fingers never stopped darting across her keyboard, even as she glanced in our direction, looked us up and down, and dismissed us as unimportant.

"We're with the After the End Times news site, and we'd like to speak to the director of this installation," I said mildly, leaning against the edge of her desk as I flashed her my ID. Becks did the same, unsmiling. "Don't worry, we can wait if we have to."

The receptionist gave us another of those quick, cold, up-and-down glances before asking, "The nature of your business, sir?" The "sir" was grudging, purely a formality to check off some internal list marked "proper procedure."

"That's for us to discuss with the director," said Becks.

"I see." The receptionist sniffed. "If you'd like to make an appointment, I'm sure we can fit you in sometime this week. In the meanwhile—"

"Sometime this week? Really? That's *awesome*." I smacked the edge of the desk for emphasis as I straightened, and was only a little gratified to see the receptionist jump. "Okay, Becks, you start setting up the cameras, and I'm going to analyze the light levels in here, see where it's best for us to start shooting."

"Excuse me?" The receptionist half rose from her seat, revealing a pencil skirt as precisely tailored as the jacket. I found myself wondering if she starched her underpants to keep them from ruining her mood through excessive softness. "What are you doing?"

"Well, this is a government building, right?" I asked, guilelessly.

"Which means that we, as citizens, are totally entitled to be here whenever and whyever we want, as long as we're not actively disrupting normal business or committing acts of vandalism? No appointments required unless there's an active state of emergency?"

"Yes, but—"

"So we're going to be streaming live from the lobby here until we get in to see your director. Let the good citizens of Portland—and the world, did I mention we're a top-rated global news site? Right, I may have left that little tidbit off when we were making introductions—see what an awesome job the CDC does responding to visitors."

"I think we can set the cameras up right over there," said Becks, stabbing a finger at a random patch along the wall.

"You can't do that!" said the receptionist. She sounded agitated. Poor thing. She'd probably sprain herself if she tried for any real facial expressions with her hair pulled back that tightly. "I'm sorry, there was a little—this is all a misunderstanding, give me a moment and I'll get Director Swenson for you."

"Thanks," I said, flashing a wide grin in her direction. "It's cool, Becks, you can hold off on setting things up."

"Check," said Becks. She re-shouldered her pack. We watched as the increasingly anxious-looking receptionist picked up her phone, muttering into it with her palm cupped around the receiver, like that would magically keep us from hearing what she was saying. It worked, a little; most of her side of the conversation was too garbled to understand, although I was pretty sure I caught the words "crazy," "reporters," and "threatening to." As press went, it wasn't bad, and might actually give the director an idea of what he was about to be dealing with.

Nothing could ever prepare him for you, said George.

"Flatterer," I murmured. The receptionist shot me a wary look, hand still cupped around the receiver. I smiled at her. Brightly. She looked away again.

"Yes, sir; of course, sir," she said, and set the receiver back into its cradle, not looking in our direction as she said, "Director Swenson is on his way down and apologizes for any inconvenience that you may have experienced in being forced to wait so long."

"It's cool," I said.

The receptionist didn't say anything. She leaned slightly forward, shoulders hunched as she focused her attention on her computer. It was obvious that she couldn't entirely dismiss our presence as a bad dream—we were a little too solid for that—and it was equally obvious that she was giving it the old college try. I rocked back on my heels, content to let her ignore us. There's pushing the envelope of polite behavior to get what you want, and then there's just plain being mean. I try not to cross the line when it can be avoided.

We'd been waiting less than five minutes when the sound of crisp footsteps echoed through the lobby and an immaculately groomed man in a white lab coat stepped around a corner and into view. He was dressed like a generic midlevel bureaucrat at any corporation in the country, assuming you could overlook the lab coat: gray slacks that were probably some sort of insanely expensive natural fiber, white button-up shirt, sedate blue-and-green tie, and immaculately polished black shoes. Even his lab coat looked like it was tailored for him, rather than being the standard off-the-rack lab wear. If the CDC was running in the red this season, his wardrobe definitely wasn't feeling the pinch.

Neither was his plastic surgeon. His hair was thick and well-styled, but still uniformly silver, and his unwrinkled skin had the characteristic tightness of a man in his late fifties paying through the nose to maintain the illusion that he was a well-preserved thirty-seven or so. He walked to the receptionist's desk with the calm assurance of a man who knows himself to be in absolute control of his environment, extending a hand in my direction. "Shaun Mason, I presume?"

"The same." I took his hand and shook it. Even with all the training I've had to desensitize me to the necessity of occasional contact
with strangers, the gesture felt *wrong*. You aren't supposed to touch
people you don't know. Not unless they've just demonstrated their
infection status with a successful blood test, and maybe not even
then. "This is my colleague, Rebecca Atherton. She works with our
action news division."

"Ah, an Irwin," said the man, reclaiming his hand and turning to
study Rebecca. His gaze started at her face, swept down her body, and
returned to her face again, all without a trace of hesitation or shame.
"You know, I've always liked that term. Irwin, for the late, great
Steve Irwin. He died in the field, you know. Just the way he would
have wanted to go."

"No shit, asshole," muttered Becks.

"Actually, sir, I'm pretty sure the way he would have wanted to go
was in his sleep, sometime in his late nineties, but that's beside the
point." Something about him was putting my hackles up. Maybe it
was the way he looked at Becks. Maybe it was his tone, which was
slick enough to grease a rusty chainsaw. "I'm guessing you're
Director Swenson."

"Precisely so. I apologize for making you wait. Next time, please
be sure to call ahead. That will allow us to avoid these little delays."

Yeah, because we'll never get past security again.

I forced my expression to remain composed as I said, "I'll keep
that in mind. If you don't mind, though, my colleague and I were in
the area and had some questions we wanted to ask you—in person,
hence the dropping by. Is there a place where we could talk?"

A flash of discomfort crossed his face, there and gone before I
could blink. "Of course," he said, smoothly. "If you'd both come with
me, I believe one of the conference rooms is available. Miss Lassen,
as you were."

The receptionist—Miss Lassen—nodded, looking deeply relieved as Director Swenson turned and began retracing his steps, leaving the front lobby behind. She might not have been able to keep us out, but at least we weren't going to be her problem anymore. Becks and I exchanged a look, shrugged, and followed the director to the back of the lobby, around a corner, and into a nondescript hall that seemed to stretch on for the better part of a mile.

Director Swenson walked past three identical doors before stopping at a fourth and pressing his thumb against a small sensor pad. The light above the door changed from red to green, and the door swung open. "Past this point, you'll need blood tests as well as someone with the proper clearances to open any doors, including the restrooms," he said, sounding self-indulgently amused. "I recommend not wandering off unescorted."

"I'll keep that in mind if I need to pee," muttered Becks. I gave her a speculative look, which she met with a glare.

Funny, normally you're the one pissing off the natives, said George.

I bit my lip to keep myself from answering as we followed Director Swenson through the door and into one of the long, featureless white hallways characteristic of CDC installations everywhere. It's like they're afraid to spend money on interior decorating when there's such a good chance of the place needing to be hosed down with bleach at any moment. We didn't pass any doctors, although we did walk past several large glass "windows" looking in on empty patient rooms. White walls, white beds, white floors— white everything. I woke up in one of those rooms once, after the CDC team picked us up outside of Memphis. I thought I'd died and gone to the sterilized afterlife.

Director Swenson stopped in front of a door that looked exactly like every other door in the place, except for the larger, more elaborate-looking testing unit built into the wall next to it. "The cycle takes approximately fifteen seconds," he said, pressing his palm flat against the test pad. "Once I go through, the door will close and the unit will reset. Please don't try to follow without a clean test. I'd really rather not send the entire facility into lockdown today."

"It's cool," I said. "We know how to do our jobs."

The light over the door turned green and the door swung open with a hydraulic hiss, saving Director Swenson the trouble of answering me. Instead, he raised an eyebrow and stepped through the doorway before the door swung closed again.

"Scale of one to ten, how stupid is this?" asked Becks, pressing her own palm against the testing panel.

Ten, said George.

"Oh, five, tops," I said, and smiled brightly. "Don't worry about it. We're just here to ask the scientists some questions about science. Scientists like that sort of shit."

"Right," said Becks dubiously as the light turned green and the door hissed open again. She stepped through.

"Hey, George," I muttered, flattening my hand against the testing panel. "Check this out."

When does telling the truth become an act of terrorism? At what point does a lie become an act of mercy? Is it cruel to tell a parent their child will die, even if it's true? Is it kind to tell an accident victim they're going to recover, even though all evidence says they won't? Where's the line dividing honesty from harm, deceit from decency, and misinformation from malice? I don't know. All the clever wordplay in the world won't somehow grant me that knowledge. I'm sorry. I wish it would.

This is what I do know: A lie, however well-intended, can't prepare you for reality or change the world. The accident victim will die whether they're promised recovery or not, but the parent told that their child is dying may have time to prepare, and may be able to treasure those final days together even more. To tell the truth is to provide armament against a world too full of cruelties to be defeated with simple falsehoods. If these truths mean the world is less comforting than it might have been, it seems like a pretty small price to pay.

It seems to me we owe the world—more, we owe ourselves—the exchange of comfort for the chance that maybe the truth can do what people always say it can. The truth may, given the opportunity, set us free.

—From *The Kwong Way of Things*, the blog of Alaric Kwong,
April 16, 2041

We had another meeting with the senator today. We're about to head out, and he wants to be sure that we all understand our roles in the campaign. I don't think he trusts us to have our heads in the game right now, and frankly, neither do I. Shaun is barely talking to anyone, including me, and Buffy simply isn't talking. I keep running the footage of the attacks so far over and over again, looking for something that we might have missed, looking for some clue to who is responsible for all of this.

When I sent in the application for this position, I thought I was doing us a favor. I thought I was giving us the opportunity to make a name for ourselves, and that we could change the world by telling the truth. I thought I was doing the right thing. But now I watch Shaun punching the walls, and I wake up as tired as I was when I went to bed, and I just wish that I could take it back. I wish I could take it all back. I'm tired, and I want to go home.

But oh, God, I'm so afraid that we're not all going to make it home alive.

—From *Postcards from the Wall*, the unpublished files of Georgia Mason, originally posted April 18, 2041

Thirteen

The CDC conference room lived up to the design aesthetic I was coming to expect from them: white on white on white. It was like they'd looked at the uniforms American nurses wore during World War II and said "Yeah, that's what we're talking about." Maybe they bleached the place on such a regular basis that they didn't want to deal with paying to have all the furnishings re-dyed. Whatever the motivation, the combination of white walls and white carpet with a glass-topped conference table and white faux-leather chairs was enough to make me feel grubby and unwashed. CDC employees probably took a lot of showers, just to keep themselves from feeling like they were too dirty to be allowed to touch the furniture.

Director Swenson walked the full length of the conference table to sit at the head. Alpha male posturing if I'd ever seen it. The gesture was designed to say "This is mine and I am in charge here"—I was sort of surprised he didn't lift his leg and piss on something. Urine's a natural bleaching agent, right? It would explain how they kept everything so damn white.

Becks and I trailed along behind him like good little peons, finally sitting down next to each other on the left-hand side of the table.

Becks took the seat closer to the director. Sure, I was technically in charge of our little fact-finding expedition, but of the two of us, I was the one more likely to launch myself for his throat, and we wanted to avoid that if at all possible. Attacking high-ranking CDC officials isn't really the best way to get what you want.

"Now, then," said the director, gracing us with a fatherly smile as warm as it was artificial. "What can I do for the two of you? I'll admit, I was a bit surprised that you didn't phone ahead. That's standard for most representatives of the media."

"Yeah, we're really sorry about that," I said, not bothering to inject the slightest note of apology into my tone. "See, we'd usually call ahead, only I managed to leave my address book—where did I leave that again, Becks?"

"In your office," said Becks promptly. She knows her cues. With as long as we've been working together, she'd better.

"Right, in my office." I bared my teeth at Director Swenson in an approximation of his smile. The corners of his mouth twitched downward, confusion flickering in his eyes. That was good. I wanted him off balance. "That's sort of the problem, since my office is—my office *was*, I guess—in Oakland, basically right at the center of the zone that got firebombed. We were out camping when the quarantine came down, but not all my people made it out."

"I see." Director Swenson leaned back in his chair, expression smoothing into careful neutrality. The confusion in his eyes faded, replaced by wariness. "You're very fortunate. That outbreak was particularly bad."

"Yeah, how *did* that happen as fast as it did? Isn't the CDC supposed to prevent things like that?" asked Becks. I shot her a sharp look. She ignored me, attention focused on Director Swenson like a sniper focuses on a target.

She had friends inside the blast zone, said George. *Not just Dave. Civilian friends.*

It was all I could do not to wince. I'd been withdrawn since George died, which meant I never really bothered getting to know the neighbors in our bucolic little part of Oakland. Becks was a hell of a lot more gregarious. She probably knew everyone on our block, not just in our building, and could recite the names of the deceased without cross-referencing the Wall. And now we knew, beyond a shadow of a doubt, that the CDC was involved in something nasty. Put it all together, and I'd basically primed her to go off. The question was whether being stuck in the blast radius was going to be a good thing or a bad thing.

"It appears that someone in the area had been illegally breeding American pit bull terriers for use in dogfights," said Director Swenson, smoothly as you please. "From what we've been able to reconstruct, one of the dogs became infected and attacked the others. The pack attacked their handler when he came to see what all the noise was about. The dogs were able to escape, and those large enough to amplify went on to infect individuals all around the area. It became too large to contain shortly after."

It was a textbook example of a no-win infection scenario. That was the problem. Textbook examples almost never happen in the real world. I saw Becks opening her mouth, probably to say just that. I clamped my hand down on her thigh under the table, squeezing hard. The pressure was enough to cut her off. She shot me a confused look. I tried to look like I was ignoring her, and cleared my throat.

"Would've still been nice if you'd sent, I don't know, a rescue helicopter or something for folks inside the blast radius, but that's beside the point," I said smoothly, keeping my hand clamped on Becks's thigh. "Anyway, I'm sure you understand why we couldn't call ahead, having lost your number in the explosion and all."

The explosion didn't wipe the CDC's phone number off the Internet, but that didn't really matter; my excuse was plausible enough that Director Swenson couldn't get away with calling me a liar, and artificial enough that we both knew I was lying. His nostrils flared slightly from the strain of keeping his expression neutral. I smiled.

"Yes, absolutely," said Director Swenson. "Now, to what do we owe the honor of this visit?"

"To get a little background, make sure we're on the same page and everything, you remember my sister, Georgia Carolyn Mason?" Becks winced at the sound of George's name, probably thinking of my recent tendency to fly off the handle whenever George came up in conversation. In the back of my head, George snorted with brief amusement but didn't say anything. This was my party. She was going to let me be the one to send out the invitations.

Director Swenson nodded. "I've seen her file. Her death was—any death is tragic, but what she accomplished, even after the point of initial amplification, was—it was amazing. You must be very proud."

"She died in the field," I said, as flatly as I could. "Just the way she would have wanted to go."

"I'm sure that must be a great comfort to you." He sounded like he meant it, too. My hand clenched tighter on Becks's thigh. It took every inch of self-control I had to peel my fingers away. She didn't make a sound, even though the way I was squeezing must have hurt.

"To be honest, I'd rather have her alive and pissed off than dead and happy," I said, putting my hands flat on the table before I could grab hold of Becks again. "If you've seen her file, you must know she suffered from retinal Kellis-Amberlee."

"Yes, I saw that. It's amazing that she accomplished so much, given her disability."

I somehow managed to smile at him. I may never know how I did that. "She did a lot with her life, it's true. Now I've got to soldier on and take care of the things she wasn't able to finish."

"Oh?" Director Swenson gave me an attentive look. "What was she working on?"

"Reservoir conditions. See, she knew a lot of people through her support groups and mailing lists—"

Support groups? asked George, sounding horrified. *I never joined a support group in my life.*

I ignored her. "—and she started noticing this crazy pattern." Was it my imagination, or was Director Swenson going still? "It was like her friends died faster than anybody else's. I mean, even faster than *my* friends, and most of my friends are Irwins, which is sort of like waving a big red flag in the face of Darwinism. So she started to dig."

"Funny, I don't remember seeing any received queries in her file," said Director Swenson. His voice had gone completely blank, neither excited nor cold. The voice of a man in the process of disconnecting.

"She didn't query the CDC," said Becks, before I could open my mouth. I decided to let her take the conversation and run. Her training was better for this bluff than mine was. "She figured that if there wasn't a pattern, she didn't want to bother you, and if there was . . . " She let the sentence trail off before lifting her shoulders in a "What are you going to do?" shrug, and said, "It was a pretty big scoop. If the reservoir conditions were that dangerous, and somebody was going to break the story, why couldn't it be her?"

"I suppose her notes were lost along with your address book," said Director Swenson, looking at me.

"Oh, no, not at all," I replied. "I've been studying them, actually. I mean, they're a little outside my reading level, but hey, what's life without learning? She's right, too. The death rate is, like, crazy. Some of these people, statistically, should have lived to see their great-grandkids. Which means either the overall mortality rates for the country need to be recalculated, because we're calibrating something really, really wrong, or folks with reservoir conditions are dying at a *really* accelerated rate." I gave him my best big-dumb-Irwin face, and asked, "Which do you think it is?"

"Well, now that you bring it up, there is some documentation to support your sister's conclusions. I only wish she'd brought them to us before she died. It would have been a real pleasure working with her." Director Swenson stood, motioning for Becks and me to stay where we were. "If you two will excuse me for just a moment, I'll go and get the files that relate to this particular issue. I think you'll find them very enlightening."

"We'll chill here," I said, offering him a half-salute. Director Swenson mustered a wan smile and turned, walking quickly out of the conference room. He shut the door as he exited. Probably another of those crazy CDC security precautions . . . or he wanted us to think so, anyway.

Relaxing in my chair, I pulled out my phone and fiddled with it, saying carelessly, "It's cool that he's going to share his research, huh?" as I texted Becks with *He's up to something. Watch yourself.*

Becks didn't look even slightly surprised when her phone started buzzing. Unclipping it from her belt, she read the screen and started to key in a reply as she said, "I told you the CDC was the place to go with this. They're going to have files on anything and everything she could have found on her own, if she just hadn't been so damn stubborn." *You think? That man couldn't have rushed out of here faster if you'd been spurring him on with an electric prod. He's not happy that we're here, and he's really* not happy *about this line of discussion.*

"You know George. Stubborn to the end." *At least this confirms that it's more than just Memphis. Did you keep track of escape routes on the way in?*

"It was her best quality." *There really aren't any, other than the way we came. These buildings are designed as giant kill chutes. If there's an outbreak, staff is supposed to hole up and stay where they are until help shows up.*

"You can say that again." *Isn't that fucking* awesome. While Becks keyed in her response, I dipped a hand into my pocket and withdrew one of our increasingly limited supply of Buffy-built bugs. You can buy listening devices from sources both legal and extralegal all over the world, and mail order makes it possible to make those purchases essentially untraceable. None of them hold a candle to Buffy's work.

Hey, you're the one who thought coming here was a good idea. I was following your lead. Do we want to scout while we wait for him to come back and get us?

I can't imagine it would be a worse idea than coming here in the first place. I snapped the bug onto the bottom of the table, flattening its edges until they were flush to the frame. The CDC would need to be looking real hard to stand even a chance of finding it.

Got it. Becks glanced up from her phone, asking, "You think Director Swenson is going to be back soon? I need to tinkle, and he didn't show us where the bathrooms were."

I bit my lip to keep from laughing out loud. Everything gets funnier when you're waiting to find out whether you're in mortal danger, and Becks saying "tinkle" would have been hysterical under the best of conditions. This was, after all, a woman who once pissed off the side of a moving RV while fleeing from a mob of hungry zombies. On camera, no less. We got a lot of downloads that day, even with the modesty filters in place. "Well, last time we went to a CDC office, they were—hell with it, he won't mind if I show you, and it'll be faster this way." I stood, sliding my phone back into my pocket.

"Thanks, Shaun." Becks followed me. She was doing her best to look embarrassed, and she was doing a decent job. I would have believed it if I'd been watching the scene through a security feed, and if I hadn't known her so well. "It'll only take me a minute."

"It's cool. Keeps me from getting twitchy while we wait." I hesitated, looking at the door. Something about it was wrong in a way that was so weird that I couldn't figure out what it was. It was like waking up one morning to find that my hair had changed color—impossible, and hence invisible, at least for a little while.

Look at the light, advised George.

The light above the door—the light that should have been green, signaling that the standard security features were active, and that the door would open after a successful blood test had been run—was glowing a strong and steady yellow. I nodded toward it, watching as Becks followed the direction of the gesture. She went pale. A green light means everything is good, all systems go. A red light means a lockdown: Either there's live viral material in the room with you or there's live viral material right *outside* the room, where you don't want to go. Either way, if you sit tight, the problem will resolve itself. A yellow light ... I wasn't sure what a yellow light could possibly mean, beyond the chilling "this door has not been properly locked."

Ignoring the testing panel waiting for my palm, I reached out and gently grasped the doorknob. Nothing shocked or stung me. The light didn't change. I gave a gentle tug. The door swung just as gently inward. There was no hydraulic hiss; the hydraulics were not engaged.

"I don't think there's a place anywhere on this planet where that's a good thing," said Becks, reaching under her jacket to rest her hand against the grip of her pistol. "Suggestions?"

"I suggest we go and find Director Swenson, let him know that he's having some kind of security problem—and I don't mean two reporters loose in his building. You're going to have to wait for that tinkle."

"I can hold it," said Becks gravely.

"Good."

We left the white-on-white confines of the conference room for the white-on-white of the hall we'd come in through. There was no one in sight in either direction, making it seem like we might be the last two people on Earth.

Something isn't right here, said George.

"Got that right," I muttered, drawing my own pistol and releasing the safety. Becks was looking at me intently, waiting for me to clarify whether I was talking to George or to her. I gestured down the hall in the direction we'd come from. "I think I can get us out if we go this way. But I'll bet you a dollar our good director went the other way."

"Then that's the way we're going," said Becks, turning to scan the hall ahead of us. "Looks clear from here."

"I think that's the problem." I started walking, keeping my pistol at a low, defensive angle. Technically, it's legal for me to be armed anywhere I want to be, since I've passed my tests and I keep my licenses up-to-date at all times. Less technically, I'm not sure it's a good idea for anyone, be he blogger, God, or the president of the United States, to go around waving a gun in a government building. It tends to give them the crazy idea that you might shoot, and things tend to get real unpleasant real fast after that happens.

The not-rightness of the situation became more and more apparent as we walked. We passed labs, break rooms, and more of the one-way windows into rooms intended for patient care. We passed bulletin boards, signs, and even the bathrooms. What we *didn't* pass was anyone who demanded to see our IDs and asked what we were doing wandering around the building un-escorted. Near as I could tell, the Portland CDC had been quietly and effectively deserted. All we needed was a creepy minor-key soundtrack to reinforce the idea that this was a bad situation. George waited silently inside my head, not making any comments that might distract me. That was good. I was already jumpy enough.

"We should be catching up to the director soon, assuming he hasn't taken a turn we missed," I said. "If he has, we better hope there's an emergency exit somewhere in this place."

"Pessimism doesn't become you."

"But I'm so *good* at it." We kept walking, Becks trailing about three feet behind me and turning every few steps to sweep the corridor. If anything came lunging after us, she'd have time to gun it down before it caught up. "Hey, did you ever see those fucked-up first-person shooter games that were so big before the Rising? The ones with the zombies chasing you through government buildings and creepy old houses and shit?"

"Shut up, Shaun."

"That's what this feels like. One big maze, and we're the rats unlucky enough to be in it." A reassuring exit sign marked one of the doors ahead, and the light above it was a steady, reassuring green. I started to think that maybe there was an innocent explanation for all this, like a broken circuit somewhere that had required a quick, quiet evacuation of the unsecured areas. The director might have been intending to come back for us.

Yeah, and pigs might fly. I slapped my hand down on the test panel as soon as it came into reach. The metal was cool and nonresponsive. No needles appeared to sample my blood, no anesthetics sprayed to numb the nonexistent sting. The light over the door stayed green. "Fuck."

"What?" Becks stepped closer, still scanning the halls around us for signs of movement. "What's it doing?"

"Nothing." I took my hand off the panel. The light over the door went out. A moment later, so did the lights in the hall, plunging us into total darkness.

Fuck, said George.

"Yeah, tell me about it," I muttered, trying the door handle. It was unsurprisingly locked. It didn't deliver an electric shock or shoot a sedative needle into my palm—both standard defensive measures for a sealed door in a government compound—but that was all I could say in the positive. I pulled my hand away and started rummaging through my pockets for a flashlight. "We could really use your eyes about now. Done being dead yet?"

Sorry, no.

"Shaun?" An amber light clicked on to my left as Becks produced the field light from her backpack and held it up between us. She still had her pistol in her other hand. That was probably a good idea. "I hate to interrupt, but can you maybe focus on the living for a little bit? I'd like to keep breathing long enough to get mad at you for this shitty idea."

"You went along with it." My fingertips grazed the hard metal base of my portable flashlight. I pulled it out and clicked it on, aiming it for the floor. The amber field light was night-vision friendly, but we'd need the extra illumination at floor level if we didn't want to risk tripping over something in the dark.

"I never said I was the smart one. Thoughts?"

"These places are designed as kill chutes—they're supposed to herd you deeper, so the infected can be picked off easily and the uninfected will stand a chance in hell at getting themselves to safety." I gestured back toward the conference room with my pistol, keeping my flashlight pointed down. "We walk this way and hope we trip over a maintenance guy."

"And if we don't?"

"Then we hope we trip over an exit."

"This plan sucks."

"I know."

We started back down the hall, me leading, Becks so close behind that her shoulders brushed mine every time she turned to do another sweep behind us. George had gone silent again. That was good; that let me narrow my focus until there was nothing that mattered but the sound of our slow progress. Field training involves learning how to step lightly and breathe slowly, so as to reduce your auditory impact on the environment. Viral amplification doesn't give zombies superpowers, but it makes them really focused. Consequentially, they're occasionally capable of feats of tracking that seem to border on the unnatural. They're not. They're just incredibly good at homing in on the little things. The little things are what get people killed.

We hit the first corner. I spun around it, raising my flashlight to light up the entire hallway ahead. What it cost us in night vision was more than balanced by its effectiveness as a defensive weapon: The retinal condition that kept George behind prescription sunglasses for most of her life is universal among the infected. They can adjust to going out during the day, but they always prefer to stay in the dark when possible, and having a flashlight shine directly into their eyes is never fun.

An empty hall greeted my sweep. I lowered the flashlight. "Clear," I said, and we walked on, following the gently herding design of the CDC building. We were walking into a kill chute. Sadly, it was the smartest thing we could do. Going the other way would just take us farther from any help that might be waiting for us—assuming there was any help to be had.

We repeated the same procedure at the next three corners we reached. Each time, I spun around to blind any lurking infected with my flashlight, while Becks watched my back and got ready to start shooting. Each time, the light revealed nothing but featureless, utterly empty hallway. The white walls glimmered like ghosts through the dimness as we walked. My skin crawled, claustrophobia and paranoia beginning to speed my heart rate. Not enough to put me in danger of panic, but enough that I could feel it rising. From the way Becks's breath was starting to hitch—just a little, every third inhale—she was in a similar state. It's not the action that kills you. It's the *waiting*.

At the very next corner, the waiting ended.

It started out like the turns before it: Becks braced to shoot, while I stepped around the corner and swept my flashlight over the hall. Only this time, the hall in front of us extended for only about five feet before splitting into a T-junction ... and this time, something up ahead and to the left responded to the light with a moan. It was still out of sight around the turn, but that didn't matter; once you've heard the moaning of the infected, you never forget it. It's the sort of sound that hardwires itself into your primitive monkey brain, and the message it sends is simple: run.

I took a hasty step backward, keeping my flashlight pointed in the direction of the moan. It wouldn't ward off the infected—nothing stops a hungry zombie once it has an idea of where a free lunch can be found—but the pain would slow them down. "Becks?"

"Yeah?"

"Is the other direction clear?"

"I think so."

"Good. Becks?"

"Yeah?"

"Run."

There was no grace or artistry in our flight. Becks was running almost before the word was out of my mouth, waiting only for the confirmation that I didn't have a better idea, and I was only half a heartbeat behind. We ran as fast as we could, our footfalls echoing off the walls around us and making it impossible to tell whether we were running for safety or into the arms of another mob. The moaning started behind us, distant at first, but growing louder with bone-chilling speed. That's one thing the old movies got wrong. Real zombies—especially the freshly infected kind—can *run*.

Call for help!

"What?" I gasped, still running. Becks shot me a look. I shook my head, and she returned her attention to the serious business of running for her goddamn life.

You have a phone! Think, *Shaun!*

It was hard to focus on running and think about what George was trying to tell me at the same time. She was always the smart one, and that's held true even now that she's nothing but a ghost in my machine. I struggled to make sense of her words, and nearly stumbled as it hit me.

"Oh, mother*fuck*," I said, causing Becks to shoot me another sharp look. "Becks, I need you to buy us some time. Don't worry about the interest rates."

"Got it," she said, obedience winning out over confusion. She turned to face the direction of the moaning, still pacing me down the hall. If she tripped, it was all over, but that didn't seem to bother her. Her hands were steady as she pulled a ball-shaped object from her belt. The motion was followed by the distinctive sound of a pin being pulled, and then she flung the grenade in the direction of the moaning. She whipped around as soon as she let go, grabbing me by the arm. It was her turn to haul me down the hall, and she did it with admirable force. "*Run!*"

I ran.

The grenade Becks had thrown exploded about six seconds later. It wasn't a big enough boom to come with a back draft but it was big enough to fill the hall briefly with light. I risked a glance back over my shoulder. The walls were burning. That should be enough to slow the infected for at least a little while. "Cover me," I said.

Becks nodded, slowing enough to let me pull a few feet in front of her before speeding up again, holding a position about a foot and a half behind me. I felt like a total shit putting her between me and the danger we knew, but I needed the breathing space. It might be the one thing that could save us.

Fumbling an ear cuff from my jacket pocket without dropping my flashlight wasn't easy, especially not at a dead run. Somehow, I managed. I slammed the ear cuff into place, pressing the Call button as I snapped, "Secure connection, command line 'Hi, honey, I'm home,' open channel to Alaric Kwong."

The ear cuff beeped. For a long, undying moment, the only sounds were footsteps, harsh, exhausted breathing, the distant moans of the infected, and the overstrained beating of my heart. We couldn't run forever. Eventually, the kill chute was going to close, and if we were in the wrong place when that happened . . .

The ear cuff beeped again as Alaric came on the line: "Secure connection confirmed, please verify your identity before I hang up on you."

"Fuck you, Alaric, I don't have the *time* to remember some stupid code word." That was a lie: "some stupid code word" was the current call sign. If the CDC was recording, which they probably were, this might make them think our security wasn't as good as it really was. I could hope, anyway. "We're in a little bit of trouble here. Is the Doc there?"

"Shaun? Why are you breathing like that? What's—"

"I need you to put the Doc on the line *right fucking now*, Alaric, or you're getting a goddamn field promotion! Am I making myself clear, here, or do I need to get footage of the zombies trying to eat our asses?"

"I'll get her," said Alaric. The line beeped again, going silent.

Becks pulled up almost even with me. Sweat was adding that new-penny shine to her cheeks. "What are you *doing*?"

"CDC installs are all built on the same basic floor plan, right?" Another T-junction came into view ahead of us, my flashlight barely illuminating it enough to give us warning before we hit the wall.

"Right, but—"

"Doc gets us out or we're dead, Becks." The moaning from behind us was still getting louder, and that wall was getting closer. "Keep running!"

The ear cuff beeped, and Kelly's hesitant voice took the place of the silence, asking, "Shaun? Is that really you?"

"In a pickle, Doc! Zombies are chasing us through the Portland CDC, and we need out before we're on the menu! There's a T ahead of us—which way do we go?"

I had to give Kelly this: She recovered damn fast to what must have seemed like a totally random question. "Have you already passed a T-junction?"

"Yes! We went right!"

"You went—damn. Okay. At the T ahead, take the left, and try the third door you pass. Is the place in lockdown yet?"

"Do you mean 'Are the lights all fucking out, and did half the doors go amber before the power failed'? Because then yeah, we're in lockdown!" I grabbed Becks by the wrist, hauling her along as I veered left. "What kind of door?"

"Same size as the rest, but it should open when you push it."

One door flashed by on our right, followed about six feet later by a second door, this one on the left. I slowed to keep from overshooting the third door and grabbed for the knob, all too aware of the advantage I was throwing to our opponents if Kelly was wrong. The zombies weren't going to slow down just to keep the playing field even.

The knob turned without any resistance and the door swung inward, nearly spilling me—and by extension, Becks—into a pantry-sized room with glowing amber tubes running all along the edges of the ceiling, like supersized versions of the portable field light. I recovered my balance and stumbled fully into the room, thrusting Becks behind me before slamming the door shut. There were three old-fashioned deadbolts on the inside, the kind of things that can never go down, not even in a power failure. I slid all three of them into the closed and locked position before I'd even finished processing the impulse to do it.

"Shaun?" Kelly's voice was strident enough to make me wince. "Where are you? Are you okay?"

"We're in some sort of weird closet." I backed away from the door, keeping my pistol trained just above the knob. If the infected started trying to batter their way inside, I'd make them pay for every inch they gained.

"Are the lights red, yellow, or green?"

"Yellow." It was close enough to the truth, and closer than either of the other options.

Kelly sighed in obvious relief. "That means the security system is engaged, but you're not in one of the sections already locked down. The door is soundproof, scent-proof, and splatter-proof, so as long as everyone inside is clean, you should be okay."

"As long as we don't mind dying like rats in a cage, you mean. How do we get *out* of here, Doc?"

"There should be a door directly opposite the one you came in through."

The wall was blank and featureless. "No door."

"Touch the wall."

"What?"

"Just do it."

If Kelly was trying to kill us, she wouldn't have given us a bolt hole. I nodded toward the far wall, saying, "Doc wants us to touch it."

"Touch it?"

"Yeah."

"Anything's better than going back out there." On this philo-sophical note, Becks slapped her left palm flat against the wall—which immediately wavered and turned translucent, revealing a second wall behind it. There was a door at the center, twin to the one we'd entered through.

Becks yanked her hand away, swearing loudly. In my ear, Kelly said, "I hear shouting. Do you see the real wall now?"

"You could've warned us!" The newly revealed wall included three testing panels, all with reassuringly green lights shining next to them.

"I wasn't sure it would be there," said Kelly. Her tone was sincere; either she really meant it, or she was a much better actress than she'd been letting on. "Put your hands against the test panels. You're going to need to check out as clean if you want the glass to lift. If you're not . . ."

If we weren't, we'd never get out of this room. "Are you sure the tests will work?"

"It's a secondary system. It doesn't run off the main grid. If the screen was still in place and the interior lights are on, it should work."

"I'm trusting you on this one, Doc. Don't fuck us." I holstered my pistol and walked over to join Becks at the wall, slapping my hand against one of the testing units. She lifted her eyebrows. I nodded to her, and she mimicked the motion. From her grimace, the needles bit into both of us at the same time. These tests were built for crude effectiveness, not reassurance. They didn't waste time with any of the niceties like stinging foam or pre-test hand sterilizer—or full-sized needles. The feeling of the test engaging was like brushing my palm across the surface of a cactus, all tiny pinprick stings that didn't hurt because they didn't last long enough to totally register. They just itched like a sonofabitch.

"Step away from the testing center," intoned a pleasant female voice.

Becks and I exchanged a look as we took a long step backward. "Doc, the room's talking," I reported.

"That's normal," she said. Somehow I didn't find that particularly reassuring.

The lights next to the two units we'd used began to flash through the familiar red-green pattern as the units themselves filtered our blood looking for live viral bodies. There was still no sound from the hall outside, which wasn't helping. Sure, we knew that we weren't going to be eaten in the next thirty seconds, but the entire infected staff of the Portland CDC could be out there, and we'd have no idea. Not the sort of thing I really wanted to be thinking about.

Breathe, said George.

I took a deep breath as the lights next to the testing units turned a uniform, steady shade of green. "Thank you," said the female voice.

"You may proceed." The glass slid to one side, vanishing into a groove in the far wall.

"This is your fucking fault, Mason," growled Becks, starting for the now-accessible door.

"How are you coming to that conclusion?"

"You're the one who said this was like a pre-Rising video game."

I had to bite my lip to keep from laughing. I didn't really want to give Kelly any reason to doubt our infection status—not when I still needed her to guide us to safety. "Okay, Doc, the clear wall's open now. There's a door. What do you want us to do?"

"Listen closely: You're in one of the secondary escape corridors. They're designed to get essential staff out if at all possible, even during an outbreak. They aren't public, and they're never used for the transport of biological materials, just evacuations. Do you understand what I'm trying to say?"

My skin crawled. "They're set to autosterilize if there's any sign of contamination, aren't they?"

"Yes, they are. My suggestion?" Kelly paused before finishing, grimly, "Go as fast as you possibly can. Follow the yellow lights. They'll lead you to an exit. As long as your infection status hasn't changed, it'll let you out."

"And if it has?"

"If anyone in the escape corridor goes into conversion, the autosterilize initiates."

"Fuckin' swell. Okay. Tell Alaric I'll call back if we're not dead." I cut the connection over her protests, yanking the ear cuff off and shoving it into my pocket as I turned to Becks. "We're pulling a last run. Once this door is open, you haul ass, and if the lava comes down while we're inside, it was nice knowing you."

"Got it," said Becks, with a small, tight nod. It wouldn't actually be lava. It would be a highly acidic chemical bath, followed by flash irradiation, followed by another chemical bath, until everything organic in the corridor had been reduced to so much inert slime. That sort of thing can't really happen in places where humans are expected to be on a regular basis, since it tends to render the environment permanently toxic, but for a rarely used, last-ditch exit, it made perfect, if horrible, sense.

I hesitated, and then offered her my hand. "It was nice knowing you, Rebecca," I said.

"The same, Shaun. Believe me, the same." She laced her fingers into mine and smiled wistfully. "Maybe when we get out of this alive, you and me can go for coffee or something."

"Sure," I said. She didn't let go of my hand, and I didn't pull away. Leaving our fingers tangled together like computer cables, I reached for the second door and pulled it open. An amber light clicked on across from us. Becks and I exchanged one final look before stepping through the doorway, into the relative darkness on the other side.

The door swung shut as soon as we were through, hydraulics engaging with a loud hiss that was almost reassuring. It meant all systems were go; even if those systems got us dissolved, they'd be doing so while fully operational. Another amber light clicked on to the left of the first one, and another, and another, until a line of tiny glittering beacons led the way deeper into the dark.

There was no other way to go, and Kelly's instructions said to follow the light. We'd trusted her this far. The worst that trusting her the rest of the way could get us was dead. "Come on," I said. We started in the direction indicated by the lights, moving as fast as we dared.

Distances always seem longer in the dark. The greater the darkness, the longer the distance. The amber lights were meant to guide us, not show us where we were going, and even my flashlight wasn't enough to beat back the shadows. We probably traveled no more than a few hundred yards, but it felt like ten or twelve times that.

Our breath was impossibly loud in the confines of the tunnel, and my toes kept catching on the floor, which wasn't completely level. After the third time I almost tripped, I realized we were running across the floor of an enormous shower, complete with drains every ten feet. They'd be essential if the CDC ever needed to sluice the place down—say, after melting a few unwanted guests. I sped up, pulling Becks along with me. She didn't argue. She was smart enough to want out of there as badly as I did.

The amber lights winked out about thirty seconds after we passed them, winking on ahead of us at the same rate. After the second time I looked back into the encroaching darkness, I forced myself to stop looking. It wasn't doing a damn bit of good, and it was doing damage to my nerves that I really couldn't afford.

I'm here, said George.

I squeezed Becks's hand and kept going.

The amber lights led us around a corner and into a narrower hallway with lights lining the walls on either side. They were still small, but they were plentiful enough to show the outline of Becks's face and shoulders. Being able to see her walking beside me lowered my stress levels like nothing else. I saw her head turn toward me, and I felt her fingers relax around mine as the same wave of relaxation washed over her. Maybe it was going to be okay.

The lights continued lighting up in front of us, finally circling a door frame directly ahead. Becks and I broke into a sprint at the same time, heading for the exit at full speed. I got there half a step before she did, purely by virtue of having longer legs, and I grabbed the door handle with my free hand. Needles stung my palm, biting deep and then—unlike every other blood test I'd ever taken—staying where they were as the light above the door flashed between red and green. The light stopped on green, and then went out, replaced by a single green bulb off to the left. The needles withdrew. The door didn't open.

"Oh, those slick bastards," I muttered, pulling my hand away. "Your turn, Becks. They're not going to let us out of here until we're both clean."

"Yippee," she deadpanned, and stepped up to take my place. The lights repeated their flickering dance, and a second green bulb came on next to the first. The latch released and the door swung inward, knocking us both back a step. Cool air rushed into the hallway like a benediction. I took a deep breath, glorying in the taste of clean air, and let Becks pull me for a change, hauling me into the light.

Kelly's emergency exit let out on the edge of the employee parking lot. About a dozen people were already there, most wearing lab coats . . . and there, off to one side, was Director Swenson. He was standing in a small cluster with two of the people in lab coats and Miss Lassen, the receptionist. She was the first to see us. Her shoulders went stiff as she straightened, whispering something urgently to the director. He turned his head in our direction, and his eyes widened before he could compose himself.

Becks squeezed my hand. I hadn't even realized she was still holding it. "Don't," she whispered. "We have what we need. The recorders were running the whole time. This story will end him. We have everything we need."

I nodded curtly as I pulled my hand away. Then I smiled. "Director Swenson!" I called, raising my arms and waving them overhead like I was signaling a plane to land. "Good to see you made it out! What happened, dude?"

"Mr. Mason—Ms. Atherton," said the director. He'd managed to compose his face, but there was still a quaver in his voice. The bastard really didn't think we'd make it out. "I'm so glad to see you both. I was so afraid you wouldn't realize what had happened in time to make it to an exit." His eyes flickered toward the door that we'd emerged through. "I had no idea that you knew about the evacuation tunnels."

Which explains why he didn't have them purged while you were still inside, said George. She sounded furious. No one threatened me and got away with it.

"We've done our homework." I kept smiling. It was that or punch him in the face, and that seemed a hell of a lot less productive, if a hell of a lot more fun. "So seriously, dude, what happened? Was it pit bulls again? Another illegal breeding program like the one in Oakland?"

"I—we're not quite sure yet." Director Swenson's eyes darted toward the door again. He clearly hadn't prepared a cover story. Why should he have bothered? We weren't intended to survive. "There will be a press release as soon as we have a better idea of what went wrong."

"Cool. Make sure we get a copy. Oh, and also, that documentation you said you had, the stuff that related to Georgia's research? I'll expect copies, since we couldn't, y'know, go over it together. I guess if I don't get it, I'm going to have to assume you've got something to hide." I turned, still smiling, and started for the visitor parking area.

"Wait—where are you going?"

I turned back to Director Swenson long enough to flash him the biggest shit-eating grin I could muster. It felt more like I was baring my teeth. Maybe it looked that way, too; he took an involuntary step backward, eyes going wide. "We're going to do what we're paid to do," I said. "We're going to go and tell everybody the news." I waved to the rest of the survivors of the Portland CDC and kept on walking, with Becks following close behind me. Neither one of us looked back as we got to the bike, stowed our gear, put on our helmets, and drove away.

Fuck you all. If that's the way you want to play things . . . If that's the way you want things to go . . . Then fuck you all. You have no idea what you're dealing with. You have no idea what I'm capable of. And you have no idea how little I have left to lose.

You're about to be sorrier than you could possibly believe, and I am going to laugh while I'm pissing on your grave.

—From *Adaptive Immunities*, the blog of Shaun Mason, April 18, 2041. Unpublished.

Fourteen

According to the bike's GPS, the drive from the Portland CDC to Maggie's place should have taken a little over five hours on the main highway. It actually took us closer to eight. Since the chances that we were being tracked by the CDC had just gone way, way up, we stuck to the back roads, keeping our cameras off and avoiding checkpoints whenever we could. I won't say we drove through the ass-end of nowhere, exactly, but we had to stop twice to gun down the zombie deer trying to chew their way through the fence between the road and the undeveloped land around us.

"I wish to God I could post this," bemoaned Becks, shooting another infected herbivore squarely between the antlers.

"Yeah, well, I wish to God I had a cup of coffee," I replied, and gunned the bike's engine. "Come on."

There was a time when I thought George was paranoid for asking Buffy to build a jammer into her bike's tracking system. I'm over it, especially since that jammer allowed us to duck back onto the highway three times for fuel and twice more for caffeine. Becks kept scanning through the newsfeeds as I drove, listening for reports of the outbreak in Portland. "We can't be too careful," she said when we stopped for drinks and enough greasy snack food to get us to Maggie's without crashing. I agreed with her. We'd come too far to die because we weren't paying attention to the news.

None of the initial reports mentioned our presence. They were all bland, tragic, and carefully sanitized. We'd been on the road for about two hours when the "official record" began admitting that perhaps some journalists had been present for the outbreak, but they didn't identify us by name and they didn't try to pin things on us. That was good. That meant it would be a little longer before we needed to kill them all.

George stayed uncharacteristically quiet during the drive. She wasn't gone—that would've left me too shaken to control the bike, especially after everything that had happened since Kelly's arrival—but she wasn't talking, either. She was just quiet, sitting at the back of my head and brooding over God knows what. I figured she'd tell me when she was through working it out for herself. Maybe it says something about my mental health that I didn't find the idea even a little strange. We were too far away from normal for strange to have any meaning anymore.

The sun was hanging low in a mango-colored sky when I turned onto Maggie's driveway. I had to keep one foot on the ground to keep the bike upright while we navigated the various security gates, until my clutch hand was cramping and I started to feel like we would have made better time if we'd ditched the bike on the street and made the rest of the trip to the house on foot. Becks clearly shared my frustration. By the time we cleared the ocular scanner, she was all but twitching with the anxious need to be back in the safety of friendly walls.

The fifth gate was standing open, just like it was when we first arrived as refugees from the ashes of Oakland. A casual observer might have thought Maggie never closed the damn thing. They would have been proven wrong almost immediately, because as soon as I coasted to a stop, the gate slid slickly shut. The sound of the locks engaging was the sweetest thing I'd ever heard.

Becks barely waited for the bike to stop before she dismounted; my foot was still on the kickstand when she hopped off. She stayed where she was for a few brief seconds, jittering in place as she worked the feeling back into her legs. Then she grabbed her bag off the side of the bike, announced, "I'm going to go take a shower," and took off for the kitchen door. I watched her go without commenting. She didn't want to give the live breakdown on what happened at the CDC, and, since I was the boss, she was leaving that little luxury for me.

"She's such a sweetheart," I said dryly.

Be careful. George sounded concerned. I jumped. It wasn't just the worry in her tone: She'd been quiet for so long that I'd almost forgotten she was there, like sitting in a room with someone who hasn't spoken in hours, until they finally get up to leave. *I don't think you really understand what's going on with her.*

"What, are you saying she might be working with the CDC? I don't think so. I'm usually better at reading people than that."

Shaun . . . I could almost see the exasperated shake of George's head, the way she'd be glowering at me behind her sunglasses. *I don't think Becks is a traitor, but you need to be careful with her. Okay? Can you do that for me?*

"Sure, George." I slid off the bike, stretching. The muscles in my calves and thighs protested the movement but were overruled by my ass, which was so sore from the drive that I doubted I'd ever sit down again. "Whatever you say."

One nice thing about working with people who know how crazy I am: Maggie, Alaric, and Kelly were in the kitchen when I stepped inside, all three of them in easy view of the window, and not one of them commented on the fact that I'd stopped to talk to myself before following Becks into the house. It's a lot easier to deal with people who are already used to me.

"Becks tore through on the way to the shower," said Maggie. She was next to the sink, drying the last of the dinner dishes. The kitchen smelled of savory pastry and fresh-cooked chicken. My stomach rumbled, reminding me that all I'd eaten since leaving Portland was some soy jerky, half a bag of potato chips, and a candy bar. The corner of Maggie's mouth turned up in a smile. "There's a potpie for each of you in the oven. We left them there so they'd stay warm."

"Awesome. Thanks." George was hovering at the back of my mind, casting a veil of anxiety over everything. I walked to the fridge and opened it. Someone had gone to the store while Becks and I were out; there was a twelve-pack of Coke on the bottom shelf, and what looked like sufficient fresh provisions for us to survive a siege, so long as no one cut the power.

I grabbed a can of Coke and swung the door shut, turning toward the table as I popped the tab. "Hey, guys," I said, as amiably as I could manage. "So how were things while Becks and I were on location?"

"Mahir announced the hiring of 'Barbara Tinney' and helped Kelly get her first post up while I monitored the footage you were beaming out of the CDC," said Alaric.

"Really? Cool. What was it about?"

"The psychological impact of isolationism on the development of human relationships," said Kelly. I looked at her blankly. She amended: "Cabin fever makes people shitty roommates."

"I'm sure it's a real ratings grabber," I said, after a suitable pause. "Alaric?"

He took the cue with grace, saying, "I was able to get about a dozen reports cobbled together after things went south, and we had them online before anyone else picked up on the outbreak. Mahir has every on-duty Newsie and about half the Irwins running follow-ups now. The CDC's only comment so far called it 'an avoidable tragedy,' and said they were looking into possible failure of the airlock seals that are supposed to separate the treatment areas from the employee locker room."

"Which is bullshit," said Kelly. "Those air locks were designed to withstand a nuclear war. There's no way they could just *fail*."

"Good to know," I said, sipping my Coke.

Ask whether any of the reports include the conference room, said George, with a sudden, strange urgency in her tone.

"Okay," I muttered. More loudly, I asked, "Uh, hey, Alaric? Did any of the reports Mahir put together include footage of me and Becks sitting in the conference room waiting for the director to come back?"

Alaric blinked and nodded. "How did you know? That was the second one he put up. He said the time stamp was important to get out there in the public record."

George started to explain. I cut her off, saying, "The time stamp on the conference room footage means they can't try to pin the outbreak on us. There's no way for us to have spent that much time sitting together, waiting, *and* be the ones who damaged the air lock seal."

You're learning, said George, approvingly.

"Time stamps can be forged," said Maggie. Alaric, Kelly, and I all turned to look at her. She shrugged. "You just shouldn't put too much faith in the time stamp. It's not going to save you by itself. That's what my family has lawyers for."

"Thanks for that little ray of sunshine, Maggie." I turned to Kelly. "So, Doc, was there any way to know that we were walking into a deathtrap? I mean, at this point, I trust the CDC about as far as George can throw you, but it still seems a little extreme, burning a whole installation to take out two reporters."

Kelly frowned. "But Georgia is—oh." She stopped midprotest, comprehension flooding her expression. "No. I didn't. I'm starting to realize that my ... my former employers"—she spat out the word "former" like it tasted bad—"may be capable of some pretty horrible things, but I never suspected they'd do anything like that. I wouldn't have let you go if I knew."

"The sad part here is that I bet they have more nasty surprises for us. Just wait." I sipped my Coke, studying Kelly's face for signs that she was fraying. The Doc was holding up better than I expected; all I saw in her eyes was exhaustion, both physical and mental. The rest of us were tired, but we were also trained for this sort of shit—or as trained as you *can* be for something that's never supposed to happen. "Well, we got out alive. That's something. Alaric, how's our market share?"

"Up four points last time I checked, with the expected uptick in our closest competitors," said Alaric, not missing a beat. "Three of them are crying hoax and two more are claiming that we're endangering our licenses by behaving recklessly in hopes of increasing our ratings."

I snorted. "Because 'behaving recklessly' is suddenly not in the job description? Amateurs. Let 'em find their own potentially fatal government conspiracies."

"Can we not?" Maggie picked up a stack of plates and began putting them away in the cupboard. "I think one is more than enough at any given time, and since they have a tendency to spread, I'm not sure a second one wouldn't wind up getting all over us, too."

"Fair enough." I tossed my empty can into the recycling bin. "You said there was a potpie?"

"Yes, and you said you'd tell us what happened." Maggie put away the last of the plates before taking down the oven mitts and opening the oven, producing a covered ceramic dish that smelled like it was less than half a mile shy of Heaven. She set it down on one of the open spaces at the table.

"Caffeine, then food, then exposition." I grabbed a fork from the dish drainer before moving to sit down. The potpie smelled even better up close. The bulldogs agreed: two promptly appeared from the next room, sitting by my feet in perfect, implacable begging positions. "Remind me again why we didn't all move in with you years ago?"

"Because I live in the middle of nowhere, and that isn't actually an asset for anyone who isn't a pure Fictional." Maggie went back to putting dishes away. "Now talk, or I'm going to take back your dinner."

"Anything but that." I stabbed my fork into the piecrust. "How much of the footage have you guys watched?"

"Enough," said Alaric grimly.

I nodded. "Okay, then." I took a bite of potpie, swallowed, and began talking, starting with the point where Becks and I drove away from the motel. Most of our time at the CDC had been fairly well-documented by the cameras we carried, but they'd been simple recorders, not full-on field deployments. There were things they missed, like most of Director Swenson's reactions, and everything in the emergency tunnels.

"Your recording feeds cut off as soon as you went through that second door," said Alaric. "They picked up again once you were outside."

"Really?" I glanced to Kelly. "Did you know that was going to happen?"

"No, but it makes sense. Those tunnels are heavily shielded, to prevent contamination if there's ever need for an actual flush. We're not even supposed to stay in them during drills, if we can help it."

"Radiation?" asked Alaric.

Kelly shrugged. "I really don't know. I'm sorry."

I took advantage of their brief side-conversation to shovel another few bites of potpie into my mouth, barely chewing. Finally, I said, "Okay, so you didn't get any of that footage. It wasn't bright enough in there to get much worthwhile, but unless their shielding fried our electronics—" I glanced at Kelly. She shook her head, indicating that it shouldn't have done anything of the sort. That made sense, since the CDC probably had recording devices of their own in the tunnels. They'd need to know what went wrong if there was ever an emergency purge. "You should be able to extract the audio track."

"Don't forget the pretty amber lights. Those are probably worth a screenshot or two." We all turned toward the sound of Becks's voice. She was wearing one of Maggie's bathrobes, knotted loosely around her waist, and her hair was still half-wet, tousled from the post-shower drying. "Is there another potpie, Maggie? I'm hungry enough to eat a dog."

"Please don't," said Maggie. "It's hard enough to socialize them without making them think that people will decide to randomly eat them. Your potpie is in the oven."

"You're an angel." Becks arrowed for the oven, dismissing the rest of us in favor of food.

I stabbed my fork into my own potpie, spearing a chunk of chicken as I focused my attention back on Kelly. "So, Doc, that was a good job you did, getting us to the tunnels. Pretty quick thinking, too."

"We do evacuation drills and infection simulations every month in order to minimize the loss of life in case of an outbreak," said Kelly. "There are differences between offices, but they're reasonably minor, and the central floor plan doesn't change. Plus, they shuttle us to different offices once a year to run evacuation trials there, to make sure we don't get too hung up on familiar landmarks."

"What, like the white door, the white door, or, that old favorite, the white door?"

Kelly cracked a slight, brief-lived smile. "Something like that. It's amazing how much two identical halls can differ when you work in them every day for a year or more. We have to learn to strip them down to nothing but the architecture."

"Does that mean you have entire installations memorized?" asked Alaric, suddenly interested. Kelly nodded. "Could you draw a map if I gave you some basic drafting software?"

"I think so. Why?"

"Because that may not be our last trip into the CDC, and I'd rather we didn't need to count on an open phone line to get us out next time," I said. Kelly's attention switched back to me. "Alaric, get her that drafting software and see if you can find some public databases to check her work against."

"The public databases won't have the emergency access tunnels," said Kelly.

"It's still never a bad idea to have a backup plan." I flashed her a toothy smile. "Besides, the public databases will have full blueprints of the general-access areas, and that should be enough to jog your memory. It's not that I don't trust you to tell us the truth as you see it, Doc. It's just that after what we learned from Dr. Abbey, I don't trust you not to leave things out if you think they're too sensitive for us."

Her expression hardened. For a moment, I thought she was going to challenge my authority. The others saw it, too: Alaric pushed his chair back from the table by a few inches, while Maggie and Becks both stopped moving around the kitchen, their attention going solely to Kelly. The house seemed to hold its breath. Finally, grudgingly, Kelly shook her head.

"Fair enough. We're in this together, whether we like it or not. I guess we're all going to need to learn how to trust each other."

"There's the spirit," I said.

"I just have one question," said Alaric. "How do we know the CDC isn't going to run an audio comparison on your call and figure out that Kelly's still alive? The last thing we need is another major raid."

"No, the *last* thing we need is them figuring out where we are.

Them figuring out that the Doc's still breathing is second to last, at best." I pushed my half-eaten potpie away and stood. "I guess we'll need to keep an eye on the news feeds, see whether anything comes through accusing us of identity theft."

"Can you steal your own identity?" asked Kelly.

"Guess we'll find out." Becks moved to take my seat as I stepped away. "Becks, you need to update as soon as you finish eating. I'm going to go and get the untransmitted footage loaded to the server. Alaric, I want you cleaning and screenshotting inside the hour."

"Got it," said Alaric.

"I've got a few poems and a bunch of garden pictures to put up," said Maggie. "I'm officially still in mourning for Dave, which is why I'm all alone here in my big, spooky old house."

"Good," I said. "Doc, work with Mahir and get started on another post about whatever the hell psychology crap you're writing about. See if you can come up with a plausible excuse for why we don't have a picture of you. I don't want anyone getting overzealous and looking for you in the public broadcast footage."

"All right."

I grabbed another Coke from the fridge and went back to the living room, where the computer wouldn't argue with me, ask me questions, or do anything but help me clear my head. George was still quiet, her normally constant presence numbed to a dull ache at the back of my skull. It didn't hurt, precisely. It just felt weird as hell.

The computer woke at the touch of a finger. I navigated the company log-in menus to reach my mailbox, which was comfortingly overfull of spam, date offers, naked pictures, suggestions of things that would make good articles, and the seemingly obligatory elevator pitches on places I should go and dead things I should bother. Sometimes it seems like the entire world is out to get me back into the field. What they don't understand—and I can't tell them—is that I've lost one of the integral traits of a good Irwin: I'm not having any fun. When I wind up in the field, it's a chore to be survived, not an adventure to be relished. Without that little spark of gosh-golly-wow to drive me on, I'm essentially a dead man walking. Don't think I don't see the irony. George is the one who stopped breathing, but I'm the one who gave up on living.

The forums were as big a mess as I'd expected from Alaric's report. The moderators were trying to be six places at once, and failing pretty spectacularly. I sat back for a few minutes sipping my Coke and watching the message notifications as they popped up next to thread after thread. The team currently on duty were all beta bloggers, trying to prove their credentials by doing the sort of shit job that George and I used to do back when we were still bylines on the Bridge Supporters site. In those days, we couldn't think of anything we wanted more than to be out on our own, telling the stories we wanted to tell, not answering to anybody but ourselves.

"Look at where *that* got us," I muttered, leaning forward in the chair and reaching for the mouse. "Stay where you are, guys. You'll be a hell of a lot happier in the long run."

George didn't say anything, and kept not saying anything as I went back to my in-box and started skimming, looking for messages that actually needed my attention. I needed to start editing footage. I needed to post and let people know that I was still alive, but most of all, and first of all, I needed to calm down a little bit. My heart-beat was starting to speed up as my body realized that the running away was over—we'd reached our destination, and now it was finally safe for me to freak out.

My hand was shaking. I sat perfectly still, waiting for the tremors to pass. I didn't have time for another breakdown. One a month is about my limit, and since this one was unlikely to come with the extra-bonus "full visual hallucinations of your dead sister," I didn't see the point of doing it again. Eventually, the shaking stopped, and I started again.

I hit Important when I was halfway down my in-box. It was buried in thread updates, private messages from the moderators, and random posts from my mailing lists, and I almost didn't click because I didn't recognize the sender's e-mail address. "Who the fuck uses 'TauntedOctopus' for a handle, anyway?" I asked myself. It wasn't entirely a rhetorical question. I was hoping the sheer stupidity of it would be enough to make George speak up.

Instead, it was enough to make me stop, swear, and open the message. Who uses "TauntedOctopus" as a handle? Probably a woman who wears T-shirts telling you not to do it. Dr. Abbey.

From: TauntedOctopus@redacted.cn.com
To: Shaun.Mason@aftertheendtimes.com
Subject: Aren't you a busy boy?

I admit I was surprised when I heard that the Portland CDC had been overrun by the infected less than twenty-four hours after you left me. You don't waste time, and I respect that. Then again, it's not like you have much time to waste. You're not the only one who knows how to operate a camera, and I bet you dollars to donuts that somebody got footage of you and your little band of Merry Men on the trek out here. It's just a matter of time before somebody figures out we were in contact, and then the shit you're in will be so deep that it'll make your current shit look like chocolate pudding. Don't come back. We started tearing down the lab as soon as you left, and by the time you get this message (assuming you live long enough to get this message, which is by no means guaranteed), we'll be on our way to a new location. The little "arrangement" I have with the CDC depends on a certain status quo, and you're playing in dangerous enough waters that I can't count on it right now. So hurry up and get your answers or get yourselves killed, will you?

The attachments on this message contain everything I've done to date involving mapping the structure of Kellis-Amberlee against the autoimmune oddities that cause the formation of stable reservoir conditions. I don't have a mechanism for reversing them, or a reliable way to induce them in adult subjects, but there's more than enough to prove that reservoir conditions are the result of the immune system beginning to learn to cope under supposedly impossible conditions. Most of the research won't make any sense to you, but it'll make perfect sense to the little CDC flunky who introduced us. Make sure she sees it. Tell her it all goes public if you think she's holding out on you. See what she has to say after that.

You're a brave idiot, Shaun Mason, and I'm sorry I never got to meet your sister. Almost as sorry as I am that you never got to meet my husband. Give my regards to the Merry Men, and tell them to sleep with one eye open, because you're well on the way to pissing off some pretty damn important people. Good for you. Keep doing what you're doing. Somebody has to.

Best wishes, and stay the fuck away from me,
Dr. Shannon L. Abbey

A flare of guilt rose, washed over me, and died as I contemplated the fact that talking to us cost Dr. Abbey her lab. She knew what she was doing when she let us through her door. Maybe she didn't invite us to come for a visit, but once we were there, she was perfectly happy to tell us what she knew. If she wasn't going to blame us for showing up, I wasn't going to feel bad for doing it.

The attachments on her message downloaded clean, and they opened to reveal huge, detailed medical charts and graphs that made about as much sense as abstract art. I recognized some of the labels, but that was about it. That was okay because Dr. Abbey was right: It didn't matter if her research made sense to me. What mattered was that her research would make sense to *Kelly*, and once she'd seen it, maybe she'd know where we needed to look next. Given the situation we were in, every little bit was about to start counting, big time.

I forwarded Dr. Abbey's message to Alaric and Mahir with a priority flag, printed copies of the attachments, and returned to cleaning out my in-box. Nothing else was nearly as interesting as that message, which wasn't much of a surprise. "Here's my Kellis-Amberlee research, enjoy" was a pretty hard act to follow.

According to the site log, Mahir was logged in, which meant that either he was awake or I had reasonable cause to think he might be. That was good enough for me. Leaning back in my chair, I dug my phone out of my pocket and snapped it open.

Luck was with me: Mahir, not his wife, answered the phone. "Shaun. Thank God."

"Hey, Mahir. There a reason you always feel the need to invoke the divine when I call you? Is that just how they're saying hello in London these days?"

"It's four o'clock in the bloody morning, Shaun, and I'm awake to take your call. That might tell you a little something about how worried I've been." A door closed in the background, and the sound of distant traffic filtered through the phone. "Try remembering that I'm eight hours off your time zone and give me the all-clear a little sooner next time, won't you?"

"Hey, sorry, dude. I figured Alaric would keep you posted." One of the London magazines did a profile on Mahir after the Ryman election—he was a local boy involved in a huge American political scandal, which was sort of a big deal. The picture they ran with the article was of him standing on the wide balcony outside his apartment, looking out over the River Thames with the sort of serious "I am an intellectual artist" expression that George and I always used to make fun of. That was the scene I pictured now, listening to the traffic rushing past behind him: Mahir on the balcony, surrounded by the weight of the London night, while cars packed with paranoid commuters went whizzing past below.

"He did. So did Magdalene. But at the end of the day, Shaun, the only person I trust to tell me your condition is you."

"I'd feel flattered if I didn't know that you expected me to die."

"Isn't that your intention?"

I stopped for a moment, suddenly and sharply aware of George's silent presence at the back of my head. Lying to Mahir would border on impossible, even if George was willing to let me, and in the end, I didn't bother trying. "Eventually, yeah. But not until after we've found the people who killed George. Did you get those files I sent you?"

"I did," Mahir admitted. "How much of them did you understand?"

"Not enough. I'm guessing you understood a little bit more."

"Enough to make me think I'll never sleep again."

"That's good—means the files are what Dr. Abbey said they were. I need you to do something for me."

"What's that?"

"Find a virologist with nothing left to lose and get them to check her work."

Now it was Mahir's turn to fall briefly silent. Finally, tone wary, he asked, "Do you understand what you're asking me to do?"

"Yeah, I do. I feel like a total ass for doing it, but I do."

Mahir went silent again. Honestly, I couldn't blame him.

North America lost a lot during the Rising. Big chunks of Canada and the lower parts of Mexico have never been reclaimed from the infected. We held the line in Alaska as long as we could, but in the end, the infection was too strong and we had to let the entire state go. Almost every part of the United States has its little dead zones, places that are too damn dangerous to take back. None of that can hold a candle to what India lost. Because what India lost ... was India.

The conditions in pre-Rising India formed a perfect model for pandemic spread of Kellis-Amberlee. We studied it in school as part of the standard epidemiology curriculum: Combine highly concentrated populations with large stretches of rural farmland, a polluted water supply, and large, unconfined animals, and you were basically setting up the ideal conditions for losing everything. According to the reports—the ones that made it out of India, anyway; there aren't many—the virus first started showing up in Mumbai, where it went from zero to chaos in the streets in less than thirty-six hours. While India was throwing all its resources at trying to save the city, the infection was taking hold in the country, claiming villages and small towns so quickly that no one had time to sound the alarm. By the time anyone realized that the quarantine couldn't possibly have held, it was way too fucking late to do anything but evacuate.

The first handheld blood testing unit was invented by an Indian scientist named Kiran Patel. Dr. Patel had isolated his family when the first signs of trouble started to show; thanks to his quick thinking and willingness to use lethal force against the infected, he managed to keep his entire apartment building clean of the live virus during a six-day siege that should have left them all casualties. When he wasn't standing watch, Dr. Patel was modifying his own diabetes kits to look for something a little more crucial than blood sugar. By the time the UN soldiers fought their way into that sector of Mumbai, he had a crude but reliable way of proving someone's infection status in minutes. The whole building checked out. Two of the troops who'd come to their rescue didn't. Acceptable losses for a piece of technology that no one else had even taken the time to think about, much less put together.

Dr. Patel went into a diabetic coma on the helicopter that airlifted him and his family out of the city. He never made it out of India. His widow went to the UN and demanded refuge for the survivors of her country in exchange for her husband's notes. She got everything she asked for. The people who made it out of India were allowed to settle anywhere they wanted, bypassing all the normal citizenship requirements. The Indian consulates stayed open and issued passports to the children of the survivors; as far as I know, they still do. When the disease is defeated, they say, they'll be ready to go home.

Whether that's true or not, London has one of the largest Indian communities on the planet, second only to Silicon Valley—although Toronto is a pretty close third. Mahir was born in London. He's never been to India, and as far as I know, he's never wanted to go. That's not true for everyone. A lot of people want to reclaim their heritage. They may like living where they are, but they want it to be a choice, not an exile. There are doctors and scientists in the Indian community who answer only to the government of a nation that currently doesn't exist, pursuing research whose only motive is "get us home." But racism doesn't die just because the dead start walking, and there are some folks who watch the displaced communities carefully for signs that they might be "turning against us." If Mahir did what I was asking him to do—if he went to one of the virologists who was working out of his home, rather than out of a government lab, and asked him to explain Dr. Abbey's work—he was putting them both at risk of a terrorism charge.

Finally, Mahir said, "I'm going to ask a question that sounds insane, Shaun, and you're going to answer. Refuse, and I hang up, and we both pretend this conversation never happened."

That sort of thing never works. Once you're past the age of five, you can't make something unhappen just by refusing to think about it. "Sure," I said. "Whatever you say."

"All right." He laughed, a little unsteadily, and asked, "What does Georgia have to say about this plan?"

Mahir had never questioned the fact that George still talks to me, but he'd never gone out of his way to address her, either. Maybe my crazy was starting to rub off on the people around me. Is crazy contagious? "Hang on. I'll ask her." *George,* I thought, *if you're just being quiet because you're pissed or something, I could really use your help right about now . . .*

Sorry. I was thinking. Tell him . . . She hesitated. *Tell him that if this research means what I think it means, the world has a right to know, and without his help, we might not be able to tell them. This is for everybody.*

" . . . okay." I cleared my throat. "She says that if this research means what she thinks it means, the world has a right to know, and that if you're not willing to help, we might not be able to figure out enough to know what to tell them. She says this is for everybody." I paused before adding, "And I say it looks like they were willing to blow up Oakland and infect an entire CDC facility to keep the news from getting out without it looking like they were trying to hide something. I want to get at least part of the work off this continent, so somebody can keep on going after they drop the bomb on Maggie's place."

"I swear, I'm going to move to San Francisco just to make you people stop using me as your off-site backup." Mahir sighed deeply. "Fine."

"Fine? You mean you'll do it?"

"I'm clearly out of my mind, and I'm going to regret this for the rest of my life, and my wife is probably going to leave me, but yes, I'll do it. Someone has to. I'm going to have to involve my local beta bloggers. This is a rather large project."

"Whatever you need, but keep it limited to people you know and can trust, okay? We can't risk this getting out early."

"Silence is expensive."

"That's not a problem. I'm sure if we shake the merchandising hard enough, the money will fall out." If nothing else, I had a standing offer to print a book of George's posts from the campaign trail. I'd been refusing—somehow that felt more like making money off her corpse than continuing to run her blog did—but it would be a good way to make some reasonably quick cash. And then there was Maggie's trust fund. Normally, I wouldn't think of going there. These were some pretty special circumstances.

"Oh, believe me, I wasn't intending to worry about the budget, and if I'm still married when this is over, you're financing the second honeymoon it's going to take for me to stay that way."

"Totally fair. Thank you. Really, thank you. You're a good guy."

"Your sister had excellent taste in men. Now update your damn blog, Shaun. Half the readership thinks you're dead, and I'm entirely out of the passion it takes to refute conspiracy theories." The sounds of distant traffic cut off as Mahir killed the connection, leaving me listening to nothing but the sound of my own breath. I clicked the phone shut and slid it back into my pocket, staring thoughtfully at the computer screen. Dr. Abbey's research looked back at me like the world's deadliest abstract art. The lines of it were strangely soothing when I looked at them long enough. They reminded me of the faint traceries of iris surrounding George's pupils, little lines of brown that no one got to see unless they got close enough to look past her glasses.

Lifting my hands, I tugged the keyboard toward me and began to write.

I like to think of myself as a reasonable man. I suppose that's true of everyone. Even the people we'd paint as the villains of the piece, given leave, doubtless consider themselves reasonable. It's a part of the human psyche. Still. My needs are simple. I have my flat, which is paid for. I have my work, which I enjoy and do reasonably well. I have a beautiful wife who tolerates the strange hours and stranger company I keep. I love the city I live in, its sights and sounds and brilliant culture, which has managed to not only recover but to thrive under adversity. London is the only place I have ever truly wished to be, and I am privileged beyond all measure to call it home.

I like to think of myself as a reasonable man. But I have buried too many friends in the too-recent past, and I have seen too many lies go unquestioned, and too many questions go unasked. There is a time when even reasonable men must begin to take unreasonable actions. To do anything else is to be less than human. And to those who would choose the safety of inaction over the danger of taking a stand, I have this to say:

You bloody cowards. May you have the world that you deserve.

—**From *Fish and Clips*, the blog of Mahir Gowda,**
April 20, 2041

Fifteen

Writing up the events of the day was enough to leave me utterly exhausted. I just wanted to go upstairs, shower, go through a proper decontamination cycle, and crash for six to eight hours before something else demanded my attention. If I did that, though, my post would go up in plain text and I'd have eager beta bloggers flooding my in-box with offers to "help." Their "help" would probably end in tears—theirs, after I dismissed them from the site for pissing me off beyond all hope of recovery. It was easier to force myself to stay where I was and go combing through the footage of the day, looking for suitable clips and screenshots.

There are times when I miss Buffy. I mean, I always miss her—she was one of my best friends, right up until she sold us out—but there are times when I *really* miss her. I could have handed her my report and told her to make it pretty, and she would have had a multimedia extravaganza ready to go almost before I could finish making the request. She was the best at what she did. Everything she did, which was sort of the problem, since in the end, what she did included betraying us and getting a lot of people killed. She said she was sorry when she came clean. I believed her then, and I believe her now. Sometimes people make mistakes, and sometimes those mistakes are the sort that don't allow for second chances.

Doesn't make her any less dead, or make me miss her any less.

In the end, I chose three short film clips and ten stills and called it a day, slapping them into my article in the places where they'd have the most impact, or at least look like they were there for a reason. I dropped a note in the mod forum to let folks know I'd be going off-line for a few hours and that I was only to be disturbed if the world was ending. Even then, they were supposed to get clearance from Mahir before they called me. That wouldn't guarantee I'd be left alone, but it would slow people down. Sort of like setting a snooze button on reality.

It wasn't until I stood that I realized how sore I was. I stretched until something in my shoulders popped. That was the cue for half the muscles in my body to start complaining, while the other half seemed to turn to jelly. "Fuck. I'm not getting any younger," I said, and walked toward the kitchen.

Alaric was gone, probably off doing his time on the message boards. I'd say better him than me, but I've done that gig more times than I can count, and it's not something I'd wish on anybody. Becks and Maggie were still sitting at the table, watching the uncomfortable-looking Kelly the way cats watch mice. She turned toward me when I entered the kitchen, expression going pathetically relieved. If I was her idea of salvation, things must have been really nasty while I was in the other room.

"Hey," I said. "I'm going to go upstairs and get a shower."

Kelly's look of relief died. "Don't you want to finish your potpie?"

"No, I'm good. Maggie, can you take care of any comments I get for the next few hours? I need to catch some sleep or I'm going to be useless tomorrow."

"Absolutely." Maggie smiled. "Now go. You're running yourself too hard."

"You're probably right." I paused, a thought hitting me. "Maggie, tell Alaric to check on the bug we planted in the conference room. It should be showing up on the live index now, and I want to know the second it picks anything up."

"Decontamination will take a few days," said Kelly. If she had opinions about the legality of bugging CDC installations, she was keeping them to herself. "You won't be getting anything until that's done."

"Well, then, I guess I'll have plenty of time to catch up on my beauty sleep. All of you, good night, and try to get some rest."

"I will," said Becks, giving me a thoughtful look as I turned to go.

Making it up the stairs took more effort than it should have. I was so damn tired. It seemed like too much trouble when I could sit down and sleep perfectly well on the steps. I knew I needed to shower. Strict field protocols said I should have showered the second I got to the house, like Becks did. It can really screw up your insurance if you don't go through proper decontamination after every logged trip into the field, but there are loopholes to the law, if you know how to use them. We didn't log the trip to Dr. Abbey's lab, and CDC offices are counted as some of the few public places *not* considered hazard zones. My failure to scrub up like a good little boy was strictly legal, and I was aware enough of my exposure risks to know that I hadn't been dangerously close to anything infectious. I just didn't want to go to bed feeling like I'd never be clean again.

The showers in Maggie's house are another amazing example of what you can achieve if you have enough money and don't care how much of it you spend. The showers in the Oakland apartments were bare-bones, consisting of air locks, computer-controlled water sprays, and simple blood test panels. Using them was like getting scrubbed down by industrial robots that didn't give a damn whether you were comfortable with the process. They didn't quite perform involuntary enemas, but God, they came close. Maggie's place, on the other hand . . . When her parents set her up with a place of her own, they took "spare no expense" seriously. Some of the bells and whistles she had were things I'd seen only in magazines and in articles about people with more money than sense.

The entire bathroom was decorated in pre-Rising tile, with genuine porcelain fixtures, the kind that can get broken or splinter, thus becoming infection risks and requiring full replacement. It was easy to miss at first glance that the room was divided into two sections, since the main section contained the toilet, a full-sized sink, and an antique claw-footed bathtub. All you had to do to get inside was open the door—no blood tests required. If you were the sort of person who could ignore the heavy curtain covering one wall, you could pretend that it really *was* a pre-Rising bathroom, and that all that zombie nonsense had never actually happened.

I closed the bathroom door and crossed to the sink, where I emptied my pockets into one of the mesh baskets Maggie keeps for exactly that purpose. Once I was sure I wouldn't accidentally sanitize my press pass or something, I stripped, tossing my clothes—shoes and all—into the bathroom hamper. As soon as I activated the shower, a chute in the bottom of the hamper would open and send my clothes for automatic sterilization. No human hands would touch them until they were certified infection-free. I glanced at my reflection and scowled. I looked exhausted, and I was starting to develop bags under my eyes. Good thing I wasn't doing the Irwin circuit anymore. An Irwin who looks tired is an Irwin who's losing merchandising points with every frame of footage he posts.

Pulling back the curtain revealed the hermetically sealed air lock door separating the shower from the rest of the bathroom. There was a testing panel to one side. I pressed my hand against it, feeling the needles bite into the base of my palm. The light over the shower began flashing between red and green. I cleared my throat, and said, "Shaun Mason, guest, requesting standard decontamination protocols."

There was a pause as the shower's computer ran my blood sample and checked my voice print against the house logs. The light stopped flashing, settling on a steady green. A chime rang, and a pleasant voice that sounded suspiciously like Maggie said, "Welcome, Shaun. Please enter." The air lock hissed as the seal released and the door swung slowly open. I shuddered as I stepped through. The sound of hydraulics wasn't going to sit easily with me for a while—not until something else horrible happened to make me forget about the events of the Portland CDC.

The door swung closed behind me, locking with a second, louder hiss. Once the decontamination cycle started, there was no way to cut it short.

"What sort of shower would you prefer?" The voice of the shower came from a speaker set high in the rear wall. Everything but the air lock door was tiled, the floor and ceiling in white, and the walls in a soothing shade of blue. There were four showerheads, set at levels ranging from shoulder height to almost ceiling level. A recessed nook in the left-hand wall held shampoo, conditioner, and a variety of shower gels.

"Hot, short, thorough," I said. I hesitated before adding, "Please." It never pays to insult computers that are smart enough to form sentences. Not when they're in control of the locks, and especially not when they have the capacity to boil you in bleach.

"Absolutely," said the shower. "Please close your eyes." That was all the warning I got before the water turned on, cascading with a vengeance from all four showerheads. I closed my eyes half a second too late and sputtered as I tried to wipe them dry. At least this shower started with water. Some of them just go straight to bleach.

The initial blast of water lasted for thirty seconds, letting me get warmed up before the shower announced, still politely, "I will be commencing sterilization on the count of three. Please prepare yourself."

"Got it," I said, and screwed my eyes more tightly shut. The liquid raining over me cooled, taking on the sharp smell of industrial-strength bleach. I did my best not to breathe too much as I scrubbed myself down, working the bleach into my skin. It stung like a bitch, just like it always does, but it was a good sting; it was the sting of getting all the way clean and staying alive for another day.

The bleaching stuck to the absolute legal minimum, lasting only a few seconds longer than the water. Finally, the shower said, "Normal bathing cycle is beginning. You have four minutes. Please speak if you want to extend this time."

The bleach stopped immediately, replaced by rapidly warming water. I rinsed my face clean before saying, "Four minutes is fine, thanks."

"You're welcome, Shaun," said the shower.

Creepy. I hate it when machines get chatty with me. I wiped my eyes before opening them and reaching for the shampoo. George and I used to have shower races. Who could get in and clean and out again in the shortest amount of time. All the guys we went to school with insisted that their girlfriends and sisters took forever in the bathroom, but George always beat me. She could scrub down in under three minutes if she was in a hurry and hadn't been out in the field—bleaching added time to both our totals, so we started subtracting it when we compared times. It was the only way to keep the contest fair. Of course, once a month or so, she'd take over the bathroom for an afternoon to dye her hair back to its original color, which inevitably resulted in her shouting for me to come in and help her dye her roots. The sink on our old bathroom was stained a permanent shade of brown by the time we were sixteen, and we ruined so many towels—

The water cut off, leaving me with soap behind one ear and a goony expression on my face. I hadn't realized four minutes could go so quickly. "Thank you for showering with me today, Shaun," said the shower, as the air lock door unsealed and hissed open. "It's been a pleasure serving you."

"Uh, thanks," I said, stepping out. "Same here."

I grabbed two towels from the pile by the sink. I wrapped one around my waist and used the other to dry my hair, rubbing briskly all the way around my head before slinging the towel around my shoulders. I needed to sleep. The basket full of my crap would be safe on the counter for the night, and it was long past time for me to get to bed.

I started for the door, and stopped in the process of reaching for the doorknob. "Oh, crap." When we arrived, Maggie apologized for having only three guest rooms—one each for Alaric, Becks, and Kelly. That left me sleeping on the front room couch, which was fine, when I had, y'know, clothes. Nudity was definitely going to be an issue if I was intending to sleep there again, and since I hadn't exactly taken time to pack when the building was exploding, I didn't have spare jeans.

I was too damn tired to make a decision. I was still standing there, trying to figure out what to do, when somebody knocked on the bathroom door. I let out a relieved sigh; saved. Clearly, Maggie had realized I was going to have a problem and was bringing me a bathrobe, if not actual pants left behind by one of her Fictional houseguests. "You have no idea how glad I am that you're here," I said, opening the bathroom door.

Becks was on the other side. She looked at me with wide, solemn eyes, and said, "I hoped you would be." Then, before I had a chance to react or say anything, she stepped into the bathroom and closed the door behind herself.

She stayed there for a moment, one hand behind her back and

clutching the doorknob, the other hand resting against her upper thigh. It was somewhere between a pose and a pause, and I had no idea what it meant.

"Uh." I took a step backward, making room for her to do, well, whatever it was she was getting ready to do. "Hey, Becks, are you okay? I was just about to clear out, so if you need the bathroom—"

"Shut up, Shaun." She let go of the doorknob and walked toward me. Once she reached me, she took the towel from my shoulders and tossed it carelessly to one side. "For once in your life, just *once,* why don't you. Just. Shut. Up." She stepped a little closer, leaning up onto her toes, and kissed me.

I wasn't expecting the kiss. I didn't have a chance to step aside or deflect it. So, no, I couldn't have prevented it from starting . . . but I could have pulled away from her. I could have stopped it right there.

Instead, I kissed her back.

Becks pressed herself hard against me as soon as I started to respond to her kiss, arms tightening around my shoulders and holding me where I was. I wrapped my arms around her waist, as much to have a place to put them as anything else, and almost involuntarily pulled her closer. The heat coming off her skin felt like it would steam the remaining dampness from the shower right off me. Through it all, she kept on kissing me, the urgency in her movement growing with every second. Suddenly exquisitely aware of how close to naked I was, I raised my hands and took hold of her forearms, pushing her gently away. She fought to maintain the kiss for another few seconds before the distance between us made it impossible.

Her eyes were bright and her cheeks were flushed. She was still wearing the bathrobe she'd borrowed from Maggie, and the belt was half-untied, letting the top gape open enough to give me a really good view of her cleavage. I swallowed. Hard. Tired or not, I was still male, and it had been a long damn time since I'd had a look at that particular vista. Parts of my anatomy that I'd been willing to write off completely were waking up and announcing their interest in the situation. Loudly.

"Becks, I don't know if—"

"Do you want me to stop?" She twisted out of my grasp, moving with a simple grace that made my breath catch in my throat. Then she reached up to take my hands, sliding her fingers into mine. "I'll be totally honest. I don't want to stop. But I will, if that's what you want."

"I . . . I don't know, I just . . . " I looked at our joined hands, studying the short, practical shape of her nails. She had the nails of an Irwin. That made me feel better, oddly enough. I was just another hazard zone for her to explore. "I don't know if this is such a good idea."

"Hey. Look at me." I raised my head. Becks met my eyes and said, "I'm not going to ask you for a commitment. I don't want to go steady. You're my boss, and you're my colleague, and I respect that. But we almost died today, and I'd like to remind myself that we didn't." She stepped back, still holding my hands. "I'm lonely. Don't you ever get lonely?"

It was suddenly hard to breathe. "Every damn night," I said, and closed the distance between us with a step, yanking my hands free before wrapping my arms around her waist again. This time, I was the one initiating the kiss; this time, I was the one pressing with increasing urgency as she kissed me back, bringing one hand up so she could curl her fingers through my hair and pull my head a little farther down. We kissed until my lips felt bruised and my chest hurt with the effort of continuing to breathe.

Becks pulled back, fingers still knotted in my hair. "Does that mean you don't want me to stop?"

"Don't stop," I managed, and kissed her again.

Somehow we made it out of the bathroom and down the hall to

the guest room where she'd been sleeping. I managed to keep the towel on until the door was closed behind us, when Becks resolved the question of what I was supposed to do with it by removing it from my waist and throwing it to one side. She untied her bathrobe and pressed herself hard against me before resuming her frantic kisses. The feeling of her skin touching mine was almost more than I could handle. I groaned. She moaned appreciatively, the sound of a living woman desiring and being desired, rather than the sound of the dead. God, I needed to hear that. I didn't spend nearly enough time among the living.

The ringing silence in my head was forgotten, drowned out by the sounds our bodies made—skin sliding against skin, fingers rustling through hair, lips meeting and parting and meeting again. Becks kept moving steadily backward, forcing me to follow if I wanted to keep kissing her. I wanted to keep kissing her, and so I kept going until she pulled me onto the bed and slung one leg over mine, keeping me there. I didn't resist. I didn't want to. For the first time since George died, I really didn't give a shit about anything but the present. It was a nice feeling. I'd missed it.

"Shaun."

I started kissing her neck, tasting the slightly salty flavor of her skin. I'd missed that, too. The taste of a woman's neck, the way it moved when she breathed—

"*Shaun.*"

It took a moment for the fact that Becks was talking to me to sink all the way into my brain. I stopped kissing her in order to push myself back and look at her face. Her hair was rumpled, making her look like she'd just finished running a marathon after holding off an entire horde of zombies with nothing but a shotgun. I was starting to understand why she kept it long. It might be impractical as hell, but it made views like this one possible, and that was worth a little inconvenience. "What? Did I do something wrong?"

"No." She smiled, a little wryly. "I just wanted to let you know that I have condoms."

I hadn't even thought that far ahead. I blinked for a moment, and then nodded. "Cool, because if I have any, they're downstairs." Actually, I wasn't sure whether I had condoms in my pack or not. I hadn't needed that sort of thing in so long that I'd stopped thinking about it, since thinking about it didn't do me a damn bit of good. Sex wasn't a factor in this post-George world. There just wasn't time.

Becks smiled a little more, looking surprisingly shy, considering that we were buck-ass naked and twisted around each other. "Will you let me up?" she asked.

"Um, right." It took some effort to untangle our limbs. She stood, stretching to give me the best possible view of her body—and I had to admit, the girl was stacked—before crossing to her pack and bending to rummage through one of the inside pockets. I stayed on the bed, feeling suddenly awkward and not exactly sure where I was supposed to put my hands. That was another thing I never had to worry about before. I wasn't even sure I was supposed to be looking at her when she wasn't in the bed. I settled for sitting up with my hands resting loosely between my thighs, looking in her direction, but trying to keep myself from really *looking*. She might get upset if I looked away. She might decide I didn't like the way she looked or something.

Jesus. When did life get so damn complicated?

"Here we go." Becks turned, a foil-wrapped condom held between her thumb and forefinger, and walked back toward the bed. "I've got a birth control implant, but you can't be too careful, right?"

"Right," I echoed, faintly. The pause had given me time to think, which wasn't such a good thing. My body was still voting in favor of going through with things, but now my brain was trying to weigh in on the topic, and it wasn't convinced that this was a good idea. It was reasonably sure that this was a really *bad* idea, and if there was any time to stop, this was it.

Becks tore the foil.

My brain found itself outvoted in a sudden upset sponsored by the body and supported by every hormone I had. I was reaching for her, and she was reaching for me, and then her fingers were unrolling the condom along the length of my cock, and then coherent thought took a backseat for a while. Its services were no longer required, or really wanted. Everything that mattered was in the bed, and none of it took the slightest bit of thinking. All I had to do was act. So I closed my eyes, cupped my hands against the side of her waist, and let the moment do the driving.

I don't know how long the moment lasted. Long enough that when it ended, I was even more exhausted. It was a better exhaustion, it was just . . . all-consuming, the kind of tired that it's almost impossible to fight. I helped clean up the mess with my eyes half-closed, fumbling as we got the damp sheets and the used condom into the appropriate hampers and waste baskets. Then I sagged back into the mattress, relaxing utterly as my head hit the pillow. It felt like all the tension was finally running out of me, leaving me floating in that wonderful horizon between half-asleep and all the way gone.

Fingers trailed down the length of my chest, coming to rest just above my navel. "Good night, Shaun," whispered a voice, inches from my ear.

God. For the first time in longer than I could remember, the world felt like it was actually back the way that it was supposed to be. I brought up a hand to brush my knuckles against her cheek, smelling the sweet-salt-sex smell of her, and smiled.

"Good night, George," I said, and slipped away into sleep.

Mankind's history is littered with singularities—big moments that changed everything, even if nobody knew they were coming. The discovery of antibiotic medicine was a singularity. Before that, it was normal for women to die of "childbed fever," a simple staph infection making them die slowly and in great agony. Cavities killed. Antibiotics changed all that, and less than fifty years later, the thought of living the way people lived before antibiotics was alien to almost everyone.

The industrial revolution was a singularity. As you sit reading this, consider that, once, electric lighting was considered a luxury, and some people weren't even sure it would catch on. The idea that someday the entire world would be run by machines was crazy, preposterous science fiction ... but it happened.

The Rising was a singularity. The way we live today isn't just a little different. It's alien. Our paradigm has shifted, and it can't be shifted back. That's why so many of the old rules of psychology don't apply anymore. Once the dead are walking, crazy's what you make it.

—From *Cabin Fever Dream*, guest blog of Barbara Tinney,
April 20, 2041

———

Tonight's watch-along film is that classic of the genre, *The Evil Dead*, wherein a truly spicy young Bruce Campbell—yum—is menaced by demons, evil trees, and his own hand. I'll be opening the chat room at eight Pacific, and live blogging the whole movie for those of you whose attention spans won't tolerate anything longer than a few hundred characters.

I hope to see you all online, and remember, last person to log on owes me a drink.

—From *Dandelion Mine*, the blog of Magdalene Grace Garcia,
April 20, 2041

Sixteen

I woke sprawled buck-ass naked on the guest room bed, surrounded by the furry mounds of sleeping bulldogs. Groaning, I pushed myself up onto my elbows. The door was open about a foot—just enough to explain my unwanted guests. I scrubbed at my face with one hand, trying to wake up enough to start worrying about my clothes. "Guess it's time to deal with another fucking morning, huh, George?"

Ringing silence answered me. I pulled my hand away from my face and sat all the way up. "George?" Still no answer. "You're start-ing to freak me out here, George. What did I do to earn the silent treatment? I'm doing what you asked me to do. I'm actually stepping up to the plate. So could you stop fucking around?"

She didn't stop fucking around. She was still there—I remember what sane felt like, and this wasn't it; sane didn't come with the con-stant low-grade awareness of George sitting at the back of my head—she just wasn't talking. I scowled.

"Fine. If you want to play silent treatment, we'll play silent treat-ment. See how *you* like it." I scooched my butt along the mattress, eventually getting to the point where my feet hit the floor. Every muscle in my legs ached. I could already tell I was going to be applying Icy-Hot and gulping aspirin like M&Ms all day. I guess that's what you get when you go and outrun an outbreak.

"And yet somehow better than the alternative," I muttered.

The mystery of how the door got open was answered by the stack of clothing and crap on the bookshelf just inside. I sent a silent thanks to Maggie's in-house laundry service—silent because with her computer systems, I was vaguely afraid the program in charge of the laundry service might respond if I thanked it out loud—and began getting dressed. Even the things I'd left in the bathroom were clean, down to the rust on my ancient Swiss army knife. I shook my head. Sometimes it's possible to be a little *too* efficient. It was unnerving to think of the house sending out tiny cleaning devices and using them to polish my thumb drive and pocket change to a mirror sheen.

At least nothing was missing. I shoved things into their respective pockets, fastened my belt, and sat down on the bed to put my boots on. That's when the reality of my position finally filtered through my sleep-addled, George-less brain:

I was the only person in the room. Where the hell was Becks? I looked back at the bed, which didn't offer any answers. From the way I'd been sprawled when I woke up, there was nothing to prove that anyone else had been in the bed to begin with. That was a little worrisome. If I'd gone even further over the edge and started hallucinating being seduced by random members of staff, the time remaining before I went totally insane was probably pretty low.

With that cheerful thought at the front of my mind, I started trying to get my boots on. The process was complicated by the dogs, who thought attacking the laces was a fantastic game. The main difference between dogs that size and cats seems to be that cats, while crazy, are at least *meant* to be little, whereas the process of shrinking dogs seems to drive them insane. "At least we have that much in common," I muttered, and stood, stretching for a final time before walking out of the room. I left the guest room door open. No point in depriving the bulldogs of a nice warm bed.

Alaric was sitting at the kitchen table with his laptop, tapping industriously away. A half a pot of coffee sat in front of him, wafting the delicious smell of hot caffeine toward me as I entered. I stopped to sniff appreciatively. The sound got his attention; he looked up, nodded briefly, and looked back down again. "Hey."

"Hey," I said. I grabbed a mug from the counter and poured myself a cup of hot black coffee. Morning is the only time I normally get coffee without complaining from my inner peanut gallery. If George wanted to sulk, maybe I could get a second cup in before going back to Coke.

A pang of guilt followed on the heels of the thought, although it wasn't enough to stop me from taking a mouthful of throat-searing liquid. I'd rather have George than all the coffee in the world. Still, if focusing on self-caffeination distracted me from the question of her silence, it was worthwhile. Alaric kept typing as I sat down across from him, seeming to ignore me completely. I sipped my coffee. He typed. George didn't say anything.

This went on for a few minutes before I cleared my throat and asked, "So what have I missed? Other than the sunrise and, apparently, breakfast?"

Alaric raised his head. "Maggie took Becks and the Doc into town to go grocery shopping. Something about us eating her out of house and home."

The image of that particular trio tackling the Weed supermarket was fascinating. I paused for a moment to ponder it. I've seen pictures of pre-Rising grocery stores. They were weird, cramped things, with narrow aisles filled with milling consumers—and of course, when the zombies came, they turned into effective little death traps, full of places for the infected to hide. Even the sprinkler systems they used to run over the vegetables worked to spread the outbreak, since all it took was a few drops of blood getting into the water system and, bam, you were literally misting live infection throughout the produce aisle. It didn't help that people kept freaking out and running for places where they could try to hole up until it was all over—like the nearest warehouse megastore. The body counts at Costco and Wal-Mart were nothing short of stratospheric.

For a few years post-Rising, everyone bought their groceries online. Some people still do that, preferring a small delivery charge to the inherent risks of going out among the rest of the population. Unfortunately for them, not everything lends itself to the online model. Fresh fruit and vegetables, meat—fish and poultry, anyway, those being the meats still sold for eating—and anything with the word "bulk" attached to it are much better bought in person. The rise of the modern grocery store has been a reflection of people's twin needs to eat and not get eaten. The layout is closer to the old megastores than anything else, but only a certain number of people are allowed in each department at any one time. Groups cycle through according to the store's floor plan, with air locks and blood testing units between each distinct part of the store. The process takes hours. Grocery shopping is not an activity for the faint of heart.

I paused. "Isn't Maggie afraid they'll be spotted?"

"I'm pretty sure her parents own the store."

"Oh, that'd do it. Has the Doc ever actually *been* in a grocery store?" I asked. My coffee was starting to cool down. I took a longer swallow, letting comforting bitterness cover the back of my throat. It was weird, drinking coffee without apologizing to George or asking permission before doing it. I took another drink, almost daring her to comment.

She didn't.

"I don't think so," said Alaric. "She turned sort of white when Maggie told her where they were going."

"God, I hope somebody's got a camera running." Or four, or five, or maybe an even dozen. We couldn't use the footage for anything, but seeing Kelly confronted with an actual fish counter would be comedy gold.

"I'm sure they do," said Alaric. "They know their jobs."

"True." I refilled my mug. "Anything else going on?"

"Not really."

"Huh. Okay. How are the overnights?"

"Good."

"Not great?"

"Really good." Alaric seemed to realize I wasn't going anywhere. He pushed his laptop to one side and reached for his own mug. "Your report got a ridiculous number of downloads. I mean, really ridiculous. Every time you go anywhere near the field, we see a ratings spike of insane proportions."

"Yeah, well, every time I go anywhere near the field, I wind up not sleeping for a month, so I guess it evens out in the end. Has the CDC said anything about what happened in Portland?"

"There's no official statement yet, but Talking Points managed to get an interview with Director Swenson—"

I snorted. Talking Points is a lousy site, and they have a reputation for editing reports to match the requests of the highest bidder. Giving them an exclusive was sort of like buying a commercial slot during prime time: a great use of your money, but a terrible abuse of the truth.

Alaric narrowed his eyes. "Mind if I continue?"

"Sorry." I waved my mug in his direction. "I'm all ears. No more interruptions, I promise."

"I'll believe that when I see it," Alaric muttered, before continuing: "He repeated the lab accident story and added a cute little 'maybe if they hadn't somehow wandered into a secure area, they wouldn't have been forced to use the emergency access tunnels' rider, trying to make it look like you and Becks had been negligent, or worse, trespassing."

"How did we answer that?"

"Mahir uploaded your footage, sans dialogue, of everything from the director leaving you in the conference room to the lights going out. Time stamps visible for the entire thing. If you were someplace you weren't supposed to be, it was because the director left you there."

"Remind me to give that man a raise."

"How about you get the rest of us out of the line of fire, first?" Alaric's tone was harsh, verging on nasty. I'd never heard him talk to anyone like that before. Not even after the time I broke his nose for suggesting that my ongoing need to talk to George was a sign of mental illness. I know it's a sign of mental illness; I knew it then, too. I just think the alternative to going crazy is even worse.

I put my mug down, frowning as I studied Alaric. He looked tired, but that wasn't really a surprise. We *all* looked tired, and with good reason. "Dude, what's going on? Did somebody decide to piss in your cereal or something?"

"I'm just not sure you have your priorities straight anymore. That's all." Alaric looked at me steadily, lips firming into a thin line. "It's not like any of us can quit at this point, is it? Not when they're blowing up buildings to make us stop poking at things."

"What, and you think that's my fault?" I waved an arm toward the front door. "I didn't ask the Doc to show up, and they started shooting at us as soon as they had a bead on where she was, remember? You can*not* pin that one on me, Alaric. You want to be pissed off at somebody, I recommend her."

"*She* brought us a hook into the greatest conspiracy of our generation! *You* just want it to be about revenge! It's not all about you, Shaun. It's *never* been all about you. You're not the only one being lied to, and you're not the only one who's lost people. I guess I'm just getting tired of you acting that way."

I blinked. "I ... what?"

"You heard me."

"I never said this wasn't everybody's fight."

"Could've fooled me."

I slammed my hand down on the table hard enough to make the coffee slosh over the lip of my mug. Alaric jumped. "Dammit, Alaric, this is *not* the time to play pissy bitches. What the fuck is bothering you? Did you get trolled on the message boards? Is your revenue share down? Do you not like the guest room you're in? What?"

"Was there a particular reason Rebecca came down the stairs this morning looking like she hadn't slept, and ran out of here the second she was given the opportunity to do so?" You could have used the edge on his voice to cut steel. Closing his laptop with one hand, Alaric continued: "You were asleep at the time. That may be why she left so quickly. Avoiding an unpleasant encounter."

"Oh, crap." Any relief I might have felt at hearing that I wasn't going crazier—Becks and I really did have sex—was destroyed by the realization that I'd hurt her in the process. I put a hand over my face, resting my elbow on the table. "Oh, fuck."

"That was what I assumed you'd been doing."

"Alaric, man—" I raised my head, looking at him. He was still glaring at me. That was fine. I felt like glaring at myself. "How upset was she?"

"I'm not sure, really. She wasn't exactly in the mood for handing out details."

That was one I owed her. Two, if you counted the monumental apology I was going to be making as soon as she got back. "I guess not. Look, Alaric, I never meant for any of that to happen, I swear. I wasn't trying to get her into bed, and I sure as hell wasn't trying to hurt her once she was there."

"I know." He sighed, deflating somehow as he looked down at the table. "I know she likes you. I've known for ages. I just kept hoping she'd see that you weren't interested. That she had better options available. But it was like she couldn't see anything but the fact that you were playing hard to get."

"I wasn't playing," I said softly. This sort of thing was easier to handle when George was around. She was always the one who noticed when girls started crushing on me, and she made them go away. One way or another. I'd never tried to deal with this sort of situation on my own before. "I really wasn't."

Alaric laughed. It was a short, dry sound, utterly devoid of humor. "The tragedy of all this is that I know. If you'd been playing, she might have gotten over you faster."

"I'll apologize."

"You'd better." He stood, taking his laptop with him. "We can't afford to be at each other's throats right now."

"No, we can't," I said bleakly, and watched as he turned and walked out of the room. Once he was gone I let my head fall to the table, forehead knocking gently against the wood. "Fuck, George. How do I get myself into this shit?"

Leaping before you look, mostly. It's always been your biggest weakness. Her laugh was superficially similar to Alaric's, all sharp, hard edges, but there was amusement there, too. The sort of amusement that comes right before the execution. *That, and me, anyway.*

"Oh, thank God." I sat up and sagged backward in the chair, closing my eyes. "You scared the crap out of me."

You needed some time to think.

"Yeah, and look how much good that did me. Now Becks is pissed, which means Maggie's going to be pissed, too, and Alaric thinks I'm an asshole."

Well, you sort of are. I told you to be careful with her.

"How was I supposed to know she was going to jump me in the bathroom?"

I love you, but there are times when I really don't understand the way your

*brain works. She's been getting ready to jump you for a while now. All the
signs were there.*

"Why would I know what the signs *were*, George? I never had to
read them before."

She sighed. *True enough. You shouldn't have called her by my name,
Shaun. This is going to complicate everything.*

"I know. Now what am I supposed to do about it?"

She didn't have an answer for that one.

Maggie's van pulled up half an hour later. I heard doors slamming
in the driveway, and then, like magic, the kitchen was full of women
with arms full of groceries, covering every flat surface with brown
paper sacks. I was still at the kitchen table, although I'd exchanged
my coffee for a can of Coke. The acidic sweetness of it was actually
pleasant for once; the fact that I was drinking it meant that George
was speaking to me again. That was worth doing a little damage to
my tooth enamel.

Becks cast a wounded look in my direction as she dropped her
armload of grocery bags onto the stove. Then she fled out the back
door, vanishing in the direction of the van. I winced and stood. "Aw,
hey, Becks, hang on a second—"

"Freeze," said Maggie, in an amiable tone.

I froze.

"Kelly, why don't you go and get Alaric. Tell him we need help
unloading the van." Maggie's voice stayed pleasant, but there was an
edge to it that made arguing with her seem like a seriously bad idea.
Kelly nodded and left the room even faster than Becks had. She
didn't even bother putting down her last bag of groceries.

I stayed where I was, watching Maggie cautiously. She put down
the bag she was holding and walked over to me, stopping a few feet
away as she studied my face. Finally, shaking her head, she sighed.

"How crazy *are* you, Shaun?"

It was an echo of the question George asked me in the van, after

Kelly dropped her little bombshell about the reservoir conditions. There was no possible way for Maggie to have heard Georgia's side of the conversation, even if she'd been listening in. I flinched all the same, answering without thinking about it: "Pretty damn crazy." I winced. "Okay, that was maybe not the best answer. Can I try again?"

"It was an honest answer, which is what I needed." Maggie looked me slowly up and down. "Did you know what you were going to do to Rebecca when you let her take you to bed?"

"God, no. Maggie, I didn't even know she was ... y'know, *interested* in me. That way."

"I thought that might be the case." Maggie sighed. "Have you ever had a girlfriend?"

That was another question without a good answer. I settled for being as honest as I could. "Not as such, no."

Again that slow look up and down before Maggie said, "I thought that might be the case, too. Will you let me give you some advice?"

"At this point?" I barked a short, bitter laugh. "I'd take advice from the bulldogs if I thought it would help. I didn't mean to fuck things up with Becks. I mean ... " It was my fault because she'd been there, and she'd been willing, and she'd been offering me something I thought I wanted. She came with full disclosure, all her baggage right there on the table. Me, I'd been hiding how far gone I was for so long that I ... didn't. She had no idea what she was getting into. I knew that. And I should have known better.

"Are you blaming her?"

"I'm blaming myself."

"Good." Maggie nodded, looking satisfied. "You're both adults, and it's none of my business what you do, as long as nobody's getting hurt. Becks got hurt. Maybe she should have been more careful about weighing the risks, but that doesn't matter right now. You need to apologize to her. You need to make this right, because if you wait for her to get better on her own, I don't think you're going to be able to work together anymore."

"Yeah, I can do that." I would even mean it. Becks deserved a hell of a lot better than the way I'd treated her, whether I meant to treat her badly or not.

She deserved a hell of a lot better than me.

"I'm glad." Maggie stepped forward and hugged me. Her hair smelled like vanilla and strawberries. She held on just long enough that I was starting to get uncomfortable before letting go and turning to start taking groceries out of bags, leaving me blinking dumbly after her. Catching my look, she arched her eyebrows, and said, "Well? What are you waiting for? Get out there and talk to her. *Go.*"

I went.

The grass was damp, probably from some overnight rainfall, and my boots were wet by the time I'd crossed it to Maggie's van, which sat in the driveway with doors open and groceries on the front seat. There was nobody there. I turned to look around, unsurprised to see footprints in the wet grass leading away, toward Maggie's vegetable garden.

I followed the trail all the way around the house and to the edge of the carefully tilled plot of ground that Maggie used for growing vegetables and fresh herbs. A few pre-Rising park benches had been set up inside the garden border, providing a decorative touch of retro chic to the place. Becks was sitting on the bench farthest from where I stood, her back to me. I wasn't quiet as I approached her, and she didn't move. I guess she'd been expecting me.

"Hey," I said, when I was close enough. "You mind if I sit down?"

"Yes, I do mind." She turned in my direction, tilting her chin up as she looked at me. Her eyes were only a little bloodshot. She'd clearly mastered the Irwin art of crying without making yourself look bad for the cameras. That just made me feel worse. "But I guess we have to do this, so you might as well." She scooted to the side, waving a hand in invitation.

"Thanks." I sat, letting my hands rest on my knees. Silence fell between us. She was waiting for me to start, and I had no clue how.

Say you're sorry, prompted George.

She'd never led me wrong before. "I'm sorry, Becks. I mean, Jesus, I'm so fucking sorry, I don't think I can even say it. I was stupid, and I was selfish, and I'm sorry."

Becks took a shaky breath. There was an edge of laughter to her voice when she spoke, like she couldn't quite believe that we were doing this. "So that's it? You're sorry? I knew you had issues, Shaun, and I'm a big girl—I thought I could handle them. I guess I was wrong. I shouldn't blame you for that." *But I do.* The subtext in her words was impossible to miss, even for me.

"Maybe you shouldn't blame me, but I should still have been smart enough to tell you that it wasn't a good idea for us to be . . . intimate like that."

"You mean we shouldn't have fucked like bunnies?"

I coughed, partly from surprise, partly to cover the phantom sound of George's laughter. "Uh, that, too. I just . . . I guess I wasn't expecting it and does that sound unbelievably lame, or is it just me?"

Becks frowned, slowly. "You really mean that, don't you? You really had no idea."

"No idea of what?"

She stared for a moment before letting her chin drop and saying, "Oh, my God. You *really* had no idea."

I was starting to get concerned. Apologizing for something I knew I'd done was one thing—I may not have much experience with girls, but I'm smart enough to know that calling them by somebody else's name is *never* a good thing, especially when that somebody else is dead and also technically my sister. Apologizing for something I didn't know I'd done was a bit more of a problem, if only because I couldn't be sure I was doing it right. "Uh, Becks, I'm sorry, but you're kinda losing me here. I'm happy to keep apologizing, but I do need to know what I'm apologizing *for*."

This time her laughter was bright and brittle, like broken glass glinting in the sunlight. "I've been throwing myself at you for *months*, Shaun. The flirting, the frilly tops, the requests for hands-on review of my reports—I mean, what the hell did you think I was doing?"

"I don't know," I replied honestly. "I figured you just wanted to make sure your facts were solid before you posted, and all that frilly stuff looked like a girl thing. Sort of like the way you wear your hair."

"I wasn't getting any ratings based on what I wore to work," she said.

I shrugged.

Becks sighed. "Fine. So you wrote all that off. What about the flirting? Did you write that off as 'a girl thing,' too?"

If I was telling the truth, I might as well go for the whole truth. I was pretty sure it couldn't get me into any more trouble than I was already in. "Until you showed up and took my towel away, I really didn't notice."

"If Dave weren't dead, I'd owe him ten bucks." Becks looked away from me, staring out at the forest past the fence. It looked completely untamed; Maggie's security precautions were very well concealed. "He said you didn't get it. I thought you were playing hard to get."

"That's what Alaric said, too. I'm really sorry. I never did the whole flirting thing."

"No, I guess you didn't, did you?" She slanted a sidelong glance my way, considering me. "You didn't need to."

I thought about lying to her. After everything else, there didn't seem to be any point. "No, I guess I didn't."

She nodded, once, mouth twisting in that too-damn-familiar way before she went back to looking at the forest. I hated that look. I'd hated it on every face that I'd ever seen wearing it. The one that said, clearly, "But she's your *sister*," and ignored the part where she was also the only person who'd ever really given a damn what I thought. About anything.

Finally, in a soft, almost contemplative tone, Becks said, "I guess I sort of knew, deep down. Maybe that's why you were so safe to chase. I didn't think I'd ever have a chance to catch you."

I wasn't sure what to say to that. I settled for what seemed like the safest of my available options. "I'm sorry."

"I am, too, Shaun. Believe me, I am too. I . . . I know we can't exactly go back to the way things were. That's my fault as much as it is yours, I guess. I just don't know . . ."

"How we're supposed to go on from here?" I ventured. She nodded. I bit back the urge to laugh, mostly because I wasn't sure I'd be able to stop again. "Dude, Becks, I've been asking myself that question pretty much every day since George died."

"Have you figured out the answer yet?"

"There isn't one." I slumped against the back of the bench, tilting my head back until I couldn't see anything but sky, going on for what might as well have been forever. "I figure I'll just keep on going the way I am until something starts making sense."

"What if nothing ever does?"

"I guess if that happens, I'll start hoping all the God freaks are right, and there's some superior intelligence up there treating us all like laboratory rats."

Fabric rustled against wood as Becks turned to peer at me. I couldn't see her, but I knew her well enough to know exactly what her expression looked like: confusion mixed with wary suspicion that whatever I said next was going to be so completely off the wall that she couldn't stand to hear it. Finally, she said, "Why are you going to start looking for God?"

"I didn't say I was going to start looking. If there's a God, there are plenty of people who know where he is." I shrugged, still watching the sky. It was easier than watching Becks. "I just want to know that he's there, so that I can die knowing there's going to be someone I can punch in the mouth on the other end."

Becks laughed. Some of the tension in my shoulders slipped away. I'd done a terrible thing to her, but I didn't mean to, and the tone of her laughter told me that maybe—despite everything—we could manage to be okay again. She was right; we'd never be exactly the same kind of okay that we were before. But we'd be more okay, and that was better than nothing.

Violence isn't the only solution, George said. She sounded as relieved as I felt.

"Sometimes it's the most fun one," I answered, without thinking about it. Becks stopped laughing. I tensed, looking away from the sky and back to her as I waited for us to start arguing again.

Instead, she just looked at me. Her eyes were hazel. I'd never noticed that before—not really. That made me feel even worse about what we'd done. I should never have slept with her if I couldn't even remember the color of her eyes. "You're pretty lucky, you know," she said.

I blinked at her. "What?"

"Most people, we lose the people that we love, and they're just *gone.* We don't get to have them anymore. But you . . . " She raised a hand, brushing her fingertips across my forehead. Her skin was cool. "She's always going to be there for you, isn't she? As long as you live."

"I don't know how to live in a world that doesn't have her in it," I said. My voice came out raw with a longing that surprised me. I never start thinking I'm getting over losing her. It still startles me sometimes, when I realize just how damn much I miss her.

"Here's hoping you never have to." Becks stood. "We're okay, Shaun. Or at least, I'm okay, and I'd like you to be okay with me."

I nodded. "I'd like that."

"Good. I'll go tell Maggie that we talked things through." She hesitated, and then added, "Keep the guest room. I'll sleep on the couch tonight." She shoved her hands into her pockets and walked away before I could say anything, footsteps plodding heavily on the damp garden earth. I watched her go, and then sagged back into the bench, closing my eyes.

"When do things get to be simple again, George?" I whispered. "Ever?"

They weren't simple to begin with, she said.

I didn't have a comeback for that, and so I just sat in the sunlight in the garden and breathed in the smell of rain-soaked grass, waiting for the world to slow down. Just a little bit. Just long enough to let us rest before the next storm came crashing through. Was that really so much to ask? I just wanted to rest.

Just for a little while.

Things it is not polite to discuss at the dinner table: politics, religion, and the walking dead.

Things we wind up discussing at the dinner table every single night: politics, religion, and the walking dead. Along with small-caliber versus large-caliber weapons for field use, personal security gear, Maggie's garden, our ratings, and vehicle maintenance. It's very claustrophobic and intense, with everyone on top of everybody else pretty much all the time. There's no real privacy, and there's so much security on the house that getting out is almost as big a production as getting *in*. It's like a fucked-up combination of prison and summer camp.

Is it weird that this is what I always dreamed the news would be like? Because, God, maybe I'm fucked in the head or something, but this is the most fun I've ever had. I want someone to remind me I said that when it all turns around and bites us in the ass.

—From *Charming Not Sincere*, the blog of Rebecca Atherton, May 9, 2041. Unpublished.

———

Check it out, folks! I can add "survived an unplanned zombie encounter while visiting the CDC to discuss the outbreak in Oakland" to my résumé! Not to brag or anything, but why don't you all download my reports, and then go fill out your Golden Steve-o nominations for the year? I'll be your best friend ...

—From *Charming Not Sincere*, the blog of Rebecca Atherton, May 9, 2041

Seventeen

Five days ticked by with little fanfare. Becks and I went shooting in the woods outside of town, clearing out a mixed mob of zombie humans and cows. Once the disease takes over, species isn't an issue anymore. Maggie spent a lot of time writing poetry, weeding her garden, and avoiding Kelly, who took over the dining room table with Dr. Abbey's research and kept muttering things none of the rest of us could understand. Alaric hung out with her, listening, taking notes, and nodding a lot. It was almost unnerving, in a geeky sort of way.

Those five days may have been the last good time for us. Maybe the universe had been listening when I made my wish out in the garden; I don't know. I just know that I asked for time to rest, and somehow, miraculously, I actually got it. Nothing exploded. There were no outbreaks and no emergencies, nothing to pull us away from the difficult task of turning ourselves back into a team. The hours turned into days, and the days blended together, distinguished from each other only by the activity in the forums and the reports we were posting.

Kelly continued her series of guest articles under the Barbara Tinney byline. It wasn't exactly a runaway hit, but it was popular—

surprisingly so. I always forget how much people like getting excuses for their crazy. The profits Kelly's column brought in went directly to Maggie, where they could help pay for our room and board. She snorted and waved it off like it was no big thing. She also took the money. It made me feel a little bit less guilty about the way we were intruding.

Becks moved into the study, saying that the air mattress was better for her back than the couch was for mine. That meant I could move to the guest room, which was a relief, since I wasn't really sleeping in the living room. And I needed my sleep. I went to bed every night with my head stuffed full of science, and woke up every morning ready to cram in some more. I needed to understand the research Dr. Abbey had given us. More important, I needed to understand the research Mahir was hopefully sweet-talking some British professor into doing. If I was going to march everyone off to get themselves killed on my behalf, I was by God going to be certain I knew what they were dying for. It was the only promise I could make that I felt reasonably sure of being able to keep.

When I wasn't studying, I was making calls. My little team of reporters might not have much in the way of manpower, but we had connections, and it was time to exploit them. Rick's ascent from Newsie to vice president of the United States isn't a normal career path for either a journalist or a politician, but hey, it's worked out pretty well for him. I started calling his office, once a day at first, then twice a day, until it became clear that he wasn't going to call me back. That wasn't like him. Not even a little bit. And that worried me.

The days rolled on. Alaric started a series on the rise of digital profiling and its applications in the medical field. Becks took a trip up into Washington, looking for zombies she could harass on camera; she came back with powder burns, bruises, and twice as many articles about her adventures. Reading the first one made my throat get tight with half a dozen emotions it was hard to put into words. That used to be me running into the woods to play tag with zombie deer and gathering "no shit, there I was" stories from truckers who remembered the roads during the Rising. That used to be all I wanted in the world. Everything changed when George died. Sometimes I read the articles that Becks posts and I wonder whether the man I used to be would even recognize the one I'm becoming. I don't think he'd like the new me very much.

I know I don't.

I told Mahir and Maggie about the silence from Rick's office, and they agreed that it was best if we kept it between us, at least for now. Everyone was freaked out enough without adding that little wrinkle to the mix. Maggie's Fictionals didn't help; at some point, she'd given at least half of them the all-clear. They went back to dropping in without warning, appearing on the doorstep and in the kitchen like they'd been there all along. Most of them brought pizza, or cookies, or samosas. I'd never met two-thirds of them before, even though they were all technically part of the site staff. They walked on eggshells around everyone but Maggie, and we started using their visits as excuses for equipment repair and trips into Weed for more groceries. Once their grindhouse parties got started, they could go for hours, watching crappy pre-Rising horror movies and eating gallons of popcorn. I didn't realize how antisocial I was becoming until the Fictionals started to descend, and all I could think of was how quickly I could get away.

The bug at the Portland CDC yielded nothing useful; either they'd managed to find and destroy it, or it hadn't survived the decontamination process. One more possible information source down the drain. The worms Alaric activated back in Oakland were doing a little bit better. They kept finding old research papers and short-lived projects buried in the bowels of one server or another. We added them to the data we already had, and kept on working.

Mahir had a few local scientists who were willing to at least discuss the situation with him; he didn't tell us their names, and I didn't press. There were some things I was better off not knowing until I had to. It seemed to be going well, at least in the beginning, but after the second day, he stopped calling or e-mailing. His reports still went up on time, and he still did his time on the forums—from the outside, everything looked fine—but he wasn't keeping up normal contact.

Don't push him, said George. I listened, more out of habit than because I agreed with her. She was usually right about when I needed to wait and when it was okay to barrel on ahead. I just wasn't sure how much longer my patience could last.

The waiting ended a little over two weeks after the destruction of Oakland and our arrival at Maggie's. The house phone rang, ignored by the humans currently present—myself, Maggie, and the Doc, who was struggling to write an article about the pros and cons of exposing children to the outside world. She was having a lot more trouble meeting her deadlines now that she didn't have Mahir to help.

The answering machine picked up after the second ring. There were a few minutes of silence, followed by the voice of the house computer saying politely, "Excuse me, Shaun. Do you have a moment?"

I hate machines that sound like people.

"Hush," I muttered. The house computer had learned not to pay attention when I spoke that quietly—I guess even machines have a learning curve for crazy—and continued to wait for my reply until I said, "Yeah, sure. What's up?"

"There is a call for you."

"I guessed that part. Who is it?"

"The caller has declined to identify himself. By his accent, there is an eighty-seven percent chance that he is of British nationality, although I am unable to determine his region of origin with any accuracy. The call has been placed from a local number. The exact number is blocked. Would you like me to request additional information?"

I stood so fast that I knocked my Coke over. Soda cascaded across the table and onto the carpet. I ignored it, lunging for the phone next to the kitchen door. Maggie was right behind me, demanding, "House, is the line secure?"

"This end of the line is secured according to protocol four, which should be sufficient to block anything but a physical wiretap. I am unable to determine the security standards of the other end of the line. Do you wish to proceed?" The voice of the house was infinitely patient, mechanical calm unbroken by the fact that Maggie and I looked like we were on the verge of hysterics.

"Yes, dammit," I said, and grabbed the receiver from the wall. Dead air greeted me. I gave the phone a panicked look. "Where is he?"

"House, *connect*," ordered Maggie.

The phone clicked, and suddenly, wonderfully, Mahir's voice was in my ear, muffled slightly, like he had his hand over the receiver. "— Promise you, sir, I'm phoning my ride now. I apologize for loitering within your isolation zone, but as my original flight was delayed, it was unfortunately unavoidable." His tone was clipped, carefully polite, and shaded with a bone-deep weariness that made me tired just listening to it.

"Mahir!" I said, loudly enough that he would be able to hear me through his hand.

There was a scraping sound before he said, "About bloody time, Mason. Come get me."

"Uh, sorry if I'm a little bit behind the program here, but come get you *where*?"

The house said the call was coming from a local number, said George sharply. *He's here. Mahir is in this area code.*

"I'm at the Weed Airport."

I froze, staring stupidly at the wall. Maggie nudged me with her elbow, and I said the first thing that popped into my head: "Weed has an airport?"

Maggie dropped her forehead theatrically into her hand. "The man's been here for weeks and he hasn't even checked the phone book . . . " she moaned.

"It had best, or I'm in the wrong place entirely." Mahir sounded like he was too tired to be amused. "I'm inside twenty minutes of being toted off for loitering, which would be a bit of a problem for me, so will you *please* come pick me up?"

"I—" I shot a glance at Maggie, who was still covering her face with her hand. "We'll be right there. Just stay where you are."

"That's not going to be a problem," Mahir said.

There was a click, and the calm, pleasant voice of the house said, "The other party has disconnected the call. Would you like me to attempt to restore the connection?"

"No, he hung up," I said, and did the same. My fingertips were numb, probably from the shock. "Maggie, you know how to find the airport?"

"I can get us there."

"Good. Doc! Get your shoes on. We're taking a road trip."

Kelly emerged from the dining room, hugging a notepad against her chest. "We are?" she asked, sounding bemused. "Where are we going?" After a pause, she added, "Why am *I* going?"

"We're going to the airport to pick up a friend, and you're coming because Maggie has to tell me how to get there." By group consensus, Kelly was never left alone in the house for any reason, not even for a few minutes. The closest we'd come was leaving her in the custody of a few of Maggie's Fictionals, and even then, it was never for more than an hour. We weren't afraid she was going to run—not anymore—but there was always the chance the CDC would finally track her down when we weren't there to protect her.

To her credit, Kelly had stopped arguing about our refusal to leave her by herself after the first week, and she wasn't arguing now. She nodded, saying, "I'll go get my coat," before disappearing back into the dining room.

Maggie and I exchanged a glance. "I didn't think he'd come *here*," she said. "I've only met him the once, at . . . the last time he came to California."

The event she wasn't naming was Georgia's funeral. I nodded, both in acknowledgment and as silent thanks for her not saying the word "funeral" out loud. "He's a good guy. If he's here, he must have found something pretty big."

"Or he's running from something pretty big."

"That's also possible." Mahir hadn't said anything about his wife being with him, and somehow I couldn't imagine that she'd approved this little jaunt without a good reason. "Let's go find out, shall we?"

"I'm pretty sure we don't have a choice," Maggie said, and patted my arm lightly before heading for the door.

I paused long enough to grab my gun belt and laptop, and followed. "I guess this means the break is over," I muttered.

I think you're right.

Maggie and Kelly were waiting next to Maggie's van when I made it outside, miniature bulldogs frolicking around their feet. Maggie smiled wryly. "They can't imagine any reason for us to be outside that doesn't involve playing with them."

"I'll throw tennis balls for an hour once we finish the debriefing," I said, holding up my hand. "Keys?"

"You're driving?" asked Maggie, as she lobbed them to me underhand.

"At least that way we'll get there alive."

Maggie's laughter was echoed by George, the two of them setting up a weird reverb that no one but me could hear. George always *hated* letting me drive, said I was trying to send the both of us to an early grave every time I swung around a corner without slowing down. I do the driving for both of us these days, by necessity, and she mostly doesn't give me shit about it, but still, the irony wasn't escaping either one of us.

Even when she was alive, George would have admitted that I was a better driver than Maggie. I've never let the car spin out just to see what would happen, for example, and I don't view rainy days as an excuse to hydroplane. I may be crazy, but I think there's a pretty good chance that Maggie's suicidal.

Kelly crawled into the backseat. Maggie and I took the front, Maggie programming an address into the GPS as I started the van. I drove slowly down the length of the driveway, pausing only for the exit checkpoint—a small, almost cursory confirmation that we were aware of the dangers inherent in choosing to leave the property— before turning onto one of the winding two-lane roads that pass as major streets in a town the size of Weed. There weren't many pot-holes. That was about as far as the civic planners went in terms of preparing the citizenry for an outbreak. In places like Oakland and Portland, there are standing defenses, blood test checkpoints, and lots of fences. In places like Weed, there are doors with locks, safety-glass windows, and room to breathe. I'd never spent much time in a stable rural area before; I always thought the people who chose to live that way were sort of insane. It was sort of surprising to realize that I liked it.

When all this is over, I'll make sure you can retire on a farm with lots of room to run around and play with the other puppies, said George dryly.

I managed to turn my laughter into a shallow cough, ducking my head to the side before Maggie and the Doc could see me smile. With as good as things had been going, I was trying not to shove reminders of my relationship with George in their faces. Knowing the boss is crazy is one thing. Dealing with it is something else.

"How far is the airport?" asked Kelly, leaning between the seats so she could see the road. Her hair was starting to grow out, and it tangled in front of her eyes in a tawny fringe. It made her look more like herself, and that made it easier for me to deal with her, especially since she was still wearing Buffy's clothes everywhere. One ghost was more than enough for me.

"About ten miles," said Maggie. She picked up the radio remote, beginning to flick through the frequencies. Our van has a sophisticated antenna array capable of picking up police and even some military bands, thanks to Buffy's tinkering and George's endless willingness to throw money into improving our access to information. Maggie's van, on the other hand, has six hundred channels of satellite radio. Prior to riding with her, I didn't know there was enough, say, Celtic teenybopper surf rock to fill a podcast, much less an entire radio station. Live and learn.

Maggie settled on a station blaring pre-Rising grunge pop, cranking the volume a few notches before she put the remote down and reclined in her seat. "That's better."

"Better than what?" asked Kelly.

"Not having the music on." Maggie twisted to face me, delivering a firm jab of her forefinger to my ribs at almost exactly the same time. "Now spill. Did you have any idea he was coming?"

"I really had no idea, Maggie, I swear." I slowed at a stop sign—not quite coming to a full stop—before gunning the engine again and going barreling down a narrow, tree-lined street at a speed that only bordered on unsafe. As long as I didn't cross that line and kill us all, I figured I was doing pretty well. "He was doing some research for me, but I honestly never expected that particular phone call."

Neither did I, and that worries me, said George.

"Who are we talking about?" asked Kelly. She sounded worried. "I'm already a little uncomfortable with the number of people who've been in the house lately. Is this guy going to be staying?"

"For a while, yeah," I said. "We're on our way to pick up Mahir Gowda. You met him at the funeral." Not that they'd had very much time to talk, or reason to; Kelly was only in attendance because the FBI had seized George's body as evidence in the case against Governor Tate, and the CDC doesn't allow human remains to be shipped without an escort. Thanks to that little rule, I wound up with two extra guests at a party I never intended to hold: Kelly and her boss, Dr. Wynne. I left George in the van and went to confront the man who really killed her—I shot her, but Tate ordered her infection, and I held Tate responsible for what happened—and I didn't see her again until she was nothing but a heap of sterile ash—

Steady, said George, breaking my black mood before it could fully form.

"Right, sorry," I muttered. Mahir's unexpected visit had me on the edge of panic, and every little thing—like the reminder of how Kelly and Mahir had first met—was enough to send me over the edge into seriously brooding. That wasn't something I could afford just now.

Maggie gave me a sidelong look that was thoughtful and, oddly, relieved. "He was the one in the really unfortunate brown pants," she said, directing her words toward Kelly.

"He flew in from London, didn't he?" Kelly paused, eyes widening. "Wait, did he just fly in from London *again*?"

"That's what it I looks like," I said. We were approaching a large green sign that read WEED AIRPORT (MUNICIPAL FIELD 046) AHEAD. I slowed to match the posted speed limit, turning into the lane that would take us to the quarantine zone.

Air travel changed a lot after the Rising. According to the history books, it used to be a pretty simple process. Older movies show airports packed with people coming and going as they pleased, and the real old ones show *really* crazy shit, like guys who aren't even passengers pursuing their runaway girlfriends through security and people buying tickets from flight attendants, in cash. Every flight attendant I've ever seen has been carrying more ordnance than your average Irwin, and if somebody ran onto a flight without the proper medical clearances and a green light from the check-in desk, they'd be dead long before they hit the floor. Working for the airlines teaches a person to shoot first and ask questions later, if ever.

People who can't hack it as Irwins because they're too violent go into the air travel industry. There's a thought to make a person want to stay at home.

Travel between the major airports requires a clean bill of health from an accredited doctor, followed by inspection by airport medical personnel before even moving into the ticketing concourse. Nonpassengers aren't allowed past the first air lock. Once you're inside, you're herded from blood test to blood test, usually supervised by people with lots and lots of guns. That's another thing that seems unbelievable about pre-Rising air travel: Nobody in those old movies is ever carrying a weapon unless they work for the police or the air marshals. Something about the fear of hijacking. Well, these days, the fear of zombies ensures that even people who have no business carrying a gun will have one when they want to get on a plane. You get on, you sit down, and you stay sitting unless one of the flight attendants is escorting you to the restroom—after a blood test, of course. It takes their clearance to even unbuckle your seat belt once the plane is in motion. So yeah, air travel? Not simple, not fun, and definitely not something people undertake lightly.

Weed's airport was tiny, three buildings and a runway, with only the minimum in federally mandated air lock and quarantine space between the airport and the curb. Several airport security cars were parked nearby. Overkill most of the time, especially for an airport this small, but I was willing to bet they wouldn't be nearly enough if a plane actually flew in with an unexpected cargo of live infected. That's the trouble with being scared all the time. Eventually, people just go numb.

I stopped the car in the space marked for passenger pick-up and drop-off, hitting the horn twice. Kelly winced, but didn't question the action. Only an idiot gets out of their car unprompted at even the smallest of airports.

We didn't have to wait long. The echoes from the horn barely had time to die out when the air lock door opened and Mahir came walking briskly toward us, dragging a single battered carry-on bag behind him. The formerly black nylon was scuffed and torn and patched with strips of duct tape in several places. At least that probably made it easy to recognize when it came along the conveyor belt at baggage claim—not that Weed's airport was large enough to *have* a conveyor belt. I was pretty sure Mahir hadn't arrived on any commercial flight.

He pulled open the van's rear passenger-side door without saying anything, putting his carry-on bag on the seat before he climbed in and pulled the door shut again. Even then, he didn't say anything, just fastened his seat belt and met my eyes in the rearview mirror, clearly waiting.

I started the engine.

Mahir held his silence until we were half a mile from the airport, and the rest of us stayed silent just as long, waiting for him to say something. Finally, closing his eyes, he pinched the bridge of his nose and said, "Magdalene, how far is it from here to your home?"

"About ten miles," she said, twisting in her seat to look at him with wide and worried eyes. "Honey, are you okay?"

"No. No, I am not okay. I am several thousand miles from okay. I am quite probably involved in divorce proceedings even now, I am present in this country under only the most tenuous of legal umbrellas, I am entirely unsure as to what time zone I am in, and I want nothing more than to rewind my life to the point at which I permitted myself to first be hired by one Miss Georgia Mason." Mahir dropped his hand away from his face, eyes remaining closed as he sagged backward. "I believe that if I were any more exhausted, I would actually be dead, and I might regard that as a blessing. Hello, Shaun. Hello, Dr. Connolly. I would say it is a pleasure to see you again, but under the circumstances, that would be disingenuous at best."

"Hello, Mr. Gowda," said Kelly. I didn't say anything. I kept driving, listening to George swearing loudly in the space between my ears. If there had been any question about what Mahir had found—whether it was good, bad, or just weird—his demeanor answered it. There was no way he'd look that beat down over anything but the end of the world, and somehow, I was starting to suspect that the end of the world was exactly what he represented.

Maggie looked around the car, a crease forming between her brows as she considered the expressions around her. Then she reached for the remote and turned the volume on the radio up. Somehow, that seemed like exactly the right thing to do, and we drove the rest of the way home without saying a word, blasting the happily nihilistic pop music of a dead generation behind us as we went.

Mahir opened his eyes when we reached Maggie's driveway, watching with interest as we passed the first and second gates. As we approached the third gate, he asked, "Does it know how many people are in the vehicle?" I hit the switch to roll down the van windows as I glanced to Maggie for her answer. Metal posts telescoped up from the bushes around the driveway, unfolding to reveal small blood test units with reflective metal panels fastened to their sides. The tiny apertures where the needles would emerge glittered in the sunlight.

"The security grid runs on biometric heat-detection, equipped with low-grade sonar," Maggie said, with the sort of rote precision that implied she knew because she'd read the manual, not because she really understood what the security system was doing. At least she read the manual. Some people trust their safety to machines without even doing that much. "It always knows how many people need to be tested. We ran a bus up here once, when we did the group trip to

Disneyland, and the gate wouldn't open until all thirty-eight of us had tested clean."

"It made you run all thirty-eight?" I asked, punctuating the question with a low whistle. "That's impressive." Also terrifying, since I was willing to bet the designers hadn't considered all the possible loopholes in that model. Maggie's security system made us each lean out the window long enough for a blood test, but it didn't actually make us get out of the car and walk through an air lock while everyone else was tested. It would be entirely possible for someone to test clean and then go into amplification while the rest of the group was still being checked out. The ocular scan at the next gate would catch them—probably—but it would increase the number of potential infected from one to everyone in the group.

Maggie smiled blithely, missing the subtext of my comment. That was probably for the best. "It's the best on the private market." She stuck her hand out the window as she spoke, pressing it down against the passenger-side testing panel.

"It's not *on* the private market," said Kelly. I twisted to look at her as I slapped my hand down on my own testing panel. She shrugged, sticking her hand out the window, and said, "This technology isn't supposed to be available outside of government agencies for another two years."

"Oopsie," said Maggie. She flashed a smile at Kelly and pulled her hand back into the van as the green light next to the testing unit flashed on. "I guess Daddy must have pulled some strings."

Again, added George dryly. I swallowed a chuckle.

"He did an excellent job," said Mahir. The light next to his testing panel flashed green. Withdrawing his hand, he slumped in his seat and closed his eyes again. "Good lord, this nation is enormous. Wake me when there's coffee."

"You'll need to open your eyes for the ocular scan in a minute," said Maggie.

Mahir groaned.

I glanced at him in the rearview mirror, taking in the fine stress lines etched around his eyes. Those weren't there a year ago. George's death was almost as hard on him as it was on me—something I wouldn't have believed possible for almost anybody else. Mahir had been her beta blogger, her colleague, and her best friend, and sometimes I got the feeling he would have tried to be more if they hadn't lived on different continents. At least I had the constant reassurance of going crazy. He just had the silence, and now, thanks to me, the strain of whatever it was he'd learned that was bad enough to drive him out of England.

"Hope this was worth it," I muttered, and started the engine again.

The ocular scanners were calibrated to test only two people at a time; it took us nearly five minutes to clear the fourth gate. Mahir and I went first—me because safety protocols say to clear the driver as fast as possible, him because I was afraid he'd actually fall asleep if we made him wait too long. His exhaustion was becoming more obvious by the moment. I wasn't going to insist he stay awake long enough to tell us everything he knew, but I wanted to know if we were looking at another Oakland. Last time we let an unexpected visitor have time to calm down before telling us everything, our apartment building got blown up, Dave died, and we wound up running for our lives. I'd like to avoid having that happen again if I get any say in the matter.

Maggie's bulldogs were waiting on the front lawn, and they mobbed our feet as soon as we got out of the van. Mahir backpedaled frantically, winding up sitting on the armrest of the passenger seat with his feet drawn up, out of reach of inquisitive noses. This didn't stop them from jumping at his shoes, yapping in their oddly sonorous small-dog voices. "Good lord, don't you keep these things leashed?"

"Not when they're at home," Maggie replied. "Bruiser, Butch, Kitty, down." The three dogs that had seemed the most intent on getting to Mahir dropped to all fours and trotted over to Maggie, tongues lolling.

"They grow on you," I said, leaning past Mahir to grab his bag. It was deceptively heavy. I'd been expecting it to weigh maybe twenty pounds, but it was heavy enough to throw me off balance for a moment. "Jeez, dude, what's in this thing, bricks?"

"Computer equipment, mostly. I hope you have a few shirts I can borrow. It seemed like a poor idea to travel with more than I could fit in a single bag." Mahir watched the dogs warily as he slipped out of the van and edged toward the house. The dogs, for their part, stayed clustered around Maggie, looking up at her with adoring eyes.

"You can borrow my shirts, my man, but you're going commando before you're borrowing my boxers." I slung my arm around his shoulders and started walking toward the kitchen door. "Coffee awaits, unless you'd rather have tea. You look like shit, by the way."

"Yes, I've gathered," said Mahir wearily. "Tea sounds fantastic."

He kept trudging onward as I glanced back at Maggie. Kelly had emerged from the van and was standing next to her, frowning thoughtfully. Maggie nodded, signaling her understanding. I answered her nod with a brief, relieved smile. I needed a few minutes alone with Mahir before he fell into an eight-hour coma, and Maggie was telling me she'd keep Kelly out of the way until I was ready for her.

The kitchen was empty. Alaric and Becks were still off-site, and all the bulldogs were outside, probably harassing Maggie into playing catch with them. I guided Mahir to a seat at the table. "You have a tea-based preference? Maggie has something like five hundred kinds. I think they all taste like licking the lawnmower, so I really can't make recommendations."

"Anything that isn't herbal will be fine." Mahir collapsed into the chair, his chin dipping until it almost grazed his chest. "Soy milk, no sugar, please."

"You got it." I kept one eye on him as I filled the electric kettle and got down a mug.

He's worn out.

"I got that," I muttered. Mahir raised his head enough to blink at me. I offered an insincere smile. "Sorry. I was just—"

"I know what you were doing. Hello, Georgia. I hope your ongoing haunting hasn't driven your brother too far past the edge of reason to justify this visit."

There's no such thing as ghosts, said George, sounding peevish.

The idea of getting into that particular argument was too ludicrous to consider, especially given my position. I got the soy milk from the fridge instead, answering, "George says hey. Your tea will be ready in just a minute. Want to tell me why you decided to be a surprise? We could've at least made up the couch for you, if we'd known that you were coming."

"I didn't want to broadcast it anywhere," Mahir said, with a calm that was actually chilling. This wasn't a spur-of-the-moment decision. I hadn't really expected it would be, but still, the tone of his voice, combined with the exhaustion in his face, made me want to put away the tea and break out the booze. "I purchased a flight from Heathrow to New York via an actual travel agency, rather than online, and flew from there to Seattle, where I switched from my own passport to my father's and caught a flight to Portland. From there, I took a private flight to Weed. The gentleman who owns the plane took payment in cash, and his manifest will show that I was a young woman of Canadian nationality visiting the state for a flower show."

"How much did that cost?"

"Enough that you should be deeply grateful I'm paid in percentage of overall site income, rather than drawing a salary, or you'd owe me quite a bit of money." Mahir removed his glasses in order to scrub at his eyes with the heel of his hand. "I'm not going to be useful much longer, I'm afraid. I've been awake damned near a day and a half as it is."

"I sort of figured." The kettle began to whistle. I turned it off, dropping a teabag from Maggie's disturbingly large collection into a mug and covering it with water before walking the mug and soy milk over to Mahir. "Give me the short form. How bad is it?"

"How bad is it?" Mahir took a moment to doctor his tea, not speaking again until he was settled with both hands wrapped firmly around the mug. Looking at me steadily, he said, "I took the data you gave me to three doctors I was reasonably sure were reputable. One laughed me out of his office. Said if anything of the sort were going on, he'd have heard about it, since the trending evidence would be virtually impossible to overlook. Further said that if anything of the sort were going on, the national census would reflect it. I challenged him to prove that it didn't."

"And?"

"He stopped taking my calls three days later. I'd wager because the national census reflected exactly what he said it wouldn't." Mahir sipped his tea, grimaced, and continued: "When I went to confront him about this in person, he was gone—and he didn't leave a forwarding address."

Well, shit, said George.

"I had more luck with the second doctor I approached—largely, I think, because he was Australian and didn't really give two tosses what the local government thought of his work. He said the research was sound, if a bit overly dramatic, and that he'd rather like a chance to test its applications in a live population."

"It had applications?" I asked, mystified.

"In the sense that . . . Well, look, it's sort of like the research they were doing on parasites at the turn of the century. They found quite a few immune disorders that could be controlled by the introduction of specialized parasites, because the parasites provided a sufficient distraction for the immune system as a whole. They kept the body from attacking itself. Part of what makes Kellis-Amberlee so effective is that it acts like a part of the body—it's with us all the time, so our immune systems don't attack it. There'd be no point; they'd rip us apart trying to kill it. The trouble is that when the virus changes states, the body still doesn't think of it as an enemy. It still regards it as a friendly component."

I frowned. "You lost me."

"If the body regards the sleeping virus as a part of itself, it isn't prepared to fight the virus when it wakes. But people who somehow survive a bout with the activated virus—those who get exposed when they're too small to amplify, for example, or those with a natural resistance—can 'store' a certain measure of the live virus in themselves, like a parasite. Something that teaches the body what it's meant to be fighting off."

"So this dude wanted to, what, go expose a bunch of kangaroos and watch to see what happened as they got bigger?"

"Essentially, yes."

"What happened with him?"

"He got deported on charges of tax evasion and improper work permits."

Silence stretched between us as I considered what he was saying—and what he wasn't. Even George was quiet, letting me think. Finally, I asked, "What about the third guy?"

"His files are in my bag." Mahir looked at me levelly as he sipped his tea. "He read the files. Three times. And then he called me, told me his conclusions and where he'd sent his data, hung up the phone, and shot himself. Really, I'm not certain he had the wrong idea."

"What . . . what did he say?"

"He said that were we braver and less willing to bow to the easy path, we might have had India back a decade ago." Mahir put his cup down and stood. "I'm tired, Shaun. Please show me where I can sleep. You can read what I've brought you, and we'll discuss it later."

"Come on." I stood and started for the hallway. "You can use my room. It's not huge, but it's quiet, and the door latches, so you shouldn't wake up with any surprise roommates."

"That's a relief," he said, following me up the stairs. His presence, strange as it was, felt exactly right, like this was exactly what had to happen before we could finish whatever it was we'd started.

We were all refugees now. None of us would stop running until all of us did.

BOOK IV

Immunological Memory

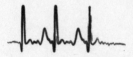

It's better to go out with a bang and a press release than with a whimper and a secret.

—GEORGIA MASON

Fuck this. Let's just blow some shit up.

—SHAUN MASON

George and I never technically knew our birthdays. The doctors could estimate how old we were and make some educated guesses about our biological parents, but it really didn't matter. We knew we were born sometime in 2017, toward the end of the Rising, when most of North America had been taken back from the infected, because the doctors said so. We knew she was older by about six weeks. Everything else was details, and details weren't important. Not to me. What was important was that I had her, and she had me, and we had each other, and that meant we could face anything the world threw at us. Sometimes I was even arrogant enough to think the Rising happened so we could be together.

It's as good an explanation as any.

As of today, no matter when my birthday really is, I've had a birthday without George. As of today, I've spent a year going to sleep and waking up in a world she isn't in, a world that seems meaningless because she's never going to make it mean anything ever again. I was always sort of afraid she'd turn suicidal when I died. I asked her once if she ever worried about me like that.

"You're already suicidal, you asshole," she said, and laughed. Only it turns out she was wrong, because losing her made me more careful about almost everything. I miss her every day. I miss her every *minute*. But if anything happens to me, she may never get the ending she deserves, and I refuse to be selfish enough to die before I'm finished taking care of the things she left behind.

Happy birthday, George. You made me better than I could ever have been without you, and you hurt me worse than I could ever have been hurt by anybody else. I love you. I miss you. And I'm starting to get the feeling that I'll see you pretty soon, because I'm starting to feel like, maybe, things are coming to an end.

God, I miss you.

**—From *Adaptive Immunities*, the blog of
Shaun Mason, June 20, 2041**

————

Anybody who messes with Shaun is messing with me. And of the two of us, I swear, I am the one you do *not* want to mess with. He'll kill you. But I will make you sorry, and I will make you pay.

Trust me. I'm a journalist.

**—From *Postcards from the Wall*, the unpublished
files of Georgia Mason, originally posted
June 20, 2041**

Eighteen

Alaric, what's your twenty?" Silence answered me. I bit back a snarl and tried again: "Alaric, where are you?" Getting mad at him for not knowing the weird mix of military and ham radio pidgin used by the Irwin community was pointless. That didn't stop me from doing it.

This time he answered, his voice coming clear and easy through the phone: "I'm finishing up my edits while Becks does some final recon for her report."

"Not an answer." I raked a hand through my hair, watching Maggie try to guide Kelly through the steps required to mix pancake batter. Either Kelly was the worst cook in the world or Maggie was really shitty at giving instructions. It could have gone either way. "Where are you, exactly?"

"Down near Mount Shasta." My silence must have told Alaric he needed to give me more information, because he added, "About an hour out. Why? Do you need us to stop at the store or something on our way back in?"

Back when Buffy was alive, we could trust our network against anyone on the planet, including the CIA. Our security isn't that stellar anymore, but thanks to upgrades cobbled from Maggie's house system, Becks's jury-rigging skills, and Alaric's computer know-how, we're pretty stable. Stable enough for what I was about to say, anyway: "Mahir's here."

It was Alaric's turn to go briefly silent. Finally, he said, "Mahir sent in a report?"

"No, dumb-ass, Mahir's *here*. Mahir is asleep upstairs in the guest room I've been using. He showed up with pretty much the clothes on his back and a suitcase full of research, and he looks like hammered shit."

Maggie looked over. "Is that Alaric? Tell him to stop by the House of Curries on his way home. I'm going to send in an order."

"Got it. Alaric, Maggie says—"

"I heard her," he said, managing to sound annoyed and astonished at the same time. "You're serious, aren't you? Mahir is actually *here*."

"Yeah, that's what I've been saying." Alaric began swearing. I listened, impressed. I hadn't realized he knew that much Cantonese. I let him go for a few minutes, then interjected, "You kiss your mother with that mouth?"

Play nice with my Newsies, or I swear I'm going to make you sorry, said George flatly.

"I am being nice."

Luckily, Alaric was still swearing, finishing off an elaborate phrase that started in Cantonese and switched to English as he said, almost wonderingly, "—son of a chicken-fucking soy farmer and a diseased convention-center security guard. How did he *get* here? Is he all right? Are we going to need to move again?"

"I'd rather wait and explain everything to you and Becks at the same time. Right now, he's exhausted but I'm pretty sure nobody's been shooting at him—yet, anyway—and that's something else I'd like us all to talk about at once. So when can you be here?"

There was a clattering sound as Alaric shoved his keyboard away, knocking something to the van floor in the process. "Give me ten minutes to get Becks back here, and I'll break a couple of dozen speed limits getting over to you."

"Don't forget to pick up dinner," called Maggie.

"Maggie says—"

"I heard her. Do you need anything else?"

"Just drive safely, don't get pulled over, and don't crash into anything. If we're going to die horribly, we're all going to do it together."

"Great pep talk, boss. Very touching. I'll always remember the day when you told me not to drive into a tree on the way home." Alaric said something caustic sounding in Cantonese—what little I remembered from my course on field communications made me think he'd just called me a goat fucker—and hung up.

Smirking, I pulled off my ear cuff and dropped it into my shirt pocket, twisting to face Maggie and Kelly. "They're on their way, and yes, Maggie, Alaric's going to pick up dinner. He said they'd be about an hour. Why are we ordering dinner if you're making pancakes?"

"It gives me something to do with my hands, and Mahir's got to be hungry after becoming an international fugitive from justice." Maggie handed Kelly another egg. "I'll tell the house to transmit our normal order, plus three."

"Fair enough." I got up and crossed to the fridge, pulling out a can of Coke. "Make me a couple of pancakes, will you?"

"Already planning to." Maggie took the bowl from Kelly. She looked inside, sighed, and started picking bits of eggshell out of the batter. "I'm assuming things are pretty bad for him to have come to us this way."

"I don't know that they're any worse than they were yesterday, but I think they're about to get pretty bad, yeah." I couldn't stop thinking about Mahir's casual mention of divorce papers. I'd given his wife shit since the day they got married, but that didn't mean I wanted her to leave him. He was risking everything to be here with us. Hell, he'd been risking everything since the day he agreed to come back to the team. I just hoped we could live up to the degree of faith that he was putting in us, because I really wasn't sure anymore.

Just keep breathing, advised George. *It's too late for any of us to turn back now.*

"Got that right," I muttered, and cracked open the Coke, taking a drink before asking, "Doc, what do you know about viral parasitism?"

Kelly stared at me. "What?"

"It was something Mahir said before he went upstairs to crash— the virus acts like a parasite in people with reservoir conditions, and that teaches their bodies how to cope with it better. I'm not quite sure what he meant, but I figure you'll be able to translate for us when we sit down for the big meeting."

"I ..." Kelly frowned thoughtfully. "It's not a *common* theory, but I've heard it before. It basically says that the virus can change its behavior, go from being a strict predator to a sort of symbiotic parasite."

"Isn't that what both source viruses were originally supposed to do?" asked Maggie, turning on the stove. She began pouring dollops of batter onto the griddle, filling the room with the hot, sweet scent of cooking pancakes. "We were supposed to catch them and then keep them forever, like ... I don't know, weird immortal hamsters that cured cancer."

"Only these hamsters developed rabies." I sipped my Coke. "If it's something people already know about, is there any reason for someone to get deported for studying it? Viral parasitism, I mean. Not hamsters."

"No," Kelly said, firmly. "There's no good reason for someone to be deported for studying viral parasitism."

"That's what I thought." I leaned back in my seat, sipping my Coke, and watched Maggie make pancakes. Kelly went quiet, a speculative expression on her face. I could almost see the wheels turning as she got herself a glass of water and sat down across from me, both of us waiting for the pancakes to be ready.

Mahir's arrival changed everything. We'd been treading water, writing our reports, studying the material we got from Dr. Abbey, and waiting for something to happen, because something always happened when we got too comfortable. We'd long since passed the point where we could back out safely—maybe we passed that point the day George and I decided it would be a good idea to go out for the Ryman campaign. I don't know—but that didn't mean we'd exactly been hurrying toward the end game. We'd been waiting to see what would happen next. Now that Mahir was with us, it was time for things to start moving again.

I wasn't ready. I don't think any of us were, or really could be. I just knew that it was too damn late to back out. It had been too late since George died.

Maybe it was too late before that, and we couldn't see it. I don't know.

Mahir hadn't come downstairs by the time Alaric and Becks showed up. The security system announced their approach long before the familiar growl of the van's engine became audible. Maggie had plenty of time to clear away the mess from the pancakes and set out dishes for dinner. "Shaun, go wake our guest," she said, starting to rummage for forks. I blinked at her, and she grinned. "I figure he's likely to hit someone if he's startled, and he'd probably feel bad if he hit a girl."

I couldn't argue with that—it was too true—and so I grunted my assent, finished off the last of my Coke, and went trudging up the stairs to the room that had been mine until just a few hours before. The door was shut, and there were no signs of motion from the other side. I raised my hand, hesitating before I actually brought it down in a knock.

"He looked exhausted," I said.

We're all exhausted, George replied. *He needs to explain things sooner or later.*

As soon as he explained all the way, any chance we had of postponing the future would be gone. It would end when he opened his bag and pulled out the files he hadn't shown me yet, and there would be no taking it back, because there never is when the truth gets involved. "Can't it be later?" The plea in my voice surprised us both, I think, me more than her; George has always known me better than I know myself. I used to do the same favor for her.

It already is, she said, quietly.

She was right, and because she was right, I brought my hand down and knocked on the guest room door. "Yo, Mahir. Alaric and Becks are here with dinner."

There was no response.

I knocked again, harder this time. "Mahir! We can sleep when we're dead, my man!" Part of me couldn't help remembering how bleak he'd looked, how deep the circles under his eyes had been. If we can sleep when we're dead . . .

Stop it. You're just freaking yourself out, and that's not going to do anyone any good. Knock again.

I didn't knock: I hammered. "*Mahir!*"

The door opened. Mahir was still dressed, his clothes no more wrinkled than they'd been before—they'd long since passed the point where a little thing like a nap was going to do anything to hurt them—and his hair was sticking up in uneven spikes, making him look like some sort of apocalyptic prophet. "Is it morning already?" he asked. Exhaustion thickened his accent, making it border on unintelligible. "I'd murder for a cuppa."

"Not sure what that is, but there's coffee and tea downstairs. Also dinner. Maggie had Becks and Alaric swing by the House of Curries on their way back from whatever the fuck it is they were doing out there." I probably should have cared more about what my team was up to when they weren't working directly on the whole "possible globe-spanning conspiracy" thing, but to be honest, I didn't have the time or the energy. I trusted them not to get themselves killed while I wasn't looking. That was all I had left to give them, and it needed to be enough.

"Right." Mahir rubbed a hand through his hair, doing nothing to improve its spiky disarray. "Is there someplace I can wash my face and slap on a couple of stimulant patches before I have to come down and face humans?"

"Bathroom's across the hall."

"Brilliant." He offered me a wan, distracted smile and stepped into the hall, heading for the bathroom. I put a hand on his elbow. He stopped, blinking at me. "Yes?"

"I'm glad you're here, even if it does mean the shit's finally hitting the fan," I said, and hugged him.

George and I weren't raised to be physically demonstrative. Having parents who treat you as a ratings stunt will do that. Mahir knew that. There was a pause no longer than the time it took for him to catch his breath, and then he was hugging me back, shoulders sagging slightly as he let go of some weight I wasn't quite aware of yet, but doubtless would be soon.

"Thank you," he said. His smile as he let me go was a little stronger. I turned to head downstairs as he walked into the bathroom, shutting the door behind himself.

The air downstairs smelled like hot curry, garlic naan, and the sweet, pasty nothingness of white rice. Maggie was unpacking bulging paper sacks from the House of Curries onto the counter while Alaric, Becks, and Kelly sat at the table, trying to stay out of her way. The bulldogs were gone, and the connecting door to the front room was closed, indicating the location of their banishment.

Hail, hail, the gang's all here, said George, quietly.

"Yeah," I muttered, pausing in the doorway and watching them. Becks was hiding a laugh behind her hand, probably in response to something Alaric had said. Maggie kept rocking onto her toes, like she was dancing to a private beat. Even Kelly was relaxed, sitting in her chair and watching the others with a faint, puzzled smile on her face. This was my team. Maybe it wasn't the one I would have put together on my own—out of all of them, Becks was the only one I really trusted in the field, and she was also still the one I had the most trouble talking to. Alaric was never actually field certified, since the shit hit the fan while he was still prepping for his tests, and Maggie had never needed to be, being a Fictional and all.

Footsteps behind me signaled Mahir's approach. I turned to face him, asking, "Hey, you're cleared for fieldwork, right?"

Mahir frowned at me. He'd slicked back his hair and done something to wipe away most of the more visible signs of exhaustion. He hadn't been kidding about the stimulant patches. He'd pay for that later. Then again, we were going to be paying for a lot of things later, assuming we lived that long.

"In the United Kingdom and European Union, yes, in the United States, no, although I can travel on my UK license for up to ninety days as a visiting journalist. Why?"

"Just wondering." I stepped to the side, sweeping one arm grandly toward the kitchen. "Ladies and gentlemen, Mahir Gowda!"

"Boss!" said Alaric, sounding delighted. As a Newsie, he answered directly to Mahir, and counted on Mahir to make me understand when I was being unreasonable. Having us both in the same house probably seemed like an excellent way to cut out the middleman. I couldn't honestly say that he was wrong.

Becks didn't do anything as gauche as shouting. Standing, she walked over to Mahir and threw her arms around his shoulders, hugging him tightly. He hugged her back, just as tightly. "I'm so glad you're here," she said.

I looked away, feeling uncomfortably like a voyeur, and found myself looking at Kelly instead. She was watching the scene in front of her with an almost wistful expression on her face, like a kid who wasn't invited to the party.

She gave up her whole life to come here and tell us what she knew, and she can never go back. The people in this room, we're all she has. And she's never going to be part of things the way Mahir is.

"Right," I muttered. Louder, pitched for an audience of people who actually existed *outside* my head, I said, "Something smells great, Maggie. Please tell me it's dinner, and not a sadistic new kind of air freshener." I brushed past Mahir and Becks, still embracing, and moved toward the counter.

Maggie flashed a smile my way. "Oh, it's dinner. All the containers are labeled, and I made sure to get extra Aloo Gobi this time, so you won't be able to eat it all."

"You're seriously underestimating my capacity for devouring curried cauliflower." I reached for a plate.

That was the signal for everyone to start grabbing plates, utensils, and whatever combination of things they were planning to eat for dinner. Mahir ate like he was starving, and the rest of us weren't much better. I wasn't the only one who understood what Mahir's arrival meant. This might be the last peaceful meal we had for a while, and none of us wanted to be the one to disrupt it.

Cramming six people around Maggie's table was surprisingly easy. I've never known anyone who entertained as much as she does, or was as willing to adjust for strangers on a moment's notice. Being in her kitchen was almost like being in one of those old pre-Rising TV shows, the ones where everyone seemed to wind up sitting around eating from the same bowl of mashed potatoes and talking about their day. We didn't have mashed potatoes, and I wasn't interested in sharing the Aloo Gobi, but we did have rice and samosas and other things to pass around. Mahir turned out to be surprisingly good at talking to Kelly, who got a little more relaxed with every minute that passed.

The best intentions weren't enough to stop the clock. All too soon, we were putting down our forks, finishing our drinks, and falling into an expectant silence. Maggie stood, starting to clear the table; Alaric and I moved to help her. She waved me back to my seat. "Stay where you are," she said. "You're going to need to ride herd on this madhouse, and that works better when you don't have something to distract yourself." She didn't wave Alaric back down. I guess she figured he could do his part from the sink if he had to.

Mahir cleared his throat. "I'll just go get a few things, shall I?"

"I think it's about that time," I agreed. "Get ready to explain some crazy science, Doc."

Kelly smiled a little. "It'll be my pleasure."

Maggie returned to the table, handing me a Coke as she sat down to my left. Alaric sat next to Becks, leaving a space between us for Mahir. The air in the kitchen seemed to be getting heavy, pressing down on us like a lead weight.

It was almost a relief when Mahir returned with an armload of manila file folders, their contents bristling with multicolored tab dividers. At least this meant that we weren't going to be waiting anymore. "I have virtual copies of everything here," he said, dropping the files onto the table without any preamble. "I didn't want to e-mail things, since there was a chance I was being watched after what happened with Dr. Christopher."

"The Australian?" I asked.

Mahir nodded. "Precisely. I might not have been under surveillance before that, but the odds increased rather substantially after I got someone deported. That's when I realized it might be best for everyone if I came here."

"Makes sense." I glanced toward Alaric and Becks, saying, "One of the scientists Mahir went to talk to about Dr. Abbey's research got kicked out of the country."

Alaric whistled, long and low. "That's not fooling around."

"No, it's not," said Mahir, with dry gravity. "What we have here is a combination of the material that was originally sent to me, the material provided by Doctors Tiwari and Christopher, some supplemental research I was able to request from Dr. Shoji of the Kauai Institute of Virology before I felt it was unsafe to make any further out-of-country contacts, and finally, the files I was able to retrieve from Professor Brannon's mail drop before it was shut down. I don't have copies for everyone, but there's enough here to keep us all predicting the end of the world until well past dawn."

"Who's Professor Brannon?" asked Becks. "Because I'm feeling a bit like I missed a memo somewhere."

"Professor Brannon ... " Alaric frowned. "He was a world-renowned expert in the behavior of Kellis-Amberlee. He spent his entire professional career identifying and studying viral substrains. He ... " Alaric's eyes went wide. "He shot himself last week. It was a devastating blow to the epidemiological community. No one saw it coming."

"I'm afraid that was my fault." Mahir handed him one of the file folders. "He'd been studying the virus in lab conditions. He'd never had the time to devote to studying it in the wild. I suppose we all require some measure of specialization in order to keep our heads above water."

Alaric started flipping through the folder in his hand, eyes narrowing in a focused "the rest of the world might as well not be here" way. I used to see that look on George's face a lot.

Kelly, meanwhile, looked horrified. "Professor Brannon is *dead*?" she asked. She sounded genuinely stunned. "But ... but ... Professor Brannon *can't* be dead. He *can't* be."

"You knew him?" I asked, reaching for a folder.

"I attended one of his lectures while I was in medical school. It was about the ways that Kellis-Amberlee inherently differs from a naturally occurring virus—" She glanced around at the rest of us, taking in our expressions, and cleared her throat before saying, "Naturally occurring viruses have a primary host, something where they, um, retreat when there isn't an outbreak going on. Like malaria, which is bacterial, but still sort of applies. Even when there isn't a malaria outbreak going on, the mosquitoes are still infected. That's how it can keep coming back, no matter how many times we think we've cured it in a human population."

"What does that have to do with Kellis-Amberlee?" asked Maggie.

"Nothing. That's sort of the point." Kelly shrugged. "Kellis-Amberlee doesn't have a natural reservoir. It's infectious across all mammalian species. Even things too small to amplify can sustain the virus—mice, squirrels, everything. It's completely endemic. Curing the human race wouldn't do any good unless we could cure the rest of the planet at the same time."

"Huh. Okay." I looked to Mahir. "So he was a lab guy, you showed him Dr. Abbey's work, and then he shot himself. Why?"

"There are several potential reasons, but I think this is the main one." Mahir began laying out a series of graphs. They didn't make much sense to me, at least on the surface; each showed two jagged lines, one red, one blue, one going up as the other went down. The red line would occasionally fight against its descent, managing a brief upward spike, but it would inevitably get quashed by the blue line as it arced unstoppably toward the top of the paper.

All of us squinted at the pages. Kelly paled, clapping a hand over her mouth. She looked like she was going to throw up. Alaric shook his head.

"This can't be right." He tapped one of the pages, next to the start of the blue line. "This strain occurred in Buenos Aires only six years after the Rising. It was one of the first signs we had that Kellis-Amberlee was mutating outside a lab setting."

Those are strain designations, said George. Her voice was very small. *Those are the strain designations for some of the most widespread varieties of Kellis-Amberlee.*

Everyone has Kellis-Amberlee, but most of us have only one strain at a time. Some are more aggressive than others and will basically wipe out an existing infection in order to take over a body. The original Kellis-Amberlee strain developed when lab-clean Kellis flu met lab-clean Marburg Amberlee. That was the first infection anybody had to deal with, the one that swept the world during the Rising. It took years of study and analysis of the structure of the virus before anyone realized that it was doing what viruses have done since the beginning of time: It was mutating, changing to suit its environment. For a while, people hoped it was becoming less virulent and that it would eventually turn into something that didn't do quite as much damage. Honestly, I think we'd have been happy if the virus just started killing people, rather than doing what it does now. At least then the dead would stay dead and the world could start moving on. Instead, Kellis-Amberlee has continued doing what it does best: making zombies and unleashing them on the world whenever it gets the opportunity.

I guess it's consistent. That's something, anyway.

"It's correct," said Mahir. His voice was dark, and there was something dangerous in his tone, something I'd never heard there before. He adjusted his glasses and continued: "There was a spike in deaths in Buenos Aires right before the substrain was isolated and identified for the first time. Eighty percent of the dead were confirmed as suffering from an early form of reservoir condition. It was five years before that substrain was identified in connection with a live reservoir condition."

Kelly paled further.

"As part of his research into the behavior of the various substrains, Professor Brannon had access to census and death records from multiple parts of the world," said Mahir. "Much of this data hadn't previously been incorporated into the model—Dr. Abbey is unable to acquire information through many normal channels, due to her lab's lack of accreditation, Dr. Christopher's focus is on treatment, not the structure of the virus itself, and Dr. Tiwari doesn't do statistics."

"I'm not following you," I said.

"I am," said Kelly. She directed her words at the wall, looking faintly stunned. "He's saying that once they were able to feed the substrain analysis and the census data into the same model, they started getting some results they didn't want to get. The kind of results a man who spent his life working to save lives would commit suicide over."

Maggie frowned. "I thought results were sort of the goal."

"They are, in the general sense, but there are negative and positive results from any analysis. Look at this." Mahir tapped the paper, shoving it toward Maggie. "Every time a new viral substrain is identified—*every* time—it comes immediately after a spike in the local death rate. Buenos Aires. San Diego. Manchester. It isn't a coincidence, and it isn't confined to any specific country or part of the world. It's everywhere, and it's every time."

Becks shook her head. "What does that prove? Maybe the new strains are more virulent when they're first getting started, and they're killing all these people."

"Unlikely." He produced another sheet of paper, this one with a brightly colored pie chart on it.

"Eye-catching," I said, tugging it closer to my side of the table.

"That was the intent." Mahir pulled another copy of the chart from his file and handed it to Alaric. "This shows the aggregate causes of death among the people with reservoir conditions killed immediately prior to the identification of a new substrain."

"These wedges are too small to read," said Alaric.

"My point exactly. There is no dominant cause of death among the victims in these regions. They just . . . die. They get hit by cars, they fall from ladders, they take their own lives, they die. As if it were any other day, as if theirs were any other deaths. The pattern is in the absolute lack of a pattern, and it's *everywhere*, and a month later, there's a new strain of Kellis-Amberlee running about, more virulent than the one that was in that region prior to the deaths. Three to five years after that, the first reservoir conditions linked to the new strain start showing up, and then it's another two years before the cycle starts over again." Mahir removed his wire-rimmed glasses, wiping them on his shirt. "Dr. Connolly, would you care to tell me what conclusions you draw from this data?"

"I can't make any firm determinations without studying the material more thoroughly, but . . . " Kelly wiped her eyes with the back of her hand, voice hitching a little as she continued: "I would say there are no naturally occurring viral substrains of the viral chimera generally referred to as Kellis-Amberlee."

"What are you talking about?" I demanded. "He just *said* there were new strains appearing all the damn time. This dead professor dude made his career studying them. They have to exist."

She didn't say they don't exist, Shaun. She said they don't occur naturally.

Georgia sounded subdued, even resigned, like this was the answer she'd been expecting all along, like the part of me that kept her with me understood perfectly and was just waiting for the rest of me to catch up. I went very still, the skin tightening into goose bumps along my arms as I looked, helplessly, at Mahir. He looked back, waiting. They were all waiting, and they all knew I'd get there if they just gave me a minute. They knew George had the answers, and I . . . well, I had her.

"They exist, but they aren't natural," I said.

"Exactly." Mahir picked up another folder and started passing its contents around the table. "These are CDC analyses of the structure of Kellis-Amberlee. They were acquired legally; they've all been published for public use. People have been trying for years to figure out how something this intricate and stable has been able to mutate without once creating a strain that behaved in a manner different from its parents. The answer is simple: It can't, and it hasn't. Every strain after the original has been created in a laboratory and has been released following what can only be an intentional culling of the individuals afflicted with reservoir conditions. It's a bloody global study, and we've all been invited to participate."

Silence fell hard. None of us knew enough to say that he was wrong, except for maybe Kelly, and she wasn't saying anything; she was just sitting there, tears running slowly down her cheeks as she looked at the papers covering the table. That, maybe more than anything, told me that Mahir's conclusions were correct. After all the years she had spent living the CDC party line, if Kelly could have argued, she would have.

Becks was the one to eventually break the silence, asking, "So what do we do now?"

"Now?" I stood, slapping my palms down on the table. "We get packing. We're hitting the road in the morning. All reports will be made while mobile—I don't want us to be sitting ducks when the shit comes down."

"Where are we going?" asked Alaric.

"The only place I think we might have half a chance of breaking into that's going to have the resources to tell us where we're supposed to go next." I looked challengingly at Kelly. She didn't look away. Instead, she nodded, acceptance blossoming in her expression.

"We're going to Memphis," she said.

I wanted to be a sport reporter. I wanted to report on sport. Sounds good, doesn't it? Rhymes a little. "Mahir Gowda, Sport Reporter." I'd watch the cricket matches and the obstacle courses and the stockcar races, and I'd write pithy little articles about them and make buckets of money, buy a huge house somewhere on the outskirts of London, and raise a family big enough to field a cricket team of my own.

Enter Georgia Carolyn Mason. She knew I'd never be happy reporting on sporting events and the lives of professional athletes. "The news is in your blood": That's what she said to me, and she hounded me until I agreed to give it a shot. A year later, when she struck out on her own, she hired me. She was right too much of the time. She was right about me, and about what I was meant to do.

I have to say as I rather wish that she'd been wrong.

—From *Fish and Clips*, the blog of Mahir Gowda,
June 21, 2041

Nineteen

It's a little over two thousand miles from Weed, California, to Memphis, Tennessee. That would have been about a two and a half days of solid driving pre-Rising, complete with miserable traffic jams and lots of rest stops. Distance is less of a barrier these days, since the average highway speed is between eighty and ninety miles per hour, and the average traffic jam involves having three cars on the same three-mile stretch.

Our problem was simpler: getting there without getting ourselves killed. Travel that crosses more than one state line needs to be registered with the Highway Commission, so that your movement can be monitored. Your updated location gets added to your file every time you stop for gas or check into a motel. It's a nifty system. George did an article on it once, and I didn't think it was completely boring. That's saying something. The trouble was that if we couldn't trust the CDC to be secure, we sure as hell couldn't trust the Highway Commission, an organization whose databases have been hacked so many times that they might as well put out a welcome mat and stop pretending they're secure.

I was the subject of a highway ambush once before—an ambush that landed me, my sister, and our friend Rick in the Memphis

CDC, ironically enough. The three of us got out alive. The other two members of our group, Georgette Meissonier and Charles Wong, didn't. If we assumed the people responsible for the destruction of Oakland were waiting for another opportunity to take a shot at us, the last thing we wanted to do was put ourselves on the open road, where accidents could—and doubtless would—happen.

Trouble was, we didn't have a choice. We couldn't take the train; the few passenger lines still in existence are luxury-oriented and would take a week to get there. Flying with Mahir and Kelly wouldn't work, since one of them was legally dead and the other was in the country under the sketchiest of legal pretenses. What's sad is that I didn't know which was the bigger concern.

Maggie's bedrock streak of practicality came to the rescue around the time Mahir and I were starting to brainstorm about stealing a crop duster and somehow riding it across the country to Tennessee. "Why don't you idiots take my van and get it over with?" she demanded, flinging her keys down on the table. "The VIN's registered to Daddy so I don't get stopped when I have to cross the border to Canada, and nobody's going to risk nuking it if they think there's even half a chance that I'm inside. Kill the heir to the Garcia pharmaceutical fortune while my parents are still alive to destroy them? No government conspiracy is *that* stupid."

Privately, I thought she was being a little complacent—anyone who was willing to nuke a *city* wouldn't hesitate before killing a pharmaceutical heir and would have the resources to make it look like an accident—but I didn't say so. I just scooped the keys into my pocket. "You really have no qualms about abuse of power, do you? Thanks, Maggie. You're badass."

"Not a single one," she said amiably. "Believe me, I know how badass I am. You'll have to leave the bike behind, you know."

I'd been trying to avoid thinking about that. The idea of leaving

George's bike when I didn't know if we'd ever make it back was almost physically painful. "I know."

"Good, just so long as it isn't going to be a fight. Now you'd better get moving. I want my guest rooms back in time for this weekend's film festival."

"What are you watching?" asked Mahir.

"All thirteen *Nightmare on Elm Street* movies, back to back," Maggie replied. "We're starting with the original and going from there."

I shuddered. "I'll take my chances with the CDC."

"I thought you might," said Maggie, and smiled.

After a day of arguing about what to pack and how many bullets we'd need, Maggie's van was loaded and ready to go. She didn't normally drive on run-flats—something about the way they changed the steering made them too much trouble for her to deal with—but one of the faceless security men we normally never saw walked up the driveway with a brand-new set and installed them before I could even ask if it was an option.

She's been expecting this for a while, said George.

I said nothing.

Kelly and Mahir were coming along, naturally; they'd both come too far and been through too much to do anything else. Becks was coming, too, despite our mutual misgivings about spending that much time crammed into a van together. We'd need another Irwin on hand if things turned bloody, and after what had happened to Dave, this was almost as personal for her as it was for me. Alaric and Maggie were staying behind.

"I'm no good in the field. I don't even have my licenses yet," said Alaric, not meeting my eyes. I think he was afraid I'd start yelling—or worse, that I'd somehow talk him into coming with us. "You'll be better off if I stay here."

"You're right."

That wasn't the answer he'd been expecting. He glanced at me, eyes gone wide.

I shrugged. "We can't pretend we're here if we're posting reports from the road, and we can't all go silent at once, either. Like that's not going to look suspicious? So we'll bounce them to you, and you can post everything from here. Same IP address. Business as usual."

"Right." Alaric smiled, either not bothering or not managing to hide his relief. "I can do that."

"While you're at it, keep digging, okay? I don't think we're at the bottom of this yet."

"On it," he said.

There was nothing to do after that but leave.

Maggie packed us a cardboard box of sandwiches and potato chips on the morning we finally started for Tennessee, along with a cooler full of sodas. She loaded everything into the backseat with Kelly before turning around and handing me two things: a large envelope packed with cash, and a debit card. "Don't use the card unless the money runs out. It draws on the company account. Seeing charges from it that match the van's movements shouldn't set off any red flags, and my parents won't care unless you buy a submarine or something."

"And here I always wanted a submarine," I said.

"Where would you put it?" asked Mahir.

"I'd have to buy a lake."

"Well, that's reasonable, I suppose."

Maggie laughed—a short, sharp sound that had a lot in common with the confused yipping of the teacup bulldogs milling at her feet—and threw her arms around my shoulders, hugging me close before I had a chance to step back. "Come *back*," she whispered, voice small and tight and right next to my ear, so only I could hear it.

We'll try, said George.

"Don't worry about us," I said. I hugged her back, feeling

awkward until she let go and stepped away, turning her face to the side to hide the tears that were glinting in her eyes. I sighed. "Maggie—"

"Go," she said.

I swallowed the things I still wanted to say and turned to walk toward the van. Behind me, I could hear Maggie and Mahir exchanging their last good-byes, too softly for me to make out the words. The words didn't matter, really, because we all knew that we might not be coming back.

Becks was in the passenger seat with a laptop propped open on her knees when I slipped behind the wheel. "File transfer and backup is almost complete; when it finishes, we'll have files stored in twenty different places, ten outside the United States." Becks kept her eyes on the screen, fingers tapping out rapid patterns across the keyboard.

I fastened my seat belt. "How solid is the encryption?"

"Solid enough that I wouldn't want to be the one who was trying to break it. Not unless I had a week to waste."

"I hope that's good enough." I slid the key into the ignition before letting my hands rest on the wheel, trying to feel the shape of it the way I felt the shape of my own van, the one George and I rebuilt almost on our own. It wasn't going to happen, but I could at least force myself to be comfortable with the idea that I was about to drive across the country in someone else's car. "Alaric's going to drop the security keys to Dr. Abbey's last known e-mail address in an hour and a half. If there's no response within half an hour, he's sending a coded message to Dr. Shoji to let him know that we need to reach her."

"Do you think it's going to work?"

"Jesus, Rebecca, I don't know. This cloak-and-dagger shit was never my first choice for a career. I think it stands a chance, anyway, and if there's any way we can get this to Dr. Abbey, we should. She'll know what to do with it."

"If we don't come back from Memphis?" Becks kept her eyes on her laptop, but I could hear the tension in the question.

"Pretty much," I said.

She didn't say anything. She just sighed, shoulders straightening a little, and got back to work. In the backseat, Kelly pulled out one of Mahir's research files and started reading. She'd been over it all a thousand times, but that didn't stop her from trying to find something the rest of us might have missed. I stayed where I was, hands resting on the steering wheel, and waited.

It can't have been more than ten minutes before Mahir pulled open the van's side door and climbed inside. It felt more like ten years. Becks kept typing the whole time, fingers dancing across her keyboard without missing a single stroke. She was brilliant, beautiful, and brave as hell. If anything proved how fucked-up I was, it was my inability to tell her any of those things. All I could do was hurt her, and having already done it once, I wasn't exactly racing to do it again.

"Right," said Mahir, settling next to Kelly as the door shut and locked behind him. "Unless we've got any more messy good-byes to make, I suppose we'd best be on our way."

I nodded and started the engine.

Maggie stayed on the lawn as we drove away, waving at first, and then just standing there, a small figure surrounded by a teeming sea of tiny dogs. Her image dwindled in the rearview mirror, disappearing and reappearing as we went around the curves in the driveway, until finally she was out of sight for good. Sanctuary was behind us, and we were well and truly on our way.

The plan called for us to drive down the length of California before cutting across through Arizona, New Mexico—the desert states. It wasn't the most efficient route, but it took good advantage of one of the bigger weaknesses of the infected: the heat. We had to cede Alaska because frostbite doesn't do much but slow a zombie down until it becomes fatal. The deserts, on the other hand, were one of the first things we managed to take back completely. The human host of the active virus still needs water, still needs shade, still collapses with heatstroke and sunstroke, still putrefies, and maybe even dies from the bite of a rattlesnake or the sting of a scorpion. There are no resident zombie mobs in the deserts of America, and while even the driest desert can sustain life, very little of that life is big enough to cross the Kellis-Amberlee amplification barrier. If we encountered any real threats, they'd be fresh ones, and that limited their potential numbers.

The relative safety of the desert made our route less suspicious, even as it meant that we'd need to stop regularly for water and watch the van to be sure it didn't overheat. It was a small price to pay for potentially making it to Memphis alive. Most of the checkpoints just waved us through, the guards too anxious to stay cool to do more than the most cursory of tests. That suited our needs perfectly.

Becks and I did the driving in shifts, six hours on, six hours off. After the first two shifts, the one who'd just finished a shift would move to the backseat to sleep, while one of the passengers would move up front to keep the driver from passing out. Mahir didn't have a license to drive in the USA, and while Kelly could drive, she didn't have her field license, and was too jumpy to drive safely. So it was just the two of us, and that meant taking turns.

Mahir and I worked on our strategy—such as it was—when Becks slept, using Kelly as a sort of a sanity check. "It's not that I'm not willing to die for this story," Mahir said, reasonably. "It's just that I'd rather not be martyred and leave the tale half-told if there's any other option." Even George had to admit that this was a sound approach, and so the four of us put our three heads together and tried to come up with something that wouldn't get us all killed for good. It was harder than it sounded, which was impressive, since it sounded pretty damn difficult. Finally, we decided to go with what we had: surprise, and the threat of going public without letting the CDC tell their side of the story.

The farther we got from Maggie's house, the dumber our makeshift plan looked . . . and the more obvious it became that there *wasn't* another way. When the corruption seems to go all the way to the end of the world, the only good approach is through the front door with a gun in each hand. No one was going to help us take on the CDC, not with our resources and reputation, and not with the radio silence coming out of the White House. That meant we needed to play to our strengths, and our strengths came from lifelong training in shoving microphones at danger and demanding that it explain itself. It wasn't much. It was going to have to be enough.

We stopped at a seedy motel in Little Rock, Arkansas, the night before we got to Memphis. They took cash and didn't look too hard at our IDs. No matter how high-tech the world gets, there will always be places designed for people who are looking to slip between the cracks. This was one of them. The man behind the desk didn't know who we were, and better, he didn't want to know. Becks and I checked in together, letting Mahir and Kelly wait in the van until the necessary transactions had been completed. The man was disinterested. He was also a modern American, which meant he might have seen Kelly's face on the news, and might well wonder what a dead woman was doing wandering around Arkansas with a couple of disreputable-looking types like me and Becks.

After the better part of two days spent driving down empty highways and eating out of truck-stop diners, all four of us smelled like road trip—that funky mix of stale corn chips, sweat, dirty hair, and ass that seems to show up any time you drive more than a couple hundred miles in one stretch. We had two rooms, which meant two of us could shower at once, after all four of us had cleared the blood test required to get inside.

Somehow, even though one room was supposed to be for the men and one for the women, Becks and Kelly managed to snag the first showers. It was like a magic trick. I asked "Does anybody want a shower?" and they were *gone*, disappearance punctuated only by the steady hiss of the water.

Mahir and I settled in the room where Kelly was taking her shower, again, just in case. We were too close to her home ground for us to want her left alone. The motel security could be worked around, and I didn't trust her to shoot her way out of a paper bag if something happened while she was unguarded.

I sat on the edge of one of the two queen-sized beds, rubbing my face with one hand like I could wipe the exhaustion away. It never worked. "So the Doc says most folks get to work around nine. The janitorial staff arrives at seven. That gives us two hours to evade one of the best security systems in the world, get inside without taking any blood tests that would announce our presence, and make our way to Dr. Wynne's lab."

"Correct," said Mahir. Paradoxically, he looked *less* tired than he did when he first arrived in Weed. The bastard. I hadn't been able to get any real sleep in the van—too many years of training telling me never to let my guard down in the field—but he'd been out like a light every time he didn't need to be working on something. The rest had been good for him. He was going to need it.

"Is it just me, or is this essentially fucking impossible?"

"If they haven't changed the timing of the security sweeps since Dr. Connolly's death, it's going to be bloody difficult, but no, I wouldn't call it 'fucking impossible.' Fucking impossible requires rather more in the way of, I don't know, ninjas." Mahir smiled. It was a small thing, half-buried in stubble and his own natural restraint, but it was there. "I'm not sure where one goes about ordering ninjas."

"Same place you get the submarines." I looked toward the bathroom door, listening to the sound of running water for a moment before I asked, "Does this shit *ever* end, Mahir? I mean, really, is there a point where we get to say 'enough' and let things go back to normal?"

"No."

I blinked at him.

He shrugged, smile fading. "Your sister trained me, and she never stood for liars. No, Shaun, I don't think this ever ends, not for us, not until we're dead. Maybe not even then. You're a haunted house pretending to be a man these days, and Georgia may be dead, but she's still not out of the game, is she?"

Bet your ass I'm not, said George. Her tone was grimmer than I'd ever heard it.

Mahir looked at my face and nodded. "I thought not. You get distant when you're listening to her. Either you're truly haunted, or you're the most reasonable madman I've ever known, and it doesn't much matter either way: The end result's the same, and she's not going to be resting in peace anytime soon."

"What if we all die here?"

"What makes you think we won't find people of our own to haunt?" Mahir dug into his pocket, producing a slim nylon wallet. He flipped it open and passed it to me. "My wife, Nandini. Nan. You never once asked to see a picture of her. You realize that? You called at all hours of the night, you drove her mad with your nonsense, and you never asked me a damn thing about her."

I took the wallet, too abashed to know what else to do. It was open to a picture of a slim, sharp-eyed woman with dark hair that she must have dyed regularly, to keep the bleach from showing. She was wearing a cowl-necked sweater the color of cherry cola, and frowning at the camera.

The resemblance wasn't perfect. Her skin was too dark and her clothing was too impractical and her nose was a little bit too long. But something in the way she held herself, something about the expression in her eyes . . .

"She looks like George."

"Yes." Mahir leaned over and plucked the wallet from my hand. I didn't fight him. "It was an arranged marriage, but she wasn't the first bride they offered me, or even the fifteenth. She was just the first one I fancied enough to have a go with. Traditional enough to suit my family, but fierce enough to be worth fighting with. I'm not sure whose parents were more relieved, hers or mine." He gave the picture a fond look, snapped the wallet shut, and slid it back into his pocket. "I told her to divorce me when I bought my tickets out of London. She's not much for listening—still, I've no doubt she listened this time, for spite if nothing else."

"I didn't mean to . . . I mean, I didn't know . . . "

"What, that I loved your sister? Of course you didn't, just like you had no idea Rebecca fancied you. You never had to go searching like the rest of us. She was haunting you a long time before she died, and if you'd been the one to go, you'd be haunting her the same way." Mahir stood as the water turned off. "We're all hauntings waiting to happen, Shaun. The sooner you realize that, the sooner you'll get past wondering when our normal lives will be starting up again."

He didn't look back as he walked out of the motel room, letting the door swing gently shut behind him. I stayed where I was, listening to the silence inside my head and the soft sounds of Kelly drying herself off behind the bathroom door. We were all hauntings waiting to happen? Really?

"I guess I can live with that," I said, to the silence.

"Live with what?"

I turned to see Kelly standing in the bathroom door, wearing an outfit I hadn't seen before. She must have bought it on one of her innumerable shopping trips with Maggie. Tan slacks, a white button-down blouse, and a pair of low, black heels. A starched white lab coat completed the illusion that she'd left the CDC only yesterday, not months before. I blinked and said the first thing that popped into my head: "What the hell happened to your hair?"

Kelly reached up to self-consciously touch her long blond ponytail. It was the hairstyle she'd been wearing when she first arrived in Oakland, if maybe a shade or two lighter. "Maggie found it for me at a beauty supply shop. Don't you like it?"

"Shit, Doc, anyone who sees you is going to think they're seeing a ghost."

Very funny, said George.

"That's the idea," said Kelly, and smiled. There was a bitterness in that expression I don't think she would have been capable of before she came to us. Even if she survived, the things she knew now had broken her, maybe forever. "Wiping my biometric information from the scanners would be expensive and time-consuming, and these people are arrogant bastards—I know, because I'm one of them. My profile will still be there. We won't have any issues with the automatic doors. The night guards don't really know any of the junior staff by name—we're just faces to them, and with all the traveling we do, it's not unusual for us to disappear for weeks at a time. As long as we don't wander into a spot check, we'll be fine."

"What about the part where we've been hiding you all the way across the country, on account of that whole 'faking your own death' thing? This seems risky as hell."

"It would be, if we were planning to deal with anyone but security, the janitorial staff, and Dr. Wynne. Security won't stop anyone the scanner says is allowed to be there, and janitorial doesn't care. We'll get past them."

"That leaves us with only the automatic systems to navigate." We'd gone over all of this before. I was so thrown by her appearance that my mouth was running on autopilot.

"So we'd better hope the servers haven't been updated." Was that doubt in her voice? It could have been. It didn't really matter either way. We were miles past the point of no return, and she was as committed as the rest of us.

"Good." I stood. "Let's get you across the hall to Becks. If we're going to invade the Centers for Disease Control, I want to do it while I'm at least remotely clean."

Kelly nodded and ducked back into the bathroom to grab her street clothes before following me to the room across the hall. It was the mirror image of the room we'd just left, with the exception of Becks. She was sitting cross-legged in the middle of one of the room's two beds, field-stripping a sniper rifle I hadn't even been aware she had. I raised an eyebrow.

Becks looked up, hands continuing their work as she glanced at Kelly and gave an encouraging nod. "That's good. You look like a CDC flunky."

"Thank you?" said Kelly, raising an eyebrow.

"That's good," I assured her. "A sniper rifle, Becks? Really?"

"Better overprepared than totally screwed."

"Fair enough." I took a step backward. "You're on Doc duty until Mahir gets out of the shower. As soon as I'm done, we can regroup and get some grub."

"Good," said Becks, and smiled. "I'm starving."

"Yeah," I said, a little dumbly. Looking at her smile, I felt a small pang of regret. We could never have really been lovers, no matter how much she wanted it or how much I tried; that just wasn't what I was wired for. But sometimes, when she smiled at me like that, I wished things could have been different.

I realized I was staring. "Later, Doc," I said, and left.

My shower was an exercise in minimalism. I spent no more time than was legally necessary under the spray of bleach and the steaming water that followed. If anyone checked the hotel's records, they'd see that the rooms had been let to four occupants, and that all four had gone through proper decontamination procedures before leaving the grounds for any reason. That's the sort of detail people don't always think about, and that makes it the sort of detail you shouldn't forget for any reason. Follow the rules whenever possible. That makes it a lot more surprising when you break them.

The bleach was cheap as hell. It stung my eyes, and even after I rubbed myself down in citrus-based lotion—designed for swimmers pre-Rising, back when they were the only people bleaching themselves on a regular basis—my skin kept itching. "Isn't this going to be an absolutely *awesome* night?" I muttered, yanking on a clean pair of khakis.

Better than tomorrow, said George.

"Yeah, I guess that's true." I hesitated. This seemed to be my night for heart-to-heart talks, maybe because I wasn't entirely sure I'd still be alive in twenty-four hours. "George—"

Yes?

I swallowed. "How long is it going to be like this? I mean, how long am I going to be your haunted house, or are you going to be my imaginary friend, or whatever the fuck the cool kids are calling it these days? Is this forever?"

George's answer, when it came, was thoughtful and slow. *Are you asking because you're scared of losing me, or because you're hoping I'm going to go away one day?*

"Yes. No. I mean . . . I mean I don't know, George, and I sure as shit need you right now, but I have to wonder sometimes if this is my life. If this is the rest of my life."

I think I'm here as long as you keep me here, Shaun. I think one day you're going to look at a mountain and say "I should climb that," or hell, look at a pretty girl and say the same thing. I think when that happens, I'll go. She laughed a little, and added, *But what do I know? I'm just the dead girl in your head.*

"You know everything, George. You always did." I put my hand flat against the steamed-up mirror. If I squinted a little, and didn't let myself really look, I could pretend it was her looking back at me and not my own blurred reflection. "I miss you."

I know. But that won't keep me here forever.

The others were waiting for me in the girls' room. Mahir was in the process of towel drying his hair, and Kelly was back in street clothes. The CDC costume was for tomorrow, when we'd storm the gates or die trying. The hair extensions were gone, and she had a baseball cap pulled low over her eyes to hide her features from any bored bloggers taking pictures for background color. Becks had put her rifle away. She was leaning against the wall next to the door, expression one of bland detachment.

"Hey," I said, stepping inside. "Who feels up for pizza?"

"What took you so long?" asked Becks.

I shrugged, smiling a little. "I had to talk something out with myself before I could come over here. That's all."

"Well, I'm starving," said Mahir, dropping the towel and grabbing his jacket off the bed. Kelly and Becks followed. I brought up the rear, pausing to close and lock the motel room door.

George didn't say anything as we walked toward the van . . . but in the back of my head, I was pretty sure I could feel her smiling.

It has been a pleasure and a privilege blogging for you over these past few weeks. Thank you for your insightful questions and for your commentary in the forums, where I have learned a great deal about what does—and doesn't!—work in this form of reporting. I promise to take these lessons, and this experience, with me in my future endeavors.

Also, while I'm being sappy . . . thank you, all of you, for continuing to care as much as you do about the world. This is the only one we're going to get, and I think it's important that we continue to give a damn about every single part of it, even the ones that aren't currently a part of our lives. You are the reason that someday, when this disease has been defeated, the amusement parks will become family fun lands once again, and people will laugh and live and love just the way they always have. Thank you for sharing yourselves with me.

Thank you.

—From *Cabin Fever Dream*, guest blog of Barbara Tinney,
June 23, 2041

Twenty

I'm not sure any of us slept that night. We were on an Internet blackout while stationary: no uploads, no message forums, nothing that could be traced to prove we were ever here. That also meant no phone calls, since turning on our phones could activate their GPS chips. We'd been scrupulously careful since leaving Weed. We just had to hope we'd been careful enough.

It was the blood tests that worried me. You can't survive in America without at least one blood test a day, and possibly—probably—more than that. We'd been taking blood tests at toll booths and convenience stores all the way across the country, and if the CDC was somehow tracking clean results, we were screwed.

Oh, the CDC swears they don't track clean results, only the ones that come back positive for a live infection, but no one knows for sure. Legally, they're not *allowed* to track clean results. It's considered an invasion of privacy. If there's nothing to indicate that a person is at risk of amplification, you can't use their tests for anything. Not tracking, and not medical profiling—which is why we have that handy little ruling to depend on. See, the insurance companies would love an excuse to analyze the blood of every person in the country, looking for pre-existing conditions. Ironically, the insurance companies may have the sort of big pockets that can normally shove something like blood test tracking through, but the pharmaceutical companies make them look like paupers, and the pharmaceutical companies didn't want to lose their customer base because people couldn't afford coverage anymore. That's one more thing we can thank Garcia Pharmaceuticals for.

We left the motel at four-thirty in the morning. The sky was still pitch-black, and the streets were deserted. We planned to arrive at the CDC about fifteen minutes before the janitorial staff, stash the van in the maintenance parking lot, and enter through a side door while the grounds were still mostly deserted. It was a risky approach, but it was no worse than any of the other ideas we'd come up with, and it was way better than some of them. Maggie's van was generic enough to be ignored, without crossing into the overly generic "plain white van with blacked-out window." That sort of thing attracts attention by virtue of being designed to be ignored.

Kelly and I were the only ones awake in the van for the first hour of the drive. She sat next to me in the passenger seat—another risky approach, since her death was big news for weeks in the Memphis area. "Local hero doctor dies in the saddle" is the sort of headline that has legs. Newsies like stories like that; they can go back to that well again and again when things get slow, milking them until they go dry. At the same time, Kelly was the one who could steer me down the frontage roads and through the shortcuts only a local would know. The thing that made her a possible danger also made her a major asset.

Then again, hadn't that been the case all along?

The sun was starting to burn a smoky line along the horizon when we hit the outskirts of Memphis. I clicked the radio on, cranking the volume as the scrambler grabbed the nearest station and blasted Old Republic through the van. "Classic rock!" I shouted to Kelly. I had to shout or she wouldn't have been able to hear me. "That's awesome! I hate this shit!"

Judging by the loud swearing now coming from behind me, Becks and Mahir hated it even more. "Turn that crap off!" shouted Becks, smacking me hard on the back of the head.

I grinned as I turned the volume down. "Good morning, sunshine." Kelly was hiding a smile behind her hand. That was good. The more relaxed we all were going into this, the better our chances of getting out alive. "Sleep well?"

"I should shoot you in the bloody head, dump you on the side of the road, and go back to the motel for another six hours of not being in this van," said Mahir.

"That's a yes. Water's in the cooler. Who needs caffeine pills?"

Everyone needed caffeine pills. Kelly handed them out, three to a person. We all gulped ours, me with Coke, Mahir and Kelly with water, and Becks dry. I didn't say anything. Some people blast pre-Rising rock music, some people put on lab coats, and some people try to prove they're the biggest badass around. If it made her feel better, I didn't have a problem with it.

The maintenance lot was just as easy to access as Kelly said it would be. Only one blood test was required to pass the gate, and it was conducted by an unmanned booth. "Can't say I think much of their security," I said. "Portland was a lot harder to get into."

"Portland was also open when you went there," Kelly said. "Trust me. It only gets worse from here."

Somehow, I didn't want to argue with her about that.

I parked as close to the building as I dared, maneuvering the van into a space tucked mostly behind a large steel generator cage. Becks was out before I'd even turned off the engine. She turned in a slow circle, pistol out and held low in front of her, where she wouldn't be slowed by the process of trying to draw. Mahir followed her out, looking less immediately aggressive as he took up his position next to the van. I glanced to Kelly.

"You ready for this?"

"No," she said, and got out of the van.

I sighed. "Am *I* ready for this?"

No, said George. *But it's too late to turn back now.*

"I guess that's fair." I opened the ashtray and dropped the keys inside. If I didn't make it out of the building, the others wouldn't need to worry about trying to hotwire the van before they could escape. "Check this out."

I opened the door and got out.

We must have made an odd sight as we made our way across the parking lot. Kelly took the lead for once, her white lab coat glowing like a banner in the dimness of the early-morning light. Becks walked close behind, covering her. She was wearing camouflage-print cargo pants, running shoes, and an olive-drab jacket with Kevlar panels sewn into the lining. She actually had her hair up, pulled back in a tight bun that would look lousy on camera but was less likely to get in her eyes than her usual waves. Mahir walked almost alongside Becks, his white running shoes the only thing keeping him from looking like a visiting professor from Oxford, and I brought up the rear in my usual steel-reinforced jeans, cotton shirt, and tweed jacket. Not exactly the sort of group that normally goes parading into the Memphis CDC before the sun is all the way up.

The first door was locked with an actual, manual lock, the sort that requires a key to open. "No blood test to get in?" asked Becks, incredulous.

"Not at this stage," said Kelly, digging in her purse. "If you're going to amplify on the property, we'd much rather you did it in the clear zone between the parking lot and the labs. That way we can catch or kill you at our leisure, and you don't eat the staff." She produced a key.

"Practical," said Mahir.

Kelly unlocked the door and we entered the CDC, Becks now taking point while I stayed at the rear. Our effective noncombatants would walk between the two of us for as much of the trip as possible. Our little formation wouldn't stop a sniper, but it might give us a chance to react before they both went down.

Taking civilians into a fire zone, said George. *What* would *your mother say?*

"That I should keep the cameras rolling," I muttered, and kept following Kelly.

That first door led to a narrow hallway, which opened after about ten feet into a wide concrete corridor that looked like it had been sliced from a pre-Rising bomb shelter. Turbines hummed in the distance. There were no windows and no natural light; instead, huge fluorescents glowed steadily overhead, protected by grids of steel mesh. Kelly kept walking, forcing the rest of us, even Becks, to hurry if we wanted to keep up.

"What is this?" asked Mahir, looking warily around.

"Isolation zone. If we lock down, this area goes airtight, and the negative-pressure venting system kicks in. It can be flooded with formalin from the central control center, or manually from any of the booths along the walls. In case of an outbreak, the doors to the main building open and the security system starts trying to herd the infected here, where they can be kept until we decide what to do with them."

"Ever hear of just shooting the damn things?" asked Becks.

"We have to get our test subjects somewhere." The statement was matter-of-fact; this was, for Kelly, another part of what it meant to work for the CDC. "We all sign body release waivers when we accept our employment offers. As soon as you amplify, you become company property."

"Because that's not creepy." I scanned the walls. "I don't see any cameras." What I did see was a series of sniper slits in the walls, probably leading to a second airtight corridor where the gunmen could be locked until their job was done and their blood tests were clean.

This was a storage room. It was also a kill chute, and we needed to remember that. "Is there one of those nifty escape tunnels here, too?"

"Underground. It lets out on the other side of the property." Kelly stopped at a door with a keypad and retinal scanner next to it. She started hitting buttons, narrating her actions, probably to keep one of us from getting trigger-happy and putting a bullet through her head. "I'm giving the system the visiting technician security code, along with the security code for Dr. Wynne's lab, and telling it I have three guests with me. This level of security doesn't distinguish between entry points. It's a known hole, but we keep it open in case we need to bring people in the back way."

"To avoid the media?" asked Mahir mildly.

Kelly reddened but kept tapping for several more seconds before she pulled her hand away. A panel opened in the wall, exposing four blood test units. "We all need to test clean before we can proceed." She slapped her hand down on the first panel, starting her retinal scan at the same time. It was a good maneuver: It cut off any further questioning, and we had *plenty* of questions. Starting, at least for me, with "How the fuck are we planning on getting out of here?"

"Too late to back out now," muttered Becks, and initiated her own blood test. Mahir and I shrugged and did the same. Becks was right; too late now.

The tests came back clean—no surprise, given that we'd only just arrived—and the door swung open, revealing a long white corridor that looked a lot more like what I expected from the CDC. Only about half the lights were on, filling the corners with shadows. A sign on the nearest door read CAUTION—BIOHAZARD.

"All the comforts of home," I said, following Mahir into the hall. I was the last one through; the door closed behind me, locks engaging with a hydraulic hiss that reminded me chillingly of Portland. The hairs along my arms and the back of my neck stood on end as I realized that we were well and truly locked in now.

"The lab is this way," said Kelly, turning to the left and starting to walk with a confidence I'd never seen from her before. We were on her home ground. Only the best and brightest actually go from medical school into careers with the CDC; she must have worked for years for the right to call these hallways hers.

This has to be killing her, said George quietly.

I nodded, not wanting to say anything out loud. George and I grew up not trusting anything anyone said to us. We always knew there were things people didn't say when the cameras were running. For Kelly, the CDC's betrayal had to feel like the end of the world. I was incredibly sorry for her ... and at the same time, I was privately glad to know that she had to be hurting like hell. The CDC was her life, and the CDC was part of the reason my sister died. I could feel bad for Kelly. I couldn't forgive her for being naive enough to believe the things she'd been willing to believe for the sake of her career.

At least she'd judged the janitorial schedules correctly. We walked the length of one hall and then another before we reached Dr. Wynne's lab, and we didn't see a single soul. I didn't see any cameras, either, and I was watching for them. Their security was incredibly well-concealed. That was a little worrisome. They'd been nowhere near this good in Portland, and in my experience, when the security cameras go invisible, that means they have something they really need to hide.

"Here," whispered Kelly, stopping at an unlabeled door with a blood test panel next to it. She started to raise her hand, and then hesitated, expression turning unsure. "We're going to have to go through one at a time," she said, slowly.

I winced. Becks scowled. Going one at a time meant that either one of us walked in ahead of Kelly—which would mean walking blind into unfamiliar territory—or we sent her through alone, which could split the party permanently. I didn't want us on opposite sides of a door when the CDC shock troops swept in and gunned us all down.

And I didn't have a choice. We'd followed Kelly's research across the world, and we'd followed her directions into the guts of the Memphis CDC. If we called it off now, a lot of people had died for nothing. "Go ahead, Doc," I said. She shot me a surprised look. "We'll be right behind you. Don't worry. We're not going anywhere."

Kelly nodded and slapped her hand down on the panel. A moment later, the light over the door flashed green and she stepped through, vanishing.

"I hope you know what you're doing," said Becks, stepping up to start her own test.

"I never have before," I said. "I figure, why start now? I wouldn't want to ruin a good thing."

The light went green before she could say anything. That was probably for the best. She still glared as she stepped through the door, and flipped me off as it slid shut again behind her.

Mahir sighed as he pressed his hand against the panel. "I do wish you wouldn't taunt her while we're in the field."

"She wouldn't know what to do with me if I didn't."

"I suppose not," said Mahir, and stepped through the newly open door, leaving me alone in the hall.

Not entirely alone. *Your turn,* said George.

"Yours, too," I said, and pressed my hand down.

The lab on the other side of the door was standard-issue CDC: equipment I didn't understand, refrigerator full of things I didn't want to know about, desk heaped with paperwork that was probably several weeks overdue. A dry-erase board, covered in what looked like meaningless gibberish, took up most of one wall. Kelly was staring at it, transfixed.

"He's figured out the settlement problem," she said, as much to herself as to the rest of herself. "I don't know how, but he's figured out the settlement problem in the immune response. This whole thing, it's so *simple*, it's so . . . "

"It's elegant," said Mahir.

Kelly smiled. "Yes, it is."

"Good for it," I said, stepping up behind her. "Want to explain it to the rest of us?"

"Oh! Well, this here—" She waved a hand at a segment of the board and began to talk, medical jargon flowing from her lips too fast for me to follow. That didn't matter. I didn't need to follow it live; I never go anywhere without half a dozen active cameras running, and I could review the recording at my leisure. Assuming we all got out of here in one piece. Since we couldn't transmit, I couldn't make backups. If we died inside the CDC, it was all for nothing.

I pushed that grim thought aside. Kelly was still talking, and at least Mahir seemed to understand whatever the hell she was saying. He interjected periodically, asking questions and restating things that had been particularly confusing when she said them.

"I love having a smart guy around," I said to Becks, sotto voce.

"Me, too," she said, and grinned, all that familiar field excitement filling her face. Irwins are never more alive than when they're five minutes away from getting slaughtered.

Kelly finished her explanation fifteen seconds before we heard the door unseal itself. It was barely louder than a whisper, but we were all so on edge that it felt like we could have heard a pin drop a mile away. I signaled to Becks, who nodded, and the two of us moved smoothly into position, flanking the doors while Mahir pulled Kelly back, out of immediate view. The door slid open and a tall man in a white lab coat stepped through, attention fixed on the clipboard he was carrying.

The door slid closed again, and Becks and I moved to stand shoulder to shoulder, pistols raised until their muzzles barely pressed against the back of the man in the lab coat. He froze. Smart guy.

"Hello, Dr. Wynne," I said amiably. "We figured you might like to know how things have been going, so we swung by to say hello."

"*Shaun?*"

"Last time I checked." I took a half step forward, digging the muzzle of my gun in a little harder. "How about you? How's it been going for you?"

"I—ah. I wasn't expecting to see you here."

"We didn't think you would be," said Mahir, stepping into Dr. Wynne's line of sight. Kelly hung back, face still hidden in the shadows. "I saw you at the funeral, but I don't believe we've been properly introduced."

"Mahir Gowda, replacement head of the Factual News Division at the After the End Times," said Dr. Wynne, not missing a beat. "I've been keeping up with the site. I must admit, I didn't expect to see you, either. Ever."

"We're full of surprises tonight," said Becks, and nudged him forward with her gun. "Move away from the door. Center of the room, hands at your sides. Please don't make any sudden moves. I'd really hate to have to shoot you."

"It's true, she would," I said. "We told her she'd have to mop up any messes she made while we were here, and Becks *hates* cleaning."

Dr. Wynne shook his head as he followed her instructions, walking to the middle of the floor before turning to face me. "Shaun, what are you doing here? You shouldn't have come."

"There was too much that didn't add up. We needed you to check our math."

Ask him about the strains.

"I'm getting to that," I muttered.

"What?" asked Dr. Wynne.

"Nothing." I flashed him a glossy photo-op smile. "Doc? You want to say hello?"

"Happily." Kelly stepped out of the shadows, heels clicking

against the floor. Dr. Wynne went white. "Hello, sir. How have you been?"

"I . . . you . . . " He stopped for a moment, composing himself, and said, "Shaun told me you died in Oakland."

"The dead have a tendency to come back these days, remember?" She looked at the whiteboard. "You solved the immune response issue. I recognize some of these figures. Every time I posited them, you said I was off base. But it looks like it worked."

"Kelly, how did you—"

She turned back to us, giving me a small nod.

That was my cue. I offered Dr. Wynne another smile, and said, "We've been doing some digging, and we didn't have a way of reaching you that wouldn't send up too many red flags, especially since the Doc wanted to be involved. We figured you'd want to know what we'd managed to find."

"And the guns were what? Just a precaution?"

"Pretty much." I lowered my gun. "You can't be too careful these days."

"You let me think Dr. Connolly was dead."

"That's true," I said agreeably. "Mahir?"

"On it." Mahir produced a handheld reader from inside his coat and walked around to offer it to Dr. Wynne. "The information you'll want to see is presently up on the screen. Read carefully. The implications can be rather unpleasant."

"When I sent Dr. Connolly to you, I expected you to disappear immediately," said Dr. Wynne, running one big hand through his thinning hair as he looked at the screen. "It would have been the smart thing to do. If you'd dropped off the grid as soon as she got there, you could have been safe."

"You know we've never worked that way," I said, surprised by the apologetic note creeping into my tone. I really *was* sorry. If we were wrong, and he only wanted to protect us—

Shaun, said George. *Shaun, stop a second. You need to stop.*

Dr. Wynne nodded as he scrolled through the material we'd collected. "This is some very good work. How difficult was this to find?"

"Not terribly," said Mahir, before I could speak. He looked at Dr. Wynne neutrally, and added, "It's amazing how much of this was out there, floating around, and simply needed to be put together in the correct order."

Shaun—

"Wait a second, George," I said softly, watching Dr. Wynne's expression. He was frowning with concentration, studying the data. "I want to hear what he has to say."

"Was any of it commissioned?" Dr. Wynne glanced up. "Is there anything here that you needed a lab or special access to find?"

All Dr. Abbey's research was conducted in a lab, and I didn't know how much of it was available to the general public. We'd released some of it in the process of getting the rest of the data, but not everything, and not in a collected format. I opened my mouth to tell him that . . . and stopped, frowning.

George spoke into the silence: *He lost track of Kelly as soon as the building blew and destroyed her ID—the ID he gave her. He never questioned her death. He must have known. Shaun—*

"I know," I whispered. And I did know, suddenly, and without room for argument: Dr. Wynne ordered the destruction of Oakland. Dr. Wynne killed Dave.

"Know what, son?" he asked.

"Nothing." I swallowed my revulsion, forcing my face to stay neutral. "Is Kelly the last living member of her research team?"

Dr. Wynne hesitated before nodding. "Yes. That's why I knew I needed to get her out of here. I was worried that something might happen to her if she stayed."

"So you sent her to us?" He would have known her arrival would bring us all in from the field; he couldn't send her out with false data—she'd know; she'd been on the research team too long for him to slip that by her—and the real stuff was more than enough to keep us stationary for hours. We were all home when Kelly got there. Even if we hadn't been, I would have called anyone who was out on assignment and demanded they come in. Let her get there. Wait a few hours. And then unleash the hounds, knowing we'd all be in one place.

"I knew I could trust you."

"Huh. Okay." I raised my gun again, aiming it at him. Mahir and Kelly blinked at me, looking startled. "See, I would have sent her to Canada. Or maybe to one of the unsanctioned labs, the ones where they'd know what to do with the stuff she had. We were grateful for the story we couldn't break and all, but it wasn't the best use of your illegal resources."

"I don't see what you're getting at, Shaun," said Dr. Wynne, looking up. His eyes widened when he saw the gun. "What's that for? We're all friends here."

"I'm starting to not be so sure about that." Becks stepped up next to me, raising her own gun into firing position. "Why did you send her to us? What the hell made us so special?"

"You were dangerous," said Kelly, and gave the dry-erase board another glance before looking toward Dr. Wynne. "That was it, wasn't it? You sent me to them because they were dangerous."

Dr. Wynne said nothing.

I gave Kelly an amiable nod. "I think that means yes. So what screwed you up, Dr. Wynne? Did somebody read the time wrong?"

Dr. Wynne frowned. "I don't understand what you mean."

"We checked the Doc real carefully for trackers, but there weren't any after we trashed the ID you gave her," I said. "If there had been, I don't think we'd have made it out. Somebody cared enough about killing us that they were willing to blow up half of downtown Oakland—"

"I think you're exaggerating a bit there, son," said Dr. Wynne.

"—but they lost track of us after that, didn't they?" I kept my gun trained on Dr. Wynne, watching his face as I spoke. "Why do you care where we got our research, Dr. Wynne? Shouldn't it be enough that we got it? If we can do it, anybody can."

"No, Shaun, not anybody." Dr. Wynne shook his head, smiling a little as Mahir snatched the reader away from him. "You'd need some pretty specialized resources. People with inside data." Kelly paled. "People who aren't bound by American law."

Mahir's eyes narrowed, expression going suddenly dangerous. "Are you saying, sir, that we were a perfect testing ground for the spread of information?"

"I'm saying I expected you to run," said Dr. Wynne. His tone was reasonable enough, still the warm, Southern-accented voice of the man who'd been there to welcome me and George back from the dead when the CDC took us off the highway. He ran a hand through his thinning hair, looking at me steadily. "I never gave you much credit for brains, Shaun—that was your sister's department, God rest her soul, and if she made any errors in judgment, it was in trusting you to watch her back—but I still thought you were smarter than this."

My throat felt dust dry, making it impossible to swallow. "You take that back," I whispered.

Don't listen to him, said George. *All he's doing is messing with you. He knows damn well that we would never have run. He didn't expect us to.*

"That's easy for you to say, George," I muttered. "You're the dead one."

Dr. Wynne's eyebrows rose. "You really do talk to her. That's . . . fascinating. I'd heard that, but I thought it was an exaggeration. Does she answer?"

I glared at him.

He raised his hands. "Now, son, I'm not trying to be insulting.

I'm just interested. It seems a bit, well, crazy, if you don't mind my saying it."

"Oh, don't worry. I've heard it all before," I said flatly.

"We've said it," added Becks. "Frequently."

"Dr. Wynne?" Kelly sounded . . . lost. For the first time since she'd shown up in Oakland, she sounded utterly and completely lost. She'd been scared, she'd been confused, and she'd been angry, but she'd never sounded like that. "Is he right? Is what Shaun's saying . . . Is he right?"

He half turned toward Kelly, lowering his hands. "It was never personal, darling. You have to believe that."

She shook her head, eyes narrowing. "I don't know what to believe . . . but I do believe you sent me out there to die. The facts aren't on your side."

"I suppose I should have considered this as a risk. They've managed to get to you, haven't they? These silly people with their silly crusade against the status quo. Well, that's why you went in blind, isn't it?" He took a step toward her. "You know I never wanted to hurt you. You were one of my favorites."

Her lip trembled as she looked at him. The urge to believe was naked in her eyes. "I just don't understand."

"Don't worry. You don't have to." He smiled a little. "Just know that you helped me a great deal with my research, and someday— when the world is ready—your work will help a lot of people. Isn't that enough?" He took another step forward.

"Stop right there," I said, sharply.

And he lunged.

I never would have guessed that a man that size could move that fast. In the time it took to shift my aim, he grabbed hold of Kelly, swinging her against his chest, and produced a gun from his lab coat pocket, pressing it against her temple. She squeaked once, sounding terrified.

"Drop it!" barked Becks.

"I don't think so," said Dr. Wynne mildly. "But thank you for asking." He took a step backward, dragging Kelly with him. "You know, Shaun, I would never have tried this if we'd hit our original target. I wouldn't have needed to. Georgia would have gotten the point when Tate made his grand, villainous exit. She would have left well enough alone."

"Don't you talk about her!" I snarled.

I didn't realize I'd stepped forward until Dr. Wynne tapped the gun against Kelly's temple again, making a "*tsk*" sound. "Now, you wouldn't want me to slip and shoot this little peach, would you? She's such an earnest girl. Never could believe the worst of anyone. That's why this was inevitable. She could be useful only so long."

Mahir, meanwhile, was gaping. "You mean . . . I always thought he was a bit overblown at the end, a bit too much of a movie-reel villain. That was *intentional*?"

"No need to look for shades of gray when an absolute black-and-white is in front of you," said Dr. Wynne, reasonably. "We offered you a perfect bad guy, with no motives to question and no thought required. You were just too damn dumb to take it."

"Dr. Wynne?" whispered Kelly.

"Hush now, darling, you be still." He took another step backward. "You like stories, don't you? Here's a story for you. Once upon a time, there was a young doctor who wanted to save the world. But worlds don't save easy, and this one needed to be damned a little longer before it would properly appreciate salvation. Salvation came with . . . complications. So he agreed to help some men who knew better than the rest of the world. Men who would be angels. And he learned that a man who controls enough can become an angel, too, in his own time."

"Okay, you win," I said. "You get to be the crazy one. I give you the crown."

Dr. Wynne shook his head. "Here's another story for you—one that's going to be the truth very soon. I was stunned when the security cameras reported a break-in. It's fortunate I came to work on time or there's no telling what sort of damage you might have done before I could stop you. Of course, we suspected you might have had some involvement with the outbreak in Portland, but it wasn't until you tried to repeat the event here that we understood just how far astray you'd gone. Without your sister to shore you up, and without a conspiracy to chase, you simply couldn't face reality. You started making monsters out of thin air."

"Why is it you assholes always feel the need to tell the media your evil plans before you kill us?" asked Becks. She sounded totally calm. I have never been more proud of her. "Is it a union requirement or something?"

"I thought you might like the truth before you died. You people are always so fixated on the truth. Like it's more righteous than a lie, even when the lie protects what the truth would destroy." His lips quirked in a regretful smile, making him look like the sympathetic figure who once greeted me with the news that I was going to live. I hated him even more for that. "I'm not afraid of being recorded. You can't transmit from here, and it's not like you'll be leaving."

I forced myself to lower my gun, saying, "How about this. We all put down our guns, you give Kelly back, and we go. Okay? Nobody needs to die. It's not like we can prove anything's actually happening here."

"Oh, but you did prove it, you did—and you exposed some holes we hadn't even considered patching. You did the work for us, and you've brought me everything we'll need to repair the situation. Half a dozen researchers, a few dozen assistants, and all this goes away for another decade. That should be more than long enough for us to make some real progress on the problem, without sending the world into a panic." He chuckled. At least he wasn't backing up anymore; his back was to the counter, Kelly locked against his chest. "You get so hung up on your precious truth that you can't see the big picture. If this information got out . . ."

"What? People would know something?" Becks glared. "Your evil plan sucks."

"Why tailor new strains of the virus?" asked Mahir. "What does it serve?"

"We'll find one that doesn't trigger reservoir behavior," said Dr. Wynne. "Once that's done, we'll be in the position to pick the virus apart at our leisure. No more pesky moral issues with shooting the infected. No more unexpected behavior. Once it's been normalized, once it *conforms*, we can finally get to work on a virus that does what *we* want it to do, that follows *our* orders, not anyone else's. We'll save the world the way we want to, in our own time, and we'll get the proper credit. The reservoir conditions complicate things, and we can't have that. Still, I'm sorry the strike on Oakland was called in early, Shaun. I really did like you. I'd hoped to spare you this very situation."

"What makes you think the information won't get out *anyway*?" I asked, mildly. "I didn't bring my whole team here. If we don't check in, it all goes public."

"Ah, but by the time it goes public, we'll have tied you to the outbreak in Portland, and possibly to the attacks on President Ryman's campaign. You may even be the reason your sister died. You won't be a hero, Shaun. You won't even be a martyr. You'll be the man who killed his sister for ratings, and the world will hate you." Dr. Wynne smiled beatifically as he let go of Kelly and reached for the counter behind them. She didn't move. Something about the gun pressed to her temple seemed to be dissuading her. "Nothing that comes out of your little tabloid press will be believed. It'll just be the final thrashings of a madman."

You bastard, whispered George.

For once, I was calmer than she was. "You're an asshole," I said.

"Yes, but I'm an asshole who's going to walk away from here alive, which is more than I can say for you," he replied. He locked his arm around Kelly again, pulling her toward the door. "Security is on the way. There's nothing you can do."

When he moved his hand, I saw what he'd picked up from the counter: two plain ballpoint pens. "What are you going to do when security gets here?" I asked. "Scribble us to death?"

Kelly's eyes widened. She didn't look lost anymore. Now she looked terrified. Even having a gun against her head hadn't elicited that response. "What?" she whispered.

"In a manner of speaking, yes," said Dr. Wynne.

"It's a *pen*," I said.

Appearances can be deceiving, said George.

Kelly looked at me, eyes still wide, and mouthed, "I'm sorry." Then she reached behind herself, fumbling a scalpel from the tray of surgical instruments before driving it into the back of Dr. Wynne's neck. He bellowed like a wounded bull, gun falling as he clapped his hand over the side of his neck. The hand that held the pens snapped upward, some sort of trigger releasing in one of them. A thin dart whistled through the air past my ear, embedding itself in the wall. Becks fired twice, one shot catching Dr. Wynne in the arm, the other going wild. I brought my own arm back into firing position and shot him squarely in the chest, right in the spot where he'd been aiming the pen at me.

The impact whipped him hard to the side, and Kelly lost her grip on the scalpel, falling back. She slammed into Mahir. Dr. Wynne, still bellowing, raised the pens again, aiming at them. Kelly screamed and shoved Mahir to the side, sending him sprawling as Dr. Wynne's knees buckled.

Dr. Wynne fell hard to the floor, and Becks immediately shot him twice in the head. That was one body that wouldn't be getting back up.

Mahir staggered to his feet, careful to avoid touching Dr. Wynne's blood. "Oh my God—"

"Mahir, are you clean?" I demanded.

He looked down at himself, scanning his clothing. "I—I think so. Nothing seems to have gotten on me."

"Great. Well, avoid fluid transfer until we can get you to a test unit. A *non*-CDC unit. Suddenly, I don't trust anything in this damn building." I lowered my gun, but didn't put it away. "Come on, Doc. We need to get the fuck out of here."

"I don't think so," she said, sounding dazed.

My head snapped up.

There was a clear plastic needle embedded in her chest, glittering with a faint, oily sheen. "He shot me," she said, staring at it. "Dr. Wynne shot me before he fell down. With the pen. Only it's not a pen—it's a defense mechanism. You can load them with knock-out darts, or lethal injections, or . . . all sorts of things." She swallowed. "All sorts of things."

"That doesn't mean anything," said Becks.

"Right. Because he obviously shot me with a sedative or something." Kelly shook her head, looking actively annoyed. "Don't be stupid. We don't have time for this."

"Fuck, Doc, just come on."

"No." She turned and yanked open a drawer, pulling out a test unit. She slammed it down on the counter, popped off the lid, and shoved her hand inside. "I'm so sorry. I swear, I didn't know. Maybe I should have known, maybe I was being a naive little idiot—I was so busy trying to do what I was supposed to do, and save the world, that I didn't open my eyes—but I didn't know."

"I believe you," Becks said, softly.

The lights along the top of Kelly's test unit were turning red, one after the other.

She pulled her hand out when the last light stabilized on red, shooting a challenging glare in our direction. "*Now* do you believe me? Dr. Wynne shot me, and I've gone into amplification. I'm done. It's over. And I really think it's time for you to leave."

I winced. "Fuck. Doc, I'm sorry." Becks raised her arm, gun up, and pointed at Kelly's head. From this distance, there was no chance she'd miss.

"So am I." Kelly pulled the needle free. She held it up for a moment, long enough for the rest of us to see it clearly, and then she dropped it to the floor. It made a faint clinking noise when it hit the tile, before rolling to a stop in a puddle of Dr. Wynne's blood. "Leave the door open when you go. I'll stay here and distract security."

I reached to the side and pushed Becks's arm slowly down, shaking my head in negation. "Doc, are you sure? Amplification's not something to fuck around with."

"I think I know that better than you do." A thin smile tilted her lips up. That, combined with the ponytail, made her look briefly, heartbreakingly like Buffy. I'd seen the resemblance when Kelly first showed up in Oakland, and now here it was again, at the worst possible time.

I guess they have more in common than we thought, said George.

Kelly shrugged out of her lab coat, letting it fall. The blood on the floor began to soak through the cotton almost instantly, but she didn't seem to notice. She just kept talking as she bent to pick up Dr. Wynne's gun. "At my body weight, you have approximately eleven minutes before I become a danger. That's long enough for you to get out of here, and that gives me long enough to make sure the security team has a really, really bad morning. Exit, take a left, and head for the end of the hall. Security will be coming from the other direction. Turn left again when you reach the T-junction, and open the fourth door you see. That should put you—"

"Same place as before?" I asked.

She nodded. Her smile faded slowly, and her lower lip quavered for a moment before she said, "The security systems in the evacuation tunnels are independent of the rest of the building, in case of malfunction or ... or something like this. As long as you can test clean, you can get out, no matter what else is happening in here."

"I remember." I took a step back, away from her. "Becks, Mahir, come on."

"Yeah." Becks hesitated before asking, "You got enough bullets?"

Kelly smiled again, this time directing it at Becks. It was a small thing, and it hurt to see, because it might be the last smile she'd ever wear. At least this one didn't make her look like Buffy. "I do. Thank you."

"If you decide you can't do this—if you want to die remembering who you are—just make sure you save one for yourself."

"I will." Kelly sighed, looking at the gun in her hands. "Under the circumstances, I think my grandfather would want me to do this. He thought the truth was important ... and so do I. I really didn't know Dr. Wynne was sending me to hurt you. And I'm sorry. I didn't want any of this."

"I know," said Becks.

I took a breath, letting it out slowly before I tried to speak. "Thanks, Doc." A whisper at the back of my mind brought a sad smile to my lips. "George says thanks, too. She's sorry she didn't trust you."

"You're welcome—and tell her it doesn't matter."

Kelly's smile faded. She stepped back, bracing herself against the cabinet before sinking to the floor. That was my last image of her, just sitting there with her knees drawn up to her chest, staring at Dr. Wynne's unmoving body like she expected it to tell her some sort of a secret—to say something that would magically make everything she'd been through start making sense.

The three of us who were still standing left the office at a walk that turned rapidly into a run and left us with no time for dwelling on what had just happened. We were too busy racing for the exit, looking for an escape from what I was raised to believe was the safest place on the planet.

We were halfway to the end of the first hall when the alarm started to blare, flashing amber lights snapping on at the top of every wall. Mahir sped up, passing us both to take the left. Becks reached back to grab my elbow, hauling me around the corner and out of sight just before the sound of running footsteps filled the hall, coming hard and fast enough to be audible under the alarm. Security was finally on the way.

"You need to keep up," she hissed. I could barely hear her; it was mostly the shape of her lips that told me what she'd actually said.

"Yeah, I know." Becks started to let go of my arm. I grabbed her hand. "Come on, you two. Let's get the fuck out of here."

Neither of them argued. We started moving again, traveling at a pace that was just short of a run as we followed a dead woman's instructions to freedom. Kelly was true to her word; she kept security busy in Dr. Wynne's lab. The sound of gunfire started as we were making our way into the evacuation grid, only to be cut off when the hidden door swung shut behind us. The secure tunnels were silent and dark, just like before.

We didn't see a soul during our escape. I still barely breathed until the outside door swung open to let us out on the far edge of the parking lot, half-hidden from the building by a short fence made of steel strips. It took me a moment to realize what it was for: If the facility had been taken by the infected, the metal would hide us from view and might give us the time to either run like hell or go back underground to wait for rescue. It was a nifty idea. Too bad "escape" didn't mean anything but getting the hell off the grounds before we were spotted.

I waited for gunshots as we ran to Maggie's van, crouched to minimize our visible profiles, with guns in our hands and ready to fire. They never came. Security was still inside, searching for Kelly's phantom guests. No one had checked the logs showing the evacuation tunnels, possibly because they hadn't compared notes with Portland, possibly because they didn't think we'd get that far. My heart hammered against my ribs, George making soothing, incoherent noises at the back of my head to try and keep me calm. It did, barely. I didn't really start breathing until we were safe inside the van with the doors closed against the outside. Then I was slamming the key into the ignition, and we were racing away into the brittle golden light of morning, leaving the CDC—and Kelly Connolly, who was naive, but never bad—behind.

We've left too many people behind. And somehow, the running never seems to end.

The sweetest summer gift of all
Is knowing spring gives way to fall
And when the winds of winter call,
We'll answer as we must.
Persephone chose to descend
Into the night that has no end,
In Hades' hands she goes to spend
Her nights amidst the dust.
For Hades holds his loved ones dear,
Away from life, away from fear,
And so when death is drawing near,
In Hades' hands we trust.

**—From *Dandelion Mine*, the blog of Magdalene Grace Garcia,
June 23, 2041**

Twenty-one

I kept my foot slammed down on the gas as we blazed along a frontage road, taking one of the more obscure ways out of town. Mahir rode in the passenger seat with a smartphone in his hand, entering alterations to our route every few minutes as he received updates from the GPS satellites. Every change had to be registered with the Highway Commission, but our credentials were in order, and unless there was a stop order out on our vehicle, registering our route was less dangerous than dealing with the smackdown if we got caught crossing state lines without the proper paperwork in place.

Our weird little hopscotch of twists and turns wasn't the fastest way to get where we were going, even if I don't think we ever dropped under eighty miles per hour, but it was definitely the most confusing. I wouldn't have been able to track us—not without an actual tracking device planted somewhere on the van, and if the CDC was that deep into our shit, we were already dead. Hacking the highway registry wouldn't give them any of the vehicles known to be registered to our site or its employees, and I seriously doubted they had a full catalog of vehicles registered to Garcia Pharmaceuticals.

Becks rode in the rear with a rifle clutched in her hands, waiting for the moment when an unmarked car would come roaring up behind us and she'd have to start shooting. Maybe we were being paranoid, but I seriously doubted it. The CDC has had a lot of power for a long damn time now. Our deaths wouldn't register on anybody's radar, except for maybe Maggie's, and there wouldn't be too much even she could do about it. Her parents had money, political pull, and a lot of patience. That didn't mean she'd be able to convince them to take on the CDC, even if she could convince them that the research we'd collected was the real deal.

I allowed the shuddering van to drop back to a more reasonable sixty miles per hour after we passed the halfway point between Memphis and Little Rock. There was still no visible pursuit. "Becks? How's the road looking?"

"Clear." I could see her in the rearview mirror. All her attention was focused on the road, shoulders tense as she waited for the moment when the ambush would be sprung. "Not a soul since we passed that tour bus."

"With your driving, the poor bastards probably thought we were running from an outbreak," said Mahir. There was a smothered chuckle in his tone. I knew that edge of hysteria better than I wanted to, although I hadn't heard it that clearly in a long time. It went away after you'd spent enough time in the field. Hysteria takes too much energy to be maintained forever. "They likely turned around as soon as they found a wide enough spot in the road."

"As long as their turn didn't take them in our direction, I don't care where they went." Becks managed to sound like she was muttering even while pitching her voice to be heard at the front of the van. It's a trick from the basic Irwin handbook: The lower and more urgent your tone, the more exciting and dangerous the situation will seem to the people at home. It's just a matter of learning to whisper as loudly as some people shout, to make sure the cameras can pick you up. I knew exactly what she was doing. I was still impressed. She was damn good at it.

"We have enough gas to get us past Little Rock—after that, I want to get freaky," I said. "Mahir, get us a route that doesn't involve the roads we used to reach Tennessee. Try to get a whole new set of states if you can."

"Why are you asking *me?*" Mahir asked peevishly. He started tapping a staccato pattern on the screen of his phone, calling up a more sophisticated GPS mapping program. "I'm the only one in this car not native to this damn continent."

"Great. That means you won't have any stupid preconceptions about what to avoid."

"What, bad neighborhoods?"

"I was thinking more like Colorado, but sure, whatever." I made a sharp turn onto yet another frontage road, causing Becks to whack her shoulder against the window. She swore, but didn't yell at me. Our escape was too important to interrupt for silly things like fighting amongst ourselves. "Becks, we still clear?"

"Unless the CDC has invisible cars, yes," she snarled.

"Good enough for me." I pulled a disposable ear cuff out of my pocket and snapped it on, tapping the side to trigger the connection. "This is Shaun Mason activating security protocol Campbell. The bridge is out, the trees are coming, and I'm pretty sure my hand is evil. Now gimme some sugar, baby."

Mahir stared at me with undisguised confusion. "What the fuck was all that about?"

"Single-use phone. I wanted to make sure I wouldn't activate it by mistake." The ear cuff beeped as the connections were made, routed through half a dozen dummy servers and half a dozen more firewalls.

Fire-and-forget phones are about as secure as it gets, providing you don't mind spending a few hundred bucks to make one call. That call can't last for more than six minutes, and it has to end with the total destruction of the phone you used to make it. But yeah, it's secure.

"Well, that's definitely one thing no one's going to say on bloody accident!"

"Exactly. Now get back to finding us a rabbit hole to dive down."

The beeping stopped, and Alaric's voice came down the line, asking, "Shaun? Is that you? Where *are* you?"

"That's a good question, and no matter how secure I think this line is, it's one I'm not going to answer. We have a maximum of six minutes talk time before we become traceable, so I want you to get Maggie and set your phone to speaker. Got me?"

"She's right here," said Alaric. There was a clicking sound. When he spoke again, his voice was tinny and a little distant, like it was coming down a tube. "Go."

"Right. Wynne sold us out. I don't know if he was always dirty or if they got to him after the election, but I'm not sure it matters. He's dead. So's Kelly." I winced as I realized that there was one more unexpected tragedy to her death. "Shit. We can't even put her on the Wall. She officially died months ago, and it wasn't because of the infected."

"Damn," whispered Alaric. The seconds were ticking away from us, but we still fell silent for a moment, considering the magnitude of the tragedy in front of us. The Wall is a virtual monument to the people who've died because of Kellis-Amberlee. It started during the Rising with bloggers and doctors, college students, and soccer moms—anyone and everyone who came out on the losing end of the zombie apocalypse. We've kept it up since then. The blog community views it as a public service and a vital reminder that none of us is safe; that it never really ended. Maybe the infected don't roam the streets the way they did once, but they're still here. They're never going away. And names keep going up on the Wall.

George's name is up there. So is Buffy's, and Dave's, since he died during an outbreak. Hell, even Tate's name is on the Wall. He killed my sister, but the Wall doesn't judge. George used to call it the ultimate monument to truth, a universally accepted model of the world as it is, not as we want it to be. There was no way we could pretend Kelly died because of any reason other than Kellis-Amberlee ... and because of that goddamn clone, she was never going to go up on the Wall.

I guess there's nothing in the world that can't lie to us, said George, sounding subdued. *I think I'm glad I died before I found that out.*

There was nothing I could say to that. I cleared my throat, shattering the silence. "We're on our way home. I can't tell you how we're going to be coming—it's not safe, and I'm not sure—but I want you to stay inside, lock yourselves down, and don't go out for *anything*. I mean *anything*."

"The dogs—" started Maggie.

"That's what you have security for! Call them out of the woods and make *them* take the little crap factories out for walkies. Dammit, Maggie, I don't think you understand how deep the shit is right now. Alaric, start backing up our databases everywhere you possibly can. Send encrypted copies to everyone in the employee database, everyone who's ever *been* in the employee database, your ex-girlfriend, your ex-girlfriend's new boyfriend, *everyone*."

"Everyone?" asked Alaric.

I hesitated.

Do it, said George.

"Yeah—everyone," I said. "Make the flat-drop. Encrypt the files first, to slow things down, but make it. We'll deal with it later, assuming there *is* a later. Both of you, make sure your wills are up-to-date. Maggie, tell your Fictionals to stay the fuck home until further notice. I don't want anyone coming within a hundred miles of Weed if they have a choice in the matter."

"All right, boss," said Alaric, quietly.

"Turn left at the next intersection," said Mahir.

"Got it." I slowed slightly as I took the turn. There were still no other cars in sight. "I'm dead serious here, guys. We're on lockdown until further notice. Treat every door and window as a sealed air lock, and open them only if your lives depend on it. Your lives probably *do* depend on keeping them closed, since these assholes have clearly demonstrated that they wouldn't know a scruple if it bit them on the ass. Mahir, how's our network security?"

"I have no fucking idea, Shaun. If you've got a way of bringing Buffy back from the dead, maybe *she* could tell you. The only thing *I* can tell you is that you've got a right turn coming up in a block and a half."

"Right. Well, the dead are walking, boys and girls, but they're not doing it in our favor, so for right now, we're on our own. I don't have a safe way of transmitting our files to you."

Maggie broke in. "I'll tell my Fictionals I've had another problem with the plumbing, and keep anything more detailed to the secure servers. Will you be able to call in again at all?"

"Maybe," I hedged. "I'm not going to promise anything, but I'll try. For the moment, assume you won't be hearing from us until we arrive, and that we won't be staying long before it's everybody out. We wouldn't be coming back at all if there was anywhere safer to go." The CDC would figure out that we'd been staying at Maggie's place, eventually. I was just praying that their fear of her parents would keep them from doing anything drastic before we had time to grab our shit and hit the road. "Pack a bag and be ready to move."

"On it."

"Good. This shouldn't be more than a three-day drive, and that's assuming we actually stop to sleep. If we're not there inside of the week—"

"If you're not here in a week, don't bother coming," she said. "We won't be here when you arrive."

"That's the right answer." I glanced over at Mahir. His attention was still focused on the phone in his hand. "Mahir? You want to send a message for your wife?"

"No." He looked up, offering me a strained smile. "She knew where I was going. She knew I might not come back. It's best if we don't complicate that further, don't you think?"

I didn't really know what to say to that. I shook my head and checked the rearview mirror. Becks was still in watch position, expression grim as she scanned the windows. "Becks? Any messages you wanted to send?"

"Fuck that shit." Her narrowed eyes met mine in the rearview mirror, almost daring me to argue. "We're going to make it home, and then we're going to take them all down."

"Sounds like a plan to me. Alaric? Maggie? You've got your marching orders. Now march. We'll check in if we can, and if we can't, just keep the porch light burning until our time runs out."

"It's been good working with you, boss," said Alaric.

"Same here, buddy, but it's not over yet."

"Your lips to God's ears," said Maggie. "All of you, stay safe, and don't pull any stupid heroics. I don't want to flee to the Bahamas with nobody but Alaric for company."

"Truly a fate worse than death," deadpanned Mahir.

"We'll do our best," I said. "Stay safe."

There was nowhere good that the call could go from there, and we were almost at the limit of what the phone's security would allow. I killed the connection before pulling off the ear cuff and dropping it into the coin tray between the van's front seats. "We'll stop and torch that as soon as we can," I said.

"Better make it sooner rather than later," said Becks.

"On it. Mahir?"

"Take the right."

I took the right.

Our original route took us to Tennessee by way of the American

Southwest, hour upon hour of desert unspooling outside the van's windows. Mahir's adjusted route followed roughly the same roads, at least until we got to Little Rock. Then things got weird. Instead of heading down to avoid the mountains and the hazard-marked farmland, we turned *up*, heading out of Arkansas and into Missouri. We stopped for gas in Fayetteville.

Mahir stayed in the van while I filled the tank and Becks visited the station's obligatory convenience store. She'd done a remarkable job of changing her appearance while standing guard against possible CDC pursuit. Her hair was down and she'd somehow managed to trade her jacket and cargo pants for a halter top and a pair of hot-pink running shorts that might as well have been painted on and left absolutely nothing to the imagination.

I didn't need to imagine what she'd looked like without them, and it was still hard to keep from staring at her ass as she sauntered toward the convenience store doors. The only aspect she hadn't been able to change were her shoes, still clunky, solid, and more "fight club" than "fashion show," but in that outfit, I doubted anyone was going to be looking at her feet.

Sometimes you're such a guy, said George.

"Yeah, well, I'm the one who isn't dead yet, remember?"

I was stating a fact, not making a complaint.

I snorted and hit the button to start fueling up. If the CDC clued to the fact that we were using a Garcia Pharmaceuticals company ID to pay our bills, we were fucked, but our cash ran out in Little Rock and it wasn't like we had another choice. The truth may set you free. It won't fill your fuel tank.

Mahir's proposed route was a good one, cutting through the corner of Missouri and into Kansas. From there, we'd travel through Colorado, Wyoming, and Utah before hitting the home stretch across Nevada. Of the six states we'd be crossing before we got to California, only two had laws forbidding self-service fueling stations, and those were the two we'd be spending the least overall time in: Colorado and Utah. If we paced ourselves right, we'd be able to avoid stopping in either state for anything longer than a bathroom break. That was good. The more we could stay away from people, the better.

While the tank filled, I washed the windshield, checked the tires, and did my best not to think about the fact that we were running from an organization that had the power to declare martial law without any justification more sophisticated than a sneeze. I couldn't believe the CDC was doing this alone, or that the entire CDC was involved—Kelly clearly hadn't been, and I was willing to bet that all the other team members who'd died hadn't been either. Still, a properly seated cabal of people willing to do anything to get their way is more than enough to be a major problem, especially when they have essentially infinite resources to throw around. At the same time, they were obviously trying to stay at least somewhat under the radar, or they wouldn't be bothering with artificial outbreaks and assassinations made to look like natural deaths. All that spy shit is necessary only when you're trying to pretend you don't exist.

Becks came sauntering out of the convenience store with a paper sack in each arm and a smug, cat-that-ate-the-canary smile curling her lips. It faded as soon as she was close enough to be out of the cashier's sight, and she yanked the van's rear door open without so much as a hello as she scrambled to get herself and our supplies inside. I unhooked the fuel pump and opened the driver's-side door, sliding myself behind the wheel.

"Any problems?" I asked, twisting to watch Becks unpack bottles of water, sodas, and snack food all over the backseat. We'd told her to buy as much as she could without attracting suspicion. Apparently, this meant focusing on things that made it look like she was heading for a bachelorette party, including a bottle of cheap Everclear knockoff and seventeen bags of M&Ms.

"Next time *you're* wearing the 'look at my titties' shirt, and *I'm* filling the tank." She chucked a bag of M&Ms at my head. I caught it and passed it to Mahir. "No, no problems. If they're running our pictures on the news, the dickhead working the counter didn't know anything about it. There's been a minor outbreak alert in Memphis, and the area around the CDC there is on lockdown, but it wasn't a big enough deal to peel Dicky's eyes off my ass."

"See, I wouldn't get the same results with that shirt. I just don't have the figure for it. Mahir might do a little better. We can try it next time we stop." I leaned into the back to grab a bottle of Coke before she could chuck that at my head, too. "We're good to go, then?"

"Should be." Becks pulled her jacket back on before opening one of the bags of M&Ms. "Mahir, make sure you're running weather projections on our route. They had a storm advisory up while I was checking out."

"Right," he said, and grabbed a drink before he started pecking away at his phone.

I slid my soda into the van's drink holder and started the engine. We'd been holding still long enough, and we had a long damn way to go before we'd be anything resembling safe.

We crossed into Kansas an hour later, and I risked pulling off the road, into the parking lot of an abandoned pre-Rising rest stop. The gate across the entrance wasn't even chained. If we wanted to go in there and get eaten, that was our problem, not the local government's. "We should report them for negligence," muttered Becks, as we pushed the gate out of our way.

"That's good," I said agreeably. "How are we going to explain what we're doing out here? Are we on a sightseeing tour of the haunted cornfields of North America or something?"

She glared at me. I shrugged and got back into the van, pulling forward until we were completely hidden from the road by the overgrown trees surrounding what must have once been a pretty nice picnic area. People used to bring kids and their dogs to places like this, letting them run wild on the grass to burn off a little energy before they got back into the car and continued their drive toward the American dream. These days, that kind of thing will get you thrown in jail for child abuse. Not even the Masons were that crazy, and they did a lot of dangerous things with me and George while we were growing up. Running around in the grass near an unsecured structure and a bunch of trees is a good way of taking yourself out of the gene pool.

Becks stood guard with her rifle while I took the fire-and-forget phone over to the remains of a barbecue pit. Mahir followed me, observing without comment as I beat the phone with a large rock, tossed it into the hole, and set it on fire. A few squirts of lighter fluid from the travel kit made sure that it kept burning, delicate circuitry and memory chips melting into slag under the onslaught of the flames.

"Hey, check it out, Mahir—the green wires burn purple. What's up with that?" No answer. I looked up. "Mahir?"

He was staring toward the low brick building that contained the restrooms and water fountains like a man transfixed. "Why haven't they torn this thing down?" he asked. "It's like a bloody crypt, right in the middle of what ought to be civilization."

"I don't know. Maybe they don't have the money. Maybe they think it's better to give the infected someplace they can hide, so they'll know where to go when they start getting outbreak reports." I squirted more lighter fluid onto my makeshift pyre. "Maybe the people who live around here would feel like it was too much like giving up. Leave the walls standing so we can build a new roof when the crisis is over. Don't tear down something you're going to want to use later."

"Do you really think people are going to want to go to places like this ever again? Even if we kill all the damn zombies, we'll remember where the dangers were."

"Will we?" I stuck the lighter fluid back into my pocket. My hands were smudgy with old ash from the barbecue pit, and I wiped them carelessly clean against the seat of my jeans. "People have pretty short memories when they want to. It'll take a few generations, but give them time, and things like this will be all the rage again. Just watch."

"Assuming we ever get to that point."

"Well, yeah. Which is going to take people not trying to kill us for a little while." The bottle of knockoff Everclear Becks picked up at the convenience store turned out to make an excellent accelerant. I dumped it out over the fire. The flames leapt up and then died back down, burning off the additional fuel in seconds.

Mahir snorted. "That would be a rather impressive change."

"Wouldn't it?" I kicked some dirt onto the remaining flames. "If we burn this place down, you think we'll get in trouble for arson?"

"I think we'll get medals from the bloody civic planning commission."

"Cool." I kicked more dirt onto the fire. That would have to be good enough; we didn't have time to dawdle. "Come on. Let's get out of here before Darwin decides we need a spanking."

Becks looked over as we approached, nodding her chin curtly toward the smoke still wafting up from the barbecue pit. "We done here?" she asked.

"Unless you want to stick around and make s'mores, yeah, we are."

She snorted. "I suppose we'd roast our marshmallows on sticks and tell each other ghost stories after the sun went down?"

"Something like that." I reached for the van door and paused, looking at Mahir, who was staring up at the sky. "What now?"

"Look at those clouds." He sounded faintly awed. Becks and I exchanged a glance, tilted our heads back, and looked.

Growing up in California meant George and I never really experienced that much in the way of what most people would consider "weather." We got more in the way of "climate." Still, even California gets rained on, and I know what a cloud looks like when it's getting ready to storm in earnest. The clouds forming overhead were blacker than any that I'd ever seen, hanging low in the sky and visibly heavy with rain. They were coming together at a disturbing rate. The sky wasn't exactly clear when we pulled off, but it hadn't been anything like this.

Becks whistled low. "That is *some* storm," she said.

"Yeah, and we get to drive in it." I opened the van door. "As long as we don't get washed away, this could actually work in our favor. If that sucker comes down as hard as it looks like it's going to, we're gonna be a bitch to track."

"Saved by the storm," said Mahir. "I suppose it's true that stranger things have happened."

Becks rolled her eyes. "I hate to be the one to get all negative on you two, but we're in Kansas, and we're planning to *be* in Kansas for hours. Isn't this where Dorothy was when that whole 'twister ride to Oz' thing happened? Does either of you know how to recognize a tornado? Because I don't. It might be a good idea for us to find a motel and hole up until this blows over."

I shook my head. "That might be the smart thing to do, but it's not an option. If the CDC is following us, they're going to expect us to wait out the storm. This could be the best shot we have at getting clear." Becks still looked unconvinced. I didn't blame her; I wasn't entirely convinced myself. "Look, we'll keep the weather advisory running on Mahir's phone. It's a nonspecific enough program that no one should be able to use it to track us, and if it starts flashing 'Get off the road, assholes,' we'll pull off until the storm passes. Okay?"

"Okay," she said, slowly. "But if we get blown to Oz, I'm going to drop a house on your ass."

"See, that's the sort of compromise I can live with." I got into the van. Becks and Mahir did the same.

You really sure this is the right plan? asked George.

"Absolutely not," I muttered, and started the engine.

We backed out of the rest area a little at a time. Once we were on the road, Mahir got out to close the gate, Becks covering him with her rifle the whole time. The highway was clear in all directions. What travelers we might have had to deal with were clearly all smarter than we were and had chosen to get out of the path of the oncoming storm. The van shuddered as the wheels left the cracked pavement of the rest area entrance for the smooth, well-maintained asphalt of US 400, running west, toward California.

The light faded out a little bit at a time, until I was driving with the lights on in what should have been the middle of the day. The wind picked up as the light slipped away, and the flatness of Kansas offered no real shelter. The van rattled and fought against me until I was forced to slow to forty miles an hour, Mahir still tapping away in the front passenger seat. Becks stayed crouched in the back with her rifle in one hand and a chocolate bar in the other, munching as she watched out the window. As long as it kept her awake, I really didn't care what she wanted to do. I was going to need her to take over driving duties before too much longer, at least if we wanted to get out of this storm without smashing the van by the side of the road.

Kansas stretched out in front of us like a bleak alien landscape, the shadows cast by the clouds turning everything strange. I turned the radio on just to break the silence, pushed down the gas a little more, and drove onward, into the dark.

We didn't know. There was nothing we could have done, and we didn't know. You can't shoot the wind. You can't argue with the clouds. There was nothing, *nothing* we could have done to stop the storm, and even if there had been, we didn't know. There was no fucking way for us to know. Nothing like that had ever happened before, and we didn't know.

It wasn't our fault. And if I say that enough times, maybe I'll start believing it. Oh, fuck.

It wasn't our fault. We didn't know.

Oh, God, we didn't know.

—From *Adaptive Immunities*, the blog of Shaun Mason, June 24, 2041. Unpublished.

Twenty-two

We crossed Kansas on the leading edge of the storm, chasing the light until the sun went down and we were driving in darkness so absolute that it was oppressive. The clouds covered the sky until they blocked out all traces of the stars, and when the rain started—about half an hour after the sun went down—visibility dropped to almost zero, even with the high beams on.

Becks took over driving after the rain started, while I moved to the back and the increasingly futile task of watching for pursuit. We hadn't spotted anybody yet, but that didn't mean no one was coming; it just meant they'd been careful enough to stay out of sight. There was a chance the rain would make them careless, driving them closer as they tried to keep from losing us. Of course, there was also a chance I'd wind up shooting myself in the leg if I tried to fire under these conditions. Sadly, that was a risk we had to take.

There was one good thing about the way the wind was howling; with Becks and Mahir in the front seat and me at the rear, they wouldn't be able to hear me over the storm. "Christ, George, will you listen to that?" I whispered. "It's like it wants to blow us all the way back to California."

I don't like it, she said, tone clipped and razor-sharp with tension.

It felt almost like I'd see her if I turned my head just a little to the side, watching the other side of the van with her favorite .40 in her hands as she scanned the road for trouble. I didn't turn. She added, *There's something not right about all this. Why aren't they coming after us yet?*

"Maybe they're not sure it was us." The excuse sounded stupid almost before it was out of my mouth. The people Dr. Wynne was working with had to know he'd sent Kelly to infiltrate us—he couldn't have triggered the outbreak in Oakland remotely, and he certainly couldn't have called in an air strike without somebody to approve it. Finding Kelly dead in his lab might confuse the legit members of the CDC, but the corrupt ones would know exactly who must have brought her back to Memphis, and they'd be watching the roads. So where were they?

This is too easy.

"I know." I took a breath, scanning what little of the road was still visible through the darkness and the pounding rain. I almost wished there was someone else out there. At least a second pair of headlights would have broken up the black a little bit. "I think we fucked up, George. I think we fucked up big."

We should have come up with a better plan. There has to have been another way. Her voice turned bitter. *If anyone should have known better, it was me.*

I didn't argue with her. George was stubborn even when she was alive. Dead, she was basically impossible to convince of anything she didn't agree with. "So now we head home, we regroup, and we head someplace where we can be invisible. We can't stay with Maggie anymore. It's not safe."

We can't leave her there alone, either. I could almost see the resignation on her face as she added, in an intentional echo, *It's not safe.*

"Fuck," I whispered, and settled against the seat, eyes still on the road.

Maggie never needed to be a blogger. She never needed to be anything. She had her parents' money and could have spent her entire life doing nothing as ostentatiously as possible. I've never been sure how she and Buffy met. It never really mattered. They were friends when Maggie joined the site, and they stayed friends right up until the day that Buffy died. She was our only real choice to take over the Fictionals, and she'd done an amazing job from day one . . . and she never needed to. Most people come to the news because there's something driving them, something that they need to find a way to cope with. Maggie was just looking for something to do with her time. She did it well, she did it professionally, and now she was in just as much danger as the rest of us.

She knew the job was dangerous when she took it, George said. She was trying to be reassuring. She was failing.

"Really?" I asked. "Because Buffy didn't."

Not even George had an answer to that one.

"Shaun?" Mahir pitched his voice just short of a shout to be heard above the roaring wind. "The wireless has gone out. We've no more GPS connection from here, so we're going to need to pray for clarity of road signs."

"That's awesome," I called back, as deadpan as I could manage. "What's our last known position?"

"We crossed into Colorado about twenty minutes ago," shouted Becks. "I'm going to go around Denver—cut through Centennial and skip Wyoming entirely. You can have the wheel when we hit Nevada."

"Deal." I crawled over the back of the seat, turning to face the front of the van. "But I have to get some sleep before I drive again. Mahir, can you watch the back? Just scream if anything looks funny."

"I think I can manage that," said Mahir, unbuckling his belt.

I stretched out on the middle seat as he worked his way past me. A bag of cheap potato chips from the first convenience store made a decent, if funky-smelling, pillow, and my jacket was a better blanket than I've had in some motels. I closed my eyes, listening to the howling wind and the sound of modern country drifting from the radio. George's phantom fingers stroked my forehead, soothing some of the tension away, and the world faded out as I slipped into a shallow doze.

I woke up several hundred miles and five and a half hours later. Mahir was asleep in the rear seat of the van, and the radio was blasting—not that you could really tell. The cloud cover seemed lighter here, allowing a few traces of what might have been sunlight to cut through. The wind was still committed to playing storm, screaming even louder than it had been when I went to sleep. I sat up groggily, rubbing the grit from my eyes, and swallowed twice to clear my throat before I rasped, "Where are we?"

"About thirty miles into Nevada," said Becks. She sounded exhausted. I was going to ask how she was still awake when I noticed the drift of Red Bull cans covering the floor. Those hadn't been there when I went to sleep.

I rubbed my eyes again. "Another supply run?" I guessed.

"Sort of." Becks met my eyes in the rearview mirror, and I realized with a start that she was on the verge of panic. "The wireless is still out. I can't get a decent radio signal. I stopped for gas about twenty minutes ago, and the place was deserted. *Open*, but there was no one there. I grabbed what I could, filled the tank, and ran."

"Did you grab anything but Red Bull?"

"Generic donuts, enough Coke to get you through Nevada, and some salmon jerky." She returned her attention to the road. "I don't think we should stop again if we don't have to. Something's really wrong out there."

"How do you mean?" I dug around between the seats until I found the bag with the Cokes. I grabbed one of those and a box of donuts, the kind so cheap that they may as well have been dipped in faintly chocolate-flavored plastic. Then I half stood and made my way to the front passenger seat, dropping down next to her.

"I haven't seen another person since Burlington," Becks said. Her hands were clenched on the wheel hard enough to turn her knuckles white. "The streets were pretty normal there, people trying to get home before the storm really hit, people trying to stock up on the things they didn't keep in the house—about what you'd expect. We rolled through Centennial so late that it wasn't weird that the streets were empty, but the sun's been up for an hour now. There should be cars. There should be *commuters*, even all the way out here. So where the fuck is everybody?"

"Maybe it's a holiday?"

"Or maybe something's really, really wrong." Becks pressed the radio scan button, scowling as it skipped through a dozen channels of static before settling back on the canned modern country station she'd been listening to the night before. "All my live news is off the air. There's nothing running but the preprogrammed music channels. I'd kill for an Internet connection right now, I swear to God. Something's really wrong."

"Have you tried to call anyone?" Making a call on an unsecured phone line could potentially blow our position. It was a last resort. With what Becks was saying, I wouldn't have questioned the choice.

She exhaled slowly, and nodded. "I did."

"And?"

"And I couldn't get a connection." Her hands clenched even tighter on the wheel. "The circuits were all full. I couldn't even get through to nine-one-one. Nobody's home, Shaun. Nobody's home anywhere in the country."

"Hey." I put a hand on her shoulder. "Take a deep breath, okay? I'm sure there's a totally reasonable explanation for all this. There usually is."

"Really?" asked Becks.

Really? asked George.

"No," I said. "But we've got a long way to go before we get back to Maggie's, so let's try to stay calm until we get there. I'd like to avoid having a fatal accident, if that's cool with you." I glanced back at Mahir, who was still flopped in the rear seat with his eyes closed. He was using one of Kelly's sweaters as a blanket. I guess there was no reason for him not to. It's not like she was going to be wearing it again.

Becks sighed. "I guess you're right."

"You know I'm right. It's the most annoying thing about me."

She actually smiled a little at that one. "True."

"When did Mahir go down?"

"Half an hour or so outside of Centennial. I figured there wasn't any harm in it. The only thing that's going to kill us on a road this empty is an air strike, and it's not like he could watch for that. Besides, he was falling asleep anyway. I just gave him permission to stop pretending he wasn't."

"Poor guy. He's really not used to field conditions."

"Shaun, *no one* is used to this kind of field condition. Zombie mobs, abandoned malls, skateboarding through ghost towns, sure, we're trained for that. Going up against the Centers for Disease Control in order to figure out who's behind a global conspiracy? Not so much. That's not why I became an Irwin."

"So why did you?"

She blinked at me, surprised. "What?"

"Why *did* you become an Irwin?" I waved a hand at the windshield, indicating the storm. "Worrying about what may or may not be going on out there isn't going to get us to Weed any faster. Now tell me why you became an Irwin while I try to get enough caffeine into my system to be safe behind the wheel."

"Right. I—right." Becks took a deep breath, drumming her fingers against the wheel. "How come you never asked me this before?"

"We were already busy when you hired on with the site, and then the Ryman campaign kicked into overdrive and there wasn't time. After that . . . I don't know. After that, I guess I was too busy being an asshole to realize it was something I needed to ask about. I'm sorry. I'm asking now."

"Okay." Becks shook her head a little. "Okay. You know I'm from the East Coast, right?"

"Yeah. Westminster, like the X-Men."

"No, Westchester, in New York. No mutants. Lots of money. *Old* money." She glanced my way. "My parents aren't in the same weight class as the Garcias, but they're well-off enough that my sisters and I had what must have looked like a fairy-tale childhood. Dance lessons at three, riding lessons at five—yes, on actual horses. That may have been the only dangerous thing my parents ever approved of. I was supposed to go off to school, get a degree in something sensible, and come home to marry a man as well-bred and well-mannered as I was."

"So what happened?"

"I went to Vassar. My concentration was in English, with a minor in American history. Wound up getting interested in the way the nation has changed, and realized that what I really wanted was to go into the news." Becks slowed as she swerved to avoid a fallen tree branch that spanned half the road. "So I told my parents I wanted to study politics at New York University, transferred, and went for a degree in film, with a journalism minor. My parents disowned me when they found out what I was really doing, naturally."

"Naturally," I echoed, disbelieving.

Becks continued like I hadn't spoken. Maybe that was for the best. "I'd been freelancing for about eight months when I saw the job posting for the Factual News Division at your site. I was doing Action News, I was doing Factual News . . . I was doing everything but supporting myself. I was living in a walk-up in Jersey City, eating soy noodles for every meal. I applied almost as a Hail Mary. And I got the job."

"George was really excited about your application," I said.

"Thanks." Becks smiled a little. "I knew the Newsies weren't for me after my second press conference. I kept wanting to slap people until they got off their asses and *did* something. So I started trying to transfer. I just wanted . . . I don't know. I guess I wanted to do something fun for a change. I wanted to have a life before I died."

"Cool." I finished my Coke in one long swallow before wiping my mouth with the back of my hand and tossing the bottle into the back. "Thanks for telling me. I'm ready to drive, if you want to pull over."

"Yeah, well, I figure we're past the point of keeping secrets, right?" Becks began to slow. "Which reminds me. What's the flat-drop you told Alaric to do?"

I grimaced.

She shot a sharp look in my direction as she pulled the van to a stop on the shoulder of the road. "Hey, I answered yours."

"I know, I know. It's not that I don't want to answer. It's just that it's complicated." I unfastened my belt as I spoke and moved to slide between the seats, creating the space for Becks to move to the passenger side. "So. You know the situation with the Masons, right? The whole thing where they adopted George and me after their biological son died in the Rising?"

"I've read Georgia's essays on the adoption process," said Becks carefully, as she moved to take the seat I had so recently vacated.

"Yeah, well, after she died, they tried to take her files away. We even went to court over her estate. They lost. George had a really solid will. But they weren't happy about it."

"So the flat-drop—"

"Was to the Masons." I fastened my seat belt and resettled the seat, adjusting it to my height before taking the wheel. "Once those ratings-hounds get involved, there's no way this story is getting buried again. Hell, maybe we'll get lucky, and if anybody else needs to die, it'll be them."

"That's a pretty horrible thing to say about your parents."

"If they were my parents, I might feel bad about it." I looked over at Becks. "Get some sleep. I'll get us home from here."

She nodded, an expression I couldn't identify on her face. It might have been understanding. Worse, it might have been pity. "Okay."

I didn't look at her again as I pulled away from the shoulder and back onto the highway. The rain made the asphalt slick and a little hazardous, but it had been raining long enough that most of the oil had washed away, and the very structure of the highway was working in our favor. Roadwork got a lot more dangerous after the Rising, and the American highway system wound up getting some adjustments that hadn't been necessary before zombies became an everyday occurrence. In areas where flooding was a risk, the roads were slightly raised, and the drainage was improved over pre-Rising standards. It would take a flood of Biblical proportions to knock out any of the major roads, and that included the one that we were on. Let it pour. We'd still make it home.

Becks was right about one thing: The roads were deserted. I didn't see anyone else as we roared across Nevada. Even the usual police patrols were missing, which struck me as more disturbing than anything else, and every checkpoint had been set to run its blood tests on unmanned automatic. I expected the cars to come back when the rain tapered off, but they didn't. Driving along an empty, sunlit road was even more disturbing than driving alone through the darkness. At least when the storm was hanging overhead, I could blame it for the sudden desertion of America.

The radio remained mostly static, with a few stations playing pre-programmed playlists, and I couldn't restart the wireless when I was the only one awake. I kept trying the phone, but the lines were all tied up. It didn't change when we crossed the border into California, although Mahir woke up around that time, moving up to the middle seat before he asked, blearily, "Where are we?"

"California, and we're about to need to stop for gas. Becks got donuts. They're crap, but they're edible. In the bag behind me."

"Cheers." Mahir fished out a box of donuts covered in something that claimed to be powdered sugar. I didn't want to take any bets on what the covering really was. I also didn't want to put it in my mouth. Mahir didn't have any such qualms. A few minutes passed in relative silence before he asked, through a mouthful of donut, "'ow much 'ther?"

"Don't talk with your mouth full, dude. That's disgusting. We've got about another five hours to go. There's a truck stop ahead. I'll fill up while you get the wireless working, cool?"

He swallowed, and nodded. "Absolutely."

"Good."

I didn't want to admit it, but I'd been afraid to stop the van with both the others asleep. Something about the world outside the van was just too eerie, and somehow, deep down, I knew that if I stepped into that emptiness alone, I'd never come back.

The truck stop didn't help with that impression. The diner was closed, metal shutters drawn over the windows and locked into place. There were no vehicles in sight. I kept one hand on my gun during the fueling process, and I didn't mess around with wiping down the windows or checking the grill. Something about this whole thing was making my nerves scream, and you can't be a working Irwin for more than a few months without learning to trust the little voice in the back of your head that tells you to get the fuck out of a bad situation.

This is not good, said George.

"You got that right," I muttered, and got back into the van. "Mahir, what's the story with the wireless?"

"No luck. All the local networks are either locked down tight or off-line. I think we're running blind until we get home."

"Because we really needed this day to get worse." I jammed the key into the ignition. The van started easily—thank God, car troubles were the one thing we hadn't been forced to deal with—and we got back out on the road.

We reached the base of Maggie's driveway an hour before sunset. Becks was driving, and I was in the passenger seat, while Mahir sat in the back with his laptop plugged into the car charger, tapping relentlessly away. He'd been writing for about four hours, recording everything we'd seen or heard in true Newsie fashion. It was a comforting sound. George used to do the same thing, back when she still had fingers.

The first two gates opened like they were supposed to, recognizing our credentials and letting us drive on through. "Looks like we're home free," said Becks. "Just a little farther and—holy shit!" She hit the brakes, hard. I slammed forward, my seat belt keeping me from hitting myself on the dashboard. There was a crash from the back as Mahir—who wasn't wearing a seat belt—went sprawling.

"Jesus, Becks, what the fuck?" I demanded.

She didn't answer me. She just raised one trembling finger and pointed to the driveway ahead of us. I turned to look where she was pointing, and stared.

Normally, the third gate on Maggie's driveway is the first one that requires authorized visitors to interact with the security system. The normal system wasn't in operation today. Instead, the gate stood open, and three men in full outbreak gear stood to block the road, assault rifles at the ready. Their faces were concealed by the biohazard masks they wore, filtering their air and blocking them from all fluid or particle attacks. That, more than anything else, told me this wasn't a drill. Those masks are hell to wear. Nobody would do that without good reason.

One of the men beckoned for us to come closer. Becks crept forward until the same man waved for us to stop. He walked over to the van and tapped the muzzle of his rifle against the glass of my window. "Please lower the window, sir," he said, in case his message hadn't been clear enough.

Swallowing hard, I did as I was told. "Uh, hey," I said. "You're one of Maggie's security ninjas, aren't you? I was starting to think you were a myth."

"Credentials."

"Right." I dug out my wallet and handed him my license card.

"All three of you."

"Got it. Becks? Mahir? A little help here?"

"Here," said Becks, shoving her card into my hand. Mahir followed suit.

I passed both cards to the security ninja. "So does this have anything to do with the total disappearance of the population of the American Midwest? Because we're a little creeped out right now, and I'd really like to get to the bathroom." I was babbling to cover my sudden conviction that something, somehow, had happened to Maggie and Alaric. We were driving into a murder investigation. We had to be. It was the only thing that made sense.

The security ninja didn't answer me. He fed our cards into a handheld reader, one at a time, before handing them back to me and waving one of the other men forward. This man carried a stack of top-of-the-line blood testing units—the same model we used to confirm that George had been infected.

"Please distribute these to the rest of your party," said the first man, as the second man carefully passed the test units through the window to me. He avoided touching my fingers, like I might be carrying a contagion that could somehow travel through his triple-lined Kevlar gloves and burrow into his skin. Not even Kellis-Amberlee can do that. The live virus has only ever traveled through direct fluid contact, thank God, or we'd all have been shambling our way around the world a long damn time ago.

I handed a test unit to Becks and held another out behind me, waiting until I felt Mahir take it out of my hand. I didn't take my eyes off the man in the outbreak gear. This wasn't outbreak *protocol*. They shouldn't have been outside at all, and if they were, they should have started firing as soon as we came into range. "What's going on?"

"Please open your test unit."

There were three security ninjas I could see, which meant there were probably half a dozen more that I couldn't. If they were all armed as heavily as the ones guarding the road, making trouble would be a good way to get dead without actually accomplishing anything. I frowned and popped the lid of the testing unit up, sliding my entire hand inside. The lid clamped down, holding my hand in position with the fingers spread for optimal sampling. Small snaps from beside and behind me told me that Becks and Mahir were doing the same. I kept watching the security ninja, trying to figure out what was going on.

The security ninja's mask wasn't directed toward my face anymore. It was directed at the lights on my testing unit. I realized with a start that his companions had moved to flank the van, putting them into position to shoot any one of us the second a test came back positive. That would fill the interior of the van with blood, turning it into a mobile hot zone, filling the enclosed space with the sharp tang of gunpowder—

Blood drying on the walls in half a dozen different shades, reds and browns and oh, God, George, I don't think that I can do this without you. I don't think I'm allowed to do this without you. So take it back, okay? Take back the blood, open your eyes, and if you've ever loved me, come back, take the blood away and come back—

George's voice cut through the sudden jangle in my head with clear, soothing calm: *That was a long time ago; that was a different van. Your test is clean.*

"What?" I said, before I could remember that talking to myself in front of strangers isn't a good idea.

The security ninja either didn't notice or had been briefed on my little idiosyncrasies. "I appreciate your cooperation, Mr. Mason," he said. A fourth man had appeared from somewhere—I wasn't sure I wanted to know exactly where, or how many friends he had lurking out there. He was carrying a large biohazard bag. "If you would collect the units and return them, we'll be glad to allow you to continue on your way."

"Uh, yeah." I took the bag with my free hand, dropping my green-lit testing unit inside before passing the bag to Becks. "Now do you want to tell us what's going on? Because seriously, we have no idea, and you're freaking me out more than a little."

"Me, too," contributed Becks.

"Myself as well," said Mahir. He leaned forward to drop his testing unit into the bag in Becks's hands. "I think we can safely declare this the worst vacation I have ever taken."

"Mr. Mason, Ms. Atherton, Mr. Gowda." The security ninja held out his hand. After a pause, Becks handed the bag back to me, and I handed it to him. He pulled it out of the van, handing it to the fourth man, who promptly vanished back into the brush surrounding the road. "If you would please continue on to the house, Ms. Garcia is anxiously awaiting your arrival."

And had probably been notified by the security system as soon as we passed the first gate. "You're not going to tell us what's going on, are you?"

"Please continue on to the house." The security ninja paused. When he spoke again, he sounded a lot more human, and a lot more frightened. "It isn't safe for you to be out here. It isn't safe for anyone to be out here. Now roll up those windows, and *go*."

"Got it. Thanks." I rolled up my window and turned to Becks, who looked like she couldn't decide between being terrified and being furious. "You heard the man. Let's get the hell out of here before they decide to shoot us just to be sure."

"Oh, right." Becks slammed her foot down on the gas, and we roared onward, up the circling driveway.

The other gates were standing open, each one flanked by a pair of men in outbreak gear. Whatever was happening, it was bad enough to mobilize the private security force that Maggie's parents maintained for her. That was terrifying, in and of itself.

Maggie's door was closed, and all the shades were drawn. They didn't twitch as we pulled to a stop in front of the house. Becks turned off the engine and simply sat there, staring through the windshield.

"Now what?" she asked.

"Now we grab whatever we absolutely can't live without and run for the house," I replied, picking up the bag with my laptop and guns in it. "Whatever the fuck is going on, it's bad enough to have men in outbreak suits on Maggie's driveway. Assume that once we're inside, we're not coming out again for anything short of the apocalypse."

"Funny, that," said Mahir. "I'm rather concerned that's what we're going in to hide from."

On the count of three, said George.

"Okay. One, two—" and I was out of the van, slinging my bag over my shoulder as I ran for the house. Doors slammed behind me as Becks and Mahir followed, the one only slightly faster than the other.

There was no blood test required to get inside the house. Once you were past the security on the driveway, you were clean—or that had always been the assumption before, anyway. I swung open the front door to find myself staring at an emergency air lock, the kind that can be slotted into place to block any standard hallway or door frame. This one was set far enough into the front hall that it left room for the three of us, and not much more than that.

There was no doggy door in the air lock. Whatever was going on, the bulldogs weren't being allowed out either.

Mahir and Becks piled in behind me while I was still staring at the air lock in dismay. As soon as Mahir was past the door frame, the door slammed itself shut. He twisted to try the knob, eyes widening. "The bloody thing's gone and locked on us," he said.

"Somehow, not surprised."

"Greetings," said the air lock.

We all jumped.

It was Becks who collected herself first, clearing her throat before she said, "Hello, house. What do you need us to do?"

"Please remove all exterior layers of clothing and place them in the chute for sterilization." A panel slid open at the base of the air lock, displaying a metal box.

"You want us to *strip?*" The words burst out before I could stop them.

"Please remove all exterior layers of clothing," repeated the house, with the infinite patience of the mechanical. "Once all potentially contaminated materials have been placed in the chute for sterilization, blood testing can begin."

Mahir cleared his throat. "Excuse me, but—"

"Failure to comply will result in sterilization."

Okay, maybe not *infinite* patience. "What about our equipment?" I asked. "Our laptops can't survive a full sterilization."

A second panel slid open next to the first. "Please place your equipment inside," said the house. "Anything that is not contaminated will be returned to you. All fabrics will be isolated and sterilized. Any materials that test positive for contamination will be destroyed. You have five minutes remaining in which to comply."

"Let's stop arguing with the creepy house and just do what it says, okay?" I slung my bag into the equipment chute before hauling my shirt off over my head and stuffing it into the clothing chute. "I don't really feel like getting sterilized today."

"The things I do for journalism," muttered Mahir, and took off his shirt.

In under a minute, the three of us were standing there barefoot in our underwear, trying to look at anything but each other. Since we were crammed in like sardines, that wasn't easy. The panel in the air lock door didn't close until the last of our clothing had been shoved through. "Please place your hands on the test panels," said the house, voice still mechanically calm. "Your testing will commence as soon as everyone is in compliance."

"I fucking hate talking machines," I muttered, and slapped my palm down on the nearest panel.

Getting Mahir and Becks access to their respective panels practically required us to play a game of standing Twister in the hall. I'd never noticed how narrow the damn thing was until I was penned in it. Finally, all three of us were in skin contact with the house security system. Three sets of lights clicked on, beginning to cycle rapidly between red and green.

"We haven't encountered any contagions between here and the gate," said Mahir. He sounded uncertain. I didn't blame him. I wasn't feeling all that certain myself.

"What if that's the problem?" asked Becks, giving voice to the one thought I was trying desperately not to have. "Maybe that's why there was no one on the roads—why those men were all wearing masks. Maybe the virus has finally gone airborne."

"It's already airborne," I said. That was true—Kellis-Amberlee is an airborne virus with a droplet-based transmission vector—but it wasn't the point. Becks wasn't talking about the passive, cooperative version of Kellis-Amberlee, the one that protects us all from colds and cancer. She was talking about the live version, the one that turns us into shambling zombies who'd eat our own families in order to fuel the virus powering our bodies.

"I suppose we'll know in a moment, won't we?" said Mahir. As if on cue, the lights started settling on green. Becks was the first, followed by Mahir's. Mine kept flashing for a few seconds more, just long enough to start making my chest get tight. Then the light settled on green, and the air lock hissed as it unsealed.

"Thank you for your compliance," said the house.

I directed my middle fingers at the ceiling.

Mahir and Becks pushed past me while I was distracted by telling the house to go fuck itself, stepping out of the air lock and into the living room where Maggie and Alaric were waiting. Becks ran to hug Alaric, while Mahir stepped off to one side, crossing his arms over his chest and looking self-conscious. I stepped out of the air lock, looking cautiously around.

Inside the house, it was obvious that the shades weren't just drawn; they were locked down, reinforced with sheets of clear plastic. The floor was practically covered with diminutive bulldogs, the entire pack forced inside by whatever emergency was at hand.

Maggie walked calmly over to me, slapped me hard across one cheek, and then, while I was still staring at her in confusion, throwing her arms around my shoulders. "We thought you were dead," she hissed, through gritted teeth. "You didn't call, and you didn't call, and we thought you were *dead*. You *asshole*. Next time, find a way to send a fucking message."

"How about there's not a next time? Can we do that, instead?" Maggie was clothed. I essentially wasn't, which was making this hug even more awkward than it would normally have been. I extricated myself from her embrace, looking around the room again. "I know we said to close the windows, but I didn't mean you had to go quite this far."

"Wait—what?" Alaric pulled away from Becks, looking utterly bemused. "What do you mean? After you told us to close the windows—don't you know what's going on out there?"

Maggie studied my face for a moment, horror dawning in her

expression. "Oh, my God," she whispered. "You really don't know. You have no idea, do you?"

"No idea about what?" I shook my head. "We haven't seen anyone since Kansas, but we thought it was just the storm keeping people inside—"

"It's not just the storm." Alaric walked across the room with sharp, jerky motions and grabbed the television remote, turning the TV on. He hit another button and the infomercial that had been playing disappeared, replaced by CNN.

The picture showed a flooded street, helpfully labeled "Miami— Live Footage." A newscaster was speaking in a low, anxious tone, saying something about death tolls and tracking survivors. I didn't really hear him. I was transfixed by the picture, my brain refusing to accept what my eyes were telling me.

As always, it was George who grasped the reality of the situation first, and her understanding allowed me to understand. *Oh, my God . . .* she said, horrified.

I couldn't argue.

The street was choked with debris and abandoned cars, brown-and-white water swirling everywhere as it tried to force itself down clogged sewer drains. They should have been cleared before the flooding could get this bad, and the city had tried to clear them; that much was obvious from the number of people in fluorescent orange shirts who were shambling down the street, moving jerkily along with the rest of the mob. I had never seen that many infected in one place. I counted fifty before my brain shut down, refusing to process any more.

"—we repeat, the federal government has declared the state of Florida a hazard zone. Uninfected citizens are urged to stay in your homes and await assistance. Anyone found on the street may be shot without warning. Anyone leaving their home will be assumed infected and treated with the appropriate protocols. Please stay in your homes and await assistance. Please ... " The newscaster faltered, losing the rhythm of his carefully prepared statement. The footage of the flood was silent. Even recorded moaning can bring zombies to your position.

Recovering himself, the newscaster said, "Reports of similar outbreaks are coming in from Huntsville, New Orleans, Baton Rouge, and Houston. We don't have numbers yet, but the death tolls are estimated to be in the thousands, and are climbing steadily." He paused again, longer this time, before saying, "Some sources are referring to the event as the second Rising. God forgive me, but I'm not so sure they're wrong. God forgive us all."

There was a rattling noise, like someone putting a microphone down, and then the sound of footsteps. The silent footage of the flood, and the infected, continued to play.

"That's what's going on," Alaric said. His voice was toneless, and I remembered with a start that his family lived mostly in Florida. "The second Rising. You drove right through the middle of it, and you didn't notice."

"Oh, my God," I whispered, echoing George's earlier statement. The picture on the TV jumped, the label at the bottom changing to "Huntsville." The newscaster didn't return. "Is this for real?"

"It's real," said Maggie.

It's the end of the world, said George, and I silently agreed.

Maggie was crying without any sign of shame, tears running down her cheeks. Her nose was chapped; she'd been crying off and on for a while. She reached for my hand, and I didn't pull away, letting her lace her fingers through mine. Becks moved to stand next to Alaric, and he took her in his arms again, holding her against his chest. All five of us stood transfixed, staring at the television.

Staring at the end of the world.

BOOK V

The Rising

The one thing I have absolute faith in is mankind's capacity to make things worse. No matter how bad it gets, we're all happy to screw each other over. It's enough to make me wonder if we should have let the zombies win.

—SHAUN MASON

I believe in the truth. I believe in the news. And I believe in Shaun. Everything else is extra.

—GEORGIA MASON

Shaun had a close call today.

He won't tell me exactly what happened; I wouldn't even know anything *had* happened if it weren't for the glitches in his video feed, the places where the picture cut out and picked back up again a few hundred seconds later. The footage he posts from the field is usually seamless, smooth and easy and effortless looking. Not this. This is amateur-hour stuff, and that tells me more clearly than anything else possibly could that whatever happened out there, it was bad.

He came home stinking like bleach and rank terror-sweat, the kind that comes after the adrenaline fades, and he didn't stop hugging me for almost ten minutes. I stopped laughing and trying to get away when I felt his shoulders shaking. My own shoulders started shaking when I realized what that sort of fear from Shaun—Shaun! Who once called a zombie in our backyard the best present I'd ever given him—actually meant.

Maybe life was always fragile and easy to lose, and maybe all those people who talk about how good things were before the Rising are full of crap, but we don't live in that world; we live in this one. And in this world, it takes only one slip, one unguarded moment, to lose everything. I don't know how close I came to losing him today. He won't tell me, and maybe this makes me a coward, but I'm not going to ask. This is one truth I have no interest in knowing. There are some truths we're better off without.

I don't know what I'd do without him. I really don't. I'd never tell him to stay out of the field—I know how much it means to him—but one day, the close call is going to cross the line into "too close," and after that ... I don't know.

I just don't know.

—From *Postcards from the Wall*, **the unpublished files of Georgia Mason, originally posted June 24, 2041**

———

My parents, Yu and Jun Kwong, are dead.

My brother, Dorian Kwong, is dead.

My colleague, Dr. Barbara Tinney, is dead.

While reports are currently sketchy, it is entirely possible that the state of Florida, and much of the surrounding region, is dead.

Welcome to the end of the world.

—From *The Kwong Way of Things*, **the blog of Alaric Kwong, June 24, 2041**

Twenty-three

"Yes, I'll hold," snarled Mahir, and continued pacing. I barely noticed. I couldn't take my eyes away from the television, where CNN continued to faithfully record the worst disaster to strike the human race since the summer of 2014, when the dead first decided to get up and nosh on the living.

Maggie sat next to me on the couch, even more fixated on the news than I was. Her interest in the situation was a little more proprietary than mine; Garcia Pharmaceuticals owned three factories and a research center in the affected area, and with the fatality reports updating every few seconds, a moment's inattention could mean missing the deaths of people she'd known her entire life.

Alaric and Becks had retired to the kitchen after the first hour. Alaric was trying to get the wireless up and running, while Becks was cleaning her guns and checking the catches on the windows— just in case. It was a sentiment I could appreciate, even if I couldn't find it in myself to move.

That's enough, said George abruptly. The television was showing a school bus packed with refugees being besieged by the living dead. The people inside were screaming; I could see their faces through the windows. As long as they were screaming, they were still essentially human. They were past saving. I hoped that infection took them quickly, or that someone had enough bullets to—

Shaun! George's shout was enough to shock me out of my stupor. It's amazing how loud something like that can seem when it's coming from inside your head.

I turned to glare at the air to my left. Maggie, sunk deep in her own fugue state, didn't appear to notice. "What?" I demanded.

George folded her arms and glared back. "You're not doing anyone any good sitting there like a media consumer, you know. You need to be finding out what the hell is going on."

"And how do you suggest I do that, huh?" I spread my arms, indicating the television and Mahir—still pacing and snarling into his phone—with the same gesture. "Things are sort of shitty right now, George, in case you failed to notice."

"Oh, trust me, I noticed, I just don't see where I need to *care*." George grabbed my arm and hauled me to my feet. "Come on. You've got work to do." Giving me a slow look, she added, "And some clothes to put on. God, Shaun, are you really sitting around watching television in your boxers? That's just sad."

"If there's all this work, why don't you do it?"

"Because I'm dead, remember?" She kept hold of my wrist as she spoke, pulling me toward the kitchen. "You need to ask Alaric whether Maggie moved our van into the garage before things locked down." Catching my blank expression, she sighed. "Come on, Shaun, try to keep up for, like, thirty seconds while you're losing your mind, okay? If we can get to the van without going outside, we can get to our emergency wireless booster."

My eyes widened. "Crap, you're right. We still have that thing, don't we?"

"Unless you threw it away in a moment of unrepeated sanity and then didn't tell me about it, yeah, we do."

Being on a news team with Buffy Meissonier meant dealing with a girl who was occasionally twenty pounds of crazy crammed into a ten-pound sack, and who eventually sold us out to the government conspiracy that got George killed. It also meant working with the best espionage technician I've ever encountered, either in the private sector or working for the government. She could make computers do things I'm not sure even science fiction considers possible, and she did it all while wearing holo-foil butterflies in her hair and T-shirts claiming that some dude named Joss was her master now. People say Buffy was good. They're wrong. Buffy was *great*.

Mahir was still shouting at the phone when George pulled me past him. He gave me a harried glance and nodded, eyes skipping straight past George. That made sense, I guess, since it's not like she was really there.

"I'm pretty sure this represents a whole new level of fucked-up crazy," I muttered, as George yanked me into the kitchen.

"I'm not the cause of your psychotic break; I'm just a symptom," she replied waspishly, and shoved me toward Becks and Alaric.

Becks, like Mahir, had managed to dress while I was staring at the television and was wearing combat boots, a black tank top, and camouflage pants—the Irwin equivalent of a uniform. She and Alaric were sitting at the table, him with his laptop pulled as close to his body as it would go, leaving the rest of the space for her. She had what looked like a small armory spread out in front of her, and was in the process of reassembling a semiautomatic handgun that had yet to be legally cleared for private ownership. They looked up when they heard my footsteps.

"What's the update?" asked Becks. She snapped the magazine into place with a *click* that echoed through the kitchen, eliciting a startled yip from one of the bulldogs sprawled next to the sealed-off door.

"Nothing that's good," I replied. George had released my wrist when she got me where she wanted me, and I realized without surprise that she was gone again. That was okay by me. Her appearing and physically hauling me around the house represented a whole new level of crazy, and I wanted to avoid thinking about it for as long as possible. "Forever" seemed like an excellent place to start. "They've declared martial law in the areas that haven't been officially marked as hazard zones, and it's starting to look like they're going to mark the entire damn Gulf Coast as a Level 1 hazard."

Alaric paled. "They can't do that."

"Yes, they can." Becks put down the gun she'd been working on. "In case of an outbreak confirmed to impact more than sixty percent of the population in a given area, USAMRIID and the CDC will both recommend that a Level 1 designation be applied for the protection of the surrounding area. The government reserves the right to take their recommendation." A smile that looked more like a grimace twisted her lips upward. "Our parents voted that little jewel into law, and we never repealed it, because why should we? Outbreaks are tiny things. Bad things. It's better if we can let fifteen people die and save five thousand, right?"

"Only this time, we're going to let fifteen million die," I said. "That sounds a little different, don't you think? Alaric."

He turned to me and blinked. He was pale and stunned looking, like he still couldn't believe what was happening. That was understandable. I couldn't believe it either. "What?"

"Where's the van?" His expression didn't change. I took a careful breath, and amended, "Where's *our* van? Did Maggie have you move it to the garage after we left, or is it still parked out back?"

If the van was parked outside, there was no way I'd be able to get at it. Maybe one of Maggie's security ninjas—but that would mean trying to talk them through finding the wireless booster, and I wasn't sure my memory was good enough for that.

"I . . ." Alaric stopped, frowning. "It's in the garage. It was out back until you called—Maggie wanted to keep the garage open for her Fictionals when they came through—but she got spooked when you told us to hole up, and she had me move it inside, where it wouldn't be visible to satellite surveillance."

"God bless justified paranoia," I said fervently, and started toward the garage door. The bulldogs lifted their heads and whined, watching me.

"Where are you going?" asked Becks, half-rising.

"The van." I looked between them, noting their matching blank looks, and explained, "I'm pretty sure Buffy's old wireless booster is still out there. If I can get it running—"

"—we can get back online," said Alaric, his eyes widening in comprehension. "I forgot all about that thing!"

"We haven't exactly needed to use it in the last year." I started walking again. "I'll be right back. If I'm not right back, well . . . fuck, I don't know. If I'm not right back, throw some gas grenades into the garage and call for the security dudes to come and shoot me until I stop bleeding."

"We'll shoot you ourselves," said Becks, causing Alaric to shoot her a distressed look. She ignored it. You learn to shrug that sort of thing off after you've been in the field for a while. That, or you stop trying to talk to people who aren't Irwins.

"Thanks." I opened the garage door, shoving a bulldog aside with my foot before it could sneak by me, and slipped through.

The garage lights were motion-activated white fluorescents. They clicked on as soon as the door to the kitchen swung shut, filling the enclosed space with an even, sterile glow. I scanned the area, automatically assessing the load-bearing capacity of the shelves lining the walls and the security of the pipes connecting to the water heater and emergency backup generator. Maggie used the garage primarily for storage, cramming most of the shelves with boxes and using the ones nearest the door as an extension of the pantry. One entire floor-to-ceiling shelving unit was dedicated to bags of dried dog food. At least the bulldogs wouldn't be going crazy with hunger anytime soon.

Our van was sitting at the center of the room. It had been washed before it was put away, and its paint almost gleamed in the antiseptic light. I took a step toward it.

"Hello, Mr. Mason," said the voice of the house. It managed to sound chiding, which was a nice trick, since it didn't have normal human intonations. I stopped where I was, looking vainly for the speaker. "I am afraid the house is presently in a sealed state. You will be unable to exit, and should return to the interior."

"That's cool. I'm not trying to get out." I forced myself to relax, one inch at a time. "I just need to get something from the van."

"Attempts to break the isolation seals will be met with necessary force."

"Necessary force" was a polite way of saying that the house security system would shoot me where I stood if I looked like I was trying to get the doors open. "Noted," I said. "I'm not trying to get out, I swear. The van is right there, and I won't even be turning on the engine. Promise."

"Your compliance is appreciated," said the house, and went silent. I waited a few seconds to see if it was going to try to evict me from the garage. Nothing happened. I started for the van, moving faster this time—if the house decided I was dawdling, it might decide I was planning to escape, and then things could get really messy, really fast. Use of lethal force by private security systems has been authorized since some jackass in Arizona loaded his house guns with dummy bullets and got himself ripped apart by a pack of starving infected. His estate tried to sue the security firm that managed his defenses, and the security firm turned right around and sued the state, saying they hadn't been allowed to do the things they had to do if they wanted to keep their client alive.

"*Mangum v. Pierce Security v. the State of Arizona*," supplied George.

She reached the van a few steps ahead of me, folding her arms as she leaned against the door. "Do you remember where Buffy kept the booster?"

"Hi, George. Nice to see you." I pressed my thumb against the scanner, letting the van identify me as an authorized driver. The locks clicked open. "So does this mean I'm finally going *really* crazy?"

She shrugged. Her face still looked wrong without her sunglasses, alien and familiar at the same time. "I think it means you already have a way of coping with things that are too big for you to handle. So Maggie goes into vapor lock, and Mahir shouts at the embassy trying to get a call through to his wife, and you . . ."

"I see dead people walking around and giving me orders. Great." I offered her a pained smile as I pulled the van door open. "At least I like having you here. This would get old damn fast if you were Mom."

George grimaced exaggeratedly. "There's a bright side to everything."

"Really? What's the bright side for Florida? Because I'm really not seeing one." Our field equipment was piled haphazardly around the van's interior, stacked on counters and taking up most of the floor space. It would take an hour, maybe more, to get the thing ready for an excursion. I couldn't blame Maggie and Alaric for putting it away in this condition—they weren't expecting to leave the house without a lot of notice, and they weren't field operatives—but I still had to grit my teeth when I saw that the weapon racks hadn't been properly secured. If we had to run for any reason, we'd all wind up getting killed by our own carelessness.

"If you're not seeing one, I can't see it either. You know that."

I bit back the urge to swear at her. Fighting with George used to be one of my best ways of blowing off steam. I've mostly tried to avoid it since she's been gone; it doesn't seem fair to start something when neither of us can really leave the room. Besides, in my saner days, I was always afraid I'd say something unforgivable and she'd leave me alone with the dark behind my eyes, and no more George, ever. I wasn't so much afraid of that anymore. We just didn't have *time* to fight.

"Hey, George, do me a favor, will you? Either go away, or stop pointing out how you're just a figment of my imagination and help me find the damn booster. I can't handle having you hanging around calling me crazy. I get enough of that from everybody else."

"Your wish is my command," she deadpanned, before climbing up to join me in the van. She couldn't touch anything, naturally, but her feet still made soft echoing sounds when they hit the floorboards, and her shadow on the walls moved just the way that it was supposed to. I had to admire the realism of my hallucinations, even though I knew that probably wasn't what most people would consider to be a good sign.

"Really? 'Cause right now, what I'm wishing for is a tank." I paused. "Maybe two tanks. Becks will probably want one, too, and I don't want to be greedy."

"Always thinking of others, that's you." Her fingers brushed the back of my neck as she moved past me. I shivered. "The last time I saw the booster, Buffy was stowing it back here, with the rest of the backup network hardware."

"We moved that around Valentine's Day, when Becks did her 'romantic places to take an Irwin' article series." I snapped my fingers. "The lockboxes!"

George leaned against the counter to watch as I dropped to my knees, rolled back the industrial rug covering the van floor, and pried up the trapdoor it had been concealing. We don't have a complete second floor in the van—the weight would have been prohibitive, not to mention the structural instability it would have introduced—but we had a few extra storage compartments built in for a rainy day during the first major retrofit. They made good hiding spots for contraband when we were doing certain types of articles, and the rest of the time, they were a convenient place to hide snack foods . . . or excess hardware.

The first compartment held nothing but weird-looking cartoon porn and Russian girlie magazines. I smiled despite myself. "Damn, Dave. You had smarts and you had guts, but what you did *not* have was taste."

"He was pretty much in love with Magdalene," said George.

I amended: "Most of the time, what you didn't have was taste. Sometimes, you were spot on." I pried open the second compartment. A metal box with half a dozen antennae welded to the sides was nestled in the bottom, padded by wads of duct tape. I reached down to wriggle it loose, lifting it carefully out of its cradle. "There we go."

"Remember, there's supposed to be a detached battery pack that goes with it."

"Right." I stuck my hand into the welter of duct tape, rummaging for a moment before pulling up a small metal square with a power adapter at one end and a USB port at the other. "Got it!" I held it up, turning to show her.

George was gone. Again.

I stopped for a second, looking at the space where she'd been—hadn't been—had appeared to be—only a moment before. Then I sighed, lowering the battery pack as I picked the wireless booster back up and pushed myself to my feet. "This stage of the crazy is going to get real old, real fast, you know."

Sorry. But you're still too sane to sustain that sort of breakdown for very long.

"Guess this means that whole 'not forever' thing we talked about before is sort of moot, huh?" My hands moved automatically as I spoke, pulling a bag from under the counter and sliding the wireless booster inside.

I think that depends on you, said George apologetically. *I'm not the one who needs to move on. I'm the one who's here because you still need me.*

"Yeah, well, right now? Right now, I think being crazy may be the only thing that's keeping me sane. Come on."

I closed the van door and made my way back across the garage. The house security system didn't say anything. I guess it was smart enough to recognize that I hadn't gone near any of the exits. That, or it just wasn't in the mood to argue with me. I didn't care either way.

Alaric and Becks were still at the kitchen table, in the exact positions they were in when I went into the garage. There was one difference: Half of Becks's guns were gone, making room for me to put down the bag. "Alaric, you got an extension cord?"

"In my laptop bag," he said. As he bent to retrieve it, he asked, "Did you find the wireless booster?"

"I did. Got any idea how it works?"

"Not really."

"That explains why we stopped using it. I guess we're going to have to hope that my classic 'smack it until it works' approach can save the day." I sat, unpacking the wireless booster and connecting it to the battery pack. Alaric passed me an extension cord. I hooked it to the battery, and Becks took the other end, plugging it into the wall.

Try not to break anything you can't fix.

"Hush, you," I said vaguely. "Working now."

Becks and Alaric exchanged a glance, but didn't say anything. That was probably the best thing they could have done.

Buffy built all her own equipment. That would have been fine— a lot of people build their own equipment—if it weren't for the fact that her idea of what equipment should look like was almost completely defined by pre-Rising television. She could put more wires, switches, and buttons on a single remote than anybody else I've ever met, and each one had a specific purpose. She also understood that by her standards, she worked with a bunch of ham-handed techno-illiterates. After the fifth time George tried to reboot a server by putting her foot through it, Buffy started putting idiot buttons on everything. They wouldn't provide access to the more complicated functions, but they'd get things going.

"Red," I mumbled. "Red, red, red . . . " Red buttons used to be common. They were visible, hard to miss, and universally understood as important. After the Rising, red took on another meaning: It became the color of infection, the color of danger . . . the color of death. Red buttons were installed on things that needed the capacity to self-destruct, and they represented the things that you should never, under any circumstances, touch. So of course Buffy, with her perverse sense of humor and pre-Rising aesthetic, made all the really good stuff red.

The center button on the booster's control panel was a glossy shade of strawberry red. Becks and Alaric knew Buffy by reputation and through staff meetings, but she was dead before they joined the standing office team. They never learned some of her little quirks. So it wasn't really surprising to see Alaric come halfway to his feet when I hit the button. Becks managed not to stand. She did have to stop herself before she grabbed my arm, but hey, at least she stopped herself.

I took my finger off the button. The wireless booster made a cheerful beeping sound as it started scanning the local network, looking for exploitable cracks in the security. I looked from Becks to Alaric, smiled, and stood.

"Give it five minutes," I said. "I'm going to get myself a Coke. Either of you want anything?"

Neither of them did.

The wireless booster clicked to itself, occasionally beeping as it verified some part of the network structure to its own satisfaction. It had been running for three of the five minutes I'd requested when Mahir came into the kitchen, rubbing his face with one hand. His glasses were propped up on his forehead, and he looked exhausted. Seeing the beeping, blinking box on the kitchen table, he slid his glasses back down and frowned. "What in bloody hell is that thing supposed to be, and what is it doing?" he asked.

"Hey, Mahir." I took a swig of Coke before saluting him with the can. "The embassy get you a connection?"

"No." He scowled. "All international lines are locked down until the cause of this incident can be determined. The damned government's thinking terrorist action, naturally. I've just had an offer of extraction back to Britain. As if the United States could hold an Indian citizen against his will."

"If this is declared an act of terrorism, I think they can," said Alaric.

Mahir paused. "You may be right," he said finally. "I'll try to avoid thinking about that for the moment. Now, does someone want to tell me what that thing is supposed to be?"

The wireless booster beeped, louder this time, and the lights along the top turned a bright sunshine yellow. I pushed away from the counter. "Hey, Alaric, check your connection."

"On it, boss." He tapped his keyboard. Then he punched the air, thrusting his arms up in a victory salute. "We have Internet!"

"Girl was a genuine genius." I finished my Coke and tossed the empty can into the sink. "That 'thing' is the original Georgette Meissonier wireless Internet booster and satellite access device. I have no clue how it works. I don't *care* how it works. All I know is that you have no signal, you plug it in, you get it to turn on, and then it finds you a signal. It—"

None of them were listening to me anymore. Alaric was typing furiously, while Becks and Mahir were in the process of hauling out their own laptops and setting to work. I looked around and shook my head.

"Thank you, Shaun. We really appreciate your getting us back into contact with the rest of the world, Shaun. You're awesome, Shaun," I said dryly.

Becks flipped me off.

"You're welcome," I said, and walked out of the kitchen.

My laptop bag was on the couch next to Maggie, who was still staring, transfixed, at the television. Her lap was full of bulldogs. I hadn't noticed that before. I touched her shoulder. She didn't react. "Hey. Maggie?" Still no response. "Maggie, hey, come on. You need to stop looking at that now. It's not doing you any good, and I think it's probably doing you a lot of bad." She still didn't react. "George . . ."

Just do it.

"Gotcha." The remote was on the arm of the couch. I picked it up and switched off the television before stuffing the remote into my pocket, where no one would be able to get it without my knowledge.

Maggie's protest was immediate. "Hey!" she exclaimed, looking blindly around for the missing remote control. "I was watching that!"

"And now you're not," I replied. "We have Internet again."

"We do?" Brief hope suffused her face. "Are things . . . did we . . . ?"

"I dug Buffy's semi-legal wireless booster out of storage. We're probably tapped into a Department of Defense satellite or something, but I think there's a good chance your parents own the satellite, so I don't give a shit. If they get pissed, you can bat your eyelashes at them and say we're sorry. Alaric's already online, Becks and Mahir are in a footrace to join him, and I figured you might want to log in and check your Fictionals. Make sure they're okay." Or as close as anyone was likely to be, under the circumstances.

Maggie isn't the sort of person who falls apart often, or for long. Her eyes cleared when I mentioned her Fictionals, and she nodded. "I'm not sure how many of them will have connectivity, but the ones who do will be worried sick." She lifted the bulldogs from her lap and set them on the couch. Two jumped down to the floor and went trotting off on unknowable bulldog errands. The third one made a fussy grunting noise, curled up, and went back to sleep.

I've never envied a dog before.

"The cities must still be online," I said. "If they knocked San Francisco off the network, they'd have riots to go with their zombies. I figure we lost connection because we're too far out in the boonies for anyone to give a shit about what happens to us."

These cold equations, said George, with a sigh.

"Exactly," I said.

Maggie pretended not to notice as she stood, brushed the dog hair from her legs, and said, "If we have Internet, we have VOIP again," she said. "I'm going to go call my parents."

I blinked. Maggie was generally happy to spend her family's money, but I'd never heard her say she was going to contact them. That was a part of her life that the rest of us really weren't invited into. "Really?"

"Really." She gave me a wry look. "Unless you want a private army descending to extract me."

"Go call your parents."

Half the dogs followed Maggie out of the living room, leaving the other half sprawled around in various stages of repose. I sat down on the couch, bracing my elbows on my knees and dropping my head into my hands as I tried to figure out our next move. No pressure or anything. It was just the end of the world.

I went through a science fiction phase when I was in my teens, around the time George was having her American history and angry beat poetry phase. We always shared the best stuff, so she learned a lot about ray guns, and I learned a lot about revolutions. There was this one story—I don't remember who the author was—about a dude who was flying a bunch of vaccine to a sick planet. The fuel was really precisely calculated, because fuel was expensive and the ship was pretty small. And this teenage girl who didn't understand stowed away on his ship. She wanted to get to her brother. Only there wasn't enough fuel to get them both to the sick planet, and she didn't know how to land the ship or deliver the vaccine. If she lived, everybody died. That was the cold equation. How many lives is one person, even a totally innocent person, going to be worth? We used to argue about that, more for fun than anything else, but we never managed to get that equation to equal anything but death.

If the outbreak was bad enough, they'd start diverting all but the most essential services to the big cities. Cold equations again: An outbreak in Weed would have a limited amount of fuel to feed it, and be geographically isolated enough to mop up without too much secondary loss of life. An outbreak in Seattle or San Francisco would kill millions, and then spill out of the city to kill millions more. We were the stowaways on this ship, and there was only enough fuel to get one person safely to the other side.

"You should call a staff meeting," said George, sitting down next to me and resting her head against my shoulder. She was affectionate like that only when we were alone, even when we were kids. She never wanted the Masons to see.

"I know." I left my head in my hands. "Maggie's crew won't be the only worried ones."

"Did we have anyone in Florida?"

"Not Florida, but we had a Newsie in Tennessee, and I think a couple of Irwins in Louisiana. They were doing the bayous." Their faces flashed behind my eyes, still photos that would have looked totally natural up on the Wall. I was grimly afraid they'd be going up there soon. Alana Cortez, who loved reptiles and had been bitten by more venomous snakes than any person has a right to survive encountering, and Reggie Alexander, a walking mountain of a man whose biggest claim to fame was the time that he punched a zombie and survived to brag about it. They were both solid, well-trained, and on the way to having lucrative careers in the news. But they'd been in Louisiana. And Louisiana wasn't there anymore.

"That makes calling a meeting even more important. If we've lost anyone, people are going to be convincing themselves that we've lost everyone."

I sighed. "Yeah, I know."

George put a hand on the back of my neck. Maybe I should have been disturbed by the fact that I could feel it, but I just couldn't work up the energy. I was too busy being grateful that she was there at all.

"Hey, George?"

"What?"

"That stuff I said before . . . before." Before Kelly died, before Dr. Wynne turned on us, before we fled the CDC hours ahead of a disaster of Biblical proportions—before everything. Before the world changed.

"Yeah?"

"I didn't mean it. I really, really didn't mean it." I lifted my head and she was there, looking at me with open anxiety, alien eyes grave. "Don't leave me. Please don't leave me. I can't do this without you, and if you try to make me, I don't think I'm going to be okay."

"Don't worry about that." Her smile was sad, and her hand continued to rest against the back of my neck, feeling solid and warm and alive. If this was crazy, God, I wasn't sure I was capable of wanting anything else. "I'm not going anywhere."

"Good," I whispered. I sat on the couch with my dead sister, listening to the voices from the kitchen, and wondered just how the fuck I was going to get us through this one in one piece.

... fuck it. I don't have the energy to be profound right now. Turn off your goddamn computer and go spend some time with your family before the world decides to finish ending. That's about the only profound thing that I have left.

We ran out of time, and we didn't even know that it was being metered.

———

What he said.

Twenty-four

The feeling of George's hand against the back of my neck eventually faded. I looked up to find myself alone. Even the usual soft sense of her at the back of my mind was gone. That didn't worry me the way it would have, once; I'd had plenty of time to adjust to the idea that her presence came and went depending on how stressed I was, how much pressure I was under, and I guess how sane I was feeling at any given moment. If she wasn't there, that must mean I was feeling better.

In the kitchen, Mahir and Alaric were typing furiously, while Becks was finishing the reassembly of what looked like her last gun for the day. Maggie was wearing a wireless headset and sitting in front of her laptop, chattering in a rapid mixture of English and Spanish. She sounded calmer. That was good, since the speed of her responses implied that whomever she was talking to wasn't calm in the least.

I hooked my thumb in her direction as I walked toward the coffee machine. George being out of the picture for the moment meant I could down a cup of real caffeine before I had to go back to caffeinated sugar water. "Who's on the line?"

"Her folks," said Becks, glancing up. "They've been talking for half an hour." The subtext—that I'd been sitting by myself in the living room for half an hour—wasn't subtle. Somehow, I didn't really care.

"Good job with the wireless booster." Mahir kept typing as he spoke, his head bowed in what could have been either concentration or prayer. "I believe Mr. Garcia was on the edge of commanding an armed extraction when she was finally able to get through and notify them as to her continuing safety."

"I could do with a little armed extraction." I took a large gulp of coffee, letting it sear the back of my throat before adding, "As long as they were willing to stay and be our private army. You think they'd stay and be a private army?"

"No," said Alaric tonelessly.

Mahir did look up at that, shooting a worried glance toward Alaric before turning to me and saying, "Internet journalists have been largely expelled from the impacted areas, and those attempting to take pictures or live blog from inside have been cited with practicing journalism without a license."

"What?" I straightened. "That's not legal."

"Becoming a blogger requires only that one establish a blog, and not necessarily even that, if one is willing to exist solely through commentary on the blogs of others. Becoming a journalist requires that one take the licensing exams, take the marksmanship exams, pass accreditation, and possess a license sufficient to allow entry to any given hazard zone, lest fines and possible charges be applied."

"Well, yeah, Mahir. Everybody knows that. What does that have to do with—"

"The individuals involved were in established hazard zones, taking actions of the sort that journalists must be properly licensed to perform." Mahir shook his head, light glinting off his glasses. "They're being held while charges are brought against them."

I gaped at him. "Wait—so—what, they're saying that when you

combine 'has a blog' with 'is inside a hazard zone,' you automatically become a journalist?"

"Poof," muttered Becks.

"That's insane!"

"Insane, and very, very clever, as it's going quite a long way toward reducing the number of unapproved reports making it out of the impacted areas." Mahir's gaze skittered toward Alaric. Just for a moment, but long enough for me to see where he was looking. "Reduction doesn't mean elimination, thankfully. Some things are still getting out."

"Some things always do," I said, putting my mug down. I wasn't thirsty anymore. "Alaric? You okay, buddy?"

"The updates to the Wall started this morning," he said. Tears ran down his cheeks as he turned to look at me. He didn't bother wiping them away. Maybe he knew that drying his face wouldn't be enough to make the crying stop. "My little sister posted for our parents and our brother. Dorian shot our parents, and Alisa shot Dorian, after he'd started to turn. I always knew getting her shooting lessons for her birthday was a good idea, even if Mother wanted her to take dance classes."

I winced. "Fuck, Alaric, I'm—"

"Did it help you when I said I was sorry George died?"

Everyone said they were sorry when George died, even the Masons. And not a single apology had made a damn bit of difference. "No. It didn't help."

"Then don't say it." He looked back to his computer. "The forums are exploding. We're one of the only major sites that has people actually responding to queries."

"That's because we don't know anything."

"That's not entirely true," said Mahir. "We know the outbreak started when Tropical Storm Fiona made landfall—and that it spread with the storm. *Only* with the storm."

"Wait, what?"

"All the index cases have matched up with the initial footprint of the storm."

I stared at him. What he was saying didn't make sense. An outbreak starting when a major storm hit was reasonable, if horrifying. Storms cause devastation, they cause injuries, and they can cause a hell of a lot of cross-contamination. There have been documented cases of someone being injured in a major storm, only to have the wind carry their infected blood onto a bystander before anyone knew what was happening. But that outbreak would be geographically contained, and even though it would be horrible, it wouldn't be anything unique enough to cause the sort of devastation they were showing on the news.

If the live state of the virus had gone airborne, it would be reasonable to assume that it would spread with the storm. It would also spread *without* the storm, and while its initial footprint might have been defined by Fiona, it wouldn't stay that way. If this was a purely airborne outbreak, it should have been breaking out of any containment not defined through a complete absence of uninfected bodies.

"Wait ..." I said again, slow dread worming its way into my stomach. I hadn't realized I still had the capacity to be frightened. Somehow, it wasn't a welcome discovery. "Alaric, your sister. You said she posted to the Wall. Is she all right?"

"She's scared out of her mind, and she's alone in the attic of the family condo, but she's physically fine." Alaric looked up, expression challenging me to say something as he added, "She's using the company server to chat with me."

"Good. Make sure she has a log-in of her own. If she wants to co-author reports with you on what's going on out there, use your own discretion, but I say let her. It may take her mind off things until she's evacuated. Can you ask her a question for me?"

Alaric eyed me suspiciously. "What do you want me to ask?"

"Ask whether any of them had been outside since the start of the storm." The idea that was unfolding in the back of my head wasn't a pleasant one. It also wasn't one that I could categorically ignore.

Alaric frowned. "I don't think—"

"Please."

He hesitated, then turned back to his computer and began to type. Mahir and Becks looked up from their respective tasks, watching him. Maggie continued to chatter in the background for a few minutes more before saying her good-byes and walking over to stand beside me. "What's going on?"

I gestured toward the still-typing Alaric. "Alaric's asking his sister a question for me."

"The one in Florida?" She gave me a sidelong look. "That seems a little . . . "

"I know how it seems. But it's important."

"All right," said Alaric. "Alisa says Dad was the first to . . . he was the first to get sick, and he went outside just after the storm started, to bring in the recycling bins before they could blow away."

"Did she say whether anyone else went outside before they got sick?"

"No. I mean, no, no one else went outside. Mother was trying to make Dad feel better—no one really understood what was happening; Kellis-Amberlee doesn't *transmit* like that—when he bit her. Dorian tried to separate them, and Dad bit him, too."

"So only your father went outside, and only your father got sick without a recognizable vector?"

Alaric was starting to scowl. "*Yes*. I just told you that."

Becks and Mahir kept looking at me blankly. It was Maggie—daughter of pharmaceutical magnates, fan of bad horror movies, the girl who'd grown up steeped in the medical community—whose eyes widened with a shocked horror that perfectly mirrored my own. "You can't be serious."

"I wish I weren't." I could feel George at the back of my head

again, watching the proceedings. I moved to grab a Coke out of the
fridge as I said, "Alaric, tell your sister to close all the windows she
can get to, and not to open the door for *anyone*. How long is it to sunrise there? Another five hours or so?"

He nodded mutely.

"Okay. If I'm right—and let's all hope I'm not—it should get a
little safer after the sun comes up." I started for the door back to the
living room.

"Hey!" Becks half rose. "Where are you going?"

Maggie didn't look at her. She just kept watching me, suddenly
paler than I'd ever seen her. "He's going to go send an e-mail, aren't
you, Shaun?"

"Yeah." I nodded. "I am. Mahir, hold the fort, keep everybody
working—and if anybody sounds off from the hazard zones, tell them
to stay inside and close the windows. I'll be back in a few minutes."

No one else spoke up as I left the kitchen; no one but George. *How
sure are you?* she asked, voice tight.

"Sure enough to know that I'd give just about anything to be
wrong." I stepped over piles of bulldogs on my way to the house terminal, where I sat and tapped the keyboard to wake the computer
from its slumber. "But I don't think I am wrong. That's the problem.
I really don't think I am."

I'm sorry.

I laughed, a little wildly. "Times like this, I really wish you
weren't dead, you know. When you were alive, I could count on you
to think of these things first. Then I got to sit back looking shocked,
and let you do all the doom-saying."

Sorry my deadness is inconveniencing you.

"Don't worry about it. It was probably my turn to do the shit
jobs." I logged in and called up my e-mail client, ignoring the multiple messages flashing *Urgent* as I scanned for a single sender. She
wasn't there.

"Damn," I sighed, and opened a new message window. I paused long enough to be sure that I wanted to do this and, when no other ideas presented themselves, began to type.

From: Shaun.Mason@aftertheendtimes.com
To: TauntedOctopus@redacted.cn.com
Subject: The current outbreak.

Hey, Dr. Abbey. I know you said we needed to stay away from you and all, but we have sort of a problem, and I was hoping you were the person who could tell me what's up with it.

I'm pretty sure you've heard about the outbreak on the Gulf Coast. It's been eating all the news cycles for at least a day, and maybe longer. I can't say for sure, since we spent the first chunk of it on the road running away from the CDC—oh, right, remember what happened in Portland? Well, it sort of happened again, in Memphis this time. The doctor who sent Kelly to us turned out to be on the side of the bad guys. Kelly died. The rest of us (Mahir, Becks, me) got away. I sort of wonder whether that would have been possible if the storm hadn't hit; if maybe the storm is what distracted them from following us. But whatever. You can't base a report on maybe. That's what George always says, and I need to get some facts.

Alaric's family was in Florida when Tropical Storm Fiona hit. His father went outside after the storm made landfall, and he got sick. Two more members of Alaric's family got sick after he bit them, but the only one to actually amplify without a confirmed vector was the father.

The outbreak is spreading with the footprint of the storm— with the *wind*. It's moving with the wind, and not against it, and not away from it, even though the survivors are doing their best to get away. I've been trying to think of every disease vector I've ever encountered, and I'm coming up with only one that works for this. You're the one who understands the structure of this virus. You're the one who can infect anything. So I'm asking you, and I think the whole world may depend on your answer:

Dr. Abbey, is it possible for Kellis-Amberlee to be spread via an insect vector?

Please reply. I need to know.

Shaun Mason

I clicked Send and sat back in my chair, leaving my hands resting limp against the keyboard. More mail was pouring into my client. The view refreshed every few seconds as things passed the filters and landed in my in-box, their subject lines screaming for attention. For the most part, I ignored them. I was waiting for an answer, not another death notice or demand for information.

You really think it's insects?

"I don't think anything else has this kind of distribution pattern." One of the few saving graces of Kellis-Amberlee has always been the fact that it's a very hands-on virus. Unless you're in the unfortunate two percent of the population at risk for spontaneous amplification, you have to either die or get bitten by someone who's been infected before you have a problem. Giving it any sort of a distance-based vector changed the entire game ... but it was still a speed killer, taking over bodies and rewriting instincts in a matter of hours. With modern quarantine procedures and our constant, comfortable societal paranoia, even an airborne strain could be controlled.

But an insect vector changed everything. Just ask the people living in parts of the world where malaria is still a problem. Ten-dollar mosquito nets can save entire families from a slow, agonizing death—assuming they don't get torn. Or stolen. Or left ever so slightly ajar one night, allowing one tiny bug to slip unnoticed through the mesh and deliver a stinging bite filled with microscopic death. But malaria's a parasitic infection. That's part of why it does so well with the whole mosquito gig. It's little and it's quick and it's very well-suited to the life cycle it's evolved for. Kellis-Amberlee is a huge, unwieldy virus, microscopically speaking, and it doesn't have the flexibility of malaria. Marburg Amberlee provided most of the structure when it combined with the Kellis flu strain, and it was a filovirus. They're *big*. So I had to be wrong. I had to be totally off-base, taking swipes at shadows. I just needed Dr. Abbey to tell me that, so we could move on to looking for answers in someplace a little bit more realistic.

Shaun? George sounded almost timid for a change. She didn't like this theory any more than I did. *Check your mail.*

I allowed my eyes to focus on the screen. The top item in my in-box was from an e-mail address I recognized all too well, and it was flagged *Urgent.* The little status marker was blinking bright red, which meant every possible "read this immediately" switch had been flipped, some of them maybe more than once. I took a breath, sent a silent prayer to anyone who might be listening, and opened the message.

For a long moment, everything was silent.

Oh, said George, finally. *I guess that answers that.*

"Yeah," I said. "I guess it does."

From: TauntedOctopus@redacted.cn.com
To: Shaun.Mason@aftertheendtimes.com
Subject: Re: The current outbreak.

Ten points, kid: You got it faster than I expected you to. The yellow fever epidemic of 1858 happened after a tropical storm blew infected *Aedes aegypti* mosquitoes over from Cuba. The city of Memphis was nearly wiped out. Hundreds of thousands died.

Tropical Storm Fiona originated in Cuba.

This time is going to be much, much worse, because the mosquitoes may have been blown in by the storm, but they're not tethered to it—some of them are probably already breaking away and infecting random people in the countryside. It's just not enough to cause the mass horror we're seeing in the storm zones. People and their shotguns can keep up with it, and as long as Fiona keeps going, the majority of the bugs will stay with the winds. That means they're concentrated, creating a steady critical mass of new infected to share the joy and make it a real community barbecue.

My lab has moved. If you need to evacuate your current location, download the attached file and upload it to a GPS unit you don't mind destroying. The directions will last for approximately five hours before the virus included with the file burns out your CPU. Attempts to extract the directions without uploading them will result in the file self-destructing and possibly giving you a nice little surprise as an added "you shouldn't have fucked around with me when I'm in this kind of a mood" bonus.

If you must go outside while the sun is down, wear long sleeves and bug spray. I recommend Avon Skin-So-Soft. It's a bath product. It smells like someone fed a Disney Princess through a juicer, but it works better than anything else on the market. Really, I recommend DDT and prayer. Sadly, those aren't available for sale.

You have twenty-four hours before I move again. I will not transmit directions a second time.

Good luck. You assholes are going to need it.

Dr. Shannon L. Abbey

I read the e-mail twice, making sure I understood exactly what it said. Finally, I sent two copies to the house printer and leaned back in my chair, bellowing, "*Mahir!*" A minute passed with no reply. I tried again: "*Mahir!*"

"What in the bloody blue blazes are you shouting about *now*?" he demanded, shoving open the kitchen door and storming toward me. The bulldogs scrambled out of his way, demonstrating more in the way of self-preservation than I would have credited them with. One small brindle even mustered the courage to bark at Mahir's ankles. I felt an unexpected pang. We were going to have to evacuate. If not immediately, then soon. The CDC knew where we were, and in the chaos of the second Rising, not even Maggie's parents would have the reach to keep us all safe.

Between the van and George's bike, we could easily take the five surviving members of the team. But there was no way we'd be able to take the dogs.

"I need a thumb drive," I said.

Mahir stared at me. "Do you mean to tell me," he said, in a measured tone, "that you just yelled like there was some sort of emergency on—when there *is* an actual emergency on, no less, which means we're all a trifle jumpy—because you needed a *thumb drive*?"

"Sort of, yeah." I held out my hand. "Got one?"

"I always thought the stories my staff told about you being impossible to work with were exaggerated, you know." Mahir dug a hand into his pocket and pulled out a thumb drive, which he slapped down on my palm. "This isn't the time to be acting the bastard, Shaun."

"I know." I plucked a sheet of paper from the printer and held it out to him. "Here's the latest from the lab of Dr. Abbey, crazy-ass scientist who knows more about the structure of Kellis-Amberlee than anybody else I've ever met. Just in case you needed a few more things to keep you awake at night."

Mahir took the paper wordlessly and started to read. I took advantage of the lull and uncapped the thumb drive, plugging it into an open USB port. It checked out clean, so I started downloading Dr. Abbey's embedded file for transfer. We'd need a way to get the information to the GPS when the time came.

That takes care of one GPS, said George. *Are you leaving the bike?*

"I'll follow the van," I replied, disengaging the thumb drive. It was another cold equation, and one that I liked just as little as I'd liked the first one. The more times we copied the information, the higher the odds were that someone could get hold of it. The van would be better armed and better-equipped to get away if something went wrong. The only person on the bike would be me, and I . . .

I wasn't quite at the end of my usefulness, but with the way I'd been slipping, I wasn't sure how much longer that was going to be true. If only one vehicle could reach Dr. Abbey's safely, it wasn't going to be mine. I was oddly okay with that.

That made one of us. *Shaun, you'd better not be thinking what I think you're thinking.*

"Or what? You'll haunt me?" I chuckled. "You're gonna have to do better than that."

George's rebuttal was cut short as Mahir raised his head and stared at me. The circles under his eyes were standing out like bruises against his suddenly pale skin. I'd thought he looked tired when he first came off the plane, but compared to this, he'd been in top fighting condition. We'd been running for too long. I wasn't the only one running out of go.

"Good lord, Shaun," he said. His voice was shaking. Not for the first time, I wished that I'd died and George had lived—at least she could have given him a hug and told him things might not be all right but they'd take a few of the bastards out with them. I didn't even know where to start. "Is this woman serious?"

"I don't think she's ever not serious. I also don't think she's ever wrong where Kellis-Amberlee is concerned. She's the one who collected most of the data I gave you. She's crazy. She's dangerous. But I think she's right."

"But I . . . " He stopped, licking his lips nervously before he said, "If she's right, we can't stay here."

"That's true."

"So what are we going to do?"

"Well, we can't stay here, and we can't go home." I stood, slipping the thumb drive into my pocket. "I suggest it's time we head off to see the Wizard. The wonderful Wizard of Jesus We Are All So Fucked."

I don't think you can make that scan, said George.

"I don't think so either," I replied. Mahir gave me an odd look. I ignored it. We were past the point of me feeling self-conscious about talking to someone nobody else could hear. "Dr. Abbey's right about the Avon Skin-So-Soft—it's sold as a cosmetic, but it's the best bug repellent on the domestic market. I have a couple of bottles in my kit. So should Becks."

Mahir blinked. "Kellis-Amberlee has never *had* an insect vector. I'm not sure I'm willing to believe that it has one now. Why are you already carrying this stuff?"

I smiled thinly. "Because it's the best bug repellent known to man. When you're an Irwin, poking into places men were not meant to poke, being chased by the living dead, the last thing you want to do is stop to deal with mosquito bites all over your ass."

"I suppose that makes sense."

"I'm going to go get the others up to speed. We need to start packing, and we need to give Maggie time to tell the house security systems to stand down." If I doused myself in bug repellent and wore my full-field armor, I'd be able to take the bike. Any mosquito that could bite through Kevlar deserved to get a piece of me. "We're taking the work van. If it doesn't fit in there, it isn't coming."

"What are you talking about? We need to wait—"

"The sun rises in five hours. The instructions will wipe themselves in five hours. If we want to get to Dr. Abbey alive, we need to leave now."

Mahir hesitated, eyes searching my face. Finally, carefully, he said, "Shaun, are you sure? I mean, are you really sure we should be going to this woman, rather than staying here, where it's safe?"

"*Is* it safe here? Maggie's folks know where we are. The security staff knows. It's only a matter of time before one of us slips and our readership knows. We're on the verge of full-blown martial law, which means that eventually some asshole at the CDC is going to put two and two together and realize that we're sitting ducks. It's going to be Oakland all over again. They just have to make sure their fall guy knows enough to be believable as the one who pressed the button and blew the only heir to Garcia Pharmaceuticals to hell. If we want to stay alive through this, we need to get the fuck out of here."

"I . . ." Mahir stopped. Squaring his shoulders, he looked me in the eye, and asked, "What is it you need me to do?"

"Check with your Newsies. See who's posting what and how much they have ready to go up. Also see who can play phone-tree. We're going to want to hold a short staff meeting before we get out of here—and by 'we,' I mean you, me, and Maggie." Becks and Alaric weren't department heads. They could be packing the van and gathering any essential supplies from the house while we made the requisite reassuring noises and made it seem like we'd be staying where we were for the foreseeable future. I hated the idea of lying to my crew, I *hated* it, but I didn't see any alternative. Not if we wanted to stay alive. I didn't think any of them were secretly working for the enemy—Buffy was a special case—and I was pretty sure they were all willing to do whatever it took to help us spread the truth. George had a gift for hiring good people, and the best thing about hiring good people is that they'll recommend other good people when it comes time to expand.

I would trust our staff with my life, and had, on several occasions. But we couldn't take them all with us, and that meant they couldn't know where we were going. More cold equations. If someone came looking, it was important there be no one who could give our location away.

Mahir was clearly doing the same math I was because he looked stricken before he nodded. "I'll get them to report in, and I'll pass the word about the staff meeting. How long do you think we need?"

"Tell 'em to be online in fifteen minutes. Anyone who isn't there when we get started can join late and try to catch up as best they can." I paused. "Also . . . tell them I'm not my sister. I'm not going to pull a grand gesture like she did. But if they want to quit without consequences, now would be the time to do it."

George called a staff meeting when we first started to realize the size of the conspiracy we were facing. She made sure everyone was connected—and fired them all. Anybody who wanted to stay on could stay, but they had to sign another contract first. They had to *understand* what they were getting into. It was a big deal. It was incredibly important. And there just wasn't time for that kind of theater. They'd stay or they wouldn't. Anyone who'd signed on during the meeting with George knew the score, and so did anyone who'd signed on since.

"All right," said Mahir. He was already moving toward the house terminal, my printout clutched in one hand.

I leaned over and plucked it from his grasp, offering a wan smile in his direction before I turned and started for the kitchen. It was time to get everybody on the same page, get Maggie to start packing, and get ready to go on the run.

Bet you wish we'd never signed up for the Ryman campaign, huh?

"The thought has crossed my mind," I admitted. "When you said,

'Hey, Shaun, let's be journalists,' I'm pretty sure this part wasn't in the brochure."

Would it have made any difference?

I paused with my hand raised to push the kitchen door open. Mahir and Buffy, Maggie, Alaric, and Becks, we knew them all because of what we'd chosen to do with our lives. More important, they were *our* lives, not mine. If I'd said no, that I wanted to be something else when I grew up, George would still have become a blogger, and I would have lost her long before I actually did.

"Not a bit," I said, and stepped into the kitchen.

I am a poet, and I am a storyteller, and it is with these two callings in mind that I make the following statement, which comes from my heart, my soul, and my middle fingers:

Fuck you people and the horses you rode in on. You better watch yourselves, because we are done screwing around, and we are going to take your bitch asses down.

This is for Dave.

—From *Dandelion Mine*, the blog of Magdalene Garcia, June 24, 2041

———

The world has gone insane, and you can't get a decent pint of lager anywhere in this bloody country. I think I can safely say that my schoolmates were correct when they predicted my eventual destination, and I am now in hell.

—From *Fish and Clips*, the blog of Mahir Gowda, June 24, 2041

Twenty-five

The staff meeting went better than I was afraid it would. That's about the only good thing that I can say about it. Everyone was scared, and everyone was expressing that fear in a different way. The Irwins were restless and pissed off about being forbidden to go into the field. The Newsies were split into two distinct camps—the ones who wanted to grab an Irwin, get outside, and find out what the hell was going on out there, and the ones who were happy to stay as far away from the disaster zone as possible but wanted information to flow freely while they stayed indoors. That's the kind of Newsie attitude that's always pissed me off, since it seems to come with a blanket assumption that the Irwins are overjoyed to be risking their lives for the benefit of the Newsies' careers.

The Fictionals, on the other hand, were uniformly glad to be staying inside, but were all scared out of their minds and spent half the call going off on tangents that required all business to come grinding to a halt while Maggie calmed them down. She was good at her job, maybe better than I ever realized, and not even she could keep them on track for more than a few minutes at a time. After twenty minutes, I was ready to kill someone—and I wasn't all that picky about who.

Mahir saved everyone's asses. He took over the call and led it with calm and grace, pausing when Maggie needed to play kindergarten teacher, and otherwise keeping us moving forward. He fielded every question that was tossed his way, somehow prompting the rest of us to speak up just often enough that no one forgot we were there. If he'd wanted to go into event planning instead of journalism, he probably could have made a fortune.

The whole time the call was going, Alaric and Becks were packing up supplies and moving them to the back of the kitchen, just outside the closed garage door. Maggie and Alaric had done a lot of packing before the rest of us got there, but neither of them was an Irwin, and Becks felt the need—probably rightly—to go through everything and make sure that we had enough supplies to reach our destination in one piece.

"All right, folks," I said, breaking into the fifth near-identical argument over who was getting more screwed by the current embargos, the Newsies or the Irwins. "I'm glad we're all on the same page now, but the wireless booster is about to shut down from lack of juice, so I figure we should wrap this up. I don't know how long it'll be before they get our little slice of the Internet back online. In the meantime, everybody has their assignments, and we have our temporary department heads. Are there any questions?"

There were no questions. That was practically a goddamn miracle. Our three temporary department heads—Katie in Connecticut, for the Fictionals; Luis in Ohio, for the Newsies; and Dmitry in Michigan, for the Irwins—were nervous enough that their tiny digital pictures looked faintly ill. Still. We wouldn't have asked them to do the jobs if we didn't think they were ready. Not that anyone could really be considered ready to take over one-third of a major news site during a disaster this large, but they were about as prepared as the rest of us, and no one was shooting at them yet. That had to count for something.

"Okay, then, I'm going to shut this baby down before something manages to actually catch fire and we have to kill it with sticks." I looked at my screen. The faces of After the End Times looked back at me, all filled with the same anxiety. The world might actually be ending. That was a bit more than we were used to dealing with on a normal workday.

Say something inspirational, prompted George. *They need to hear it from you. You're the leader.*

That was a job I never applied for. I managed to bite back the words "Like what?" before they could quite escape, and cleared my throat instead, trying to think of a single damn thing to say. My mind was a blank. This was a threat way too big to prod with a stick.

You can do it, said George, quietly.

I cleared my throat again. "Guys ... " Everyone looked at me expectantly. I faltered, losing my place for a second before I tried again: "This has been one hell of a year. For those of you who hired on with us after the campaign, I'm sorry. You've never seen me at my best. Hell, if it weren't for the fact that we have the best damn administrative staff in the known universe, you would never have seen me at all, because we would have gone under a long time ago."

"He's quite right about that," said Mahir.

Ignoring him seemed like the best idea, so I did. "And for those of you who've been with us since the beginning, I know this isn't what you signed on for. Hell, it's not what *I* signed on for, and you'd think I might have some say in what we do, right? But the thing is, regardless of when you came on with us, whether it was day one or yesterday, you have all done an amazing, amazing job. If I were asked to put together a team to record the end of the world, there's not one of you who I wouldn't want to have on board—and yeah, I don't know all of you that well, but I know the people who recommended you, and since I would trust them with my life, I figure you're worth taking the gamble on."

Laughter followed this statement, some nervous, most not. A few people were nodding. That was sort of unnerving.

"I don't know how much worse things are going to get before they get better. We're in the same place now that we were in twenty years ago—the dead are rising, the situation looks grim as hell, and no one really knows what's going on. I won't lie to you. If the first Rising is anything to go by, we're not all going to live to see the end of this. Some of us will be going up on the Wall before this is over." I paused, the litany of the dead running in the back of my mind. Buffy, Georgia, Dave, Kelly. The convoy guards in Eakly, Oklahoma. All our neighbors back in Oakland. Alaric's family. Too damn many people. "Some of us already have. But see, the thing is, that isn't what matters. What matters is that we're going to keep doing what we do. We're going to keep getting the news out. We're going to keep telling the truth. And if we go up on the Wall, we're by God going to know that we did the best we could—and that we've left behind as much information as we can for the ones who'll tell the truth after us."

There was a long pause. *Well said,* said George.

And then someone—one of the Irwins, I think, since we're the ones trained to start making noise whenever we get the excuse—cheered. Several more people joined in, and the ones who didn't clapped their hands, or just grinned. I stared at them, dumbfounded.

They like you.

I kept staring.

Mahir saved me by leaning forward and saying, "That's the end of our motivational speaking for the day, and the end of our power supply, I'm afraid. Ladies and gents, it's been fabulous chatting with you all, and we'll do our best to keep updating you as things progress here, but for now, assume that we're off-line for the foreseeable future. Ask your interim department heads if you have any questions or troubles, and stay safe." He moved his mouse cursor to the button for Terminate Conference, and clicked.

The screen went black, all those little windows blinking out in an instant. It felt weirdly final, like I'd never speak to any of these people again. In some cases, I probably wouldn't. I coughed into my hand to clear the tightness in my throat, and straightened.

"Okay," I said. "Let's go."

Packing the rest of the equipment took less than ten minutes. Maggie spent the time in the living room, feeding treats to the bull-dogs and telling them how good they were. They were happy to receive the attention, if a little confused by all the fuss that she was making; people came and went all the time, after all, and she didn't normally make such a big deal out of it. To their canine minds, this excursion didn't look any different from the hundreds of others she'd taken. Maybe it was better that way.

While she was dealing with the dogs, I went upstairs to the guest room and changed into my body armor. I slathered Avon Skin-So-Soft over every inch of skin I had, even the skin that would be covered by three layers of Kevlar and leather. I was going to be as soft as a baby's ass, and more important, I wasn't going to get infected if I had any choice in the matter.

I paused in the doorway before heading back down to join the others, looking at the guest room. The bed was made, the nightstand was empty, and there was nothing to indicate that I'd ever been there at all.

"Will we ever stop just passing through?" I asked aloud.

George didn't answer, and so I went back downstairs.

Maggie had joined the others in the kitchen while I was getting changed. She offered me a nod, wiping her eyes with the back of one hand before turning to walk up to the back door. "House," she said, clearly, "please contact Officer Weinstein. Tell him it's time for the matter we discussed earlier."

"All right, Magdalene," said the house. Its tone was blandly pleas-ant as always.

"Thank you, house." Maggie looked over her shoulder to me. "I warned Alex we might need to go, and that we'd need it to be as quiet as possible. He's been waiting for my word."

"And the house will let us out?" asked Becks.

"If the security crew outside says that we're opening the isolation lock, even for a few minutes, the house won't have a choice. My security logs are only uploaded if there's an unapproved breach, so unless the infected take the house, no one will know for sure that we're gone." Maggie wiped her eyes again. "I hate this."

"I know," I said, quietly.

The house speaker crackled as someone switched to manual, and a man's voice came through, asking, "Ms. Garcia? Are you sure this is what you want to do?"

Maggie smiled unsteadily at a point just above the door—probably the location of a hidden security camera. "No. But I'm sure it's what I have to do. Please let us out, Alex."

"Your father—"

"Signs your checks, but you work for me, remember? That was always the deal. Now please, just give us ten minutes to get out of here, and you can lock the place down again."

He sighed heavily. "If anything happens to you, your father will have all our asses. You understand that, right?"

"I do."

"Just checking. You have ten minutes. Now please, try not to make me regret this."

The speaker crackled again as he hung up his end, and the house said, sounding almost perplexed, "The isolation order has been rescinded. Thank you for your patience. You are now free to leave the premises if you so choose."

"Grab your gear, folks," I said, picking up a duffel bag with one hand and my helmet with the other. "We need to get rolling."

"On it," said Alaric, grabbing the wireless booster.

Becks didn't say anything. She just picked up a box filled with dry cereal and cans of soda and kicked the garage door open.

The van was inside, which was good. The bike was outside, which was not good. Working in tight tandem, the five of us were able to load the van in just under five minutes, cramming boxes and bags into every inch of available space. I didn't question the amount of stuff that we were bringing. Since the odds of us coming back were pretty damn slim, we needed to take everything that was even potentially useful and assume that it was easier to throw shit away than it would be to find it once we were on the road.

We were halfway through the packing process when Alaric realized there wasn't going to be room for everyone. "Wait," he said. "We need to leave some of this. We're filling the backseat."

"It's all good." I raised my helmet. "I'm taking the bike."

"But—"

"We need someone riding point. And besides," I said and grinned, "you know I'm going to get the *best* footage."

He gave me an uncertain look. "You're going to be exposed."

"We've all basically bathed in insect repellent—if they bite me, I probably deserve it. Now come on, finish packing the van. We have a pretty narrow time frame here, and we need to get out before it closes."

Becks lobbed a duffel bag at him. He caught it with an *oof*, and gave me a wounded look before turning to resume packing the van. I didn't really care if he thought I was being an idiot. Maybe I was. I was also being a realist.

When the last box was wedged into place and the last bag was stowed, the four of them got into the van, rolling the windows all the way up. I put on my helmet, sealing it tightly before nodding to activate the intercom. "How's our connection?" I asked.

"Loud and clear," Mahir replied.

"Great. Now let's roll."

The garage door rolled smoothly upward in answer to some unseen signal from Maggie, and the night air came flooding in, chilling me even through my leathers. It wasn't the temperature so much as the uncertainty that the air represented: the risk of a kind of infection we'd never been afraid of before. Kellis-Amberlee was a known quantity; it was, for lack of a better phrase, a safe virus, something that could kill you, but which we understood. The thought of a new vector made it all terrifying again.

Becks started up the van engine and turned on the headlights. I didn't need them to see where I was going, since the exterior house lights were turned up so far that it practically looked like noon out in the yard. I walked over to the bike and swung my leg over it, balancing myself. "Go," I said, into the microphone in my helmet. "I'll be right behind you."

The van pulled out of the garage. I let them get to the first gate before I started the ignition and followed.

The trip down the driveway was harrowing. We moved slowly enough that I had to walk the bike about two-thirds of the time. When that wasn't possible, I had to coast, trying to keep from either overbalancing or stalling out. Neither would be good. And I'd be dealing with it alone either way, since there was no way I was letting the others stop the van to help me. That wasn't part of the plan.

All the gates stood open, allowing us to keep moving through as we wound our way toward the street below. Maggie's security guards flanked the open gates, their guns held at the ready. I'm not sure they really believed that we were going until we'd passed the third gate. That was when they started locking things down behind us, each gate sliding shut and sealing itself with a clang that was audible even through my helmet. The guards moved forward as the gates closed, reforming their ranks around each new opening.

They stayed behind as we passed the last gate. One of them— Officer Weinstein, most likely—raised his assault rifle in salute. Then

Becks hit the gas, speeding off down the road in answer to the instructions in the van's GPS, and I had to gun the throttle in order to catch up. It took only a few seconds for the house to recede entirely out of sight. The view of the hill that it was on lasted for a little longer, slipping in and out of sight as we followed the curve of the road.

The lights from the house stayed visible even after the house itself was out of sight. They blazed up into the night, painting the clouds with tiered bands of light and shadow. I was relieved when they finally faded. They reminded me too much of everything that we were leaving behind.

The speaker in my helmet beeped to signal an incoming call. I nodded to activate it. "Go."

"We're heading for I-5 toward Portland," said Becks, right in my ear. "We're going to have to take the main highway for about forty miles, just to get past the worst of the forest."

"Got it." Under most circumstances, taking the highway would have been the safest thing to do. It was well-guarded, was well-maintained, and had access to multiple emergency services, including bolt holes we could flee to if things took a turn for the worse. It was also the single route most likely to be monitored by anyone who was watching to see if we were on the move and, because of the nature of modern highway design, would be relatively easy to isolate from the rest of the grid. It was possible that some innocent bystanders might be caught up in an attack designed to target the five of us . . . and after everything we'd been through, I no longer had any illusions that the people we were running from would care.

"Watch yourself out there," said Becks. Then the connection was cut and the van sped up, racing away from the lights of Weed, racing into the darkness up ahead.

The only thing I could do was follow her.

I-5 was eerily deserted. Even the guard stations were dark, proving once again that, when faced with a true national emergency, no amount of "duty" is going to be sufficient to get people to leave their homes. Half the men who should have been guarding the road were likely to be charged with treason if they were caught, and right now, they had absolutely no reason to care. Treason wasn't as bad as infection and death. At least treason was something you stood a chance of surviving. We took the automated blood tests and rolled on.

Every time the occupants of the van had to roll down a window, I stopped breathing, waiting for the screams to start. They never did. We were far enough outside the footprint of the storm that we were probably safe . . . but "probably" isn't something I believe in banking on. Thank God for bug repellent.

With the road empty and both of us driving as fast as we dared, we cleared forty miles of highway driving in just under thirty minutes. From there, Becks led us onto a frontage road that paralleled I-5 but was mostly concealed by the concrete retaining wall meant to protect passing motorists. I guess if you were one of the people who lived in the tiny houses and aging trailer parks we passed, you were shit out of luck. That's something almost everyone does their best to forget: The world may have changed, but some people still can't afford to come in out of the cold. The poor didn't have advanced security systems or hermetically sealed windows, and now that Kellis-Amberlee had found itself a new vector . . .

It didn't really bear thinking about.

We were passing Ashland, Oregon, when my helmet beeped again. "Go," I said.

"Shaun?" Becks sounded uncertain. "The GPS just gave me our final destination."

"And?"

"And it's Shady Cove."

I managed to keep control of the bike, but only because I had George to take care of the vital business of swearing like a madwoman at the back of my head while I focused on the road. "Are you *sure?*"

"I'm sure." There was a long pause before she asked, "What are the odds that she's driving us into a trap?"

"I don't know. What are the odds that we have anywhere else to go?" She didn't answer me. "I figured as much. We're going to Shady Cove, Becks. Tell everybody to take off the safeties and keep their eyes on the mirrors."

"I hope to God you know what you're doing, Mason," said Becks, and cut the connection.

"So do I," I muttered. "So do I."

A lot of small towns were declared uninhabitable after the Rising. They're little dead zones scattered around the map of the world, places where no one goes anymore—no one but well-prepared, heavily armed Irwins looking for a story, and even then, we never go in at night. Going into a dead zone at night is like signing your own death warrant. Santa Cruz, California, is a dead zone. So is most of India. And so is Shady Cove, Oregon. It used to be a small but comfortable town of about two thousand people, surrounded by woodlands, comfortably close to the popular tourist attraction of several state and county parks. They did okay.

Until the zombies came, and the very things that made it such a nice place to live turned Shady Cove into a deathtrap. The same thing could have happened to Weed, if not for the fisheries, and Shady Cove didn't have anything that vital to the local economy. It just had people. We lost a lot of people in the Rising. A town that size was barely even a blip in the statistics.

This is bad, said George. *We need to turn back.*

"This makes perfect sense. If Dr. Abbey is trying to go off the grid, a dead zone is the best place to do it, and Shady Cove was never burned." I forced a smile. "Besides, you only know the place exists because of the number of times I begged you to let me go there."

There's a reason I always said no.

"I know. But it's not like we've been left with a whole lot of options."

George didn't have an answer to that one.

The frontage roads gave way to smaller frontage roads, which gave way in turn to roads that were barely even paved. The lights of the freeway guard walls stayed in view the whole time, almost taunting me with the idea of smooth surfaces and well-marked exit signs. We were still within Dr. Abbey's time frame, and the GPS was clearly still feeding Becks directions, because she kept driving and didn't stop to yell at me for getting us into this mess.

When I drove past a sign reading SHADY COVE — 5 MILES, I actually started to believe that we might reach our destination alive.

Then the first zombie came racing out of the woods on my left.

It was moving with the horrible, disjointed speed that only the freshly infected can manage. A normal human will always be faster in a short sprint, but the freshly infected win every time in a long race. They don't care about pain, and they don't really notice when their lungs stop pulling in enough air. The uninfected will eventually stop chasing you. A zombie will run until it collapses from exhaustion, and there's a good chance that even that won't keep it down for long.

The van swerved to avoid the zombie. I did the same. I was so busy trying to keep the bike upright that I didn't see the other three infected lunging out of the shelter of the trees until one of them was scrabbling at the handlebars of my bike, with absolutely no awareness of the sheer stupidity of attacking a man on a moving motorcycle. "Holy—"

I slammed on the brakes, sending the zombie tumbling away from me. The van was back on track, moving away at top speed. I twisted the throttle, starting after them, only to come up short as an arm was hooked around my neck and I was jerked off the bike.

The Kevlar jacket I was wearing absorbed most of the impact with the road, but it couldn't save me from the hands that were pulling me down, uncoordinated fingers trying to find an opening in my body armor. I smacked them away, flailing to get free. If I could get to my guns, either of them, I would stand a chance of getting away from this. Not a good chance, but a chance.

My questing fingers found the grip of a pistol. I yanked it from the holster hard enough to break one of the snaps and fired it into the face of the first zombie without pausing to aim. The report was loud enough to make my ears ring, even through the still-sealed helmet. The zombie fell back, leaving me with just enough leverage to push myself into a sitting position and shoot the zombie to my right. That left—crap. That left at least three, by a quick count, and all of them focused entirely on me. The bike was on its side up ahead. There was no way I'd be able to get it righted and running again unless I took all the zombies out, and the numbers were *not* on my side.

Don't be an idiot. You've survived worse.

"Says you," I muttered, and took another shot.

I was so focused on the zombies I could see that I forgot one of the first rules of dealing with any zombie mob larger than three: Remember that they're smarter than you think they are. Surprisingly strong hands grabbed me from behind, jerking me back.

Maybe it was the fall I'd taken earlier, and maybe it was just a natural flaw in the construction of my body armor, but when the zombie pulled, I heard something tear. I whipped my head around, looking for a shot, and saw to my horror that the entire left sleeve of my jacket was ripped along the main seam, leaving my arm—protected only by a flannel shirt—exposed.

The infected who was holding me hissed, showing me his shattered, blackened teeth, and brought his head down as I brought my gun up. The bullet caught him in the crown of the head, blowing a jet of brain matter out onto the pavement. The zombie's hands went limp, and he fell, a look of comic bewilderment on the remains of his face. More infected were coming out of the woods. For the moment, however, I wasn't sure how much concern I could spare for them.

Most of my concern was for the new hole in my flannel shirt, and the blood welling up through the fabric. The pain hit half a second later, but the pain wasn't really that important. The blood had already told me everything I needed to know about the situation.

I grabbed the sleeve and yanked it back into place before running toward the bike, shooting as I went. The speaker in my helmet was beeping insistently. I didn't know how long that had been going on. The encounter felt like it had started years ago, even if I was reasonably sure it had been only a few seconds. I nodded sharply.

"—there? Shaun, please, are you *there*?"

"I'm here, Mahir." I shot another zombie as it ran for me, and snickered. "Hey, did you know that rhymes? Where are you guys?"

"We're coming back for you. Can you hold your position?"

"I can, but I gotta tell you, buddy, that's not the best idea you've ever had."

He took a sharp breath. "Shaun, please don't tell me . . . "

"No test results yet, but I'm definitely bleeding." The lights of the van blazed back into sight ahead of me. I groaned. "I told you not to come back!"

"Not in so many words, you didn't, and if you think we're leaving you without a test, you're an arsehole. Now down!"

Mahir's command was sharp enough that I obeyed without thinking, hitting the road on my hands and knees a second before bullets sprayed through the air where I'd been standing. The rest of the undead fell in twitching heaps. The gunfire stopped, leaving the night silent.

"Get on the bike and go," said a voice in my ear. For a dazed second, I couldn't tell whether it was George or Mahir. Then it continued: "We want the turnoff for Old Ferry Road."

"Mahir, I really don't think—"

"If you amplify before we get there, you'll lose control of the bike. If you don't, I'm sure Dr. Abbey will appreciate the chance to check your blood for signs that this is a new strain." Mahir's voice gentled. "Please, Shaun. Don't make us leave you out here."

"This is idiotic," I said.

"Yes."

"Just wanted to be sure you were aware." I nodded again to cut the connection and took a moment to pull my sleeve closed as best as I could before righting the bike and getting back on. It started easily. There went that excuse for staying behind. I could want to protect them, but I couldn't lie to them.

"Well?" asked George, next to my ear. "Are you going to follow them, or what?"

"I'll follow," I said.

The van turned laboriously around on the narrow road, taillights gleaming red through the darkness as Becks hit the gas and started forward once again. I squeezed the throttle, whispered a prayer for swift amplification, and followed them.

We took a tour of the government zombie holding facility on Alcatraz today.

A lot of people don't like having it there, even though it's been scientifically proven that Romero was wrong about at least one thing: Zombies can't survive without oxygen. Since they're too uncoordinated to swim, and they don't know how to operate boats, if there were ever an outbreak, it would be naturally confined. That doesn't matter. "Not in my backyard" comes out loud and clear where the dead are concerned.

I looked through the safety glass into the pens, into the dozens of eyes that looked just like mine, and I searched them as hard as I could for a sign of something, anything that would tell me they were still human. There was nothing there. Only darkness.

If I pray for anything tonight, it will be that when Shaun eventually does something insane and gets himself bitten, I'll be there to shoot him. Because I couldn't live with myself knowing I'd allowed him to amplify. No one deserves to end up like that. No one.

—From *Postcards from the Wall*, the unpublished files of Georgia Mason, originally posted June 24, 2034

Twenty-six

The building housing Dr. Abbey's new lab must have started life as the local forestry center. The front looked like pure glass until you got close enough to see that it was backed with sheet metal. Better yet, the trees had been cut back on all sides, making room for a massive parking lot that provided clear sightlines for anyone trying to guard the building from the infected ... or, as we pulled up to park near what looked like the front entrance, from us. There was even a structure on the roof that might have started out as an observatory but would make a damn good shooter's nest, if necessity demanded.

Becks was the first out of the van, and she had a gun pointed at my head before I could get my helmet off. I could have kissed her for that, if it weren't for the history between us and the fact that I was probably contagious. Field protocol said I was to be kept under constant guard until I could be confirmed as uninfected, and somehow that didn't seem likely to me.

I pulled off my helmet. The night air was cool, and even cold where it hit the sweat on the back of my neck. "Hey," I said, wearily. My throat was a little dry, but that was all; I wasn't experiencing any of the other symptoms I knew would signal the start of amplification.

Just my luck. I would have to go and develop a sturdy immune system.

"Hey," Becks agreed, with a small tilt of her head. "How are you feeling?"

"Like I want to go redline a test and get this over with." Mahir, Alaric, and Maggie got out of the van, all three looking shaken and nauseated. I offered them a nod. "Hey, guys, you know how to set up a guard formation?"

"Yes," said Alaric.

"No," said Maggie.

"I have absolutely no idea," said Mahir.

"That's fine. Becks, Alaric, you guard me. Mahir, you guard Maggie." I stepped away from the bike, leaving the helmet on the seat, and linked my hands behind my head. "Let's go tell Dr. Abbey she has guests, shall we?"

I felt almost like we were parodying our approach to the CDC as we walked toward the building. Mahir and Maggie went first, followed by Becks, who walked backward so as to keep her gun trained on me. Alaric brought up the rear, his own gun out and, I knew, pointed at my head. If I showed any signs of turning, they'd take me down before I could do any serious damage. It was reassuring.

At least they're well-trained, said George.

"There's that," I muttered. Them being well-trained might actually keep them alive for a little bit longer, now that they weren't going to be my responsibility anymore.

We were still about ten yards away when the door opened. Dr. Abbey stepped into view with a shotgun braced against her shoulder and Joe the Mastiff standing next to her, looking more massive than ever. Maybe she'd been feeding him trespassers.

"So you came after all," she said, eyes flicking over the group before settling on me. Her eyebrows rose. "And you're under armed guard because ... ?"

"I was bitten about five miles back," I replied. "There was a pack of infected in the woods. I'm pretty sure we killed them all, but you may want to send a cleanup crew, just to be certain."

"We didn't run a blood test because we didn't want the results uploaded to the CDC database," said Mahir. "Given the circumstances, it seemed somewhat . . . less than wise."

My stomach sank. I hadn't even considered that. "Shit," I whispered.

Nobody expects you to be doing any heavy thinking right after a zombie tried to take your arm off.

"Says you."

"So you brought him here?" Dr. Abbey shrugged, lowering her gun. "I would have settled for a bottle of wine, but I guess a new test subject and the location of some fresh corpses will do. Come on, all of you. Shaun, don't try to touch anyone, or my lab techs will have to blow your head off."

"That's fair," I agreed.

"Good boy." Dr. Abbey smiled and stepped back, letting Becks lead the rest of us inside.

The new lab wasn't as established as the old one, which meant it was more cluttered, with boxes everywhere, and didn't yet have that ground-in "science" smell—strange chemicals, bleach, sterile air, and plastic gloves. This lab smelled rather pleasantly of cedar wood. That would change as things got up to speed. Maybe they could hang some of those little air fresheners, try to bring it back.

Of course, that assumed they were going to have *time*. Most of the shelving units had a distinctly temporary look to them, like this was just a stop on the way to some more distant destination. The mad science equivalent of pitching camp for the night.

Lab-coated assistants scurried here and there, unpacking boxes, carrying trays of samples from one place to another. The assault rifles they all had strapped around their waists were new, making it clear just how seriously they were taking their situation. That was a bit of a relief. I wouldn't be leaving my team with no one to defend them.

"Molena, Alan," said Dr. Abbey, flagging down two of the nearest techs. "Take this group to the cafeteria. Get them coffee and blood tests, and see if you can't scrape together something resembling food. *Not* that god-awful lasagna we had for dinner. That's not even suitable for feeding to the pigs."

"Yes, Dr. Abbey," said the taller of the lab techs. He turned to the group. "If you'll come with me?"

"Of course," said Mahir. "Shaun——"

"Don't." I gave him a pleading look. "All of you, please, don't. We've said everything that needs to be said. So don't, okay?"

"All right," he said, and turned to follow the lab tech. Maggie cast an uncertain glance back in my direction and did the same.

Alaric lingered for a moment, shifting his weight from foot to foot. Finally, he said, "Say hello to Georgia for me," and fled, leaving only me, Becks, and Dr. Abbey behind. And Joe, of course. He sat next to Dr. Abbey, tongue lolling and tail wagging. He was the only one of us not equipped to understand the gravity of the situation, and I sort of envied him that.

Dr. Abbey looked at Becks. "Not hungry?"

"I'm not leaving until I know what you're going to do with him." She kept her gun trained on me as she spoke, professional to the last. Her hand was shaking only slightly. I didn't do as well when I was in her position.

"Fair enough. Come on, Shaun." Dr. Abbey waved for me to follow her as she turned and started down the nearest hall. She didn't call for anyone else to keep an eye on me. I guess she figured Becks would be enough.

We walked maybe twenty yards deeper into the building, moving around towers of cardboard boxes and past hastily constructed metal racks. Lab techs moved past us constantly, grabbing this and that and vanishing down hallways or through doors. I guess moving an entire virology lab isn't a simple task.

Dr. Abbey grabbed a blood testing unit from one of the shelving units and kept walking, offering nods and quiet greetings to some of the lab techs we passed. She stopped only when we reached a door labeled ISOLATION III. "In here," she said, and opened it. I didn't move. "What are you waiting for, an invitation? Get in."

"I thought—"

"We're not going in there with you. Don't be an idiot." She held the unit out toward me. "Go inside, sit down, and start your test. You won't be able to get out. You can't hurt anyone."

Relief washed over me, strong enough to make my shoulders unlock. "Thank you," I said. I flashed Becks one last smile, aware that it was strained, and not really that concerned about it. I wasn't going to hurt anyone. That was all I needed to know.

Becks smiled back. She was crying. I was sorry about that, but there was nothing I could do about it. So I stepped forward to take the testing unit from Dr. Abbey's hand and walked past her into the darkened isolation room.

The door swung shut behind me, the locks sealing with a hydraulic hiss that went on long enough to make it clear that this wasn't casual security. This was the real thing. The hissing stopped and the overhead lights clicked on, illuminating a room about the size of my bedroom back when George and I still lived with the Masons. The walls were painted a shiny, neutral beige, and there were three pieces of furniture: a narrow cot against one wall, a metal table bolted to the floor, and a folding chair. There was a blanket and a small pillow on the cot. Make the condemned as comfortable as possible, I guess.

I wasn't interested in comfort. I walked to the chair and sat down, placing the testing unit on the table in front of me. It seemed to stare back accusingly, like it didn't understand why I wasn't getting on with it already.

"It's not like this is important or anything," I said sourly, and unfastened my gloves, dropping them on the table. Blood had run down my left arm and onto the hand, crusting under my nails. I looked at it and shuddered, wishing there were some way to wash it off. After I amplified, I probably wouldn't care, but until then, I'd know it was there. I flexed my fingers, checking my joints for stiffness, and turned my attention to the testing unit.

It wasn't a model I'd seen before—if anything, it looked like the pictures of Dr. Patel's original design, the one that just measured your viral levels but didn't give you real-time results, and definitely didn't upload anything. I picked it up, checking it for lights, and didn't find any. Apparently, once I was in the isolation room, I didn't need to know whether I was infected or not. I scowled. "Isn't this just dandy?"

"Get it over with," said George, beside me.

I jerked my head up, looking for her. She was nowhere to be seen. I scowled more. "I don't exactly feel like rushing right now."

"The results won't change if you wait." Her voice came from the other side this time. I somehow managed not to look. I just sighed.

"Can you just appear already?"

"No. I'm sorry, but that's your choice, not mine."

"Okay. Right. Well . . . if you won't appear, will you at least stay?"

I felt the ghost of her hand brush the back of my neck, there and gone in an instant. "Until the end. I promise."

"Okay," I said, and popped open the lid on the unit. "One . . ."

"Two . . ."

I slammed my hand flat on the metal pressure pad, triggering the needles to start their business. They bit deep, and I hissed, biting my tongue against the pain. I thought amplification was supposed to make this sort of thing easier. I didn't feel any difference at all. Blood tests always hurt, but this one was worse than most, maybe because the unit was so primitive.

When the last of the needles disengaged, I pulled my hand away. The test unit beeped once and was silent. No lights, no alarms, nothing to indicate whether I'd passed or failed. Not that I really needed the confirmation that I was infected—"Get a bite, say good-night," as they said when I was in training—but it still would have been nice. You were supposed to see your results. That was how the testing worked.

"Hey." George put her hand on my shoulder. "Why don't you go lie down? You're exhausted."

I shrugged her hand off. "No, I don't want to sleep through this. If this is the end of me being me, I don't want to miss it." A thought struck me, and I chuckled bitterly. "I can't be too far gone if I'm still hallucinating you, can I? You're a pretty complicated delusion. Zombies probably can't manage this quality of crazy."

"Thanks a lot."

"You're welcome."

She fell silent, and so did I. I was too tense to carry on a conversation, even with a dead person who lived only in my head. I'd just keep trying to pick a fight, and she'd keep trying to stop me, until we wound up screaming at each other and I spent the last minutes of my conscious life arguing with the one person I least wanted to argue with. I just wanted to know that she was there, and that I wasn't going through this alone.

So I stared at the test unit instead of talking to her, willing it to develop lights and tell me what I needed to know. All I needed was for it to confirm that my life was over. Nothing difficult. Nothing any fucking toaster couldn't manage these days.

I don't know how long I sat there staring at the test unit, feeling my throat getting dryer and waiting for the other symptoms to set in. The difficulty breathing, the sensitivity to light, the murkiness of thought—all the little dividing lines that separated human from zombie. Dryness of the throat was only the beginning, and my training was extensive enough to tell me exactly what the progression would be. Every little step along the way.

The door opened.

My head snapped up, tensing as I waited for the gunmen to enter. I wondered whether they'd send Becks to shoot me; I wondered whether she'd insist. We'd been colleagues for a long time, and Irwins tend to view shooting infected comrades as part of the job. It's a sign of respect.

Dr. Abbey stepped into the room.

I stopped breathing for a second, eyes going wide. They went even wider as Joe pushed past her, his tail wagging wildly from side to side. "You're going to let him be in here while you put me down?" I asked. "That's cold. I mean, not that I'm one to judge, but that's *cold.*"

Dr. Abbey smiled. "Hello, Shaun." She shut the door behind herself, waiting until the locks finished hissing before she walked over to the other side of the table. She was carrying a folding chair, which she set up and sank into, watching me the whole time. "How are you feeling?"

"You shouldn't be in here," I said. Joe walked around the table and shoved his enormous head into my crotch in canine greeting. I barely remembered the blood on my hand in time to stop myself from pushing him away. "This isn't safe."

"Oh, right. You're contagious." She reached into the pocket of her lab coat, pulling out a can of Coke and putting it down on the table between us. "You must be thirsty. You've been sitting in here for a while." I stared at her. "No, really, open the can. I want to see how good your manual dexterity is."

Still staring, I reached out and picked up the can. Its cold heaviness was soothing, even before I popped the tab, closed my eyes, and took a long, freezing drink. It was the best thing I'd ever tasted, sugary syrupy sweetness and all.

Dr. Abbey was watching me intently when I opened my eyes. "How's the throat feeling, Shaun?" she asked.

"A little dry. I don't understand what you're doing—" I stopped. The dryness in my throat was gone, replaced by the residual carbonated tingle that always came after I drank one of George's Candyland hookers. "—here," I finished, more slowly. "Dr. Abbey?"

"I'm here because I wanted to talk to you about your test results, Shaun." She reached into her pocket again, this time producing a standard, run-of-the-mill field testing unit. Catching my surprise, she said, "Don't worry. It's been modified so it won't upload—it'll think it has, but it won't. This won't give our position away to the CDC, or to anybody else."

"I don't understand. Did something go wrong with my first test?"

"No, nothing went wrong with your first test. Now please." She gestured toward the unit. "Humor the woman who's willing to risk her life by offering sanctuary to your team, and take the goddamn test."

"Right." At least this one had lights. I popped off the lid, whispering, "One," and waiting for George's answering *Two*, before pressing my hand against the pressure pad. The needles bit in, quick and painful as always, and the lights began to flash through their complex analytic series of reds and greens. They flashed fast to begin with, then slowed as they settled on their final determination. It only took about thirty seconds for the last light to stop flashing.

All five of them settled on green.

I frowned, looking up at Dr. Abbey. Joe shoved his nose into my hand. I ignored him, focusing on her instead. "Is this a side effect of blocking the transmission? You change something internally so it registers negatives as positives?"

"No, Shaun. I didn't." Dr. Abbey calmly picked up the lid to the testing unit, snapping it back into place. She watched my face the entire time, moving with slow, methodical gestures, so that I

wouldn't be surprised. She didn't really need to worry. I was somewhere past surprise by that point. "None of the adjustments we've
made to our equipment would do something as suicidal or idiotic as
showing a positive result as a negative one. We'd just disable the
readouts, like we did with your first test. Those results came to my
computer, and no one else's. I was able to study your entire viral profile."

"What are you trying to say?"

"I'm not *trying* to say anything. What I *am* saying is that your
test results—both times, the ones you didn't see and the ones you
just witnessed—came back clean." Dr. Abbey looked at me gravely,
a wild excitement barely contained in her expression. "You're not
sick, Shaun. You're not going to amplify.

"I don't know what your body did, but it encountered the live
virus . . . and it fought it off. You're going to live."

I didn't know what to say. So I just stared at her, the green lights
on the testing unit glowing steadily, like an accusation of a crime I
had never plotted to commit. I'd been right all along; amplification
would have been too easy an exit, and when given the chance, my
body somehow refused to do it. I was going to live.

So now what?

Coda: Living for You

I have no idea what's going on anymore. When did the world stop making sense?

—SHAUN MASON

What the fuck is going on here?

—GEORGIA MASON

One of the Fictionals asked me this morning, if I could have one wish—any wish in the world, no matter how big or how small— what would I wish for? This would be a universe-changing wish. I could wish away Kellis-Amberlee. Hell, I could wish away the Rising if I wanted to, restore us to a universe where the zombies never came and we never wound up hiding in our houses, scared of everything we couldn't sterilize. And I stared at him until he realized what a stupid question that was and went running off, probably figuring that I was going to start hitting next.

He wasn't wrong.

If I could have any wish, no matter how big, no matter how small, I'd wish to have George back. Without that, nothing else I could wish for would be worth a fucking thing. And if you don't like that, you can shove it up your ass, because I don't care.

—From *Adaptive Immunities*, the blog of Shaun Mason,
January 5, 2041

Twenty-seven

I woke up in a white bed in a white room, with the cloying white smell of bleach in my nose and the tangled white cobwebs of my dreams still gnawing, ratlike, at the inside of my brain. I sat up with a gasp, realizing as I did that I was wearing white cotton pajamas and covered by a white comforter with no buttons or snaps. I took a breath, then another, trying to force my heart rate down as I looked around the room, seeking some clue as to where I was.

The only furnishings were the bed I was in and a single bedside table with rounded edges. I reached out and gave it an experimental shake. It was bolted to the floor. The bed probably was, too. Nothing in the room could be used as a weapon, unless I wanted to try strangling myself with the sheets. Even hanging was out of the question, since there was nothing for me to hang myself from.

A huge, inset mirror that almost certainly doubled as an observation window took up one entire wall. That sort of fixture in this sort of room can mean only one thing: medical holding facility, probably owned by the CDC. That fit with the dreams I'd been having, horrible, tangled things about some sort of major outbreak. No, not a major outbreak—there weren't that many people involved, at least not when we closed the doors. And we had to close the doors. We had to close the doors, because—

"I see you're awake."

The voice came from a speaker in the wall above the mirror and caught me entirely by surprise. I screamed a little, clutching the blanket against my chest before I realized I was being an idiot. Whoever had me in here could do a lot worse than talk to me, if they decided that was what they wanted. I eyed the speaker suspiciously, letting go of the blanket.

"I'm awake," I confirmed.

"Good, good. Now, you may be a little shaky at first. I don't recommend trying to walk before you've had a little time to get adjusted."

I was out of the bed before the voice was finished with its warning, stalking across the floor toward the mirror. Then I stopped again, stunned by the sight of my own reflection in what should have been—for me—a completely transparent surface. My eyes make one-way glass a pretty fiction.

Or they're supposed to, anyway. Only for some reason, things weren't working that way this time, and instead of looking at the hallway beyond the glass, I was looking at myself.

The pajamas I was wearing were at least two sizes too big, or maybe it was just that I'd lost weight: I looked like I was recovering from a long illness, all pale skin and bird-boned limbs. The lines of my collarbone stood out like knives, making me seem downright frail. My hair was too long, falling to hit my shoulders in those annoying thick curls that always seemed to form when I let it grow out, and my eyes ... There was something wrong with my eyes. Something very, very wrong.

I was still staring at my reflection when the speaker crackled on again. The voice from before came smoothly into the room, saying, "We're very glad to see you up and about. Some disorientation is normal at first, and you shouldn't let it bother you. Now, the speakers in your room are voice-activated; you don't need to look for a button or anything like that. Just speak loudly and clearly, and we'll understand you. Can you please tell us your name, and the last thing that you remember?"

I took a deep breath, holding it for a moment before letting it slowly out. Looking directly into my reflection—and hence, directly at anyone who happened to be standing in the hallway outside the one-way mirror, watching their little test subject, I answered.

"My name is Georgia Mason," I said. "What the *fuck* is going on here?"

Acknowledgments

Writing a follow-up volume to *Feed* was both elating and terrifying, and it wouldn't have been possible without the assistance of a wonderful group of people. I can't thank them enough. They ranged from medical professionals who worked with both humans and animals to gun experts and epidemiologists. *Deadline* is the work of many hands, and I am grateful to each and every one of them, because they were the ones who made this all possible.

Michelle Dockrey is a longtime editor of mine who chose to sit out *Feed* because it included zombies. Upon reading it, she promptly demanded the manuscript for *Deadline*, and just as quickly used her red pen and insightful eye for blocking to improve the book beyond all measure. (Also, I no longer need to worry about her trying to "sit this one out." I win at proofreader.) Brooke Lunderville stepped up to become primary medical consultant on this volume, and her keen sense of what you should and shouldn't do with a syringe can be seen on every page.

Alan Beatts joined the proofing pool as my new weapons expert, and his patient efforts to make me understand why a shotgun isn't the ideal zombie-fighting weapon did a lot to improve my combat scenes. I am incredibly grateful, especially given that it was really,

really late in the process when I decided to say, "Hey, do you think you could ..." Thanks also to Torrey Stenmark, Dave Tinney, and Debbie J. Gates for their well-timed, well-considered technical suggestions.

The Machete Squad must also, and always, be thanked. Amanda Perry, Rae Hanson, Sunil Patel, Alison Riley-Duncan, Rebecca Newman, Allison Hewett, Janet Maughan, Penelope Skrzynski, Phil Ames, and Amanda Sanders were all on tap for general proofreading and plot consultation. Through their efforts is this book made incalculably better. Meanwhile, at Orbit, DongWon Song was applying a keen editorial eye to the text, Lauren Panepinto was rocking the cover design, and Alex Lencicki was just plain rocking. Thanks so much, guys. I couldn't have done this without you.

Finally, acknowledgment for forbearance must go to Kate Secor, Shaun Connolly, and Cat Valente, who put up with an amazing amount of "talking it out" as I tried to make the book make sense; to my agent, Diana Fox, who remains my favorite superhero; to Betsy Tinney, for everything; and to Tara O'Shea and Chris Mangum, the incredible technical team behind www.MiraGrant.com. This book might have been written without them. It would not have been the same.

If you're curious about the American yellow fever epidemic and mosquito-based vectors, check out *The American Plague: The Untold Story of Yellow Fever*, by Molly Crosby.

Rise up while you can.

extras

orbit

www.orbitbooks.net

about the author

Born and raised in California, Mira Grant has made a lifelong study of horror movies, horrible viruses, and the inevitable threat of the living dead. In college, she was voted Most Likely to Summon Something Horrible in the Cornfield, and was a founding member of the Horror Movie Sleep-Away Survival Camp, where her record for time survived in the Swamp Cannibals scenario remains unchallenged.

Mira lives in a crumbling farmhouse with an assortment of cats, horror movies, comics, and books about horrible diseases. When not writing, she splits her time between travel, auditing college virology courses, and watching more horror movies than is strictly good for you. Favorite vacation spots include Seattle, London, and a large haunted corn maze just outside of Huntsville, Alabama.

Mira sleeps with a machete under her bed, and strongly suggests you do the same. Find out more about the author at www.mira-grant.com.

if you enjoyed
DEADLINE

look out for

BLACKOUT

book three of Newsflesh series

also by

Mira Grant

BOOK I

From the Dead

People like to say things like "It wasn't supposed to go this way" and "This isn't what I wanted." They're just making noise. In the end, there's no such thing as "supposed to," and what you want doesn't matter. All that matters is what really happened.

—GEORGIA MASON

I honestly have no idea what's going on anymore. I just need to find something that I can hit.

—SHAUN MASON

My name is Georgia Carolyn Mason. I belong to the vast, unspoken class of people known as the Orphans of the Rising, individuals who were under two years of age when their parents were killed. Individuals who were too young to remember anything about where they came from. My biological family is presumably listed somewhere on the Wall, living people transformed into one more simple footnote of a dead world. Their world died in the Rising, just like they did. They didn't live to see the new one.

My adoptive parents have raised me to question the world around me, understand the realities of my situation, and, in times of necessity, shoot first. They have equipped me with the tools I need to survive, and for that I am grateful. Through this blog, I will do my best to share my experiences and, yes, my opinions in as open and honest a way as I can. It is the best way to honor the family that raised me; it is the only way I have to honor the family that lost me.

I'm going to tell you the truth as I understand it. You can take it from there.

—From *Images May Disturb You*, the blog of
Georgia Mason, June 20, 2035

———

So George says I have to write a "mission statement" for this blog, because apparently, our contract with Bridge Supporters says that I will. I am personally opposed to mission statements, since they're basically one more way of sucking the fun out of everything. I tried telling George this, but all she said was that it's her job to suck the fun out of everything. She then threatened physical violence of a type that I will not describe in detail, as it might unsettle and upset my theoretical readership. Suffice to say that here I am, writing a mission statement. So here it is:

I, Shaun Phillip Mason, being of sound mind and body, do hereby swear to poke dead shit with sticks, do stupid things for your amusement, and put it all on the Internet where you can watch it over and over again. Because that's what you want, right?

Glad to oblige.

**—From *Hail to the King*, the blog of Shaun Mason,
June 20, 2035**

One

My story ended where so many stories have ended over the course of the last two decades: with a man—in this case, my adoptive brother and best friend, Shaun—holding a gun to the base of my skull as the virus in my blood caused my body to betray me, transforming me from a living, thinking human being into something better suited for a horror movie. I remember the feeling of the hypodermic needle biting into my arm, and the cold, absolute dread as I watched the lights on the blood test unit as they went red, one after the other. I remember the look on Shaun's face when he realized that this was it, this was really happening, and there wasn't going to be any clever third-act solution that got me out of the van alive.

I remember the gun pressing against my skin. It was cool, and it was soothing, because it meant that Shaun was going to do his duty. No one was going to get hurt—no one who hadn't been hurt already. This was something we'd never planned for. I always knew that one day he'd push his luck too far, and I'd lose him. Neither of us ever dreamed that he'd be the one losing me. I wanted to tell him it would be okay. I wanted to lie to him. I couldn't. There wasn't time.

I remember starting to write. I remember thinking that this was it; this was my last chance to say anything I wanted to say to the world. This was the thing I was going to be judged on, now and forever.

I remember feeling my mind start to go. I remember the fear.

I remember the sound of Shaun pulling the trigger.

By all rights, I shouldn't remember anything after that because that's where my story ended. Curtain down, save file, that's a wrap. Once the bullet hits the spinal cord, you're out, you're done, you don't have to worry about this shit anymore. You definitely shouldn't find yourself waking up in a room that looks suspiciously like a CDC holding facility, with no one to talk to but some unidentified voice on the other side of a one-way mirror. So what the hell did I do to get so lucky?

The room was practically barren, containing nothing but a bed with white blankets and a rounded white bedside table—bolted to the floor, of course. Wouldn't do to have the mysteriously resurrected dead journalist throwing things at the mirror that took up most of one wall. The only wall with a door, naturally. It was locked. I'd tried the knob, and then I'd searched the walls around it for a blood test unit, in the vain hope that checking out clean would make the locks let go and release me. There weren't any. That was chilling all by itself. I grew up in a post-Rising world, one where blood tests and the threat of infection are a part of daily life. I'm sure I'd been in sealed rooms without testing units before. I had to have been. I just couldn't remember any.

There was something else the room was lacking: clocks, or windows, or anything else that might let me know how much time had passed since I woke up, much less how much time had passed *before* I woke up. There was a voice from the speaker above the mirror when I first woke up, an unfamiliar voice that asked my name and what the last thing I remembered was. I'd answered him—"My name is Georgia Mason. What the *fuck* is going on here?"—and then he went away, cutting off communication without answering my question.

That might have been ten minutes ago. It might have been ten hours ago. The lights overhead glared steady and white, not so much as flickering as the seconds went slipping past.

That was another thing. The light was hard and white, the sort of industrial fluorescent lighting that's been popular in medical facilities since long before the Rising. It should have been burning my eyes like acid by now. I was diagnosed with retinal Kellis-Amberlee when I was a kid, meaning that the same disease that causes the dead to rise had taken up permanent residence in my eyeballs. It gave me excellent low-light vision, and a tendency to get migraines if I so much as tried to watch normal television without my sunglasses on.

Well, I wasn't wearing sunglasses, and it wasn't like I could dim the lights in a room with no light switches or computer controls. Even if it had been only ten minutes since I woke, that was long enough for me to risk permanently damaging my eyesight, if not destroying it entirely. But my eyes didn't even itch. All I felt was thirsty, and a vague, gnawing hunger in the pit of my stomach, like lunch might be a good idea sometime soon. There was no headache. I honestly couldn't decide whether or not that was a good sign.

My palms were starting to sweat as the anxiety really set in. I scrubbed them hard against the legs of the unfamiliar white cotton pajamas. *Everything* in this room was unfamiliar—even me. I've never been heavy—a life spent running after stories and running for your life doesn't allow for carrying excess weight—but the girl I saw reflected in the one-way mirror was thin to the point of being wrung-out and scrawny. She looked like she'd be easy to break. Her hair was dark enough to be mine, but it was also too long, falling in thick curls to her shoulders. I've never in my life allowed my hair to get that long. Hair like that is a passive form of suicide when you do what I do for a living. And her eyes . . .

When I looked at the face reflected in the mirror, I could see a ring of copper-brown all around her pupils. That, more than anything else, was making it all but impossible to think of the face as my own. Because I don't *have* visible irises. I have pupils that fill all the space not occupied by sclera, giving me a black, almost emotionless stare. Those weren't my eyes. But my eyes didn't hurt. Which meant that either those *were* my eyes, and my retinal KA had somehow been cured, or Buffy was right when she said the afterlife existed, and this was hell.

I stared at the unfamiliar eyes in my reflection for a moment more before I went back to what seemed to have become my primary activity: pacing back and forth and trying to think. The fact that I had to do it quietly, with no one to talk to or bounce things off, made it a hell of a lot harder. I've always thought better when I do it out loud, and this was the first time in my adult life that I'd been anywhere without at least one personal recorder running. I'm an accredited journalist. When I talk to myself, it's not a sign of insanity; it's just me making sure I don't lose important material before I have the chance to get to a keyboard and write it all down.

None of this was right. Even if they had some sort of experimental treatment that could reverse the effects of amplification, there would have been somebody there to explain things to me. *Shaun* would have been there. There it was: the reason I knew that this, whatever it was, was a long way from being right. I remembered him pulling the trigger. Even assuming it was a false memory, even assuming that never happened, *why wasn't he here?* Shaun would move Heaven and Earth to be with me. I briefly entertained the notion that he might be off forcing the voices from the intercom to tell him where I was, and then regretfully dismissed it.

Something would have exploded by now, if that was the situation.

"Goddammit." I scowled at the white wall in front of me, turned, and started walking in the other direction. The vague hunger was getting worse, and was accompanied by a new, more frustrating sensation: the need to pee. If someone didn't let me out soon, I was going to have a whole new set of problems to contend with.

"Run the timeline, George," I said, trying to take some comfort in the still-familiar sound of my own voice. Everything else may have changed, but not that. "You were in Sacramento with Rick and Shaun, running for the van. Something hit you in the arm. One of those syringes like they used at the Ryman farm. The test came back positive. Rick left. And then . . . then . . . " I faltered, having trouble finding the words, even if there was no one else to hear them.

Everyone who grew up after the Rising knows what happens when you come into contact with the live form of Kellis-Amberlee. You essentially go rabid, becoming a mindless slave to the virus and its needs. You become a zombie, and you do what every zombie exists to do. You bite. You infect. You kill. You feed. You don't wake up in a white room, wearing white pajamas, and wondering how your brother was able to shoot you in the neck without even leaving a scar.

Scars. I stopped in my tracks before wheeling and stalking back to the mirror, pulling the lids on my right eye apart while I studied its reflection. I learned how to look at my own eyes when I was eleven. That's when I got my first pair of protective contacts. That's also when I got my first visible retinal scarring, little patches of tissue that had been so scorched by the sun that they would never recover. We caught it in time to prevent there being any major vision loss, and I got a lot more careful after that. The scarring was there to remind me every day, creating small blind spots at the center of my vision. Nothing major. Nothing that prevented my working in the field. Just . . . little spots.

My pupil contracted to almost nothing as the light hit it. The spots weren't there. I could see clearly, without any gaps.

"Oh," I said, lowering my hand. "I guess that makes sense."

When I first woke up, the voice from the intercom told me that all I had to do was speak and someone would hear me. I looked up toward the speaker. "A little help here?" I said. "I need to pee really bad."

There was no response. I hadn't honestly been expecting one. Turning my back on the mirror, I walked to the bed and settled into a cross-legged position atop the mattress, closing my eyes. And then I started waiting. There was still no mechanism in the room for marking time, but if anyone was watching me—and someone *had* to be watching me—this might be a big enough change in my behavior to get their attention. I wanted their attention. I wanted their attention really, really badly. Almost as badly as I wanted an MP3 recorder, an Internet connection, and a bathroom.

After I'd been waiting for what felt like hours but, again, might have just been minutes, the need for a bathroom had crept substantially higher on that list, as had the need for a drink of water. The fact that the human body can demand both of these things at the same time is proof that evolution has no erase button.

I was beginning to consider the possibility that I might need to somehow cover the mirror with one of the blankets while I used a corner of the room as a lavatory when the intercom clicked on again. "Miss Mason? Are you awake?"

"Yes," I said, without opening my eyes. "Do I get a name to call you by?"

He ignored my question like it didn't matter. Maybe it didn't, to him. "I apologize for going silent before. We were a little surprised by your vehemence. We'd expected a slightly longer period of disorientation."

"Sorry to disappoint you."

"Oh, we weren't disappointed," the voice said, hurriedly. It was a male voice, with the faintest traces of a Midwestern accent. I couldn't place the state, but I knew I'd never heard it before. "I promise you, we're thrilled to see you up and coherent so quickly. It's a wonderful indicator for your recovery."

"A glass of water and a trip to the ladies' room would do a lot more to help my recovery than a bunch of apologies and evasions."

Now the voice sounded faintly abashed. "I'm so sorry, Miss Mason. We didn't think . . . Just a moment." The intercom clicked off again, leaving me in silence once again. I stayed where I was, and kept on waiting.

A new sound intruded on my silence: the hiss of a hydraulic lock unsealing itself. I opened my eyes, turning my head to see a small panel slide open above the door, revealing a single red light. The hissing continued, and the door, at long last, swung inward, revealing a skinny, nervous-looking man in a long white lab coat. He was holding his clipboard against his chest like he thought it afforded him some sort of protection, and his eyes were wide behind the lenses of his glasses.

"Miss Mason? If you'd like to come with me, I'd be happy to escort you to the restroom."

"Thank you." I unfolded my legs, ignoring the protest of pins and needles in my calves, and walked toward the man in the doorway. He didn't quite cringe as I approached, but he definitely shied back, looking more profoundly uneasy with every step I took in his direction. Interesting.

"We do apologize for making you wait," he said. His words had the distinct cadence of something recited by rote, like telephone tech support asking for your ID and computer serial number. "There were just a few things that had to be taken care of before we could proceed."

"Let's worry about that *after* I get to the bathroom, okay?" I sidestepped around him, out into the hall, and stopped as I found myself looking at three hospital orderlies in blue scrubs, each of them pointing a pistol in my direction. I put my hands up, palms outward. "Okay, okay, I get it. I can wait for my escort."

"That's probably for the best, Miss Mason," said the nervous man, whose voice I now recognized from the intercom. It just took me a moment, without the filtering speakers between us. "We're all a bit jumpy right now. I'm sure you understand."

"Yeah. Sure." I lowered my hands as I fell into step behind the nervous man. The orderlies followed us down the hall, their aim never wavering. I did my best not to make any sudden moves. Having just returned to the land of the living, I was in no mood to exit it again before I had a few answers about what, exactly, was happening. "Am I ever going to get something I can call you?"

"Ah ..." His mouth worked for a moment without a sound escaping before he said, "I'm Dr. Thomas. I've been one of your attending physicians since you first arrived at this facility. I'm not surprised that you don't remember me. You've been sleeping for some time."

"Is that what the kids are calling it these days?" The hall we were walking along was built along the model I've come to expect from CDC facilities, with nothing breaking the sterile white of the walls but the occasional door and the associated one-way mirrors that looked into patient-holding rooms. All of them were empty.

"You're walking well."

"It's a skill."

"How's your head? Any disorientation, blurred vision, confusion?"

"Yes." He tensed. I ignored it, continuing: "I'm confused about what the hell I'm doing here. I don't know about you, but I get a little twitchy when I wake up in strange places with no idea of how I got there. Will I be getting some answers soon?"

"Soon enough, Miss Mason," he said, looking relieved. We had stopped in front of a door with no mirror next to it. That implied that it wasn't a patient room. Better yet, there was a visible blood test unit to one side. I never thought I'd be so happy for the chance to be jabbed with a needle. "We'll give you a few minutes. If you need any-thing—"

"Using the bathroom, also a skill," I said, and slapped my palm down flat on the test panel. Needles promptly bit into the heel of my hand and the tips of my fingers, and the light above the door changed from amber to red and finally to green. The door swung open. I smiled at Dr. Thomas, which just seemed to make him even more nervous, and I stepped into the bathroom, only to stop and scowl at the one-way mirror taking up most of the opposite wall. The door swung shut behind me.

"Cute," I muttered. There was no way to cover it, and the need to pee was getting bad enough that I didn't have time to protest the situation. I glared at the mirror the entire time I was using the facilities, all but daring someone to watch me. See? I can pee whether you're spying on me or not, you sick bastards.

Other than the mirror—or maybe because of the mirror—the bathroom was as much standard-issue CDC as the hallway outside, with white walls, a white tile floor, and white porcelain fixtures. Everything was automatic, including the soap dispenser, and there were no towels; instead, I dried my hands by sticking them into a jet of hot air that activated as soon as the water turned off. It was one big exercise in minimizing contact with any surface. When I turned back to the door, the only thing I'd touched was the toilet seat, and I was willing to bet that it was in the process of self-sterilization by the time I started washing my hands.

No blood test was required to leave the bathroom. I guess they assumed you wouldn't go into amplification while alone in a little white room. The three orderlies had arrayed themselves in a loose semicircle, with an unhappy Dr. Thomas between them and me. If I did anything bad enough to make them pull those triggers, the odds were good that he'd be treated as collateral damage.

"Wow," I said. "Who did you piss off to get this gig?"

He flinched, looking at me guiltily. "I'm sure I don't know what you mean."

"Of course not. Thank you for bringing me to the bathroom. Now, could I get that water?" Better yet, a can of Coke. The thought of its acid sweetness and the snap of bubbles on my tongue was enough to make my mouth water. It's always good to know that some things never change.

"If you'd come this way?"

I gave the orderlies a pointed look. "I don't think I have much of a choice, do you?"

"No," he said, guilty expression growing. "I suppose you don't. It's just a precaution. You understand."

"Not really, no. I'm unarmed. I've already passed one blood test. I don't really understand why I need three men with guns covering my every move."

"Security."

"Why is it people always say that when they don't feel like giving a straight answer?" I shook my head. "I'm not going to make trouble. Please, just take me to the water."

"Right this way," he said, and started walking back the way we'd come. Interesting.

More interesting was what awaited us in the room I first woke up in, distinguishable from the others only by the messed-up bedclothes and the fingerprints on the inside of the one-way mirror. There was a tray on the bolted-down table. It held a plate with two pieces of buttered toast, a tall tumbler filled with water, and, wonder of wonders, miracle of miracles, a can of Coke with condensation beading on the sides in tiny, enticing droplets. I made for the tray without pausing to consider how the orderlies might react to my moving at something faster than a casual stroll. None of them shot me in the back. That was something.

The first bite of toast was the best thing I'd ever tasted, at least until I took the second bite, and then the third. Finally, I crammed most of the slice into my mouth, barely chewing. I managed to resist the siren song of the Coke long enough to drink half the water. It tasted just as good as the toast. I put down the glass, popped the tab on the can of soda, and took my first postdeath sip of Coke. I was smart enough not to gulp it; even that tiny amount was enough to make my knees weak. I slowly turned to face Dr. Thomas.

As I'd expected, he was standing in the doorway, watching me carefully and making notes on his clipboard. Wouldn't want to miss a moment, after all. There were probably a few dozen video and audio recorders running, catching every move I made, but any good reporter will tell you that there's nothing like real field experience. I guess the same thing applies to scientists.

"How do you feel?" he asked, lowering his pen. "Dizzy? Are you already full? Did you want something besides toast? It's a bit early for anything overly complicated, but I might be able to arrange for some soup, if you'd prefer that . . ."

"Mostly, what I'd prefer is having some questions answered, if you don't mind." I shifted the familiar weight of my Coke from one hand to the other. If I couldn't have my sunglasses, I guess a can of soda would have to do. "I think I've been pretty cooperative up to now. I also think that could change, if you're not willing to play fair with me."

Dr. Thomas looked uncomfortable. "Well, I suppose that will depend on what sort of questions you want to ask."

"Oh, this one should be pretty easy for you. I mean, it's definitely within your skill set."

"All right. I can't promise to know the answer, but I'm happy to try. We want you to be comfortable."

"Good." I looked at him levelly, missing my black-eyed gaze. It always made people so uncomfortable. I got more honest answers out of those eyes . . . "You said you were my attending physician."

"That's correct."

"So tell me: How long have I been a clone?"

Dr. Thomas dropped his pen.

Still watching him, I raised my Coke, took a sip, and waited for his reply.

Subject 139b was confirmed as bitten on the evening of June 24, 2041. The exact time of the bite was not recorded, but a period of no less than twenty minutes elapsed between exposure and initial testing. The infected individual responsible for delivering the bite was retrieved from the road. Posthumous analysis confirmed that the individual was heavily contagious and had been so for at least six days, as the virus had fully amplified through all parts of the body.

Analysis of blood taken from the outside of Subject 139b's hand confirmed that infection had been successfully passed when the bite was delivered. (For proof of viral bodies in Subject 139b's blood, please see the attached file.) Amplification appears to have begun normally and followed the established progression toward full loss of cognitive functionality. Samples taken from Subject 139b's clothing confirm this diagnosis.

Subject 139b was given a blood test shortly after arriving at this facility and tested clean of all live viral particles. Subject 139b was given a second test, using a more sensitive unit, and once again tested clean. After forty-eight hours of isolation, following standard Kellis-Amberlee quarantine procedures, it is my professional opinion that the subject is not now infected, and does not represent a danger to himself or others.

With God as my witness, Joey, I swear to you that Shaun Mason is *not* infected with the live state of Kellis-Amberlee. He should be. He's not. He started to amplify, and he somehow fought the infection off. This could change everything ... if we had the slightest fucking clue how he did it.

—Taken from a letter sent by Dr. Shannon Abbey to Dr. Joseph Shoji at the Kauai Institute of Virology, June 27, 2041